CET 710分

大学英语六级测试
试题集
（新题型版）

College English
Practice Tests(CET-6)

张增健　　吴建蘅

U0140818

W 上海外语教育出版社
外教社 SHANGHAI FOREIGN LANGUAGE EDUCATION PRESS

图书在版编目（CIP）数据

大学英语六级测试试题集（新题型版）/张增健，吴建蘅编著.
－上海：上海外语教育出版社，2007（2008重印）
ISBN 978-7-5446-0421-5

Ⅰ.大… Ⅱ.①张…②吴… Ⅲ.英语－高等学校－水平
考试－习题 Ⅳ.H319.6

中国版本图书馆CIP数据核字（2007）第006161号

出版发行：上海外语教育出版社
（上海外国语大学内） 邮编：200083
电　　话：021-65425300（总机）
电子邮箱：bookinfo@sflep.com.cn
网　　址：http://www.sflep.com.cn　http://www.sflep.com
责任编辑：杨自伍

印　　刷：上海华文印刷厂
经　　销：新华书店上海发行所
开　　本：787×1092　1/16　印张20.5　字数371千字
版　　次：2007年3月第1版　2008年6月第2次印刷
印　　数：8 000 册

书　　号：ISBN 978-7-5446-0421-5 / G · 0209
定　　价：37.00 元（附MP3光盘）

本版图书如有印装质量问题，可向本社调换

前　言

  根据有关通告,改革后的大学英语六级考试(以下简称"新六级考试")定于2006年12月正式开考,届时将有部分试点院校学生接受新题型的首次检测。报考新六级的考生中,有一部分刚通过新四级大学英语考试,他们对测试题型的改革以及考试流程的变化,有切身体会,临考时可得"驾轻就熟"之便。但也有相当数量的考生,是早先通过大学英语四级考试的,他们对于改革后的考试项目,可能并不完全熟悉。为配合大学英语新六级考试的推广,帮助考生熟悉新设定的题型、顺应测试流程的变化,我们参照考试委员会所编印的(CET-6)考试样卷,对《大学英语六级测试试题集》(第三版)从内容到形式,作了全面的修订。2007年《大学英语六级测试试题集》(新题型版)所提供的模拟卷,不仅在卷面题型、试项安排方面,与样卷保持一致,而且在设计过程中,更着眼于体现考试改革方案的精神——从写、听、读、译等方面考查学生的语言实际运用能力,进而切实有效地推动大学英语教学的全方位改革。

  为了更好地发挥本试题集的作用,我们觉得有必要简单介绍一下新六级题型设计方面的某些特点及其用意。

  和新四级考试一样,新六级考试最显眼的一个特点,是将"写作"(Writing)列为首考试项。就"写作"这一题型本身来说,并没有什么变化:依然是要求考生就某一社会"热点"现象,按所列(汉语或英语)提纲表述自己的意见。我们知道,写作最能反映考生的语言综合使用能力,至于作为考试项目,是用来"开场"还是用于"压轴",照理说并无关大局。但问题是,写作乃是目前大学英语教学中最薄弱的环节之一。平时学生疏于练笔,教师也少有点评。单凭试前的几周辅导和苦练,正式应考时似乎很难在30分钟内,写出一篇让人满意的短文来。如果开局没找准感觉,势必会影响到整场考试的正常发挥。所以"写作"虽说是旧题型,但还得有充分的实战准备才行。再说,从命题内容到写作要求,难度皆有所提高。

  新六级考试的另一显著特点,是将"快速阅读"单独立为一个试项:要求考生在15分钟内读完一篇千余字的文章,并就十道试题即时作出回答。严格说来,Skimming 和 Scanning 本应包含在整体的阅读技能之内。之所以在新六级考试中被设为一单独试项,想必是为了强调这两项技巧的实际应用价值。而在目前的大学英语教学中,对这两项技巧的训练、培养,并未给予应有的重视:精

1

读、泛读课程固然很少顾及，就连快速阅读课程本身，也未将其定为强化训练的重点。该试项所着重考查的，是考生对通篇文章的整体理解（Skimming）及信息检索时的定位能力（Scanning）。该试项的设置，会对今后的快速阅读教学起到一定的促进推动作用。

"仔细阅读理解"（Reading in Depth）试项中的第一部分，在新四级考试中采用的是"选词填空"，而在新六级考试中采用的则是"简答题"（Short Answer Questions）。"简答题"原属供选用的题型，现改设为固定题型。其目的不但着眼于考查学生对各种阅读技能的具体运用，能否在语篇层面上领会所读文章的主旨和内涵，而且还进一步要求考生以最直接、简约的言词，对问题作出"一语中的"式的回答。平时教学中，学生比较习惯于"多种选择题"的练习，较少做这类问答题的练习，现在似有必要强化这方面的针对性训练。

新六级考试中变量最大的，当属"听力理解"（Listening Comprehension）。该试项由原来的两个组成部分，扩展为三个组成部分。第一部分原含十组短对话，现在改由八组短对话和两组长对话构成。"长对话"（Long Conversation）是新六级考试增设的内容，用于检测考生捕捉、提炼信息的能力。第二部分"短文听力"，仍保持原样。至于第三部分"复合式听写"（Compound Dictation），原属供选用的题型，在新六级考试中则转为固定题型。

新六级考试的最后一项题型变化，是以"汉译英"替换原有的"英译汉"。就目前"汉译英"的测试内容来看，并不要求考生作整句翻译，而是侧重考查英语常用词、短语和基本句型的掌握以及语法知识在语言表达时的实际运用。

很显然，改革后的大学英语六级考试，更加注重考察学生的语言实际运用能力。从客观效果来看，考试改革方案的逐步实施，也确实对大学英语教学改革，起到一定的推动促进作用。大学英语教学中的某些薄弱环节正逐步得到强固。我们还该注意到，大学英语新六级考试除了题型、内容方面的变化，对各试项的分值比例也进行了调整。例如，"听力理解"从原来的 20%，增加至 35%；"阅读理解"内容扩充、题量增多之后，分值比例却由原有的 40%，降为 35%；"写作"加"翻译"，占 20%；"词汇及结构"（Vocabulary and Structure）试项全部撤除；而以词汇、语法运用为主要测试内容的"改错"（Error Correction）项目，仍保持原有的 10%。我们应该由此意识到，新的大学英语六级考试正是通过上述两方面的变化，在向我们传递这样一个信息：向来以语法、阅读为核心的大学英语教学，现在正朝着语言技能全面并举的方向倾斜。

总的来说，新六级考试题型繁多，题目分散，考生应把握好考试流程的节奏。2007 年《大学英语六级测试试题集》（新题型版），能在一定程度上满足大学英语新六级考生的需求。本试题集为考生提供了一个系统复习、进行适度模拟测试的机会。这不仅能帮助我们熟悉各种新题型、顺应新的流程变化，而且还使我们的英语运用能力在实际训练中得以巩固、提高。

最后，我们恳切希望使用《大学英语六级测试试题集》（新题型版）的教师和同学，能在使用过程中及时提出宝贵的批评和建议。

编　者
2007 年 2 月

CONTENTS

COLLEGE ENGLISH PRACTICE TESTS (CET-6)

Practice Test 1

Part I Writing (30 minutes)

Note: The topic and directions for writing are shown on *Answer Sheet 1*.（注意：此部分试题在**答题卡**１上。）

Part II Reading Comprehension (Skimming and Scanning) (15 minutes)

Directions: *In this part, you will have 15 minutes to go over the passage quickly and answer the questions on **Answer Sheet 1**.*

For questions 1 – 4, mark

Y *(for YES)*   *if the statement agrees with the information given in the passage;*

N *(for NO)*   *if the statement contradicts the information given in the passage;*

NG *(for NOT GIVEN)*   *if the information is not given in the passage.*

For questions 5 – 10, complete the sentences with the information given in the passage.

Workplace 2020

— By Susan Paynter

It's a summer morning in the year 2020 and not yet 7:30 a.m. Jane Hanson, flushed from her early morning run along the river, sets down in her work station at home. She is still in her sweats, and this is the first day all week she has slid her knees under a desk.

For Jane and millions of other so-called knowledge workers, the job is wherever she is. Today, it's at home. A graphics designer, Jane has a current assignment to develop a new logo for a sports shoe for a client. She's delighted to have the project, since it gives her a chance to work with Aki, her international partner in Yokohama（横滨）, Japan. Today, Aki's face pops up on her computer screen as she checks "see-mail," a type of communication that replaced E-mail a few years ago. With a click, Jane can call up the video image and voice of each person who left her a message the previous night.

This morning, Jane calls Aki back and they see and hear each other via video phone. They collaborate on an interactive screen almost as if they are standing side by side at the same drawing board.

Jane's husband, George, can often be found working at home as well. "Going to the office" has become an option, not a necessity, with the advent of the wireless computer. George teaches at a nearby university, and often broadcasts his lectures via satellite. But this morning he is at an on-campus seminar. The kids are also out of the house today attending classes at a nearby language and science lab. Jane is grateful to have the house to herself today as she and Aki work on the logo.

The Virtual Office

Twenty years from now, as many as 25 million Americans — nearly 20 percent of the workforce — will stretch the boundaries between home and work far beyond the lines drawn now. Technology has already so accelerated the pace of change in the workplace that few futurists are willing to predict hard numbers. But nearly all trend-trackers agree that much of the next century's work will be decentralized, done at home or in satellite offices on a schedule tailored to fit worker's lives and the needs of their families. Even international boundaries may blur as the economy goes truly global.

Between 1990 and 1998, telecommuting doubled from about 3 percent to 6 percent of the working population — or about 8.2 million people. The numbers are expected to double again in far less time, with as much as 12 percent of the population telecommuting by the year 2005, says Charlie Grantham, director of the Institute for the Study of Distributed Work in Windsor, California.

Wireless computers and seamless communications systems are already in the works and fueling the trend. The video phone is not far off, an advance that many futurists believe will make even more companies comfortable with employees working from home. "Now, we communicate at the level of radio," says Gerald Celente, author of *Trends 2000* and director of The Trends Research Institute of Rhinebeck, New York. E-mail and the telephone are primitive, he argues, and make people feel cut off from co-workers. But once everyone can see each other on the screen, long-distance relationships will feel more intimate.

What about the office? "Today's offices are a direct descendant of the factory," says Gil Gordon, a consultant based in Monmouth Junction, New Jersey, who has spent nearly two decades advising companies on how to institute telecommuting and more flexible work patterns. "They may be better lighted, but they're much the same."

Still, Gordon does not think the office building will vanish altogether. Rather, the office of 2020 will be just one place for focused work that requires true collaboration. It will also be a key site for socializing and cementing the relationships that keep a business going.

Physically, however, it may look quite different. The typical office today allocates about 80 percent of the space to offices and cubicles, with the rest given over to formal meeting rooms, Gordon says. That will soon change to 20 percent for individual work stations and 40 percent for "touch-down spaces" to land in but not to move into. We may sit still only long enough to check E-mail and access data.

Gordon predicts the remaining 40 percent of space will be devoted to sites used by teams and groups, including conference rooms. But they will not look like today's dull conference rooms. Instead, many will be designed to promote connection and creativity.

It's also likely that companies will share space. Instead of more high-rise office towers, there will be more multi-use centers shared by several firms. "You will call ahead and reserve a space and check-in time, and a kind of concierge (服务台职员) will assign you a spot and make sure that, as of seven a.m. that day, your phone rings there."

With all this mobility, employees may long for a sense of belonging. Transitional workspaces may become more individualized, according to Gordon. "A lighted panel may display pictures of your family, your dog or your sailboat." Futurist Lisa Aldisert, a senior consultant with a New York-based trends analysis firm, suggests that, through sophisticated microchip applications, a roving employee will be able with the flick of a switch to alter wall colors and room temperature to fit her mood.

New Work Relationships

The benefits of these changes, for both workers and companies, are already evident to many. Compelling studies have convinced many companies that telecommuting is a plus for the bottom line. Aetna, for example, finds that the people who process its claims produce about 20 percent more when they work outside of the office.

What will some other side effects be? No one can guess yet just how the legal relationships between workers and employers will change. Many workers may move from a salary system to an independent contractor system. Or they may sign on with different clients on a project-by-project basis. Companies might continue to provide benefits to many workers to assure their loyalty. In any case, companies will still try to find ways to foster a sense of identity with their products and services. To do their best, workers will still need to feel part of a team, says Leslie Faught, president of Working Solutions, a work/life benefit company based in Portland, Oregon.

Some futurists also note that technology may change the hierarchy of most workplaces. In fact, work may become much more democratic, as companies share more information to get the job done. Introducing software to streamline communications within a company, for example, can also mean allowing access to information that was formerly held by one or two people. That can be threatening to some managers at first, but many change their minds, once they see how much better working relationships can be. "Once they get on board, many managers realize their own lives are better too," says Kathy King of the Oregon Office of Energy whose job is to promote telecommunicating from an environmental standpoint.

New Social Life

A growing number of American workers have already had a taste of the future. Leslie Faught "talks" via E-mail with customers and partners scattered across South America, Canada and Asia. She says being able to see them via video phone and work with them via interactive computer will only strengthen personal connections she has already forged.

Nonetheless, being part of a virtual community will never entirely replace the need for in-person connections right here at home. That's why workers of the future will also flock to satellite work centers in their neighborhoods. Many will have amenities (福利生活区) — provided by companies or entrepreneurs — that bring people together, as they used to gather around the water-cooler. It's already easy to see prototypes in places like Seattle, where Kinko's and Tully's Coffee are next door, and people bounce in and out while they do both work and community projects.

At the heart of all these changes, says Gil Gordon, is the fact that we have finally begun to separate the idea of work from the place where we do it. And that will make blending work and family a lot easier for many people. Like Jane Hanson and her husband, many families will find life less hectic and more integrated.

Note: Please put down on *Answer Sheet 1* your answers to the questions in this part. (注意：此部分试题请在**答题卡** 1 上作答。)

1. This article begins with an episode taken from a sci-fi story with Jane Hanson as its heroine.

2. The development of technology is speeding up the pace of changes in the workplace.

3. In the years to come, the percentage of telecommuters will grow far beyond the futurists' wildest expectations.

4. Realizing the potential benefits, executives are expecting those changes in the workplace with even greater enthusiasm.

5. From the context we may figure out that "telecommuting" means _____.

6. It appears that being flexible in work patterns, telecommuters tend to be _____ in efficiency than their office-based counterparts.

7. Regardless of other workplace changes, employees may long for _____ and workers will still need to _____ in order to do their best.

8. Offices in the future tend to look different and serve different purposes; they will most likely be designed to _____.

9. The main advantage of the video phone over E-mail and the telephone is _____.

10. With all these possible changes in the workplace or work patterns, people may find it easier to _____ between work and family life.

Part III Listening Comprehension (35 minutes)
Section A

Directions: *In this section, you will hear 8 short conversations and 2 long conversations. At the end of each conversation, one or more questions will be asked about what was said. Both the conversation and the questions will be spoken only once. After each question, there will be a pause. During the pause, you must read the four choices marked A), B), C) and D), and decide which is the best answer. Then mark the corresponding letter on **Answer Sheet 2** with a single line through the center.*

Note: Please put down on **Answer Sheet 2** your answers to the following questions. (注意：此部分试题请在**答题卡 2** 上作答。)

11. A) He's upset because he has cut himself.
    B) He can't face the physics instructor any longer.
    C) He wants the woman to cut out science courses.
    D) He doesn't have the ability to be a scientist.

12. A) She should be careful about her money.
    B) She should buy the brown suit.
    C) She should find another job to make more money.
    D) She shouldn't buy the brown suit.

13. A) One hour.   B) Two hours.
    C) Three hours.   D) Four hours.

14. A) He has hurt his hand.
    B) He can't fix it.
    C) He is very busy at the moment.
    D) He wants the woman to give him a hand.

15. A) It's raining.
    B) She doesn't like playing tennis.
    C) She doesn't want to get sunburned.
    D) It's a hot day.

16. A) A plumber.   B) An automobile mechanic.
    C) A doctor.   D) A hair stylist.

17. A) Apologetic.   B) Grateful.
    C) Disappointed.   D) Angry.

18. A) Three years ago.   B) This year.
    C) Last year.   D) In December.

Questions 19 to 21 are based on the conversation you have just heard.

19. A) Training.   B) Typing.
    C) Computer skills.   D) Word-processing.

20. A) Just like an advanced typewriter.
    B) Equipped with a memory.
    C) Used as a filing cabinet.
    D) Easier to check and correct mistakes.

21. A) A couple of weeks with the computer first, and a few months with
       the word-processor later.
    B) About one month with the word processor first, and a two-month,
       part-time period with the computer use.
    C) About two months with computer first, and a one-month, part-time
       period with the word processor later.
    D) About a two-month, part-time period with the word processor and
       computer.

Questions 22 to 25 are based on the conversation you have just heard.

22. A) Because he has pneumonia.   B) Because his wife told him to.

C）Because he feels tired.　　　D）Because his wife feels tired.

23. A）A couple of days.　　　　B）Four days.
    C）Six months.　　　　　　　D）Two weeks.

24. A）When the doctor told him to.　B）When his wife told him to.
    C）When he had to.　　　　　　D）When he felt better.

25. A）Being on sick leave.
    B）Staying in hospital for further tests.
    C）Changing his job.
    D）Taking some new medications.

Section B

Directions: *In this section, you will hear 3 short passages. At the end of each passage, you will hear some questions. Both the passage and the questions will be spoken only once. After you hear a question, you must choose the best answer from the four choices marked A), B), C) and D). Then mark the corresponding letter on **Answer Sheet 2** with a single line through the center.*

Note: Please put down on **Answer Sheet 2** your answers to the following questions.（注意：此部分试题请在答题卡2上作答。）

Passage One
Questions 26 to 28 are based on the passage you have just heard.

26. A）Jobs on Wall Street.
    B）How schools are changing to reflect the economy.
    C）Types of graduate degrees.
    D）Changes in enrollment for MBA schools.

27. A）Princeton.　　　　　　　B）Yale.
    C）Harvard.　　　　　　　　D）Stanford.

28. A）Lack of necessity for an MBA and an economic recession.

B) Low salary and foreign competition.

C) Fewer MBA schools and fewer entry-level jobs.

D) Declining population and economic prosperity.

Passage Two

Questions 29 to 31 are based on the passage you have just heard.

29. A) In the later 1920s.   B) In the mid-1950s.

     C) In the 1970s.   D) In the mid-1980s.

30. A) It will act as a computer as well.

B) It will do away with stereo equipment.

C) It will provide a better picture.

D) It will replace transistors.

31. A) There have been three major changes in TV technology since 1927.

B) Basic TV technology nowadays is quite different from that of the first TV set.

C) Digital TV sets incorporate computer technology.

D) Digital TV technology originated in the U.S.

Passage Three

Questions 32 to 35 are based on the passage you have just heard.

32. A) Power.   B) Academic degree.

     C) Wealth.   D) Diligence.

33. A) The change of lifestyle.

B) The change of the nature of occupations.

C) The increase of social wealth.

D) The increase of job opportunities.

34. A) Politicians.   B) Clerks.

     C) Manual workers.   D) Lawyers.

35. A) Farm workers.   B) White-collar workers.

C) Blue-collar workers.   D) Not mentioned.

Section C

Directions: *In this section, you will hear a passage three times. When the passage is read for the first time, you should listen carefully for its general idea. When the passage is read for the second time, you are required to fill in the blanks numbered from 36 to 43 with the exact words you have just heard. For blanks numbered from 44 to 46 you are required to fill in the missing information. For these blanks, you can either use the exact words you have just heard or write down the main points in your own words. Finally, when the passage is read for the third time, you should check what you have written.*

Note: The questions in this section are all shown on *Answer Sheet 2*; please put down your answers on it as required. （注意：此部分试题在**答题卡**2上；请在**答题卡**2上作答。）

Part IV   Reading Comprehension (Reading in Depth) (25 minutes)

Section A

Directions: *In this section, there is a short passage with 5 questions or incomplete statements. Read the passage carefully. Then answer the questions or complete the statements in the fewest possible words on Answer Sheet 2.*

Questions 47 to 51 are based on the following passage.

In a sense the university has failed. It has stored great quantities of knowledge; it teaches more people; and despite its failures, it teaches them better. It is in the application of this knowledge that the failure has come. Of the great branches of knowledge — the sciences, the social sciences and humanities — the sciences are applied. Strenuous and occasionally successful efforts are made to apply the social sciences, but almost never are the humanities well applied. We do not use philosophy in defining our conduct. We do not use literature as a source of real and vicarious （通过他人而间接获得的） experience. The great task of the university in the next generation is to learn to use the knowledge we have for the questions that come before us. The university should organize courses around primary problems. The difference between a primary problem and a secondary or even tertiary (第三级即高等教育的) problem is that primary problems tend to be around for a long time, whereas the less important ones get solved.

One primary problem is that of interfering with biological development. The next generation, and perhaps this one, will be able to interfere chemically with the actual development of an individual and perhaps biologically by interfering with an individual's genes. Obviously, there are benefits both to individuals and to society from eliminating, or at least improving mentally and physically deformed persons. On the other hand, there could be very serious consequences if this knowledge were used with premeditation to produce superior and subordinate classes, each genetically prepared to carry out a predetermined mission. This can be done, but what happens to free will and the rights of the individual? Here we have a primary problem that will still exist when we are all dead. Of course, the traditional faculty members would say, "But the students won't learn enough to go to graduate school." And certainly they would not learn everything we are in the habit of making them learn, but they would learn some other things.

Note: Please put down on *Answer Sheet 2* your answers to the questions in this section. (注意：此部分试题请在**答题卡**2上作答。)

47. According to the author, the university's greatest shortcoming lies in its failure to _____.

48. It can be inferred that the author presupposes that the reader will regard a course in literature as a course _____.

49. What does the expression "this one" in Paragraph 2 refer to?

50. In this passage, what does the author mention as an example of the possible misuse of scientific knowledge with serious consequences?

51. The development discussed in the passage is primarily a problem of _____ philosophy.

Section B

Directions: *There are 2 passages in this section. Each passage is followed by some questions or unfinished statements. For each of them there are four choices marked A), B), C) and D). You should decide on the best choice and mark the corresponding letter on **Answer Sheet 2** with a single line through the centre.*

Passage One

Questions 52 to 56 are based on the following passage.

Generation gaps are nothing new. Imperfect communication between age groups plagued the ancient Greeks and current workers alike.

Many an older worker chafes at an under-30 colleague who surfs the Internet, listens to his Sony Walkman and chats on the phone or with his desk mate — all while working on a project due in an hour.

Sometimes, of course, he isn't working, and that's a whole different issue. But sometimes he is getting lots of great stuff done. In the meantime, the different work styles create a case of "Would you please shut up?" vs. "Lighten up. Get a life."

Marc Prensky, vice president of Bankers Trust and founder of its interactive learning subsidiary, Corporate Gameware, was on point in *Across the Board*, a publication of the conference Board. The business research organization titled Prensky's article "Twitch Speed," a reference to the fast pace of video game play.

Today's under-30 workers likely grew up in a multimedia, technology-rich, twitch-speed environment. Prensky says they simultaneously did homework, watched TV and listened to music; this exposure changed the ways they receive and process information.

Baby boomers and older workers may or may not have done homework by TV, but much else has changed. Sociologists say the over-30s are more likely to want room doors closed. TV off. One thing happening at a time. Quiet, please! ·

When the two heritages clash in the workplace, it pits comfort with speed and "multitasking" against comfort with deliberation and focused concentration.

Sound familiar? If the gap has become a chasm in your workplace, it's time to talk. Both work styles can be productive, but both sides need to make accommodations so the other's productivity isn't impaired.

Note: Please put down on *Answer Sheet 2* your answers to the following questions. （注意：此部分试题请在答题卡 2 上作答。）

52. This passage mainly describes _____.
    A) generation gaps
    B) work styles of different age groups
    C) lack of mutual understanding between the old and the young
    D) imperfect communication between old and young workers

53. From the context we may figure out that the word "plagued" (Paragraph 1) means _____.
    A) annoyed   B) infected
    C) damaged   D) affected

54. According to the passage, which of the following is NOT true?
    A) Older workers often feel annoyed about their young colleagues' attitudes towards work.
    B) Younger workers always do a good job of their work though they prefer to listen to music or chat with others while working.
    C) The different work styles may sometimes lead to an unnecessary argument.
    D) Older workers are used to working in a comfortable and quiet environment so that they can fully concentrate on what they are doing.

55. The author agrees with Marc Prensky on the point that younger workers prefer a multitasking style because _____.
    A) they are smart and energetic
    B) they have the special ability to perform several tasks at the same time
    C) brought up in a special cultural background, they have developed a behavioral pattern different from that of their older colleagues
    D) they have been trained to receive and process information in a special

way

56. The author maintains that both sides should _____ if the two different work styles clash headlong.
    A) be patient and tolerant
    B) realize that both work styles are productive
    C) make efforts to avoid doing damage to the other's productivity
    D) make compromises to bridge the gulf between them

Passage Two

Questions 57 to 61 are based on the following passage.

The 1990s were all about downsizing, the practice of laying off large numbers of staff in the search for efficiency and profitability. More than 17 million workers were laid off between 1988 and 1995, although about 28 million jobs were added back to the economy.

Two economists at the Federal Reserve Bank in Dallas, W. Michael Cox and Richard Alin, reported on the 10 largest downsizers of the 1990 – 1995 period, which include Digital Equipment, McDonnell Douglas, General Electric, and Kmart. Collective output (sales adjusted for inflation) declined by almost 10 percent. On the other hand, productivity per worker rose nearly 28 percent, compared with a gain of 1.5 percent in the rest of the economy. Says Cox, "Most of the companies emerged from the downsizing more competitive than before and thus were able to provide greater security to their workers." The cost? 850,000 workers.

Yet negative outcomes prevailed at many firms. Devastatingly low morale, increased disability claims and suits for wrongful discharge (解雇), and general mistrust of management plague many companies. A study done at the Wharton School examined data on several thousand firms and found that downsizing had little or no effect on earnings or stock market performance. Far more effective were leveraged buyouts (举债全额收购) and portfolio (投资组合) restructuring.

There is some evidence that consistent focus on creating value for shareholders, which includes paring unneeded workers, actually increases jobs in the long run, "Stronger, leaner companies are able to compete in the world market more effectively, and that ultimately draws jobs back to those companies." That's the opinion of Thomas Copland, a director of McKinsey and Co., a management consulting firm that studied 20 years of data or 1,000 companies in the United States, Canada, Germany, Holland, Belgium, and France. The study revealed that, unlike those in the United States and Canada, the European firms lost jobs in the long term because their returns to shareholders fell between 1970 and 1990.

Although long-run growth is a pleasant prospect for shareholders, the short-term loss of jobs and income has left many employees and their families struggling in the aftermath of downsizing.

Note: Please put down on *Answer Sheet 2* your answers to the following questions. (注意：此部分试题请在**答题卡 2** 上作答。)

57. The term "downsizing" in this passage means _____.
    A) just cutting down to size
    B) producing smaller models or styles
    C) cutting jobs and positions for higher performance and profits
    D) cutting down on incentive programs

58. Some economists maintain that the practice of downsizing tends to _____.
    A) win immediate earnings for shareholders
    B) improve productivity and competitive edge
    C) lead to a more effective recombination of investments
    D) all of the above

59. According to this passage, downsizing will result in _____ at many companies.
    A) low morale on the part of employees
    B) disputes between labor and management
    C) general distrust of management
    D) all of the above

60. The word "paring" in Paragraph 4 is closest in meaning to _____.

A) peeling   B) firing
C) relocating   D) re-training

61. Which of the following might serve as a suitable title for this passage?
    A) Downsizing: Pros and Cons
    B) Downsizing and Competitive Edge
    C) The Cost of Downsizing
    D) Downsizing and Gains for Shareholders

Part V   Error Correction (15 minutes)

Directions: *This part consists of a short passage. In this passage, there are altogether 10 mistakes, one in each numbered line. You may have to change a word, add a word or delete a word. Mark out the mistakes and put the corrections in the blanks provided. If you change a word, cross it out and write the correct word in the corresponding blank. If you add a word, put an insertion mark (∧) in the right place and write the missing word in the blank. If you delete a word, cross it out and put a slash (/) in the blank.*

Example:

Television is rapidly becoming the litera-
ture of our ~~periods~~. Many of the arguments   1. __time/times/period__
~~having~~ used for the study of literature as a   2. _____
school subject are valid for ∧ study of televi-   3. ____the____
sion.

Note: The questions in this part are shown on *Answer Sheet 2*; please put down your answers on the **Sheet**. （注意：此部分试题在**答题卡 2** 上；请在**答题卡 2** 上作答。）

Part VI   Translation (5 minutes)

Directions: *Complete the following sentences by translating into English the Chinese given in brackets.*

Note: Please put down on *Answer Sheet 2* your answers to the questions in this part.（注意：此部分试题请在**答题卡** 2 上作答。）

72. A full-scale security operation ＿＿＿＿＿＿＿（现在正在实施之中）.

73. ＿＿＿＿＿＿＿（突然遇上一场倾盆大雨）he was wet through.

74. You can never get through negotiation ＿＿＿＿＿＿＿（用武力所得不到的东西）.

75. It is important that ＿＿＿＿＿＿＿（展览馆的工程能如期竣工）.

76. ＿＿＿＿＿＿＿（与其让他们干这事）, we prefer to do the job ourselves.

Answer Sheet 1 (答题卡 1)

Part I   **Writing**   **(30 minutes)**

Directions: *For this part, you are allowed 30 minutes to write a short essay entitled* **Schoolbags: Too Heavy for Schoolkids**. *You should write at least 150 words following the outline given below:*

1. 学生的书包越来越重
2. 造成这情况的原因
3. 如何减轻学生的负担

SCHOOLBAGS: TOO HEAVY FOR SCHOOLKIDS

Answer Sheet 1 (答题卡 1)

....

....

....

....

....

....

....

....

....

....

....

....

....

....

....

....

....

....

Part II   Reading Comprehension (Skimming and Scanning) (15 minutes)

1. [Y] [N] [NG]   5. _____   8. _____

2. [Y] [N] [NG]

3. [Y] [N] [NG]   6. _____   9. _____

4. [Y] [N] [NG]   7. _____   10. _____

Answer Sheet 2 (答题卡2)

Part III   Section A   Section B

11. [A] [B] [C] [D]   16. [A] [B] [C] [D]   21. [A] [B] [C] [D]   26. [A] [B] [C] [D]   31. [A] [B] [C] [D]

12. [A] [B] [C] [D]   17. [A] [B] [C] [D]   22. [A] [B] [C] [D]   27. [A] [B] [C] [D]   32. [A] [B] [C] [D]

13. [A] [B] [C] [D]   18. [A] [B] [C] [D]   23. [A] [B] [C] [D]   28. [A] [B] [C] [D]   33. [A] [B] [C] [D]

14. [A] [B] [C] [D]   19. [A] [B] [C] [D]   24. [A] [B] [C] [D]   29. [A] [B] [C] [D]   34. [A] [B] [C] [D]

15. [A] [B] [C] [D]   20. [A] [B] [C] [D]   25. [A] [B] [C] [D]   30. [A] [B] [C] [D]   35. [A] [B] [C] [D]

Part III   Section C

Around the world young people are spending (36) _____ sums of money to listen to rock music. *Forbes Magazine* (37) _____ that at least fifty rock stars have (38) _____ of between two million and six million dollars (39) _____ year.

"It doesn't make sense," says Johnny Mathis, one of the (40) _____ music millionaires, who made a million dollars a year when he was most popular, in the 1950s. "Performers aren't (41) _____ this kind of money. In fact, nobody is."

But the rock stars' admirers seem to (42) _____. Those who love rock music spend about two billion dollars a year for records. They pay 150 million to see rock stars in person.

Some (43) _____ think the customers are buying more than music. According to one theory, (44) _____

_____. There is no gulf between the audience and the performer. Every boy and girl in the audience thinks, "I could sing like that." (45) _____

_____. Young people are glad to pay to worship a rock star because it is a way of worshipping themselves.

Luck is a key word for explaining the success of many. In 1972 one of the luckiest was Don McLean, who wrote and sang "American Pie." McLean earned more than a million dollars from recordings of "American Pie." Then, too, (46) _____

_____.

21

Answer Sheet 2 (答题卡2)

Part IV   Section A   Part V   Error Correction   (15 minutes)

47. _____

_____

48. _____

_____

49. _____

_____

_____

50. _____

_____

51. _____

_____

_____

Part IV   Section B

52. [A][B][C][D]
53. [A][B][C][D]
54. [A][B][C][D]
55. [A][B][C][D]
56. [A][B][C][D]
57. [A][B][C][D]
58. [A][B][C][D]
59. [A][B][C][D]
60. [A][B][C][D]
61. [A][B][C][D]

It was once thought that air pollution affected only

the area immediately around large cities with factories

and/or heavy automobile traffic. Today we know that

because these are the areas with the worst air pollution,   62. _____

the problem is literally world-wide. At several occasions   63. _____

over the last decade, a heavy cloud of air pollution has

covered the entire half of the United States and lead to   64. _____

health warnings even in rural areas away from any minor   65. _____

concentration of manufacturing and automobile traffic.

What has been found that air pollution is killing trees in   66. _____

the mountains of California and melons on the farms of

Indiana. In fact, the very weather of the entire earth   67. _____

may be affected by air pollution. Some scientists feel

that the increasing concentration of carbon dioxide in

the air resulted from the burning of fossil fuels (coal   68. _____

and oil) is creating a "greenhouse effect" — holding in

heat reflected to the earth and raising the world's   69. _____

average temperature. If this view is correct and that the   70. _____

world's temperature is raised only a few degrees, much

of ice cap will melt and cities such as New York,

Boston, Miami, or New Orleans will be under water.   71. _____

Part VI   Translation   (5 minutes)

72. _____

73. _____

74. _____

75. _____

76. _____

Practice Test 2

Part I　Writing (30 minutes)

Note: The topic and directions for writing are shown on *Answer Sheet 1*.（注意：此部分试题在**答题卡** 1 上。）

Part II　Reading Comprehension (Skimming and Scanning) (15 minutes)

Directions: *In this part, you will have 15 minutes to go over the passage quickly and answer the questions on Answer Sheet 1.*

For questions 1 – 4, mark

Y (for YES)　　　　*if the statement agrees with the information given in the passage;*

N (for NO)　　　　*if the statement contradicts the information given in the passage;*

NG (for NOT GIVEN)　　*if the information is not given in the passage.*

For questions 5 – 10, complete the sentences with the information given in the passage.

A Book That Changed Our Thinking

— By Karl Krahnke

The Book

America in 1962 was still emerging from the comfortable decade of the 1950s, a time in which life generally seemed good and many technological advances of the previous twenty or thirty years promised a happier, healthier, and safer future. But clouds were on the horizon, and many of the questions and doubts that would characterize the decade of the 1960s were already apparent. One cloud that quickly became a major storm took the form of a book that was published in 1962, *Silent Spring*. *Silent Spring* is one of a few books that have changed history.

Silent Spring is about chemicals, specifically about one type of chemical chlorinated hydrocarbons — and more specifically about one famous member of that group, DDT. Many people who have grown up since the 1960s have not heard of DDT, but before *Silent Spring*, and for a number of years afterward, DDT and its relatives were important tools in the civilized world's attempt to control nature through the use of technology and chemicals. DDT is a powerful insecticide and was used throughout the world to kill insect pests of all kinds.

DDT had been discovered in 1939 and began to be widely used during the Second World War. For many years it seemed to be just one more miraculous product of modern science. DDT was used to destroy populations of many harmful insects, malaria-carrying mosquitoes, lice, and flies. There is no question that DDT and similar chemicals did, and still are doing, a lot of good. The danger from insect-carried diseases such as malaria and yellow fever has been greatly reduced, and the lives of many people have been saved and lengthened by their use.

Silent Spring, however, told about the other side of DDT and its relatives. Using carefully collected scientific evidence, the author showed that DDT and similar pesticides had at least two dangerous side effects. One of these was the tendency of pesticides to kill all of the insects in the location where they were used. Not all insects are harmful, however. Many bees, for example, perform necessary functions, such as pollinating plants and even controlling the numbers of other, more harmful, insects. When useful insects are eliminated, the result has often been greater problems than before the pesticide was used. A second problem with chlorinated hydrocarbons is that they do not disappear quickly; they are stable chemicals that accumulate in the bodies of insects and the birds and animals that eat them and continue to do harm when and where the effect was not intended. Birds are especially affected by DDT-type pesticides. Many birds eat insects and worms as food, and the chemicals that were in the insects collect in their bodies, frequently leading to their death. As *Silent Spring* demonstrated so clearly, the disappearance of many kinds of birds was due to the presence of pesticides in their food sources.

Most importantly, *Silent Spring* brought to the world at large the beginning of an understanding of modern ecology. We began to see that the natural world we live in is made up of a number of plants, insects, and animals, some good, some not so good, and that we cannot encourage or eliminate some without producing effects in many others, and even in ourselves.

Silent Spring is a powerful book, beautifully and sensitively written, and it carries a strong message. It is full of complex scientific information, but it is equally a very human and caring book. It does not try to present a balanced picture or to find excuses for the mistakes we made with pesticides. It is an argument for a new and different way of looking at nature and our relationship with nature. The book convinced many people that controlling nature was not always possible and was certainly not always a good idea.

The Author

Almost as remarkable as the story of *Silent Spring* itself is that of the book's author, Rachel Carson. Ms. Carson's background and education did little to indicate that she would affect the public's thinking about pesticides in such a dramatic way.

She was born in Pennsylvania in 1907. Although she grew up in a family of five, she was especially close to her mother, who encouraged Rachel's education and love of nature. The family's house was in a rural setting, and Rachel spent much time getting to know the wildlife of the area. She also loved writing, and even before finishing high school she was sending stories and poems to magazines for publication. Not surprisingly, then, when Rachel Carson went to college, she began as an English major with plans to be a writer. She attended a small women's college, Pennsylvania College for Women. In her second year, she discovered science and quickly changed her major to biology. As she explained, rather than losing her interest in writing, she had found what she wanted to write about.

Carson graduated in 1929 and immediately went on to a graduate program at Johns Hopkins University. Supporting herself by teaching and working as a laboratory assistant, she finished her thesis and received a master's degree in marine zoology in 1932. She taught part-time at several universities for a few years and then went to work for the U.S. government in 1936. Her first job was writing radio programs on marine life. These radio scripts were turned into a magazine article and later into a book, *Under the Sea Wind*.

Rachel Carson wrote and worked as a government biologist for a number of years. Finally, in 1951, *The Sea Around Us* was published and was highly regarded by the public and by scientists. The book is simply a detailed description of the sea and the life in it, but it is written with the warmth and skill of a writer. Carson was given a National Book Award for her work.

In 1955, Carson published *The Edge of the Sea*, a book about the shores of the oceans and the life on those shores. It, too, was extremely successful. By this time, Rachel Carson had gained a reputation as a wonderful writer with a deep knowledge of science, especially on matters related to the sea. She was liked and respected by scientists and writers, but she led a very quiet and private life away from publicity. She lived with her mother and her grandnephew.

By the late 1950s, Carson had become interested in a more controversial problem, the effect that some attempts to control insects were having on wildlife, especially birds, and on humans. She began working on *Silent Spring*. Although many of the people she had contacted for information about pesticides and their use had warned her that the book she had planned would be controversial, no one was really prepared for the attacks on *Silent Spring* after it was published in 1962. The book was as popular as her previous books had been, but many critics, especially from the chemical industry and the government, called the book untrue and exaggerated. Angry reviews appeared in newspapers and magazines, and commentators on radio and television debated the arguments made in the book. During this time Carson remained largely quiet, although she made several calm and sensible responses to the criticism. Unfortunately, she had developed cancer several years earlier, and she eventually died of it in 1965.

Rachel Carson gave us a precious gift. She changed our thinking about science and nature and how we interact with nature. She did it not just with fact and argument, but with writing that is as enjoyable to read as it is informative.

Note: Please put down on *Answer Sheet 1* your answers to the questions in this part. （注意：此部分试题请在**答题卡** 1 上作答。）

1. *Silent Spring* is a book written about the use of DDT, a powerful insecticide, and its dangerous side effects.

2. The decade of the 1960s was characterized by the ever-growing suspicion

of the civilized world's attempt to control nature through the use of technology.

3. *Silent Spring* contained so much carefully collected scientific evidence that it was widely acclaimed as a significant book when it came out in the early 1960s.

4. The book *Silent Spring*, to a certain extent, marks the beginning of our understanding of modern ecology.

5. The book *Silent Spring* has changed our thinking by providing us with an entirely new and different way of _____.

6. In her book Rachel Carson asserts that "controlling nature" _____ and does not necessarily mean _____.

7. Rachel Carson started writing before _____.

8. She studies at Pennsylvania College for Women first with a major in _____ then changed her major to _____.

9. How many books did Carson write before *Silent Spring*, and what were their titles? _____.

10. Rachel Carson's writings are both _____ and _____.

Part III　Listening Comprehension (35 minutes)
Section A
Directions: *In this section, you will hear 8 short conversations and 2 long conversations. At the end of each conversation, one or more questions will be asked about what was said. Both the conversation and the questions will be spoken only once. After each question, there will be a pause. During the pause, you must read the four choices marked A), B), C) and D), and decide which is the best answer. Then mark the corresponding letter on **Answer Sheet 2** with a single line through the center.*

Note: Please put down on **Answer Sheet 2** your answers to the following questions. （注意：此部分试题请在答题卡 2 上作答。）

11. A) At 9:00.　　　　　　　　B) At 9:45.
　　C) At 9:15.　　　　　　　　D) At 10:00.

12. A) A cab driver.　　　　　　B) A repairman.
　　C) A traffic officer.　　　　D) An automobile salesman.

13. A) The noise in the library.　　B) The heat inside.
　　C) The late hour.　　　　　D) The crowded room.

14. A) The woman doesn't like orange juice.
　　B) The woman forgot to buy orange juice.
　　C) The man was in a car crash this morning.
　　D) The man broke the container of orange juice.

15. A) She hasn't gone camping for several weeks.
　　B) She likes to take long camping trips.
　　C) She prefers not to go camping on weekends.
　　D) She takes a long time to plan her trips.

16. A) A gun store.　　　　　　B) A sports store.
　　C) A camera store.　　　　D) A lamp store.

17. A) Timid.　　　　　　　　B) Hostile.
　　C) Enthusiastic.　　　　　D) Sympathetic.

18. A) Getting the help will be difficult.
　　B) The help from the school authority will get the competition to start.
　　C) She likes ball games.
　　D) Both B and C.

Questions 19 to 21 are based on the conversation you have just heard.

19. A) He failed his last test.
　　B) He can't find his watch.
　　C) He's taking examinations soon.

D) He missed his medical checkup.

20. A) She is a medical student.
    B) She is older than he is.
    C) She has been through a similar experience.
    D) She has a sense of humor.

21. A) He has never heard of them.   B) He didn't have their number.
    C) He hasn't had the time.   D) He couldn't afford the fee.

Questions 22 to 25 are based on the conversation you have just heard.

22. A) An actress.   B) A writer.
    C) A teacher.   D) A painter.

23. A) Because Diego came from a famous family.
    B) Because Diego was highly intelligent.
    C) Because Diego was a man with a great fortune.
    D) Because he could not pay his daughter's medical expense any more.

24. A) Because she wanted to hurt Diego.
    B) Because she was told she looked better in a man's suit.
    C) Because she was an advocate of the women's liberation movement.
    D) Because she preferred modern men's suits to the traditional women's
       Mexican dresses.

25. A) She had long suffered from ill-health.
    B) She had a passion for traditional Mexican dresses.
    C) She had a strong belief in the equality between men and women.
    D) She regretted that she had married to Diego.

Section B

Directions: *In this section, you will hear 3 short passages. At the end of each
    passage, you will hear some questions. Both the passages and the questions
    will be spoken only once. After you hear a question, you must choose the best*

answer from the four choices marked *A)*, *B)*, *C)* and *D)*. Then mark the corresponding letter on **Answer Sheet 2** with a single line through the center.

Note: Please put down on **Answer Sheet 2** your answers to the following questions. （注意：此部分试题请在**答题卡 2**上作答。）

Passage One
Questions 26 to 28 are based on the passage you have just heard.

26. A) To fight against social injustice.
    B) To develop and exchange social and economic projects.
    C) To launch a campaign against environmental pollution.
    D) To preserve natural resources.

27. A) Because it has widened the gap between the very rich and the very poor.
    B) Because it has proven an oppressive economic policy.
    C) Because it has totally ignored the needs of the poorest people.
    D) Because it has caused worldwide environmental problems.

28. A) From a half to two thirds.
    B) Their share has almost doubled.
    C) By three times.
    D) Up to 86%.

Passage Two
Questions 29 to 31 are based on the passage you have just heard.

29. A) On the item.   B) In the store.
    C) On the window.   D) On the stall.

30. A) When money is offered.
    B) When the customer says he will buy them.
    C) When the merchant accepts the offer of the buyer.
    D) All of the above.

31. A) No, he is not allowed to change his mind.
    B) Yes, he has the legal right to do so.
    C) No, because he has already displayed the goods.
    D) Yes, if the customer allows him to do so.

Passage Three

Questions 32 to 35 are based on the passage you have just heard.

32. A) At three o'clock in the afternoon.
    B) At five-thirty in the afternoon.
    C) At seven o'clock in the evening.
    D) At eight o'clock in the evening.

33. A) Bloomington.   B) Springfield.
    C) Saint Louis.   D) New Orleans.

34. A) At 5:30.   B) At 6:00.
    C) At 6:30.   D) At 5:00.

35. A) Smoking is prohibited anywhere in the coach.
    B) Smoking cigarettes is permitted anywhere in the coach.
    C) Smoking cigarettes is permitted only in the last three rows of seats.
    D) Cigar smoking is permitted in the last three rows of seats in the coach.

Section C

Directions: *In this section, you will hear a passage three times. When the passage is read for the first time, you should listen carefully for its general idea. When the passage is read for the second time, you are required to fill in the blanks numbered from 36 to 43 with the exact words you have just heard. For blanks numbered from 44 to 46 you are required to fill in the missing information. For these blanks, you can either use the exact words you have just heard or write down the main points in your own words. Finally, when the passage is read for the third time, you should check what you have written.*

Note: The questions in this section are all shown on *Answer Sheet 2*; please put down your answers on it as required. （注意：此部分试题在答题卡 2 上；请在答题卡 2 上作答。）

Part IV   Reading Comprehension (Reading in Depth) (25 minutes)
Section A
Directions: *In this section, there is a short passage with 5 questions or incomplete statements. Read the passage carefully. Then answer the questions or complete the statements in the fewest possible words on Answer Sheet 2.*

Questions 47 to 51 are based on the following passage.

The role of manager is another critical component in the development of an office-systems career. One study reported that in 76 percent of the organizations surveyed supervisors were involved in career development. Because of daily contact with employees and personal contact with other managers, the manager can assist office-systems employees in their career development in many ways. Managers can delegate their subordinates' assignments which promote growth. In addition, managers can provide realistic assessments of their subordinates' career potential. Such feedback can take the form of coaching employees to strengthen any personal or professional weaknesses.

Some managers might become mentors to their subordinates, thus improving their chances for career success. A mentor usually is a superior or experienced peer within the employee's organization. The mentor assumes a professional interest in another's career and acts in an advisory capacity to that individual. Generally a mentor arranges for the employee to meet the "right people" and to make the "right moves," thus helping the employee to acquire recognition of and acceptance by the managerial network. However, even when managers show an interest in their subordinates' careers, problems can occur.

Some managers might lack sufficient power within their organizations to be successful mentors or might be reluctant to become a mentor for an aspiring（有抱负的）female employee because of the possibility of office gossip. Other managers might resist the mentor role because managers may not be rewarded by their organizations for engaging in career development activities for their subordinates.

Other dilemmas for both manager and subordinate could arise when the career development process is linked to the manager's task of performance appraisal. The career development process is not as effective when it is tied to employee assessment for job promotions and salary increases.

Most employees would be reluctant to risk revealing any career inadequacies or doubts to their evaluators. Therefore，employees should take charge of their own career development.

Note： Please put down on **Answer Sheet 2** your answers to the questions in this section.（注意：此部分试题请在**答题卡**2上作答。）

47. Managers play an important part in the development of an office-systems career because _____.

48. What does the word "delegate" in Paragraph 1 most probably mean?

49. The main function of a mentor is _____.

50. What are the possible reasons that some managers do not want to be mentors to their subordinates?

51. The chief reason why most employees are not active in the career development program is that _____.

Section B

Directions: *There are 2 passages in this section. Each passage is followed by some questions or unfinished statements. For each of them there are four choices marked A), B), C) and D). You should decide on the best choice and mark the corresponding letter on Answer Sheet 2 with a single line through the centre.*

Passage One
Questions 52 to 56 are based on the following passage.

The genetic characteristics of all life forms on earth are embodied in the chemical structure of DNA molecules. An organism's DNA molecules provide a complete blueprint for its physical makeup. Genetic engineering is the process of altering the DNA genetic code to change the characteristics of plants and animals. Through the process, scientists can literally build to order new life forms that perform desired functions. For hundreds of years, humans have engineered the development of food crops and domesticated animals through selective breeding practices. For example, the modern dairy cow is the result of centuries of carefully breeding individual animals that carried the genetic trait for high milk production. However, new technology makes it possible for scientists to restructure the DNA molecules themselves and thus obtain more rapid and more radical genetic changes than were possible in the past. This new process is commonly called recombinant DNA technology or gene splicing because it involves disassembling the DNA molecule and then recombining or splicing the pieces according to a new pattern. The gene-spliced DNA molecule may have a genetic code that has never existed before.

Although recombinant DNA technology is still in its infancy, it has already demonstrated its value. New crop breeds produced by this process are already growing in farmers' fields. Crops that are genetically engineered to resist pests, diseases, and drought could be important in efforts to alleviate starvation around the world. Scientists are trying to use genetic engineering to produce important drugs such as insulin（胰岛素）and interferon（干扰素） cheaply. They are also working on a genetically engineered generation of wonder drugs to combat cancer and other killer diseases. However, the recombinant DNA technology brings with it problems our society has not previously faced. Gene splicing could produce new disease microorganisms, deadly to us or to the plants and animals upon which we depend. The possibility of altering human genetic structure raises serious moral, political, and social issues. Genetic engineering illustrates dramatically the promises and dangers of technological development. The decisions our society makes about genetic engineering will undoubtedly have tremendous consequences in the years to come.

Note: Please put down on **Answer Sheet 2** your answers to the following questions.（注意：此部分试题请在**答题卡 2** 上作答。）

52. The best title for this passage is _____.

A) The Basic Function of Genetic Engineering

B) New Applications of Genetic Engineering

C) Recombinant DNA Technology: A New Process in Genetic Engineering

D) The Promises & Dangers of Technological Development

53. Which of the following is NOT mentioned about recombinant DNA technology?

A) It can bring about rapid and radical genetic changes in life forms.

B) It can be used to restructure DNA molecules to produce new desired plant and animal breeds.

C) It may increase the risk of producing some unexpected diseases.

D) It proves an effective way to cure cancer and other incurable diseases.

54. The word "alleviate" (Paragraph 2) is nearest in meaning to _____.

A) relieve   B) avoid

C) eliminate   D) terminate

55. It can be inferred from the passage that _____.

A) there will inevitably be a heated debate over the general application of recombinant DNA technology

B) the use of the recombinant DNA technology on human beings will be forbidden

C) the recombinant DNA technology can be traced back to hundreds of years ago

D) serious dilemmas may be generated when recombinant DNA technology is used to modify human genetic code

56. The author's attitude towards genetic technologies is _____.

A) enthusiastic   B) indifferent

C) critical   D) objective

Passage Two

Questions 57 to 61 are based on the following passage.

Until recently, the acquisition of scientific literacy and the enlargement of general knowledge on the part of the individual had only been intuitively understood and was best observed in extreme cases. Contrary to the notion of instant "creativity" that was popular in the 1960s, distinguished scientific accomplishment is a matter of opportunity and of continuous and concentrated effort over at least a decade. When Newton was asked how he had managed to surpass the discoveries of his predecessors, in both quantity and quality, he replied, "By always thinking about them." Add to this the comment of Gauss that "if others would but reflect on mathematical truths as deeply and continuously as I have, they would make my discoveries," and it becomes apparent that "instant" scientific discoveries are many long years in the making.

So, too, are accomplishments in many other areas. Psychological studies of the lives of eminent painters, writers, musicians, philosophers, religious leaders, and scientists of previous centuries, as well as prizewinning adolescents in this country today, reveal early, intense concentration on previous work in their fields, often to the near-exclusion of other activities. It appears, though, that science and mathematics, because of their highly specialized and abstract symbolism, may require the greatest concentration and perseverance.

The same fundamental thought process, moreover, appear to be required in both elementary and advanced science, as Simon and his colleagues have shown. "The development of literacy, the acquisition of information, and the problem-solving of beginners differ in degree rather than in kind from mental activities of experts. The scarce resources are opportunities and concentration rather than the amount of information available or the processing capacity of the mind, both of which, for practical purposes are unlimited.

Note: Please put down on *Answer Sheet 2* your answers to the following questions. （注意：此部分试题请在**答题卡** 2 上作答。）

57. The passage says that in the 1960s it was a widespread belief that distinguished scientific accomplishments were _____.

A) made mostly by accident

B) the results of painstaking efforts

C) the results of sudden bursts of creativity

D) made only by distinguished characters

58. What is the author's view of "instant" scientific discoveries?

A) They occur with long intervals.

B) They occur in quick succession for a long period.

C) They require long periods of time to be confirmed.

D) They are never made easily, but through long years of intense work and persistence.

59. It can be inferred from the passage that Gauss (Paragraph 1) must be _____.

A) a prominent mathematician who made important discoveries

B) a famous writer who wrote about Newton

C) a scientist who made discoveries in various fields

D) a scientist who advocated instant scientific discoveries

60. Studies of the lives of eminent persons show that their successes can be attributed to all the following EXCEPT _____.

A) careful studies of the work of their forerunners

B) complete involvement in the previous work in their fields

C) very early exposure to basic knowledge and various activities

D) total concentration on the work done previously

61. According to the passage, which of the following is of primary importance in becoming successful in the scientific fields?

A) The development of literacy.

B) The degree of problem-solving approaches.

C) Opportunity and concentration.

D) The processing capacity of the mind.

Part V　Error Correction (15 minutes)

Directions: *This part consists of a short passage. In this passage, there are altogether 10 mistakes, one in each numbered line. You may have to change a word, add a word or delete a word. Mark out the mistakes and put the corrections in the blanks provided. If you change a word, cross it out and write the correct word in the corresponding blank. If you add a word, put an insertion mark (∧) in the right place and write the missing word in the blank. If you delete a word, cross it out and put a slash (/) in the blank.*

Example:

Television is rapidly becoming the literature of our ~~periods~~ . Many of the arguments
~~having~~ used for the study of literature as a
school subject are valid for∧ study of television.

1. time/times/period
2. ——————————
3. 　　　　the　　　　

Note: The questions in this part are shown on *Answer Sheet 2* ; please put down your answers on the **Sheet**. （注意：此部分试题在**答题卡**2上；请在**答题卡**2上作答。）

Part VI　Translation (5 minutes)

Directions: *Complete the following sentences by translating into English the Chinese given in brackets.*

Note: Please put down on *Answer Sheet 2* your answers to the questions in this part. （注意：此部分试题请在**答题卡**2上作答。）

72. I don't feel well today; I'm afraid ＿＿＿＿＿＿（我得打电话请病假了）.

73. Signing the cease-fire agreement is one thing; ＿＿＿＿＿＿（实施这一协定又是另一回事了）.

74. That film is not as wonderful as expected, ＿＿＿＿＿＿（但还是值得一看）.

75. Our current educational system has not been able to ＿＿＿＿＿＿（跟上

当今世界经济和科技的发展步伐).

76. Friendship is the ideal; friends are the reality; _____ （现实总是与理想相隔很大一段距离的）.

Answer Sheet 1 (答题卡 1)

				准		考		证		号				
[0]	[0]	[0]	[0]	[0]	[0]	[0]	[0]	[0]	[0]	[0]	[0]	[0]	[0]	[0]
[1]	[1]	[1]	[1]	[1]	[1]	[1]	[1]	[1]	[1]	[1]	[1]	[1]	[1]	[1]
[2]	[2]	[2]	[2]	[2]	[2]	[2]	[2]	[2]	[2]	[2]	[2]	[2]	[2]	[2]
[3]	[3]	[3]	[3]	[3]	[3]	[3]	[3]	[3]	[3]	[3]	[3]	[3]	[3]	[3]
[4]	[4]	[4]	[4]	[4]	[4]	[4]	[4]	[4]	[4]	[4]	[4]	[4]	[4]	[4]
[5]	[5]	[5]	[5]	[5]	[5]	[5]	[5]	[5]	[5]	[5]	[5]	[5]	[5]	[5]
[6]	[6]	[6]	[6]	[6]	[6]	[6]	[6]	[6]	[6]	[6]	[6]	[6]	[6]	[6]
[7]	[7]	[7]	[7]	[7]	[7]	[7]	[7]	[7]	[7]	[7]	[7]	[7]	[7]	[7]
[8]	[8]	[8]	[8]	[8]	[8]	[8]	[8]	[8]	[8]	[8]	[8]	[8]	[8]	[8]
[9]	[9]	[9]	[9]	[9]	[9]	[9]	[9]	[9]	[9]	[9]	[9]	[9]	[9]	[9]

Part I　　　　　　　　　　**Writing**　　　　　　　　　**(30 minutes)**

Directions: *For this part, you are allowed 30 minutes to write a short essay entitled* **What a College Education Means to Me.** *You should write at least* **150** *words following the outline given below:*

1. 学习一向优异,理所当然应进大学深造
2. 大学是满足求知欲的最佳场所
3. 大学生活能开阔视野,提高思想境界
4. 高等教育为开创职业生涯做好准备

WHAT A COLLEGE EDUCATION MEANS TO ME

Answer Sheet 1 (答题卡 1)

Part II Reading Comprehension (Skimming and Scanning) (15 minutes)

1. [Y] [N] [NG]   5. _____   8. _____

2. [Y] [N] [NG]

3. [Y] [N] [NG]   6. _____   9. _____

4. [Y] [N] [NG]   7. _____   10. _____

Answer Sheet 2 (答题卡2)

Part III Section A   Section B

11. [A] [B] [C] [D]   16. [A] [B] [C] [D]   21. [A] [B] [C] [D]   26. [A] [B] [C] [D]   31. [A] [B] [C] [D]
12. [A] [B] [C] [D]   17. [A] [B] [C] [D]   22. [A] [B] [C] [D]   27. [A] [B] [C] [D]   32. [A] [B] [C] [D]
13. [A] [B] [C] [D]   18. [A] [B] [C] [D]   23. [A] [B] [C] [D]   28. [A] [B] [C] [D]   33. [A] [B] [C] [D]
14. [A] [B] [C] [D]   19. [A] [B] [C] [D]   24. [A] [B] [C] [D]   29. [A] [B] [C] [D]   34. [A] [B] [C] [D]
15. [A] [B] [C] [D]   20. [A] [B] [C] [D]   25. [A] [B] [C] [D]   30. [A] [B] [C] [D]   35. [A] [B] [C] [D]

Part III Section C

A growing number of scientists insist that answers to the world's problems will not come from a (36) _____ array of electronics and machines. Instead, as they see it, solutions must (37) _____ from a better understanding of the humans that drive the system and from a fuller (38) _____ of the limits and potential of the earth's resources.

What this means is an increased (39) _____ on the life and earth sciences, on sociology, psychology, economics and even philosophy.

More and more of the best minds in science, particularly young researchers, are being drawn into these (40) _____ fields.

Industry officials are concerned by a (41) _____ rate of innovation in technology. Patent applications by Americans have been (42) _____ in the U. S. since 1971. Yet many scientists seem to be saying: The need for better televisions, bigger power plants and faster airplanes — markers of rapid-fire technological creativity — is becoming (43) _____ at best. (44) _____

_____.

All this is not to say that technological creativity will not play a critical role in solving energy and food shortages, or that (45) _____

_____.

Where the real challenge lies is (46) _____

_____.

Answer Sheet 2 (答题卡2)

Part IV   Section A   Part V   Error Correction   (15 minutes)

47. _____

_____

_____

48. _____

_____

_____

49. _____

_____

_____

50. _____

_____

_____

51. _____

_____

_____

Part IV   Section B

52. [A][B][C][D]
53. [A][B][C][D]
54. [A][B][C][D]
55. [A][B][C][D]
56. [A][B][C][D]
57. [A][B][C][D]
58. [A][B][C][D]
59. [A][B][C][D]
60. [A][B][C][D]
61. [A][B][C][D]

Time spent in a bookstore can be enjoyable, if you are a book-lover or merely there to buy a book as a present. You may even have entered the shop just to find shelters away a sudden shower.

62. _____

Whatever the reasons, you can soon become totally unaware of your surroundings. The desire to pick up a book with an attractive dust-jacket is irresistible, even this method of selection ought not to be followed, as you might end up with a rather bored book. You soon become engrossed in some book or other, and usually it is only much later that you realise you have spent far far much time there and must dash off to keep some forgotten appointment — without buying a book, of course.

63. _____

64. _____

65. _____

66. _____

This opportunity to escape the realities of everyday life is, I think, the main attraction of a bookshop. There are not many places where it is impossible to do this. A music shop is very much like a bookshop. You can wander round such places to your heart's content. If it is a good shop, no assistant will approach to you with the inevitable greeting: "Can I help you, sir?" You needn't buy anything if you don't want. In a bookshop an assistant should remain the background until you have finished browsing. Then, only then, are his services necessary. Of course, you may want to find out where a particular section is, since when he has led you there, the assistant should retire discreetly and look as he is not interested in selling a single book.

67. _____

68. _____

69. _____

70. _____

71. _____

Part VI   Translation   (5 minutes)

72. _____

73. _____

74. _____

75. _____

76. _____

Practice Test 3

Part I   Writing (30 minutes)

Note: The topic and directions for writing are shown on *Answer Sheet 1*. （注意：此部分试题在答题卡 1 上。）

Part II   Reading Comprehension (Skimming and Scanning) (15 minutes)

Directions: *In this part, you will have 15 minutes to go over the passage quickly and answer the questions on Answer Sheet 1.*

For questions 1 − 4, mark

Y *(for YES)*　　　　*if the statement agrees with the information given in the passage;*

N *(for NO)*　　　　*if the statement contradicts the information given in the passage;*

NG *(for NOT GIVEN)*　*if the information is not given in the passage.*

For questions 5 − 10, complete the sentences with the information given in the passage.

The Magic of Memory

— By Laurence Cherry

Our memories are probably our most cherished possessions. More than anything else we own, they belong uniquely to us, defining our personalities and our views of the world. Each of us can summon thousands of memories at will: our first day at school, a favorite family pet, a summerhouse we loved. And yet the marvel of memory continues to be a tantalizing (挑逗性的) mystery. Nevertheless, within the past few years great advances have been made in understanding what memory is, how it works, and how it may possibly be improved. "We're standing at the brink of a whole new era in memory research," says Dr. Steven Ferris, a psychologist at the Millhauser Geriatric (老年医学的) Clinic. "For the first time, there's a general feeling that we're really on the right track."

For years, the prevailing theory was that remembering was somehow connected to electrical activity inside the brain. But within the past decade, it's become clear that chemical changes must also be involved, otherwise our memories could never survive deep-freeze, coma, anesthesia (麻醉) and other events that radically disrupt the brain's electrical activity. Ingenious research over the past few years has demonstrated that biochemical changes do indeed accompany learning and remembering. In one dramatic experiment, mice, who usually prefer the safety of darkness, were taught to fear the dark and were then killed. Extracts of their brains were injected into untrained mice, and they then began to shun the dark. Other experimenters have shown that the amounts of certain chemicals, such as RNA (核糖核酸), radically increase with learning, as do the amounts of certain neurotransmitters (神经传递素) — chemicals released by brain cells that help conduct nerve impulses from one brain cell to another. Memory, then, is also chemical in nature, although exactly in what way remains a mystery.

Almost all memory researchers now agree that our brains record — and on some level remember — everything that ever happens to us. Many people who've narrowly escaped sudden death, such as soldiers and mountain climbers, have reported that in the few seconds that seemed left to them a stream of long-lost memories flashed before them. The first experimental confirmation that the brain does record every experience in this minute way came some years ago from Dr. Wilder Penfield of the Montreal Neurological Institute. He hoped to cure epileptics (癫痫病人) by stimulating a part of their brains called the temporal cortex (脑的颞皮层) with a mild electric current. Because the brain is immune to pain, Penfield was able to operate with his patients fully awake. To his astonishment, simply by touching the brains of some patients with the tip of his wire-thin electrode (电极) he was able to evoke astonishingly precise and vivid memories. "I see a guy coming through the fence at the baseball game," exclaimed one patient, whenever Penfield touched the upper part of his left temporal lobe (脑叶). "It's the middle of the game, and I'm back there watching him!" Another woman reported being back at a concert she had once attended and could even hum along with the orchestra whenever her brain was stimulated.

Investigators using hypnosis (催眠术) have been as astonished as Penfield at the amazing capacity of our memories. Once in a trance (昏睡), good hypnotic subjects can report detailed recollections of events that took place days, months, even decades ago — which, when checked against old records and diaries, turn out to be accurate. "Everything, absolutely everything, is remembered," says one hypnotist.

Even senile patients, who can hardly remember recent events at all, retain the ability to remember new experiences, but only very briefly. "Give them a list of nonsense syllables to memorize, and for a few seconds they do almost as well as healthy young people in remembering," says one expert. But apparently the brains of senile subjects cannot electrochemically translate the new information and shift it into long-term storage. It seems rather as if our perceptions, in order to be remembered for more than a few seconds, must be sorted out and slid into place like folders into file cabinets. Some of the cabinets are easily opened, their contents readily available to us. Others, thanks to still unknown processes, are locked away, only to be retrieved if the files are jarred open by hypnosis or a researcher's electrode.

For years, scientists hunted for the brain's elusive "memory center," where long-term memories might be processed and stored. Above all, the hippocampi（侧脑室下角的海马状突起物）, small, seahorse-shaped structures about three centimeters long, deep within each half of the brain, were targeted as the possible center. If one hippocampus is injured, memory is temporarily affected, then eventually returns. But if both are damaged, the loss of memory is final. Patients who have lost their hippocampi live in a strange, twilight world. If they meet you, they will shake your hand and five minutes later greet you as a complete stranger. Although they can still perform well enough on IQ tests and speak quite intelligently, it's as if some crucial memory system had been cruelly short-circuited. Often they're aware something is wrong and try to hold on to their memories. But the attempt is usually useless, and even when they forget the reason for their sadness, they remain depressed.

Is it possible to improve your memory?

The surprising answer appears to be yes. Dr. Richard J. Wurtman, professor of endocrinology（内分泌学）at the Massachusetts Institute of Technology, recently discovered that the food we eat can affect the amount of neurotransmitters in our brains and — by implication — how well we can remember.

In 1985，Wurtman and his colleagues learned that choline（胆碱），a common food substance found in large quantities in egg yolks（and to some degree in meat and fish as well），has a pronounced effect on the brain's ability to make an important neurochemical called acetylcholine（乙酰胆碱），almost certainly involved in memory.

Meanwhile，new information is being gathered about memory loss among older people. With the exception of an unfortunate minority who suffer from Alzheimer's disease，a progressive ailment that leads to almost total memory loss，the news is good. "I think the most crucial thing we've learned is that it simply isn't true that you lose your memory as you get older," says Dr. James Ninninger of the Payne Whitney Psychiatric Clinic. "That's simply one of the self-fulfilling prophecies that should be dropped." At Johns Hopkins University，studies of men over many years as they grow older confirm this belief. "There are some subjects sixty-five to ninety who are just not showing any decrements," says Dr. Nathan Shock，who admits that the findings surprised him.

Although some brain changes do seem to come with age，in most cases their effect on memory is not nearly as serious as once thought. Even the idea that we begin to lose hundreds of thousands of brain cells each day past the age of 30 — with the usual grim implication that our brainpower must diminish — has recently been hotly disputed. "As a neuroanatomist（神经解剖学家），I've been intrigued by this myth of disappearing brain cells," Dr. Marian C. Diamond，professor of anatomy at the University of California at Berkeley，has said. As she points out，almost no studies of brain loss have been done in humans and only a few haphazard ones in animals. "In fact," she insists, "there is only a trivial decrease in the number of brain cells — right up through old age."

Another recent finding is that intellectual stimulation keeps memory at its peak — just as physical exercise does for our muscles. In the Johns Hopkins' studies，the people who showed the least memory impairment as they aged were those who had made problem-solving a way of life. Studies in monkeys and rats have shown the same thing：constant mental activity preserves memory. And at least until we reach the outer limits of old age，the continuous amount of new information we are always storing should help us to remember, not cause us to forget. Dr. Patricia Siple, a psychologist at the University of Rochester, has found that a large store of information helps our memories. We remember not so much words and sounds as concepts, which form a kind of indexed system to recall information.

Recent research indicates that, unlike a container that can be filled, our memory far more resembles an ever-growing tree, continually putting out new roots and connections, memory building on memory, rivaled in complexity only by the mysterious, ever-challenging brain itself.

Note: Please put down on *Answer Sheet 1* your answers to the questions in this part.（注意：此部分试题请在**答题卡** 1 上作答。）

1. An important discovery recently made in memory research is that remembering is closely related to electrical activity inside the brain.

2. Memory is chemical as well as electrical in nature.

3. Most memory researchers agree that our brains record — and remember at some level — everything that happens to us.

4. There is scientific evidence that the "hippocampi" deep within each half of the brain are the "memory center," where long-term memories are processed and stored.

5. Elderly people retain their ability to remember information briefly but are unable to turn it into _____.

6. Recent findings also indicate that _____ helps us keep memory at its height.

7. Our memories are our most important properties in that _____.

8. The magic of memory lies in _____.

9. In this article, the author relies chiefly on _____ to support his main ideas.

10. The author compares our memory first to "file cabinets" (Paragraph 5)

and then to an "ever-green tree" (the last paragraph). This special comparison is known as _____.

Part III   Listening Comprehension (35 minutes)

Section A

Directions: *In this section, you will hear 8 short conversations and 2 long conversations. At the end of each conversation, one or more questions will be asked about what was said. Both the conversation and the questions will be spoken only once. After each question, there will be a pause. During the pause, you must read the four choices marked A), B), C) and D), and decide which is the best answer. Then mark the corresponding letter on **Answer Sheet 2** with a single line through the center.*

Note: Please put down on *Answer Sheet 2* your answers to the following questions.（注意：此部分试题请在**答题卡 2** 上作答。）

11. A) Husband and wife.   B) Doctor and patient.
    C) Teacher and student.   D) Doctor and nurse.

12. A) To do whatever the committee asks of him.
    B) To make decisions in agreement with the committee.
    C) To run the committee according to his own ideas.
    D) To elect the committee chairman himself.

13. A) At 8:45.   B) At 8:15.
    C) At 8:05.   D) At 8:35.

14. A) The man would understand if he had Frank's job.
    B) Frank could help him get a job on an airplane.
    C) Waiting on tables is an enjoyable job.
    D) She is tired of waiting for him there.

15. A) It's not important how he dances.
    B) It's too crowded to dance anyway.

C) If he's careful, no one will notice.

D) No one knows the steps to the dance.

16. A) She leaves the office by 3:00 or 4:00 in the afternoon.

B) She sends her employees for regular checkups.

C) She pays her employees by check.

D) She inspects her employees' work several times a day.

17. A) She doesn't know whether the film is good or not.

B) The film is hard to understand.

C) She saw the film from beginning to end.

D) She saw only the last part of the film.

18. A) At the doctor's office.　　　　B) At the hospital.

C) At the drugstore.　　　　D) At the department store.

Questions 19 to 21 are based on the conversation you have just heard.

19. A) A little known actress and a literary critic.

B) A well-known actress and a newspaper editor.

C) A movie star and one of her fans.

D) A movie star and a TV interviewer.

20. A) They show greater interest in scandals than truth.

B) They help young actors and actresses establish their fame.

C) They are interested in the spread of false information about celebrities.

D) They ignore the journalistic ethics they should act upon.

21. A) Few people can become famous without the help of the press.

B) Readership is of vital importance to newspapers.

C) More often than not, so-called "scandalous" stories about celebrities in the newspapers are true or must be partly true.

D) Movie stars tend to become ungrateful to the press when they have become famous.

Questions 22 to 25 are based on the conversation you have just heard.

22. A) A comparison of unconscious behavior patterns.
    B) Recent trends in psychology.
    C) Reasons for certain behavior problems.
    D) Causes of anxiety.

23. A) He feels angry.   B) He wants attention.
    C) He's too quiet.   D) He's very nervous.

24. A) He's late for social occasions but not for work.
    B) He's a quiet person but likes to make grand entrances.
    C) He expects others to be on time but is usually late himself.
    D) He loses pay for being late to work but doesn't seem to mind.

25. A) Trying to get Mark to talk about his problem.
    B) Helping Mark relax and be more comfortable in a group.
    C) Waiting fifteen minutes and then leaving without Mark.
    D) Telling Mark to come earlier than the planned meeting time.

Section B

Directions: *In this section, you will hear 3 short passages. At the end of each passage, you will hear some questions. Both the passage and the questions will be spoken only once. After you hear a question, you must choose the best answer from the four choices marked A), B), C) and D). Then mark the corresponding letter on **Answer Sheet 2** with a single line through the center.*

Note: Please put down on **Answer Sheet 2** your answers to the following questions. （注意：此部分试题请在**答题卡 2** 上作答。）

Passage One

Questions 26 to 28 are based on the passage you have just heard.

26. A) On an island.   B) In the mountains.
    C) In a city.   D) By the sea.

27. A) He couldn't see the steamer clearly.
    B) He failed to attract the attention of the steamer.
    C) The steamer refused to help him.
    D) The cliff was too steep for him to climb.

28. A) The steamer took him to the harbor.
    B) He was left alone there.
    C) He was saved.
    D) None of the above.

Passage Two
Questions 29 to 32 are based on the passage you have just heard.

29. A) A driver's license.   B) A passport.
    C) An international credit card. D) A deposit.

30. A) Turning right at a red light.
    B) Driving in freeways without a local driver's license.
    C) Passing a school bus that is letting off children.
    D) All of the above.

31. A) The size of the country.
    B) Large areas of virgin forest.
    C) The rich natural resources of the land.
    D) Wild animals and plants.

32. A) Because nearly 1,000 million acres of land was burned off.
    B) Because natural resources are being used up.
    C) Because animals and plants are in danger of extinction.
    D) Because natural beauty of the land would be ruined.

Passage Three
Questions 33 to 35 are based on the passage you have just heard.

33. A) The symbolic significance of a specific color.
    B) The subtle cultural connotation of colors.

C) The influence of Westernization on Asian people's outlook.

D) Expensive lessons Western businessmen learned in Asia.

34. A) Yellow.
    B) Red.
    C) Blue.
    D) The combination of green and purple.

35. A) Good luck.　　　　　　　　B) Healthiness.
    C) Untidiness and illness.　　　D) A funeral.

Section C

Directions: *In this section, you will hear a passage three times. When the passage is read for the first time, you should listen carefully for its general idea. When the passage is read for the second time, you are required to fill in the blanks numbered from 36 to 43 with the exact words you have just heard. For blanks numbered from 44 to 46 you are required to fill in the missing information. For these blanks, you can either use the exact words you have just heard or write down the main points in your own words. Finally, when the passage is read for the third time, you should check what you have written.*

Note: The questions in this section are all shown on **Answer Sheet 2**; please put down your answers on it as required. （注意：此部分试题在**答题卡 2** 上；请在**答题卡 2** 上作答。）

Part IV　Reading Comprehension (Reading in Depth) (25 minutes)

Section A

Directions: *In this section, there is a short passage with 5 questions or incomplete statements. Read the passage carefully. Then answer the questions or complete the statements in the fewest possible words on **Answer Sheet 2**.*

Questions 47 to 51 are based on the following passage.

In the twentieth century, and particularly in the last 20 years, the old footpaths of the wandering scholars have become vast highways. The vehicle which has made this possible has of course been the aeroplane, making contact between scholars even in the most distant places immediately feasible, and providing for the very rapid transmission of knowledge.

Apart from the vehicle itself, it is fairly easy to identify the main factors which have brought about the recent explosion in academic movement. Some of these are purely quantitative: there are far more centres of learning, and a far greater number of scholars and students.

In addition one must recognise the very considerable multiplication of disciplines, which by widening the total area of advanced studies, has produced an enormous number of specialists whose particular interests are precisely defined. These people would work in some isolation if they were not able to keep in touch with similar isolated groups in other countries.

Frequently these specializations lie in areas where very rapid developments are taking place, and also where the research needed for developments is extremely costly and takes a long time. It is precisely in these areas that the advantages of collaboration and sharing of expertise appear most evident. Associated with this is the growth of specialist periodicals, which enable scholars to become aware of what is happening in different centres of research and to meet each other in conferences and symposia. From these meetings come the personal relationships which are at the bottom of almost all schemes of co-operation, and provide them with their most satisfactory stimulus.

But as the specializations have increased in number and narrowed in range, there has been an opposite movement towards interdisciplinary studies. These owe much to the belief that one cannot properly investigate the incredibly complex problems thrown up by the modern world, and by recent advances in our knowledge along the narrow front of a single discipline. This trend has led to a great deal of academic contact between disciplines, and a far greater emphasis on the pooling of specialist knowledge, reflected in the broad subjects chosen in many international conferences.

Note: Please put down on *Answer Sheet 2* your answers to the questions in this section. （注意：此部分试题请在**答题卡** 2 上作答。）

47. What does the author mainly discuss in this passage?

48. Why has academic work become more specialised?

49. The writer thinks that the growth of specialist societies and periodicals has helped scholars to _____.

50. Developments in international co-operation are often, it is suggested, the result of _____.

51. Why does the author think that interdisciplinary studies are important?

Section B

Directions: *There are 2 passages in this section. Each passage is followed by some questions or unfinished statements. For each of them there are four choices marked A), B), C) and D). You should decide on the best choice and mark the corresponding letter on **Answer Sheet 2** with a single line through the centre.*

Passage One
Questions 52 to 56 are based on the following passage.

A problem more specific to schools themselves is pervasive student passivity — a lack of active participation in learning. This problem is commonly found in both public and private schools and all grade levels.

Many students do not perceive the opportunities provided by schooling as a privilege, but rather as a series of hurdles that are mechanically cleared in pursuit of credentials（文凭）that may open doors later in life. Students are bored and much of the pervasive passivity of American students is caused by the educational system.

During this century, expanding state and federal governments favored large regional schools as more efficient means of supervising educational curricula and ensuring uniformity. Schools today, therefore, reflect the high level of bureaucratic organization found throughout American society. Such rigid and impersonal organization can negatively affect administrators, teachers, and students, and this bureaucratic educational system fosters five serious problems.

First, bureaucratic uniformity ignores the cultural variation within countless local communities. It takes schools out of the local community and places them under the control of outside "specialists" who may have little understanding of the everyday lives of students.

Second, bureaucratic schools define success by numerical ratings of performance. School officials focus on attendance rates, dropout rates, and achievement scores. They overlook dimensions of schooling that are difficult to quantify, such as the creativity of students and energy and enthusiasm of teachers. Such bureaucratic school systems tend to define an adequate education in terms of the number of days per year that students are inside a school building rather than the school's contribution to students' personal development.

Third, bureaucratic schools have rigid expectations of all students. For example, fifteen-year-olds are expected to be in the tenth grade, eleven-grade students are expected to score at a certain level on a standardized verbal achievement test. The high school diploma thus rewards a student for going through the proper sequence of educational activities in the proper amount of time. Rarely are exceptionally bright and motivated students allowed to graduate early. Likewise, the system demands that students who have learned little in school graduate with their class.

Fourth, the school's bureaucratic division of labor requires specialized personnel. High-school students learn English from one teacher, receive guidance from another, and are coached in sports by others. No school official comes to know the "full" student as a complex human being. Students experience this division of labor as a continual shuffling among rigidly divided fifty-minute period throughout the school day.

Fifth, the highly bureaucratic school system gives students little responsibility for their own learning. Similarly, teachers have little latitude in what and how they teach their classes; they dare not accelerate learning for fear of disrupting "the system." Standardized policies dictating what is to be taught and how long the teaching should be taken render teachers as passive and unimaginative as their students.

Note: Please put down on *Answer Sheet 2* your answers to the following questions. (注意：此部分试题请在答题卡 2 上作答。)

52. Which of the following statements best expresses the main idea of this passage?
    A) Most American students today are lacking in readiness for active participation in learning.
    B) The prevalent passivity of American students has much to do with the existing educational system.
    C) The bureaucratic structure of American schools has negatively affected administrators, teachers, and students.
    D) The solution to the problem of student passivity lies in humanizing schools.

53. According to the passage, American schools today have turned into _____.
    A) a typically bureaucratic organization, highly rigid and impersonal
    B) an efficient means of supervising educational curricular and ensuring uniformity
    C) a well organized system competent enough to meet the educational demands of the vast and complex society
    D) all of the above

54. The expression "numerical ratings" in Paragraph 4 can best be interpreted as _____.
    A) scores and grades
    B) formal records
    C) assessments expressed by numbers
    D) official statistics

55. Which of the following is NOT mentioned as a serious problem prevalent in today's school systems?
    A) Indifference to cultural difference within local communities.
    B) Dependence on numerical ratings of performance.
    C) Rigid expectations of all students.
    D) Lack of funding and specialized personnel.

56. In this passage the author points out that bureaucracy in American schools not only discourages initiative and creativity on the part of students, but also _____.
    A) deprives teachers of freedom of opinion or action
    B) makes teachers passive and unimaginative
    C) fosters doubts about the values of education among teachers
    D) both A and B

Passage Two
Questions 57 to 61 are based on the following passage.

It is amazing how many people still say, "I never dream," for it is now decades since it was established that everyone has over a thousand dreams a year, however few of these nocturnal (夜间发生的) productions are remembered on waking. Even the most confirmed "non-dreamers" will remember dreams if woken up systematically during the rapid eye movement (REM) periods.

These are periods of light sleep during which the eyeballs move rapidly back and forth under the closed lids and the brain becomes highly activated, which happens three or four times every night of normal sleep.

It is a very interesting question why some people remember dreams regularly while others remember hardly any at all under normal conditions. In considering this, it is important to bear in mind that the dream tends to be an elusive phenomenon for all of us. We normally never recall a dream unless we awaken directly from it, and even then it has a tendency to fade quickly into oblivion.

Given this general elusiveness of dreams, the basic factor that seems to determine whether a person remembers them or not is the same as that which determines all other memory, namely degree of interest. Dream researchers have made a broad classification of people into "recallers" — those who remember at least one dream a month — and "non-recallers", who remember fewer than this. Tests have shown that cool analytical people with a very rational approach to their feelings tend to recall fewer dreams than those whose attitude to life is open and flexible. It is not surprising to discover that in Western society, women normally recall more dreams than men, since women are traditionally allowed an instinctive, feeling approach to life.

In modern urban-industrial culture, feeling and dreams tend to be treated as frivolities (无聊事) which must be firmly subordinated to the realities of life. We pay lip-service to the inner life of imagination as it expresses itself in the arts, but in practice relegate (置于次要地位) music, poetry, drama and painting to the level of spare-time activities, valued mainly for the extent to which they refresh us for a return to work.

Note: Please put down on *Answer Sheet 2* your answers to the following questions. (注意：此部分试题请在**答题卡**2上作答。)

57. Many people are unaware that they dream because _____.
    A) their dreams fade very quickly
    B) they do not recall their dreams
    C) they sleep too heavily
    D) they wake up frequently

58. During REM periods, people _____.
    A) dream less
    B) wake up more easily
    C) remember their dreams more clearly
    D) experience discomfort

59. People who remember their dreams do so because they _____.
    A) find the content relevant   B) are awakened suddenly
    C) have retentive memories   D) are regular dreamers

60. Those who recall their dreams tend to be _____.
    A) practical   B) unrealistic
    C) disorganized   D) imaginative

61. The author believes that, in Western society, dreams are considered to be _____.
    A) shameful   B) beneficial
    C) unimportant   D) artistic

Part V   Error Correction (15 minutes)

Directions: *This part consists of a short passage. In this passage, there are altogether 10 mistakes, one in each numbered line. You may have to change a word, add a word or delete a word. Mark out the mistakes and put the corrections in the blanks provided. If you change a word, cross it out and write the correct word in the corresponding blank. If you add a word, put an insertion mark (∧) in the right place and write the missing word in the blank. If you delete a word, cross it out and put a slash (/) in the blank.*

Example:

Television is rapidly becoming the literature of our ~~periods~~ . Many of the arguments
~~having~~ used for the study of literature as a
school subject are valid for∧ study of television.

1. time/times/period
2. ——————
3. _____the_____

Note: The questions in this part are shown on ***Answer Sheet 2*** ; please put down your answers on the **Sheet**. （注意：此部分试题在**答题卡** 2 上；请在**答题卡** 2 上作答。）

Part VI   Translation (5 minutes)

Directions: *Complete the following sentences by translating into English the Chinese given in brackets.*

Note: Please put down on ***Answer Sheet 2*** your answers to the questions in this part. （注意：此部分试题请在**答题卡** 2 上作答。）

72. As usual，the correspondent is required to _____（在写报道前核对所有的事实）.

73. The waltz and tango are obviously out of fashion now. Things like the twist，jerk and hip-hop _____（才似乎是年轻人真正 感兴趣的东西）.

74. （幸好我带了足够的钱）_____ : it is more expensive than I expect-

ed.

75. Being a foreign student, _____ （他没能领会中文老师所说的
笑话）.

76. （要不是你的大力支持）_____ , we might not have faced up to the
challenge.

Answer Sheet 1 (答题卡1)

Part I   **Writing**   **(30 minutes)**

Directions: *For this part, you are allowed 30 minutes to write a short essay entitled **Energy Shortage: How to Solve It**. You should write at least **150** words following the outline given below:*

1. 能源是当今人们最关心的重大问题之一。
2. 节约使用是缓解能源短缺的手段之一。
3. 但最好的解决办法是开发新的能源。

ENERGY SHORTAGE: HOW TO SOLVE IT

Answer Sheet 1 (答题卡 1)

Part II   Reading Comprehension (Skimming and Scanning) (15 minutes)

1. [Y] [N] [NG]
2. [Y] [N] [NG]
3. [Y] [N] [NG]
4. [Y] [N] [NG]

5. _____
6. _____
7. _____

8. _____
9. _____
10. _____

Answer Sheet 2 (答题卡 2)

Part III   Section A   Section B

11. [A] [B] [C] [D]   16. [A] [B] [C] [D]   21. [A] [B] [C] [D]   26. [A] [B] [C] [D]   31. [A] [B] [C] [D]
12. [A] [B] [C] [D]   17. [A] [B] [C] [D]   22. [A] [B] [C] [D]   27. [A] [B] [C] [D]   32. [A] [B] [C] [D]
13. [A] [B] [C] [D]   18. [A] [B] [C] [D]   23. [A] [B] [C] [D]   28. [A] [B] [C] [D]   33. [A] [B] [C] [D]
14. [A] [B] [C] [D]   19. [A] [B] [C] [D]   24. [A] [B] [C] [D]   29. [A] [B] [C] [D]   34. [A] [B] [C] [D]
15. [A] [B] [C] [D]   20. [A] [B] [C] [D]   25. [A] [B] [C] [D]   30. [A] [B] [C] [D]   35. [A] [B] [C] [D]

Part III   Section C

London is the center of the international art market and Sotheby's, which has its (36) _____ there, is the world's biggest and oldest seller of art and antiques. If you were lucky enough to own a priceless "Old Master", an Impressionist, or a (37) _____ antique, and you wanted to sell it, you would probably put it up for auction at Sotheby's.

Sotheby's auctions are (38) _____ by some of the world's richest people, who spend millions of pounds on art and antiques each year. (39) _____, the company is very proud of its status and its 250-year-old (40) _____. But, earlier this year, that reputation came under threat, when a journalist (41) _____ Sotheby's staff of bringing art treasures to London illegally. If these (42) _____ are true, they will severely damage London's (43) _____ as a center of the world's art trade.

As if that were not bad enough, (44) _____ _____ from European Union regulations. If passed in Britain, the EU laws would make London a much less attractive place to purchase art treasures. Buyers and sellers would then look elsewhere for the best prices and could stop coming to London altogether.

The problems began last year, (45) _____ _____. He made his allegations in a book and television program, which used hidden camera to film Sotheby's staff. Watson says (46) _____ _____, and that the international art trade needs to be cleaned up.

Answer Sheet 2 (答题卡2)

Part IV   Section A   Part V   Error Correction   (15 minutes)

47. _____

_____

48. _____

_____

49. _____

_____

50. _____

_____

51. _____

_____

_____

Part IV   Section B

52. [A][B][C][D]
53. [A][B][C][D]
54. [A][B][C][D]
55. [A][B][C][D]
56. [A][B][C][D]
57. [A][B][C][D]
58. [A][B][C][D]
59. [A][B][C][D]
60. [A][B][C][D]
61. [A][B][C][D]

As we mentioned earlier, there is a wide variety of sports activities available to the United States both to watch and play. Most large cities have teams that play the most popular American sports — baseball, in the spring and summer, football, in the autumn and winter, and basketball, in the winter and spring. Tickets to games may be easy or difficult to obtain, depend on the team and the city. You can find the ticket news by reading the newspapers or by calling the ticket office of the teams. (These are listed in the Alphabetical Telephone Book.) Moreover, most major sporting events are on radio and television. Most hotels and motels in the United States have television sets in each room, many of them with color.

If you would rather play a sport not watch it being played, there are certainly many opportunities to do. If you are interested in swimming or any indoor sports, go to the Young Men's Christian Association (YMCA) or the Young Women's Christian Association (YWCA). These are organizations for men and women who offer sports programs to the public at inexpensive rates. During the summer months, there are public and private beaches and swimming pools available. In every city you visit, they are public parks and play areas for picnics, sports, or walks. Informations about other sports can be found in the newspapers or frequently in the Yellow Pages of the telephone book.

62. _____

63. _____
64. _____

65. _____

66. _____
67. _____
68. _____

69. _____

70. _____
71. _____

Part VI   Translation   (5 minutes)

72. _____

73. _____

74. _____

75. _____

76. _____

Practice Test 4

Part I Writing (30 minutes)

Note: The topic and directions for writing are shown on *Answer Sheet 1*.（注意：此部分试题在**答题卡**1上。）

Part II Reading Comprehension (Skimming and Scanning) (15 minutes)

Directions: *In this part, you will have 15 minutes to go over the passage quickly and answer the questions on* **Answer Sheet 1**.

For questions 1 − 4, mark

Y *(for YES)*   *if the statement agrees with the information given in the passage;*

N *(for NO)*   *if the statement contradicts the information given in the passage;*

NG *(for NOT GIVEN)*   *if the information is not given in the passage.*

For questions 5 − 10, complete the sentences with the information given in the passage.

Cigarette Makers See Future (It's in Asia)

— By Philip Shenon
New York Times Service

The Marlboro Man has found greener pastures.

The cigarette-hawking (兜售香烟的) cowboy may be under siege back home in the United States from lawmakers and health advocates determined to put him out of business, but half a world away, in Asia, he is prospering, his craggy (毛糙的) all-American mug slapped up on billboards and flickering across television screens.

And Marlboro cigarettes have never been more popular on the continent that is home to 60 percent of the world's population.

For the world's cigarette-makers, Asia is the future. And it is probably their savior.

Industry critics who hope that the multinational tobacco companies are

67

headed for extinction owe themselves a stroll down the tobacco-scented streets of almost any city in Asia.

Almost everywhere here the air is thick with the swirling gray haze of cigarette smoke, the evidence of a booming Asian growth market that promises vast profits for the tobacco industry and a death toll measured in the tens of millions.

At lunchtime in Seoul, throngs of fashionably dressed young Korean women gather in a fast-food restaurant to enjoy a last cigarette before returning to work, a scene that draws distressed stares from older Koreans who remember a time when it would have been scandalous for women from respectable homes to smoke.

In Hong Kong, China, shoppers flock into the Salem Attitudes boutique (时装商店), picking from among the racks of trendy sports clothes stamped with the logo of Salem cigarettes.

In Phnom Penh (金边), the war-shattered capital of Cambodia, visitors leaving an audience with King Sihanouk are greeted with a giant billboard planted right across the street from his ornate (装饰华丽的) gold-roofed palace. It advertises Lucky Strikes.

According to tobacco industry projections cited by the World Health Organization, the Asian cigarette market should grow by more than a third during the 1990s, with much of the bounty going to multinational tobacco giants eager for an alternative to the shrinking market in the United States.

American cigarette sales are expected to decline by about 15 percent by the end of the decade, a reflection of the move to ban public smoking in most of the United States. Sales in Western Europe and other industrialized countries are also expected to drop.

But no matter how bad the news is in the West, the tobacco companies can find comfort in Asia and throughout the Third World, markets so huge and so promising that they make the once all-important American market seem insignificant. Beyond Asia, cigarette consumption is also expected to grow in Africa, Latin America, Eastern Europe and in the nations of the former Soviet Union.

Status appears to matter far more than taste. "There is not a great deal of evidence to suggest that smokers can taste any difference between the more expensive foreign brands and the indigenous（本地产的）cigarettes," said Simon Chapman, a specialist in community medicine at the University of Sydney. "The difference appears to be in the packaging, the advertising."

He said that researchers had been unable to determine whether the foreign tobacco companies had adjusted the levels of tar, nicotine and other chemicals for cigarettes sold in the Asian market. "The tobacco industry fights tooth and nail to keep consumers away from that kind of information," he said.

Most governments in Asia have launched anti-smoking campaigns, but their efforts tend to be overwhelmed by the Madison Avenue glitz（浮华）unleashed by the cigarette giants.

With 1.2 billion people and the world's fastest-growing economy, China is the most coveted（极想得到的）target of the multinational tobacco companies.

Cigarette consumption, calculated as the number of cigarettes smoked per adult, has increased by 7 percent each year over the last decade in China. There are 300 million smokers in China, more people than the entire population of the United States, and they buy 1.6 trillion cigarettes a year.

Competing in many cases with domestically produced brands, the multinational tobacco companies are moving quickly to get their cigarettes into China and emerging markets in the rest of the developing world. Their campaign has been bolstered（支撑）by the efforts of American government trade negotiators to force open tobacco markets overseas.

Since the mid-1980s, Japan, South Korea, and Thailand have all succumbed（屈从）to pressure from Washington and allowed the sale of foreign brand cigarettes. Foreign cigarettes, shut out of Japan in 1980, now make up nearly 20 percent of the market.

"Worldwide, hundreds of millions of smokers prefer American-blend cigarettes," James W. Johnston, chairman of Reynolds Tobacco Worldwide, wrote in his company's 1993 annual report. "Today, Reynolds has access to 90 percent of the world's markets; a decade ago, only 40 percent. Opportunities have never been better."

Last year, Philip Morris, the company behind the Marlboro Man, signed an agreement with the government controlled China National Tobacco Corp.

to make Marlboros and other Philip Morris brands in China. The company's foreign markets grew last year by more than 16 percent, with foreign operating profits up nearly 17 percent. Operating profits in the domestic American market fell by nearly half.

Physicians say the health implications of the tobacco boom in Asia are nothing less than terrifying.

Richard Peto, an Oxford University epidemiologist (流行病学家), has estimated that because of increasing tobacco consumption in Asia, the annual worldwide death toll from tobacco-related illnesses will more than triple over the next two decades, from about 3 million a year to 10 million a year, a fifth of them in China. His calculations suggest that 50 million Chinese children alive today will eventually die from diseases linked to cigarette smoking.

"If you look at the number of deaths, the tobacco problem in Asia is going to dwarf tuberculosis, it's going to dwarf malaria and it's going to dwarf AIDS, yet it's being totally ignored," said Judith Mackay, a British physician who is a consultant to the Chinese government in developing an anti-smoking program.

The explosion of the Asian tobacco market is a result both of the increasing prosperity of large Asian nations — suddenly, tens of millions of Asians can afford cigarettes, once a luxury — and a shift in social customs. In many Asian countries, smoking was once taboo for women. Now, it is seen as a sign of their emancipation.

Note: Please put down on *Answer Sheet 1* your answers to the questions in this part. （注意：此部分试题请在**答题卡 1**上作答。）

1. To engage the reader's interest, the author begins his article with a picturesque description of a cigarette advertising item.

2. Before raising their voices against U. S. tobacco industry, many critics have made field trips across many parts of Asia.

3. It is, partly at least, owing to the effectiveness of cigarette giants' advertising that smoking foreign brand-name cigarettes has almost become a fashion in Asia.

4. Research has shown that foreign cigarettes do taste better to Asian smokers than native brands.

5. There is some question whether cigarette manufacturers have changed the levels of tar and nicotine for cigarettes sold in the Asian market, but the foreign tobacco companies _____.

6. China becomes the most desirable market for foreign cigarette manufacturers because _____ and _____.

7. The U.S. government has exerted great pressure on many Asian nations to _____.

8. The death rate from cigarette smoking in Asia will someday _____.

9. The major reason for the explosion of the cigarette market is _____.

10. In this article the author uses _____ to support many of his important points in the news story.

Part III   Listening Comprehension (35 minutes)
Section A
Directions: *In this section, you will hear 8 short conversations and 2 long conversations. At the end of each conversation, one or more questions will be asked about what was said. Both the conversation and the questions will be spoken only once. After each question, there will be a pause. During the pause, you must read the four choices marked A), B), C) and D), and decide which is the best answer. Then mark the corresponding letter on **Answer Sheet 2** with a single line through the center.*

Note: Please put down on **Answer Sheet 2** your answers to the following questions. (注意：此部分试题请在**答题卡**2上作答。)

11. A) He fixes bicycles.   B) He raises sheep.
    C) He sells chairs.   D) He's a gardener.

12. A) He is having a hard time letting his apartment.

B) He prefers his old tenant to the new one.

C) He is not accustomed to living with the new tenant yet.

D) He doesn't want to let his apartment to her.

13. A) Courageous.   B) Lazy.

    C) Curious.   D) Cowardly.

14. A) English husbands usually do a lot of housework.

B) English husbands usually do little housework.

C) English husbands are good at sports.

D) English husbands enjoy doing housework.

15. A) Peter will quit his job.   B) Peter is joking.

    C) Peter has sold his house.   D) Peter will not sell his house.

16. A) She's looking for her raincoat. B) She's soaking her clothes.

    C) She wants to close the window. D) She got caught in the rain.

17. A) He is interested in reading.

B) He'd like to read the book very much.

C) He has already read the book.

D) He feels sorry that the woman doesn't know him very well.

18. A) John was not at home when the woman called.

B) The woman dialed the wrong number.

C) John is a plumber.

D) John was too busy to come.

Questions 19 to 21 are based on the conversation you have just heard.

19. A) Go to university.

B) Go to a music school.

C) Start his music career as a pop singer.

D) Start a business in the music world.

20. A) Go to university and get a degree.
    B) Get into the music world as a pop singer.
    C) Start his music business after he gets a university degree.
    D) Go to university and get a qualification for his music career.

21. A) Because they can't afford to pay for him to live in London.
    B) Because they think Neil should get a university degree first of all.
    C) Because they think Neil is wasting his talent and energy singing in the pop world.
    D) Because they believe Neil will never make it in the pop world.

Questions 22 to 25 are based on the conversation you have just heard.

22. A) Local news and children's programs.
    B) Children's programs and local service programs.
    C) Documentaries and news.
    D) Documentaries and movies.

23. A) Broadcasting interviews with people from all walks of life.
    B) Training broadcasters to higher standards.
    C) Paying close attention to the quality of their programs.
    D) Improving sound quality.

24. A) Every 10 minutes.   B) Every 15 minutes.
    C) Every 20 minutes.   D) Every 25 minutes.

25. A) If the expenses are paid for him.
    B) If they will not last long.
    C) If he is specially invited.
    D) If they are held locally.

Section B

Directions: *In this section, you will hear 3 short passages. At the end of each passage, you will hear some questions. Both the passage and the questions will be spoken only once. After you hear one question, you must choose the best* *answer from the four choices marked A), B), C) and D). Then mark the cor-responding letter on **Answer Sheet 2** with a single line through the center.*

Note: Please put down on **Answer Sheet 2** your answers to the following ques-tions.（注意：此部分试题请在**答题卡 2**上作答。）

Passage One
Questions 26 to 28 are based on the passage you have just heard.

26. A) The widening gap between the haves and have-nots, in terms of high-tech equipment and knowledge.
    B) The sharp distinction between computer experts and computer illiter-ates.
    C) The gulf between the very rich and the very poor.
    D) The barrier that keeps the poor people from learning how to use a computer.

27. A) He does not think the "digital divide" ever exists.
    B) He thinks that to people in developing countries to be healthy is more important.
    C) He has given large amounts of money to help poor people use com-puters and Internet.
    D) He attended the conference held in Seattle and made an impressive speech there.

28. A) The "digital divide" is disappearing.
    B) Bill Gates made a big donation at the meeting.
    C) Big information technology companies promised to make greater con-tributions.
    D) Many organizations around the world are making efforts to reduce the digital divide.

Passage Two
Questions 29 to 31 are based on the passage you have just heard.

29. A) From the place where the agreement was signed.

B) From the people who signed the agreement.

C) From the significance it tried to find in the international finance system.

D) None of the above.

30. A) To lower their exchange rates. B) To regulate their exchange rates.
    C) To raise their regulated rates. D) To make no change of their rates.

31. A) Some developed countries.
    B) Countries that wanted to borrow money.
    C) All the member countries.
    D) The World Bank.

Passage Three

Questions 32 to 35 are based on the passage you have just heard.

32. A) No fuel.   B) Ice on the wing.
    C) Engine trouble.   D) No food.

33. A) New England.   B) Britain.
    C) Newfoundland.   D) Alaska.

34. A) None.   B) Less than two.
    C) Two.   D) More than two.

35. A) Many hours.   B) One full day.
    C) Two full days.   D) Three full days.

Section C

Directions: *In this section, you will hear a passage three times. When the passage is read for the first time, you should listen carefully for its general idea. When the passage is read for the second time, you are required to fill in the blanks numbered from 36 to 43 with the exact words you have just heard. For blanks numbered from 44 to 46 you are required to fill in the missing information. For these blanks, you can either use the exact words you have* just heard or write down the main points in your own words. Finally, when *the passage is read for the third time, you should check what you have written.*

Note：The questions in this section are all shown on *Answer Sheet 2*；please put down your answers on it as required. （注意：此部分试题在**答题卡** 2 上；请在**答题卡** 2 上作答。）

Part IV Reading Comprehension (Reading in Depth) (25 minutes)
Section A

Directions: *In this section, there is a short passage with 5 questions or incomplete statements. Read the passage carefully. Then answer the questions or complete the statements in the fewest possible words on Answer Sheet 2.*

The history of English since 1700 is filled with many movements and counter-movements, of which we can notice only a couple. One of these is the vigorous attempt made in the eighteenth century, and the rather half-hearted attempts made since, to regulate and control the English language. Many people of the eighteenth century, not understanding very well the forces which govern language, proposed to polish and prune and restrict English, which they felt was proliferating too wildly. There was much talk of an academy which would rule on what people could and could not say and write. The academy never came into being, but the eighteenth century did succeed in establishing certain attitudes which, though they haven't had much effect on the development of the language itself, have certainly changed the native speaker's feeling about the language.

In part a product of the wish to fix and establish the language was the development of the dictionary. The first English dictionary was published in 1603; it was a list of 2,500 words briefly defined. Another product of the eighteenth century was the invention of "English grammar." As English came to replace Latin as the language of scholarship it was felt that one should also be able to control and dissect it, parse and analyze it, as one could Latin. What happened in practice was that the grammatical description that applied to Latin was removed and superimposed on English. This was silly, because

English is an entirely different kind of language, with its own forms and signals and ways of producing meaning. Nevertheless, English grammars on the Latin model were worked out and taught in the schools. In many schools they are still being taught. This activity is not often popular with school children, but it is sometimes an interesting and instructive exercise in logic. The principal harm in it is that it has tended to keep people from being interested in English and has obscured the real features of English structure.

Note: Please put down on *Answer Sheet 2* your answers to the questions in this section.（注意：此部分试题请在**答题卡**2上作答。）

47. What is the topic of this passage?

48. What is the primary reason for many people in the 18th century to try hard to "control" the English language?

49. It is suggested in the first paragraph that no organization is authoritative enough to _____.

50. What does the author think of English grammars developed in the 18th century?

51. From this passage we may come to the conclusion that the 18th century saw _____.

Section B
Directions: *There are 2 passages in this section. Each passage is followed by some questions or unfinished statements. For each of them there are four choices marked A), B), C) and D). You should decide on the best choice and mark the corresponding letter on **Answer Sheet 2** with a single line through the centre.*

Passage One
Questions 52 to 56 are based on the following passage.

Some of the old worries about artificial intelligence were closely linked to the question of whether computers could think. The first massive electronic computers, capable of rapid computation and little or no creative activity, were soon dubbed "electronic brains." A reaction to this terminology quickly followed: To put them in their place, computers were called "high speed idiots", an effort to protect human vanity. But not everyone realized the implications of the high-speed idiot tag. It has not been pointed out often enough that even the human idiot is one of the most intelligent life forms on earth. If the early computers were even that intelligent, it was already a remarkable state of affairs.

One consequence of speculation about the possibility of computer thought was that we were forced to examine with new care the idea of thought in general. It soon became clear that we were not sure what we meant by such terms as thought and thinking. We tend to assume that human beings think, some more than others, though we often call people *thoughtless* or *unthinking*. Dreams cause a problem, partly because they usually happen outside our control. They are obviously some type of mental experience, but are they a type of thinking? And the question of nonhuman life forms adds further problems. Many of us would maintain that some of the higher animals — dogs, cats, apes, and so on — are capable of at least basic thought, but what about fish and insects? It is certainly true that the higher mammals show complex brain activity when tested with the appropriate equipment. If thinking is demonstrated by evident electrical activity in the brain, then many species are capable of thought. Once we have formulated clear ideas on what thought is in biological creatures, it will be easier to discuss the question of thought in artifacts. And what is true of thought is also true of the many other mental processes. One of the immense benefits of a research is that we are being forced to scrutinize, with new rigor, the working of the human mind.

It is already clear that machines have superior mental abilities to many life forms. No fern or oak tree can play chess as well as even the simplest digital computer; nor can frogs weld car bodies as well as robots. It seems that, viewed in terms of intellect, the computer should be set well above plants and most animals. Only the higher animals can compete with computers with regard to intellect and even then with diminishing success.

Note: Please put down on *Answer Sheet 2* your answers to the following questions. (注意：此部分试题请在**答题卡 2** 上作答。)

52. According to the first paragraph, human beings' attitude towards the early computers can best be described as _____.
   A) indifferent   B) ambiguous
   C) contemptuous   D) hostile

53. In the author's opinion, even if the term "high-speed idiot" was appropriate for the early computers, _____.
   A) they were worthy of our pride
   B) they were not able to think even like a human idiot
   C) they could never be compared to human brains
   D) they were still not capable of any human thought

54. The second paragraph attempts to tell us that _____.
   A) mental abilities are characteristic of humans only
   B) we are still not certain about the difference between thought and thinking
   C) all animal species are in fact capable of thought
   D) we need to research further to get an appropriate definition of the term "thought"

55. The word "scrutinize" (Paragraph 2) can be best replaced by _____.
   A) "improve"   B) "examine closely"
   C) "experiment with"   D) "make use of"

56. It can be concluded from the passage that _____.
   A) computers will be capable of thought in the near future
   B) computers think in a different way from human brains
   C) computers can never compete with humans in thinking
   D) computers possessed the ability to think at the very beginning

Passage Two
Questions 57 to 61 are based on the following passage.

Silence is unnatural to man. He begins life with a cry and ends it in stillness. In the interval he does all he can to make a noise in the world, and there are few things of which he stands in more fear than of the absence of noise. Even his conversation is in great measure a desperate attempt to prevent a dreadful silence. If he is introduced to a fellow mortal, and a number of pauses occur in the conversation, he regards himself as a failure, a worthless person, and is full of envy of the emptiest-headed chatterbox. He knows that ninety-nine per cent of human conversation means no more than the buzzing of a fly, but he longs to join in the buzz and to prove that he is a man and not a waxwork figure. The object of conversation is not, for the most part, to communicate ideas: it is to keep up the buzzing sound. There are, it must be admitted, different qualities of buzz: there is even a buzz that is as exasperating as the continuous ping of a mosquito. But at a dinner-party one would rather be a mosquito than a mute. Most buzzing, fortunately, is agreeable to the ear, and some of it is agreeable even to the mind. He would be a foolish man, however, who waited until he had a wise thought to take part in the buzzing with his neighbours. Those who despise the weather as a conversational opening seem to me to be ignorant of the reason why human beings wish to talk. Very few human beings join in a conversation in the hope of learning anything new. Some of them are content if they are merely allowed to go on making a noise into other people's ears. They have nothing to tell them except that they have seen two or three new plays or that they had bad food in a Swiss hotel. At the end of an evening during which they have said nothing at immense length, they just plume on themselves their success as conversationists. I have heard a young man holding up the monologue of a prince among modern wits for half an hour in order to tell us absolutely nothing about himself with opulent long-windedness. None of us except the young man himself liked it, but he looked as happy as if he had a crown on his head.

Note: Please put down on *Answer Sheet 2* your answers to the following questions.（注意：此部分试题请在**答题卡 2** 上作答。）

57. According to the author, conversation is by and large a grim effort to _____.

    A) prevent men thinking they are failures

    B) eradicate man's fear of silence

    C) avoid silence

D) make a man feel he has value in other's eyes

58. Why, according to the author, is a man so keen to join in conversation?
    A) In order to assert his superiority.
    B) In order to prove that he is a rational, living being.
    C) In order to communicate ideas which he considers important.
    D) To prove that he is not a worthless person.

59. The reason why one would rather be a mosquito than a mute at a party is that _____.
    A) conversation, however meaningless, is preferable to silence
    B) a mosquito makes more noise than a mute and noise is second nature to man
    C) man can achieve identity through noise
    D) the qualities of a mosquito are superior to those of a mute

60. According to the author, what part does weather play in conversation?
    A) It shows people's ignorance of purpose of conversation.
    B) It can provide a topic to break the ice.
    C) It indicates that very few people hope to learn anything new from conversation.
    D) It can provide a topic of conversation that is acceptable.

61. The author once heard a young man who for thirty minutes _____.
    A) interrupted an outstandingly witty speaker
    B) in a group of witty people, hindered a prince from making a speech
    C) in a group of witty people did not allow a prince to get a word in edgeways
    D) delayed the speech which a prince was about to deliver to a group of intelligent people

Part V Error Correction (15 minutes)

Directions: *This part consists of a short passage. In this passage, there are altogether 10 mistakes, one in each numbered line. You may have to change a* *word, add a word or delete a word. Mark out the mistakes and put the corrections in the blanks provided. If you change a word, cross it out and write the correct word in the corresponding blank. If you add a word, put an insertion mark (∧) in the right place and write the missing word in the blank. If you delete a word, cross it out and put a slash (/) in the blank.*

Example:

Television is rapidly becoming the literature of our ~~periods~~ . Many of the arguments
~~having~~ used for the study of literature as a
school subject are valid for∧ study of television.

1. time/times/period
2. _____
3. _____the_____

Note: The questions in this part are shown on ***Answer Sheet 2***；please put down your answers on the **Sheet**.（注意：此部分试题在**答题卡 2** 上；请在**答题卡 2** 上作答。）

Part VI Translation (5 minutes)

Directions: *Complete the following sentences by translating into English the Chinese given in brackets.*

Note: Please put down on ***Answer Sheet 2*** your answers to the questions in this part.（注意：此部分试题请在**答题卡 2** 上作答。）

72. "（当一个人怀有一股展翅高飞的冲动时）_____," Helen Keller once said，"one can never consent to creep."

73. Unable to defend themselves，some countries _____.（只得听凭列强的摆布）.

74. After he retired，the professor lived in _____（纽约西面的一个小镇上）.

75. When the woman reporter heard the suggestion that she attend a sales-training course，_____（她气恼得双眼直冒怒火）.

76. A college degree is not a sign that one is a finished product _____（而是个人已作好生活准备的一个标记）.

Answer Sheet 1 (答题卡1)

学校:

姓名:

划线要求

准		考			证			号						
[0]	[0]	[0]	[0]	[0]	[0]	[0]	[0]	[0]	[0]	[0]	[0]	[0]	[0]	[0]
[1]	[1]	[1]	[1]	[1]	[1]	[1]	[1]	[1]	[1]	[1]	[1]	[1]	[1]	[1]
[2]	[2]	[2]	[2]	[2]	[2]	[2]	[2]	[2]	[2]	[2]	[2]	[2]	[2]	[2]
[3]	[3]	[3]	[3]	[3]	[3]	[3]	[3]	[3]	[3]	[3]	[3]	[3]	[3]	[3]
[4]	[4]	[4]	[4]	[4]	[4]	[4]	[4]	[4]	[4]	[4]	[4]	[4]	[4]	[4]
[5]	[5]	[5]	[5]	[5]	[5]	[5]	[5]	[5]	[5]	[5]	[5]	[5]	[5]	[5]
[6]	[6]	[6]	[6]	[6]	[6]	[6]	[6]	[6]	[6]	[6]	[6]	[6]	[6]	[6]
[7]	[7]	[7]	[7]	[7]	[7]	[7]	[7]	[7]	[7]	[7]	[7]	[7]	[7]	[7]
[8]	[8]	[8]	[8]	[8]	[8]	[8]	[8]	[8]	[8]	[8]	[8]	[8]	[8]	[8]
[9]	[9]	[9]	[9]	[9]	[9]	[9]	[9]	[9]	[9]	[9]	[9]	[9]	[9]	[9]

Part I   **Writing**   **(30 minutes)**

Directions: *For this part, you are allowed 30 minutes to write a short essay entitled **The Value of Science**. You should write at least **150** words following the outline given below:*

有的人认为,科学的价值在于对人类物质生活的提高作出了巨大贡献;另一些人则认为,科学的真正价值在于它提高了人的整体素质.你的看法如何?写出你的观点,并适当举例说明你的理由.

THE VALUE OF SCIENCE

Answer Sheet 1 (答题卡 1)

Part II Reading Comprehension (Skimming and Scanning) (15 minutes)

1. [Y] [N] [NG]

2. [Y] [N] [NG]

3. [Y] [N] [NG]

4. [Y] [N] [NG]

5. _____

6. _____

7. _____

8. _____

9. _____

10. _____

Answer Sheet 2 (答题卡 2)

Part III Section A   Section B

11. [A] [B] [C] [D]   16. [A] [B] [C] [D]   21. [A] [B] [C] [D]   26. [A] [B] [C] [D]   31. [A] [B] [C] [D]
12. [A] [B] [C] [D]   17. [A] [B] [C] [D]   22. [A] [B] [C] [D]   27. [A] [B] [C] [D]   32. [A] [B] [C] [D]
13. [A] [B] [C] [D]   18. [A] [B] [C] [D]   23. [A] [B] [C] [D]   28. [A] [B] [C] [D]   33. [A] [B] [C] [D]
14. [A] [B] [C] [D]   19. [A] [B] [C] [D]   24. [A] [B] [C] [D]   29. [A] [B] [C] [D]   34. [A] [B] [C] [D]
15. [A] [B] [C] [D]   20. [A] [B] [C] [D]   25. [A] [B] [C] [D]   30. [A] [B] [C] [D]   35. [A] [B] [C] [D]

Part III Section C

In the medical profession，technology is advancing so fast that questions of law and ethics cannot be discussed and answered fast enough. Most of these questions (36) _____ ending or beginning a human life. For example，we have the medical ability to keep a person (37) _____ "alive" for years, on machines, after he or she is "brain dead". But is it ethical to do this? And what about the (38) _____? In other words，is it (39) _____ *not* to keep a person alive if we have the technology to do so?

And there are also many ethical questions involving the (40) _____ of a human baby. External fertilization，for example，is becoming more and more common. By this method，couples who have difficulty (41) _____ a child may still become parents. At a cost between $70,000 and $75,000 for the (42) _____ of one such baby, should society have to pay for this especially when there are many (43) _____ children who need parents? (44) _____; is this fertilized egg a human being? If the parents get a divorce, to whom do these frozen eggs belong? And there is the question of surrogate mothers. There have been several cases of a woman (45) _____. After delivering the baby, the surrogate mother sometimes changes her mind and wants to keep the baby. Whose baby is it? (46) _____?

85

Answer Sheet 2 (答题卡2)

Part IV   Section A   Part V   Error Correction   (15 minutes)

47. _____

    _____

48. _____

    _____

49. _____

    _____

50. _____

    _____

51. _____

    _____

Part IV   Section B

52. [A][B][C][D]
53. [A][B][C][D]
54. [A][B][C][D]
55. [A][B][C][D]
56. [A][B][C][D]
57. [A][B][C][D]
58. [A][B][C][D]
59. [A][B][C][D]
60. [A][B][C][D]
61. [A][B][C][D]

In every city and town there are people named as real estate agents who will help you find a house to rent. But they may charge a fixed number of money, such as a month's rent or a percentage of the year's rent, to help you find a place. Some companies pay the amounts for their workers; others do not. If you have a work in the United States, be certain that you ask if your company will pay for this service or not after you sign any papers with a real estate agent. You can also find a house by yourself by noticing "For Rent" signs and following newspaper advertisement. The sign will list a telephone number for you to call.

When you rent a house, in addition to the rent, you will generally be expected to pay for what we called utilities — gas and electricity, heat and hot water — besides for simple electrical and other repairs. However, this is a good idea to be sure what the rent does and does not include. As there is often the case with most house rentals, you will probably be expected to have certain demands for the care of the house, such as grass-cutting and snow removal. For example, in most cities, you, not the city, are responsible for clearing the walk of snow in front of the house within a few hours after each snowfall.

62. _____

63. _____

64. _____
65. _____
66. _____

67. _____

68. _____
69. _____
70. _____

71. _____

Part VI   Translation   (5 minutes)

72. _____

73. _____

74. _____

75. _____

76. _____

Practice Test 5

Part I Writing (30 minutes)

Note: The topic and directions for writing are shown on *Answer Sheet 1*.（注意：此部分试题在**答题卡** 1 上。）

Part II Reading Comprehension (Skimming and Scanning) (15 minutes)

Directions: *In this part, you will have 15 minutes to go over the passage quickly and answer the questions on* **Answer Sheet 1**.

For questions 1 – 4, mark

Y *(for YES)*　　　　　*if the statement agrees with the information given in the passage;*

N *(for NO)*　　　　　*if the statement contradicts the information given in the passage;*

NG *(for NOT GIVEN)*　*if the information is not given in the passage.*

For questions 5 – 10, complete the sentences with the information given in the passage.

Super-kids and Super Problems

— By David Elkind

Not so long ago, most parents wanted their kids to be like everybody else. They were often as upset if a child were precocious（早熟的）as they were if the child were slow. Precocity was looked upon as being bad for the child's psychological health. The assumption was "early ripe, early rot."

Now that has changed. For many parents today there is no such thing as going too fast, and their major concern is that their child stay ahead of the pack（一群伙伴）. Far from presuming that precocity has bad effects psychologically, they believe that being above the norm brings many benefits. The assumption is "early ripe, early rich!"

The major consequence of this new parenting psychology is that many contemporary parents are putting tremendous pressure on children to perform at ever-earlier ages. A first-grade teacher told me that an angry mother screamed at her because she had given the woman's son a "Satisfactory." "How is he ever going to get into M. I. T. if you give him a 'Satisfactory?'" the mother wailed.

Many parents now enroll their child in prestigious nursery schools as soon as the pregnancy is confirmed. And once the child is old enough, they coach the child for the screening interview. "When they count everything in sight," one nursery school director said, "you know they have been drilled before the interview." Parents believe that only if the child gets into this or that prestigious nursery school will he or she ever have a chance at getting into Harvard, Yale, or Stanford. For the same reason, our elementary schools are suddenly filled with youngsters in enriched and accelerated programs.

It is not just in academic study that children are being pushed harder at ever-earlier ages. Some parents start their preschool children in sports such as tennis and swimming in hopes that they will become Olympic athletes. A young man who attended one of my child development lectures stopped by afterward to ask me a question. He works as a tennis instructor at an exclusive resort hotel in Florida and wanted to know how to motivate his students. When I asked how old they were he told me that they ranged in age from three to five years!

The pressure to make ordinary children exceptional has become almost an epidemic in sports. I had high hopes for soccer, which can be played by all makes and models of children, big, small, and in between. But in most states soccer has become as competitive and selective as baseball, football, and hockey. The star mentality prevails, and the less talented youngster simply doesn't get to participate. Play is out and competition is in.

The pressure for exceptionality is equally powerful at the secondary level. High school students are pressured not only to get good grades but to get into as many advanced-placement classes as possible. Around the country private tutoring centers are sprouting up like dandelions (蒲公英) in the spring, offering lessons in everything from beginning reading to taking college-entrance exams. Other parents urge their children to start dating at an early age so that they will have good interpersonal skills and a better chance to win the most eligible mates.

Clearly, there is nothing wrong with wanting children to do their best. It is not the normal, healthy desire of parents to have successful children that is the problem, but the excessive pressure some parents are putting on children.

Why this push for excellence? Since parents today are having fewer children their chances of having "a child to be proud of" are lower than when families were larger. The cost of child rearing has also increased dramatically, so a successful child also protects one's investment. But most of all, many of today's parents have carved out their own successful careers and feel very much in charge of their lives. They see no reason they should not take charge of child rearing in the same manner and with the same success. A successful child is the ultimate proof of their success.

The result is that many parents are far too intrusive. By deciding what and when children should learn, they rob them of the opportunity to take the initiative, to take responsibility for their mistakes and credit for their achievements. Such practices run the risk of producing children who are dependent and lacking in self-esteem. Today's parents want super-kids, but what they are often getting are super problems.

Although correlation (相互关系) is certainly not causation (因果关系), it is hard not to connect the reported increase in stress symptoms over the last decade with the pressure on today's children to be super-kids. The stories I hear as I travel about the country are frightening. A girl who was involved in four different out-of-school activities (ballet, horseback riding, Brownies (幼年女童子军), and music lessons) developed severe facial tics (抽搐) at age eight. Irving Sigel of Educational Testing Service tells the story of a six-year-old who, while doing her homework, asked her mother, "If I don't get there right, will you kill me?" A woman told me that her seven-year-old grandson ran away from home (and all the after-school lessons) and came to her house, where he could have milk and cookies and play with the dog. One mother asked me if I could cure her six-year-old son of his nail biting by hypnosis or by teaching him relaxation. When I suggested that a less demanding extracurricular (课外的) program might help, she replied, "Oh no, we can't do that."

Such child behavior problems are symptomatic (表明……症状的) of our times. Our trouble is that we always seem to go to extremes. Parents are either too permissive (宽容的) or too pushy (一意孤行的). Healthy child rearing demands a middle ground. Certainly we need to make demands on our children. But they have to be tailored to the child's interests and abilities. We put our children at risk for short-term stress disorders and long-term personality problems when we ignore their individuality and impose our own priorities "for their own good."

I believe that we need to abandon the false notions that we can create exceptional children by early instruction, and that such children are symbols of our competence as parents. And I believe we should be as concerned with character as with success. If we have reared a well-mannered, good, and decent person, we should take pleasure and pride in that fact. More likely than not, if we have achieved those goals, the child's success will take care of itself. Each child has a unique pattern of qualities and abilities that makes him or her special. In this sense, every single child is a super-kid.

Note: Please put down on *Answer Sheet 1* your answers to the questions in this part.（注意：此部分试题请在**答题卡 1** 上作答。）

1. Many parents today assume that their children will be in an advantageous position if they start striving competitively for excellence at an early age.

2. Many people now prefer the saying "early ripe, early rich" to the saying "early ripe, early rot."

3. Many parents are pushing their children prematurely into adulthood and at ever-earlier ages they have to work hard to excel not only in academic study, but in sports and social life as well.

4. The push for excellence is powerful all the way through to higher education.

5. _____, _____, and _____ are some factors that lead parents to pursue a competitive approach to child rearing.

6. Most probably the word "intrusive" means _____.

7. Pushing a child to be a competitive high achiever at an early age will result in such negative long-term consequences as _____, _____, and

_____.

8. The author supports his belief in the "consequences" of parental pressure by _____.

9. The author strongly believes that parents should care as much about _____ as with _____.

10. According to the author, a child with _____ is an exceptional child by itself.

Part III Listening Comprehension (35 minutes)
Section A
Directions: *In this section, you will hear 8 short conversations and 2 long conversations. At the end of each conversation, one or more questions will be asked about what was said. Both the conversation and the questions will be spoken only once. After each question there will be a pause. During the pause, you must read the four choices marked A), B), C) and D), and decide which is the best answer. Then mark the corresponding letter on Answer Sheet 2 with a single line through the center.*

Note: Please put down on *Answer Sheet 2* your answers to the following questions.（注意：此部分试题请在**答题卡 2** 上作答。）

11. A) He doesn't want to help.   B) He isn't able to work.
    C) He will help the woman later.   D) He'd like to work here.

12. A) Peter is visiting his mother.
    B) Peter will be unable to come.
    C) Peter's mother is coming for dinner.
    D) Peter can't hear them.

13. A) All the students would like a formal ball.
    B) Raising money will be hard.
    C) The festival will begin the year nicely.
    D) The club needs some sports as well.

14. A) At a restaurant.

    B) In a store specializing in seashells.

    C) On a fishing boat.

    D) In the fresh ocean air.

15. A) He didn't think it a success.

    B) He was listening too attentively to the speakers.

    C) He was puzzled by what the speakers said.

    D) He had nothing to say.

16. A) She was extremely happy with her exams.

    B) She was not sure about the results of her exams.

    C) She couldn't believe the results of her exams.

    D) She was not satisfied with her exams at all.

17. A) She wants to work again tomorrow.

    B) She's willing to stop working.

    C) She wants to consider half a day's work as a full day.

    D) She's unhappy to work so long without pay.

18. A) Make his own arrangements.   B) Go to the places she likes.

    C) See a travel agent.   D) Take a spring vacation.

Questions 19 to 21 are based on the conversation you have just heard.

19. A) They had to work during the performance.

    B) They couldn't find time.

    C) They couldn't afford to go.

    D) The tickets were sold out.

20. A) The performances have been rescheduled.

    B) Student discount tickets are available.

    C) Prices for all tickets have been reduced.

    D) Ushers are needed at the theater.

21. A) She doubts it will work.
    B) She thinks they don't have enough time.
    C) She's enthusiastic about it.
    D) She's happy to get so much money.

Questions 22 to 25 are based on the conversation you have just heard.

22. A) A scientist and his assistant.
    B) A physician and a nurse.
    C) A psychologist and a news reporter.
    D) A professor and his student.

23. A) Emotional intelligence.
    B) Intelligence quotient.
    C) Applied psychology.
    D) The function of the emotional brain.

24. A) Days.   B) Weeks.
    C) Months.   D) Years.

25. A) Effective ways of growing emotional intelligence.
    B) Interactions between emotional intelligence and IQ.
    C) Correlations between emotional intelligence and IQ.
    D) Good combinations of emotional intelligence and IQ.

Section B

Directions: *In this section, you will hear 3 short passages. At the end of each passage, you will hear some questions. Both the passage and the questions will be spoken only once. After you hear a question, you must choose the best answer from the four choices marked A), B), C) and D). Then mark the corresponding letter on* **Answer Sheet 2** *with a single line through the centre.*

Note: Please put down on **Answer Sheet 2** your answers to the following questions.（注意：此部分试题请在**答题卡 2** 上作答。）

Passage One

Questions 26 to 28 are based on the passage you have just heard.

26. A) Because life in the country is more interesting.
    B) Because they are in search of the "good life."
    C) Because there are more job opportunities.
    D) Because people there are very kind to the new comers.

27. A) Life is quiet and relaxed.
    B) There isn't much to do at night.
    C) People there are living a simple and hard life.
    D) There aren't many theaters and restaurants there.

28. A) To save up some money.
    B) To enjoy yourself most before you move.
    C) To read more books to know more about the life in the small town.
    D) To spend some time in a village to make sure if you are used to the life there.

Passage Two

Questions 29 to 31 are based on the passage you have just heard.

29. A) They should not be too strict with the children.
    B) They should limit their demands on some children.
    C) They should demand more of their children.
    D) They should demand more of the bright children.

30. A) To do comprehensive exercises.
    B) To read simple sentences.
    C) To copy out from the textbooks.
    D) To do all of the above.

31. A) She assigned people to do this report.
    B) She made investigations in the 700 schools.
    C) She supported the report.
    D) She wrote this report.

Passage Three

Questions 32 to 35 are based on the passage you have just heard.

32. A) The population of elderly people.
    B) Nuclear weapon.
    C) Standard of living.
    D) Violence in crime.

33. A) Growth of violence on TV.
    B) Destructive threat from nuclear explosives.
    C) Degrading moral standards.
    D) All of the above.

34. A) People are more destructive.
    B) People are more selfish.
    C) People do what they preach now.
    D) People do not have moral principles to follow now.

35. A) Indifferent.　　　　　　　　B) Surprised.
    C) Worried.　　　　　　　　　D) Confident.

Section C

Directions: *In this section, you will hear a passage three times. When the passage is read for the first time, you should listen carefully for its general idea. When the passage is read for the second time, you are required to fill in the blanks numbered from 36 to 43 with the exact words you have just heard. For blanks numbered from 44 to 46 you are required to fill in the missing information. For these blanks, you can either use the exact words you have just heard or write down the main points in your own words. Finally, when the passage is read for the third time, you should check what you have written.*

Note: The questions in this section are all shown on *Answer Sheet 2*; please put down your answers on it as required. (注意：此部分试题在**答题卡** 2 上；请在**答题卡** 2 上作答。)

Part IV   Reading Comprehension（Reading in Depth）（25 minutes）
Section A
Directions: *In this section, there is a short passage with 5 questions or incom-plete statements. Read the passage carefully. Then answer the questions or complete the statements in the fewest possible words on **Answer Sheet 2**.*

Researchers disagree whether the "use it or lose it" philosophy holds for cognitive aging, but there is some evidence that keeping mentally active can slow age-related declines.

At Pennsylvania State University, Sherry Willis and her husband, K. Warner Schaie, have studied 5,000 people, some since 1956. People lucky enough to avoid chronic diseases may also fare better in intellectual function, they find, perhaps because chronic diseases can restrict lifestyle and reduce mental stimulation. Similarly, those lucky enough to be relatively affluent also fare better, perhaps because money can buy intellectually stimulating things like travel.

Education helps, too, researchers say, perhaps because it instills the conviction that you can always learn something new. The Schaie-Willis team also has some other observations. Being in a stable marriage with a stimulating spouse, they say, helps maintain intellectual vigor.

Flexibility counts, too. People who stay mentally vibrant are often those who do not insist that "they must do things today as they did before," Schaie says. In neuropsychological（神经心理学的）terms, the ability to see problems in new ways often yields higher scores on tests of mental function. And people satisfied with life also stay more mentally fit, he says.

If you find your mental skills sagging, consider working on specific deficits. When Willis gave 5-hour tutorials（辅导课）on inductive reasoning or spatial skills to about 200 people whose skills had declined in the previous 14 years, 40 percent regained lost abilities. That advantage held up seven years later when they were re-tested.

Other ways to stay sharp, Schaie says, are doing jigsaw puzzles to hone （磨练）visuo-spatial skills, working crossword puzzles for verbal skills, playing bridge for memory and simply matching wits at home with players on TV game shows.

Finally, remember this. Even though you may lose some mental skills with normal aging, you also gain in one key area: wisdom. The growth of wisdom — loosely defined as the maturation of intellectual abilities that comes with life experience — continues throughout the 40s, 50s and even 60s.

Note: Please put down on *Answer Sheet 2* your answers to the questions in this section. (注意: 此部分试题请在**答题卡**2上作答。)

47. What does the author mainly discuss in this passage?

48. The word "it" in the saying "use it or lose it" (Paragraph 1) refers to _____.

49. According to researchers, what factor or factors affect cognitive aging?

50. From this passage we may safely infer that _____ might help prevent mental declines.

51. According to the author, wisdom still grows even when _____ _____ and makes up _____.

Section B

Directions: *There are 2 passages in this section. Each passage is followed by some questions or unfinished statements. For each of them there are four choices marked A), B), C) and D). You should decide on the best choice and mark the corresponding letter on **Answer Sheet 2** with a single line through the centre.*

Passage One

Questions 52 to 56 are based on the following passage.

The chant of "digital, digital, digital" continues to grow in volume worldwide. Digital cameras, digital video camcorders (摄像放像机), video CD players, DVD, cellular phones, and a host of computer peripherals (外围设备) are moving the trend along at a breathtaking rate. For the average person, it may seem like a remote and puzzling phenomenon meant only for the technologically adept.

Virtually every aspect of our lives could be affected by the digital revolution. Here is a hypothetical scenario（设想）to show the possibilities: A real estate agent in Seattle uses a digital still camera to take some pictures of a house she's trying to sell. She transfers them to her computer, digitally retouches and enhances them, and posts them on her company's Internet Web site. In Singapore, a buyer sees the pictures and asks via electronic mail for more information. The agent replies via e-mail and attaches the text and a digital video clip to her message. Later the buyer flies to Seattle, inspects the property, and seals the deal.

One of the biggest marketing surprises of the current age is the digital still camera. Once prohibitively expensive, these cameras have radically dropped in price while gaining in resolution（分辨率）and other features. Although they often resemble traditional cameras, they don't use film. Instead, they store images on either a small removable memory card or on the memory chip inside the camera.

The beauty of digital photography is that while you'll spend relatively more for a digital camera, you'll save a lot on film processing costs, because there aren't any. You can also discard digital pictures and keep shooting. Better yet, you can use software to enhance or alter the image. In quality, the images consumer-level digital cameras produce do not compare to ones you'd get from a 35mm camera. For the most part, though, digital photos are meant to be viewed on a computer monitor, and so their resolution is more than acceptable. In a world where the speed at which you distribute information often means the difference between success and failure, and immediacy supersedes quality in importance, many people are finding a use for digital camera.

Note: Please put down on *Answer Sheet 2* your answers to the following questions.（注意：此部分试题请在**答题卡** 2 上作答。）

52. From the first paragraph we know the average person thinks _____.
    A）the digital age is far away
    B）digital is too complicated for him
    C）digital age is dreadful
    D）both A and B

53. In the second paragraph the author used an example to show that
_____.
   A) any real estate agent should use digital still camera
   B) digital still camera should be used together with Internet Web
   C) digital age is gaining momentum
   D) house dealing can be made easier

54. _____ could be the best summary of the last two paragraphs.
   A) Digital still camera and traditional camera
   B) Pros and cons of digital still camera
   C) Capturing the world digitally
   D) The ways to use digital still camera

55. All the following are the advantages of digital still camera EXCEPT
_____.
   A) no need of film   B) easy to carry
   C) the image can be changed   D) high resolution

56. Which of the following best summarizes the article?
   A) New Digital Age of Interactivity
   B) Digital Still Camera
   C) One Application of Computer
   D) Goodbye Analog, Hello Digital

Passage Two
Questions 57 to 61 are based on the following passage.

Most large-scale, objective measures of men's roles show little change over the past decade, but men do feel now and then that their position is in question, their security is somewhat fragile. I believe they are right, for they sense a set of forces that lie deeper and are more powerful than the day-to-day negotiation and renegotiation of advantage among husbands and wives, fathers and children, or bosses and those who work for them. Men are troubled by this new situation.

The conditions we live in are different from those of any prior civilization, and they give less support to men's claims of superiority than perhaps any other historical era. When these conditions weaken that support, men can rely only on previous tradition, or their attempts to socialize their children, to shore up their faltering advantages. Such rhetoric is not likely to be successful against the new objective conditions and the claims of aggrieved women. Thus, men are correct when they feel they are losing some of their privileges, even if many continue to laugh at the women's liberation movement.

The new conditions can be listed concretely, but I shall also give you a theoretical formulation of the process. Concretely, because of the increased use of various mechanical gadgets and devices, fewer tasks require much strength. As to those that still require strength, most men cannot do them either. Women can now do more household tasks that men once felt only they could do, and still more tasks are done by repair specialists called in to do them. With the development of modern warfare, there are few, if any, important combat activities that only men can do. Women are much better educated than before.

With each passing year, psychological and sociological research reduces the areas in which men are reported to excel over women and discloses far more overlap in talents, so that even when males still seem to have an advantage, it is but a slight one. It is also becoming more widely understood that the posts in government and business are not best filled by the stereotypical aggressive male but by people, male or female, who are sensitive to others' needs, adept in obtaining cooperation, and skilled in social relations. Finally, in one sphere after another, the number of women who try to achieve rises, and so does the number who succeed.

Note: Please put down on *Answer Sheet 2* your answers to the following questions. (注意：此部分试题请在**答题卡**2上作答。)

57. It can be inferred that the main source of men's resistance to women's liberation is the feeling that _____.

A) women are now better educated

B) women can now hold executive positions

C) men are no longer indispensable

D) men are no longer superior

58. Which of the following is TRUE according to the passage?
   A) Only few men can participate in combat activities.
   B) Only few women can participate in combat activities.
   C) There are a few modern wars which can be done by men.
   D) There are few modern wars which can not be done by women.

59. The phrase "to shore up" in the second paragraph probably means
   _____.

   A) "demonstrate"   B) "take"
   C) "strengthen"   D) "grasp"

60. According to the annual research report, _____.
   A) the area where men can have a slight advantage has increased
   B) the area where men can show their talents has decreased
   C) the area where women can make full use of their talents is expanded
   D) the area where women can not compete with men is reduced

61. What does the passage mainly discuss?
   A) The new challenge men are facing in modern society.
   B) The reasons for men's feeling that they are not superior.
   C) The role men are playing in the new situation.
   D) The contribution of new conditions to men's weakened position.

Part V   Error Correction (15 minutes)
Directions: *This part consists of a short passage. In this passage, there are altogether 10 mistakes, one in each numbered line. You may have to change a
   word, add a word or delete a word. Mark out the mistakes and put the corrections in the blanks provided. If you change a word, cross it out and write
   the correct word in the corresponding blank. If you add a word, put an insertion mark (∧) in the right place and write the missing word in the blank. If
   you delete a word, cross it out and put a slash (/) in the blank.*

Example:

Television is rapidly becoming the literature of our ~~periods~~. Many of the arguments
~~having~~ used for the study of literature as a
school subject are valid for ∧ study of television.

1. time/times/period
2. _____
3. _____ the _____

Note: The questions in this part are shown on *Answer Sheet 2*; please put down your answers on the **Sheet.**（注意：此部分试题在**答题卡 2** 上；请在**答题卡 2** 上作答。）

Part VI   Translation (5 minutes)

Directions: *Complete the following sentences by translating into English the Chinese given in brackets.*

Note: Please put down on *Answer Sheet 2* your answers to the questions in this part.（注意：此部分试题请在**答题卡 2** 上作答。）

72. Only when we have suffered a serious setback，_____（我们才会去努力克服自己的自满情绪）.

73. With _____（烟雾和蒸汽从火山口不断升起），the volcano has shown signs of life recently.

74. The houses in this residential area _____（价格在 30 万至 50 万美元之间）.

75. _____（由于电力供应不足，多达两千家工厂）had to reschedule their production to evenings or at weekends.

76. Having made this event known to the public，the reporter _____（已经从女演员的窘境中捞到了好处）.

Answer Sheet 1 (答题卡 1)

学校:		准 考 证 号														
姓名:		[0]	[0]	[0]	[0]	[0]	[0]	[0]	[0]	[0]	[0]	[0]	[0]	[0]	[0]	[0]
		[1]	[1]	[1]	[1]	[1]	[1]	[1]	[1]	[1]	[1]	[1]	[1]	[1]	[1]	[1]
		[2]	[2]	[2]	[2]	[2]	[2]	[2]	[2]	[2]	[2]	[2]	[2]	[2]	[2]	[2]
		[3]	[3]	[3]	[3]	[3]	[3]	[3]	[3]	[3]	[3]	[3]	[3]	[3]	[3]	[3]
划线要求		[4]	[4]	[4]	[4]	[4]	[4]	[4]	[4]	[4]	[4]	[4]	[4]	[4]	[4]	[4]
		[5]	[5]	[5]	[5]	[5]	[5]	[5]	[5]	[5]	[5]	[5]	[5]	[5]	[5]	[5]
		[6]	[6]	[6]	[6]	[6]	[6]	[6]	[6]	[6]	[6]	[6]	[6]	[6]	[6]	[6]
		[7]	[7]	[7]	[7]	[7]	[7]	[7]	[7]	[7]	[7]	[7]	[7]	[7]	[7]	[7]
		[8]	[8]	[8]	[8]	[8]	[8]	[8]	[8]	[8]	[8]	[8]	[8]	[8]	[8]	[8]
		[9]	[9]	[9]	[9]	[9]	[9]	[9]	[9]	[9]	[9]	[9]	[9]	[9]	[9]	[9]

Part I   **Writing**   **(30 minutes)**

Directions: *For this part, you are allowed 30 minutes to write a short essay entitled **The Newspaper: A Better Source of News**. You should write at least **150** words following the outline given below (in Chinese):*

根据一项有关人们日常信息来源的调查(a questionnaire on "ways of obtaining information"),有近乎 72%的人靠电视获取信息,只有 12%的人是通过报纸了解天下大事的。在我看来,报纸是一种更可取的信息来源。理由有三:1.新闻报道比电视新闻更具深度;2.看报纸不受时间限制;3.看报纸要动脑筋,有利于智力的提高。

THE NEWSPAPER: A BETTER SOURCE OF NEWS

Answer Sheet 1 (答题卡 1)

Part II   Reading Comprehension (Skimming and Scanning) (15 minutes)

1. [Y] [N] [NG]
2. [Y] [N] [NG]
3. [Y] [N] [NG]
4. [Y] [N] [NG]

5. _____

6. _____

7. _____

8. _____

9. _____

10. _____

Answer Sheet 2 (答题卡2)

Part III Section A

11. [A] [B] [C] [D]
12. [A] [B] [C] [D]
13. [A] [B] [C] [D]
14. [A] [B] [C] [D]
15. [A] [B] [C] [D]
16. [A] [B] [C] [D]
17. [A] [B] [C] [D]
18. [A] [B] [C] [D]
19. [A] [B] [C] [D]
20. [A] [B] [C] [D]
21. [A] [B] [C] [D]
22. [A] [B] [C] [D]
23. [A] [B] [C] [D]
24. [A] [B] [C] [D]
25. [A] [B] [C] [D]

Section B

26. [A] [B] [C] [D]
27. [A] [B] [C] [D]
28. [A] [B] [C] [D]
29. [A] [B] [C] [D]
30. [A] [B] [C] [D]
31. [A] [B] [C] [D]
32. [A] [B] [C] [D]
33. [A] [B] [C] [D]
34. [A] [B] [C] [D]
35. [A] [B] [C] [D]

Part III Section C

As heart disease continues to be number-one killer in the United States, researchers have become increasingly interested in (36) _____ the potential risk factors that (37) _____ heart attacks. High-fat diets and "life in the fast lane" have long been known to contribute to the high (38) _____ of heart failure. But according to new studies, the list of risk factors may be (39) _____ longer and quite surprising.

Heart failure, for example, appears to have seasonal and (40) _____ patterns. A higher percentage of heart attacks occur in cold weather, and more people experience heart failure on Monday than on any other day of the week. In addition, people are more (41) _____ to heart attacks in the first few hours after waking. Cardiologists first observed this morning (42) _____ in the mid-1980s and have since discovered a number of possible causes. An early-morning rise in blood pressure, heart rate, and concentration of heart (43) _____ hormones, plus a reduction of blood flow to the heart, (44) _____ .

In other studies, both birthdays and bachelorhood have been implicated as risk factors.

Statistics reveal that (45) _____ . And unmarried men are more at risk for heart attacks than their married counterparts. (46) _____ .

Answer Sheet 2 (答题卡 2)

Part IV   Section A

47. _____

_____

48. _____

_____

49. _____

_____

_____

50. _____

_____

_____

51. _____

_____

Part IV   Section B

52. [A][B][C][D]
53. [A][B][C][D]
54. [A][B][C][D]
55. [A][B][C][D]
56. [A][B][C][D]
57. [A][B][C][D]
58. [A][B][C][D]
59. [A][B][C][D]
60. [A][B][C][D]
61. [A][B][C][D]

Part V   Error Correction   (15 minutes)

The key to being a winner is to have desire and a goal from which you refuse to be deterred (被吓住).
That desire fuels your dreams and the special goal keeps you focusing.   62. _____

Deeply down we all have a hope that our destiny is   63. _____
not to be average and prosaic. Everyone talks about a good game, but the winner goes out and do something.   64. _____
To win, there has to be movement and physical action.
Attitudes and persistence can help us become who we   65. _____
want to be.

Competition is the best motivator. Because many   66. _____
people use competition as an excuse for not doing something, those who really want to success see   67. _____
competition as an opportunity, and they are willing to do the tough work necessarily to win.   68. _____

Learn to deal with fear. Fear is the greatest deterrent to taking risk. People worry so much about   69. _____
failing that their fear paralyzes them, drained the   70. _____
energy they might otherwise be using to grow.

You can cultivate self-respect by developing a commitment to your own talents. It may be necessary to do the thing you fear the most in order to put that fear in rest, so that it can no longer control you.   71. _____

Part VI   Translation   (5 minutes)

72. _____

73. _____

74. _____

75. _____

76. _____

Practice Test 6

Part I   Writing (30 minutes)

Note: The topic and directions for writing are shown on *Answer Sheet 1*. （注意：此部分试题在**答题卡**１上。）

Part II   Reading Comprehension (Skimming and Scanning) (15 minutes)

Directions: *In this part, you will have 15 minutes to go over the passage quickly and answer the questions on **Answer Sheet 1**.*

  For questions 1 – 4, mark

  Y *(for YES)*　　　　 *if the statement agrees with the information given in the passage;*

  N *(for NO)*　　　　　 *if the statement contradicts the information given in the passage;*

  NG *(for NOT GIVEN)*　 *if the information is not given in the passage.*

  For questions 5 – 10, complete the sentences with the information given in the passage.

Stress Management: Personally Adjusting to Stress

Stress is a state of imbalance between demands made on us from outside sources and our capabilities to meet those demands. Often, it precedes and occurs concurrently with conflict. Stress, as you have seen, can be brought on by physical events, other people's behavior, social situations, our own behavior, feelings, thoughts, or anything that results in heightened bodily awareness. In many cases, when you experience pain, anger, fear, or depression, these emotions are a response to a stressful situation like conflict.

Sometimes, in highly stressful conflict situations, we must cope with the stress before we cope with the conflict. Relieving some of the intensity of the immediate emotional response will allow us to become more logical and tolerant in resolving the conflict. Here are some of the ways we have for controlling our physical reactions and our thoughts will be explained.

People respond differently to conflict just as they respond differently to stress. Some people handle both better than others do. Individual differences are not as important as learning how to manage the stress we feel. The goal in stress management is self-control, particularly in the face of stressful events.

Stress reactions involve two major elements: (1) heightened physical arousal as revealed in an increased heart rate, sweaty palms, rapid breathing, and muscular tension, and (2) anxious thoughts, such as thinking you are helpless or wanting to run away. Since your behavior and your emotions are controlled by the way you think, you must acquire skills to change those thoughts.

Controlling physical symptoms of stress requires relaxation. Sit in a comfortable position in a quiet place where there are no distractions. Close your eyes and pay no attention to the outside world. Concentrate only on your breathing. Slowly inhale and exhale. Now, with each exhaled breath say "relax" gently and passively. Make it a relaxing experience. If you use this method to help you in conflict situations over a period of time, the word "relax" will become associated with a sense of physical calm; saying it in a stressful situation will help induce a sense of peace.

Another way to induce relaxation is through tension release. The theory here is that if you tense a set of muscles and then relax them, they will be more relaxed than before you tensed them. Practice each muscle group separately. The ultimate goal, however, is to relax all muscle groups simultaneously to achieve total body relaxation. For each muscle group, in turn, tense the muscles and hold them tense for five seconds, then relax them. Repeat this tension-release sequence three times for each group of muscles. Next, tense all muscles together for five seconds, then release them. Now, take a low, deep breath and say "relax" softly and gently to yourself as you breathe out. Repeat this whole sequence three times.

You do not need to wait for special times to practice relaxing. If, during the course of your daily activities, you notice a tense muscle group, you can help relax this group by saying "relax" inwardly. Monitor your bodily tension. In some cases you can prepare yourself for stressful situations through relaxation *before* they occur. Practice will help you call up the relaxation response whenever needed.

For other ways to relax, do not overlook regular exercise. Aerobic or yoga-type exercise can be helpful. Personal fitness programs can be tied to these inner messages to "relax" for a complete relaxation response.

Controlling your thoughts is the second major element in stress management. Managing stress successfully requires flexibility in thinking. That is, you must consider alternative views. Your current view is causing the stress! You must also keep from attaching exaggerated importance to events.

Everything seems life-threatening in a moment of panic; things dim in importance when viewed in retrospect.

Try to view conflict from a problem-solving approach: "Now, here is a new problem. How am I going to solve this one?" Too often, we become stressed because we take things personally. When an adverse event occurs we see it as a personal affront or as a threat to our ego. For example, when Christy told Paul she could not go to the concert with him, he felt she was letting him know she disliked him. This was a blow to Paul because he had never been turned down — rejected — before. Rather than dwell on that, however, he called Heather, she accepted his invitation, and he achieved his desired outcome — a date for the concert.

One effective strategy for stress management consists of talking to ourselves. We become our own manager, and we guide our thoughts, feelings, and behavior in order to cope. Phillip Le Gras suggests that we view the stress experience as a series of phases. Here, he presents the phases and some examples of coping statements:

1. *Preparing for a stressor.* [Stressors are events that result in behavioral outcomes called stress reactions.] What do I have to do? I can develop a plan to handle it. I have to think about this and not panic. Don't be negative. Think logically. Be rational. Don't worry. Maybe the tension I'm feeling is just eagerness to confront the situation.

2. *Confronting and handling a stressor.* I can do it. Stay relevant. I can psych myself up to handle this, I can meet the challenge. This tension is a cue to use my stress-management skills. Relax. I'm in control. Take a low breath.

3. *Coping with the feeling of being overwhelmed.* I must concentrate on what I have to do right now. I can't eliminate my fear completely, but I can try to keep it under control. When the fear is overwhelm-

ing，I'll just pause for a minute.

4. *Reinforcing self-statements*. Well done. I did it! It worked. I wasn't successful this time，but I'm getting better. It almost worked. Next time I can do it. When I control my thoughts I control my fear.

The purpose of such coping behavior is to become aware of and monitor our anxiety. In this way，we can help eliminate such self-defeating，negative statements as "I'm going to fail," or "I can't do this." Statements such as these are cues that we need to substitute positive，coping self-statements.

If the self-statements do not work，or if the stress reaction is exceptionally intense，then we may need to employ other techniques. Sometimes we can distract ourselves by focusing on something outside the stressful experience — a pleasant memory — or by doing mental arithmetic. Another technique is imaging. By manipulating mental images we can reinterpret，ignore，or change the context of the experience. For example，we can put the experience of unrequited love into a soap-opera fantasy or the experience of pain into a medieval torture by the rack. The point here is that love and pain are strongly subjective and personal，and when they are causing us severe stress we can reconstruct the situation mentally to ease the stress. In both these cases the technique of imaging helps to make our response more objective — to take it *outside* ourselves. The more alternatives we have to aid us in stress reduction，the more likely we are to deal with it effectively.

Note: Please put down on *Answer Sheet 1* your answers to the questions in this part.（注意：此部分试题请在**答题卡** 1 上作答。）

1. Stress is an imbalance of internal and external demands.

2. In most stressful conflict situations we try to manage the stress while coping with the conflict.

3. Controlling our physical reactions and our thoughts is an effective means of managing stress.

4. Human response to stress is individual.

5. Physical symptoms of stress can be controlled _____.

6. In the tension-release method of relaxation, one should tense all his or her muscles together after _____.

7. To manage stress, thoughts can be controlled by considering alternative views through _____.

8. Talking to oneself is an effective means of managing stress because it is a means of _____.

9. Imaging involves reconstructing mental image to make a situation _____.

10. The primary purpose of this article is to instruct the reader to _____.

Part III Listening Comprehension (35 minutes)
Section A
Directions: *In this section, you will hear 8 short conversations and 2 long conversations. At the end of each conversation, one or more questions will be asked about what was said. Both the conversation and the questions will be spoken only once. After each question there will be a pause. During the pause, you must read the four choices marked A), B), C) and D), and decide which is the best answer. Then mark the corresponding letter on **Answer Sheet** 2 with a single line through the centre.*

Note: Please put down on **Answer Sheet 2** your answers to the following questions. （注意：此部分试题请在**答题卡** 2 上作答。）

11. A) In a factory.   B) In a flower shop.
    C) In a heating plant.   D) In a locked room.

12. A) Student and professor.   B) Athlete and coach.
    C) Client and lawyer.   D) Patient and doctor.

13. A) A stormy ocean.   B) Calm water.
    C) Golden sand.   D) Little waves.

14. A) It must be wrapped quickly.

    B) It will arrive next week.

    C) She'd like the store to send it to her.

    D) She'll take it with her to save trouble.

15. A) You should believe everything you read.

    B) She thinks the book is excellent.

    C) She wonders which newspaper he reads.

    D) Reaction to the book has been varied.

16. A) At 9 a.m.   B) At 11 a.m.
    C) At 2 p.m.   D) At 4 p.m.

17. A) He doesn't think he'll do that.   B) He finds it difficult to do that.
    C) He has no time to do that.   D) He knows nothing about math.

18. A) On the street.   B) At the police bureau.
    C) At the gas station.   D) At the library.

Questions 19 to 22 are based on the conversation you have just heard.

19. A) Tuesday.   B) Friday.
    C) Saturday.   D) Sunday.

20. A) English.   B) History.
    C) Biology.   D) Geography.

21. A) Monday.   B) Tuesday.
    C) Wednesday.   D) Thursday.

22. A) Finish them on schedule.

    B) Browse them all during the first week.

    C) Read the relevant ones ahead of lectures or seminars.

    D) Select and read the most helpful.

Questions 23 to 25 are based on the conversation you have just heard.

23. A) With a knife.　　　　　　B) On the edge of some metal.
　　C) On some glass.　　　　　D) On a piece of paper.

24. A) The amount of skin affected by the cut.
　　B) The cause of the cut.
　　C) The number of nerve endings irritated.
　　D) The amount of bleeding.

25. A) Keep the finger wrapped.　　B) Take a pain reliever.
　　C) Let the cut dry out.　　　　D) Go to a doctor.

Section B

Directions: *In this section, you will hear 3 short passages. At the end of each passage, you will hear some questions. Both the passage and the questions will be spoken only once. After you hear a question, you must choose the best answer from the four choices marked A), B), C) and D). Then mark the corresponding letter on Answer Sheet 2 with a single line through the center.*

Note: Please put down on **Answer Sheet 2** your answers to the following questions. （注意：此部分试题请在**答题卡** 2 上作答。）

Passage One

Questions 26 to 29 are based on the passage you have just heard.

26. A) He is a commercial diver.
　　B) He is an independent photographer.
　　C) He is a camera manufacturer.
　　D) Both A and B.

27. A) Michael has been diving for nine years.
　　B) Michael dives on holidays with his parents.
　　C) Michael loves diving ever since he first tried it.
　　D) Michael has never taken any diving courses.

28. A) Taking pictures under water.

    B) Connecting pipelines.

    C) Planting seaweed.

    D) Placing explosives under the water.

29. A) Because he was never afraid of anything.

    B) Because he was protected by a special medium.

    C) Because he had enough experience.

    D) Because it was his job.

Passage Two

Questions 30 to 32 are based on the passage you have just heard.

30. A) Family phone numbers.

    B) Phone numbers of government services.

    C) Phone numbers of businesses.

    D) Phone numbers of professional services.

31. A) People can call you back if necessary.

    B) You can dial a special number free.

    C) You don't need to pay for a long-distance call.

    D) You can get a credit coupon when you give the phone number.

32. A) He will connect you to the correct number.

    B) He will charge you less for the wrong number.

    C) He will charge you no money for the wrong number.

    D) He will tell you what the wrong number is.

Passage Three

Questions 33 to 35 are based on the passage you have just heard.

33. A) English is the easiest language to learn.

    B) English is as easy to learn as your mother tongue.

    C) English can be learnt in six weeks.

    D) It is easier to learn English on radio or TV.

34. A) To speak English.

    B) To read technical books in English.

    C) To listen to English programmes on radio.

    D) To read English literature.

35. A) English learning at school usually takes a long time.

    B) More and more people want to learn English nowadays.

    C) It is not necessary for many people to go to English speaking countries to learn English.

    D) It is more difficult to learn English quickly than to learn it slowly.

Section C

Directions: *In this section, you will hear a passage three times. When the passage is read for the first time, you should listen carefully for its general idea. When the passage is read for the second time, you are required to fill in the blanks numbered from 36 to 43 with the exact words you have just heard. For blanks numbered from 44 to 46 you are required to fill in the missing information. For these blanks, you can either use the exact words you have just heard or write down the main points in your own words. Finally, when the passage is read for the third time, you should check what you have written.*

Note: The questions in this section are all shown on *Answer Sheet 2*; please put down your answers on it as required.（注意：此部分试题在**答题卡**2上；请在**答题卡**2上作答。）

Part IV   Reading Comprehension (Reading in Depth) (25 minutes)
Section A

Directions: *In this section, there is a short passage with 5 questions or incomplete statements. Read the passage carefully. Then answer the questions or complete the statements in the fewest possible words on Answer Sheet 2.*

Whoever coined the phrase "save the planet" is a public-relations genius. It conveys the sense of imminent catastrophe and high purpose that has wrapped environmentalism in an aura（光环）of moral urgency. It also typi-fies environmentalism's rhetoric excesses, which, in any other context, would be seen as wild exaggeration or simple dishonesty.

Up to a point, our environmental awareness has checked a mindless enthusiasm for unrestrained economic growth. We have sensibly curbed some of growth's harmful side effects. But environmentalism increasingly resembles a holy crusade addicted to hype（天花乱坠的广告宣传）and ignorant of history. Every environmental ill is depicted as an onrushing calamity that — if not stopped — will end life as we know it.

Take the latest scare: the greenhouse effect. We're presented with the horrifying specter（幻像）of a world that incinerates（火化）itself. Act now, or sizzle later. Food supplies will wither. Glaciers will melt. Coastal areas will flood. In fact, the probable losses from any greenhouse warming are modest: 1 to 2 percent of our economy's output by the year 2050, estimates economist William Cline. The loss seems even smaller compared with the expected growth of the economy（a doubling）over the same period.

No environmental problem threatens the "planet" or rates with the danger of nuclear war. No oil spill ever caused suffering on a par with today's civil war in Yugoslavia, which is a minor episode in human misery. The great scourges of humanity remain what they have always been: war, natural disaster, crushing poverty and hate. On any scale of tragedy, environmental distress is a featherweight.

This is not an argument for indifference or inaction. It is an argument for perspective and balance. And it does not follow that anyone who disagrees with me is evil or even wrong. On the greenhouse effect, for instance, there's ample scientific doubt over whether warming would occur over decades. Unfortunately, the impulse of many environmentalists is to simplify. Doomsday scenarios are developed to prove the seriousness of environmental dangers.

The rhetorical overkill is not just innocent excess. It clouds our understanding. For starters, it minimizes the great progress that has been made, especially in industrialized countries. The worst sin of environmental excess is its bias against economic growth. The cure for the immense problems of poor countries usually lies with economic growth. A recent report from the World

Bank estimates that more than 1 billion people lack healthy water supplies and sanitary facilities. The result is hundreds of millions of cases of diarrhea（腹泻）annually and deaths of 3 million children. Only by becoming wealthier can countries correct these conditions.

Note: Please put down on *Answer Sheet 2* your answers to the questions in this section.（注意：此部分试题请在**答题卡2**上作答。）

47. The main purpose of this article is to challenge the basic assumption that _____.

48. What does the author think about the phrase "save the planet"（Paragraph 1）?

49. By "rhetoric excesses"（Paragraph 1）the author means _____.

50. The author argues that compared with war or natural disasters, environmental problems _____.

51. In contrast to environmentalists' position and attitude, the author maintains that _____.

Section B

Directions: *There are 2 passages in this section. Each passage is followed by some questions or unfinished statements. For each of them there are four choices marked A）, B）, C）and D）. You should decide on the best choice and mark the corresponding letter on Answer Sheet 2 with a single line through the centre.*

Passage One
Questions 52 to 56 are based on the following passage.

The concept of culture has been defined many times, and although no definition has achieved universal acceptance, most of the definitions include three central ideas: that culture is passed on from generation to generation, that a culture represents a ready-made prescription for living and for making day-to-day decisions, and, finally, that the components of a culture are accepted by those in the culture as good, and true, and not to be questioned.

The eminent anthropologist George Murdock has listed seventy-three items that characterize every known culture, past and present. The list begins with Age-grading and Athletic sports, runs to Weaning and Weather Control, and includes on the way such items as Calendar, Firemaking, Property Rights, and Toolmaking. I would submit that even the most extreme advocate of a culture of poverty viewpoint would readily acknowledge that, with respect to almost all of these items, every American, beyond the first generation immigrant, regardless of race or class, is a member of a common culture. We all share pretty much the same sports. Maybe poor kids don't know how to play polo, and rich kids don't spend time with stickball, but we all know baseball, and football, and basketball. Despite some misguided efforts to raise minor dialects to the status of separate tongues, we all, in fact, share the same language. There may be differences in diction and usage, but it would be ridiculous to say that all Americans don't speak English. We have the calendar, the law, and large numbers of other cultural items in common. It may well be true that on a few of the seventy-three items there are minor variations between classes, but these kinds of things are really slight variations on a common theme. There are other items that show variability, not in relation to class, but in relation to religion and ethnic background — funeral customs and cooking, for example. But if there is one place in America where the melting pot is a reality, it is on the kitchen stove; in the course of one month, half the readers of this sentence have probably eaten pizza, hot pastrami, and chow mein. Specific differences that might be identified as signs of separate cultural identity are relatively insignificant within the general unity of American life; they are cultural commas and semicolons in the paragraphs and pages of American life.

Note: Please put down on *Answer Sheet 2* your answers to the following questions. （注意：此部分试题请在**答题卡 2** 上作答。）

52. According to the author's definition of culture, _____.
    A) a culture should be accepted and maintained universally
    B) a culture should be free from falsehood and evils
    C) the items of a culture should be taken for granted by people
    D) the items of a culture should be accepted by well-educated people

53. Which of the following is NOT true according to the passage?
    A) Baseball, football and basketball are popular sports in America.
    B) Pizza, hot pastrami, and chow mein are popular diet in America.
    C) There is no variation in using the American calendar.
    D) There is no variation in using the American language.

54. It can be inferred that all the following will most probably be included in the seventy-three items except _____.
    A) heir and heritage   B) dream patterns
    C) childrearing practices   D) table manners

55. By saying that "they are cultural commas and semicolons ..." the author means that commas and semicolons _____.
    A) can be interpreted as subculture of American life
    B) can be identified as various ways of American life
    C) stand for work and rest in American life
    D) are preferred in writing the stories concerning American life

56. The main purpose of this passage is to _____.
    A) prove that different people have different definitions of culture
    B) inform that variations exist as far as a culture is concerned
    C) indicate that culture is closely connected with social classes
    D) show that the idea that the poor constitute a separate culture is an absurdity

Passage Two
Questions 57 to 61 are based on the following passage.

Every profession or trade, every art, and every science has its technical vocabulary. Different occupations, however, differ widely in the character of their special vocabularies. In trades and handicrafts, and other vocations, like farming and fishery, that have occupied great numbers of men from remote times, the technical vocabulary, is very old. It consists largely of native words, or of borrowed words that have worked themselves into the very fibre of our language. Hence, though highly technical in many particulars, these vocabularies are more familiar in sound, and more generally understood, than most other technicalities. The special dialects of law, medicine, divinity, and philosophy have also, in their older strata, become pretty familiar to cultivated persons and have contributed much to the popular vocabulary. Yet every vocation still possesses a large body of technical terms that remain essentially foreign, even to educated speech. And the proportion has been much increased in the last fifty years, particularly in the various departments of natural and political science and in the mechanic arts. Here new terms are coined with the greatest freedom, and abandoned with indifference when they have served their turn. Most of the new coinages are confined to special discussions, and seldom get into general literature or conversation.

Yet no profession is nowadays, as all professions once were, a close guild （行会）. The lawyer, the physician, the man of science, the divine, associated freely with his fellow-creatures, and does not meet them in a merely professional way. Furthermore, what is called "popular science" makes everybody acquainted with modern views and recent discoveries. Any important experiment, though made in a remote or provincial laboratory, is at once reported in the newspapers, and everybody is soon talking about it — as in the case of the Roentgen rays and wireless telegraphy. Thus our common speech is always taking up new technical terms and making them commonplace.

Note: Please put down on *Answer Sheet 2* your answers to the following questions. （注意：此部分试题请在**答题卡 2** 上作答。）

57. Special words used in technical discussion _____ .
    A) never last long
    B) are considered artificial language speech
    C) should be confined to scientific fields
    D) may become part of common speech

58. It is true that _____ .
    A) an educated person would be expected to know most technical terms
    B) everyone is interested in scientific findings
    C) the average man often uses in his own vocabulary what was once technical language not meant for him

D) various professions and occupations often interchange their dialects and jargon

59. In recent years, there has been a marked increase in the number of technical terms in the terminology of _____.
    A) farming.
    B) sports
    C) government
    D) fishery

60. The author of the article was, no doubt _____.
    A) a linguist
    B) an essayist
    C) a scientist
    D) an attorney

61. The purpose of this passage is to _____.
    A) be entertaining
    B) describe a phenomenon
    C) argue a belief
    D) propose a solution

Part V　Error Correction (15 minutes)

Directions: *This part consists of a short passage. In this passage, there are altogether 10 mistakes, one in each numbered line. You may have to change a word, add a word or delete a word. Mark out the mistakes and put the corrections in the blanks provided. If you change a word, cross it out and write the correct word in the corresponding blank. If you add a word, put an insertion mark (∧) in the right place and write the missing word in the blank. If you delete a word, cross it out and put a slash (／) in the blank.*

Example:

　　Television is rapidly becoming the literature of our ~~periods~~. Many of the arguments
~~having~~ used for the study of literature as a
school subject are valid for ∧ study of television.

1. <u>time/times/period</u>
2. <u>　　／　　</u>
3. <u>　　the　　</u>

Note: The questions in this part are shown on *Answer Sheet 2*; please put down your answers on the **Sheet.**（注意：此部分试题在**答题卡 2** 上；请在**答题卡 2** 上作答。）

Part VI Translation (5 minutes)

Directions: *Complete the following sentences by translating into English the Chinese given in brackets.*

Note: Please put down on *Answer Sheet 2* your answers to the questions in this part.（注意：此部分试题请在**答题卡 2** 上作答。）

72. As expected, this much-talked-about match _____ （最后打成平手）.

73. In the next few years, he _____ （作为一位航天火箭专家而享有盛誉）.

74. _____ （无可否认）that this mathematician made important achievements in this field.

75. If we do not treat the natural world with greater respect, _____ _____ （我们自身的生存就有可能受到威胁）.

76. Not until now _____ （她才让我知道那年夏天究竟发生了什么事）.

Answer Sheet 1 (答题卡 1)

Part I   **Writing**   **(30 minutes)**

Directions: *For this part, you are allowed 30 minutes to write a composition based on the following graph. The title is **Schoolkids Going to Evening School**. You must write no less than 150 words and give possible REASONS for the growing number of schoolkids who learn a second language at evening school.*

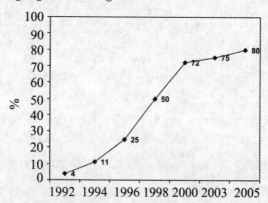

Percentage of schoolkids going to evening school in the past 15 years
— A Survey Conducted by Shanghai Municipal Education Bureau

SCHOOLKIDS GOING TO EVENING SCHOOL

....
....
....
....
....
....

Answer Sheet 1 (答题卡 1)

Part II   Reading Comprehension (Skimming and Scanning) (15 minutes)

1. [Y] [N] [NG]   5. _____   8. _____

2. [Y] [N] [NG]

3. [Y] [N] [NG]   6. _____   9. _____

4. [Y] [N] [NG]   7. _____   10. _____

Answer Sheet 2 (答题卡 2)

Part III   Section A   Section B

11. [A] [B] [C] [D]   16. [A] [B] [C] [D]   21. [A] [B] [C] [D]   26. [A] [B] [C] [D]   31. [A] [B] [C] [D]
12. [A] [B] [C] [D]   17. [A] [B] [C] [D]   22. [A] [B] [C] [D]   27. [A] [B] [C] [D]   32. [A] [B] [C] [D]
13. [A] [B] [C] [D]   18. [A] [B] [C] [D]   23. [A] [B] [C] [D]   28. [A] [B] [C] [D]   33. [A] [B] [C] [D]
14. [A] [B] [C] [D]   19. [A] [B] [C] [D]   24. [A] [B] [C] [D]   29. [A] [B] [C] [D]   34. [A] [B] [C] [D]
15. [A] [B] [C] [D]   20. [A] [B] [C] [D]   25. [A] [B] [C] [D]   30. [A] [B] [C] [D]   35. [A] [B] [C] [D]

Part III   Section C

Some people cannot learn in ordinary schools. Often some physical or (36) _____ handicap prevents a child from learning. In education today new methods are being used in special schools to help the handicapped learn.

(37) _____ the many interesting schools for handicapped persons, there is one which is being (38) _____ in the southern part of New Jersey, U. S. A. It is called the Bancroft Community. Here handicapped young (39) _____ will be trained to support themselves and to get along in the (40) _____ world.

The Bancroft Community is not (41) _____ by walls of any kind. Its director (42) _____ that it be open so that students may gradually develop (43) _____ relations with the rest of the world. Bancroft Community students (44) _____

_____. Gradually, as they become able, they will buy their own furniture, paying for it out of their own earnings. They will pay rent and pay for their food, too. (45) _____

_____.

As a step toward the goal of becoming independent, each handicapped person will decide what kind of work he wants to be trained to do. (46) _____

_____. They will be trained by townspeople for whom they will work without pay.

Answer Sheet 2 (答题卡 2)

Part IV   Section A   **Part V   Error Correction**   (15 minutes)

47. _____

  _____

  _____

48. _____

  _____

  _____

49. _____

  _____

  _____

50. _____

  _____

  _____

51. _____

  _____

  _____

Part IV   Section B

52. [A][B][C][D]
53. [A][B][C][D]
54. [A][B][C][D]
55. [A][B][C][D]
56. [A][B][C][D]
57. [A][B][C][D]
58. [A][B][C][D]
59. [A][B][C][D]
60. [A][B][C][D]
61. [A][B][C][D]

Some people, in all seriousness, say that humans will be living in space within the next hundred or so years. Planet Earth will be crowded, dirty and lack of   62. _____
resources. A sort of exodus (移居) of mankind will begin.

Spaceships will be assembled so that they revolve around the earth. Some may orbit around Mars. These space stations will be serviced by space buses. We saw the first space bus launch in April 1981. This was   63. _____
"Columbia", it made several orbits around the earth and   64. _____
then returned, landing on a huge dry lake bed in California. "Columbia" will be used again. Previous spaceships have been abandoned, only the nose cone being used to bring the crews back to earth.   65. _____

Upon established, each space station will generate   66. _____
its own atmosphere and have its own agriculture. It will need to rotation to provide an artificial gravity; people   67. _____
will be forced inwards from the centre by centrifugal   68. _____
(离心力) force.

The moon and Mars could become new sources of new materials. Driving through space will no longer   69. _____
need Earth fuel — the energy would come from the sun. This energy would be converted from electricity to   70. _____
work magnetic rockets.

That all sounds quite fantastically but, with the   71. _____
rapid development of modern technology, who knows about what the future holds?

Part VI   Translation   (5 minutes)

72. _____

73. _____

74. _____

75. _____

76. _____

Practice Test 7

Part I Writing (30 minutes)

Note: The topic and directions for writing are shown on *Answer Sheet 1*. （注意：此部分试题在答题卡 1 上。）

Part II Reading Comprehension (Skimming and Scanning) (15 minutes)

Directions: *In this part, you will have 15 minutes to go over the passage quickly and answer the questions on **Answer Sheet 1**.*

For questions 1 – 4, mark

Y *(for YES)*　　　　*if the statement agrees with the information given in the passage;*

N *(for NO)*　　　　*if the statement contradicts the information given in the passage;*

NG *(for NOT GIVEN)*　*if the information is not given in the passage.*

For questions 5 – 10, complete the sentences with the information given in the passage.

Why Men and Women Can't Communicate

— by Deborah Tannen

A man and a woman were seated in a car that had been circling the same area for a half hour. The woman was saying, "Why don't we just *ask* someone?" The man was saying, not for the first time, "I'm sure it's around here somewhere. I'll just try this street."

Why are so many men reluctant to ask directions? Why aren't women? And why can't women understand why men don't want to ask? The explanation, for this and for countless minor and major frustrations that women and men encounter when they talk to each other, lies in the different ways that they use language — differences that begin with how girls and boys use language as children, growing up in different worlds.

Anthropologists, sociologists and psychologists have found that little girls play in small groups or in pairs; they have a best friend, with whom they

127

spend a lot of time talking. It's the telling of secrets that makes them best friends. They learn to use language to negotiate intimacy — to make connections and feel close to each other.

Boys, on the other hand, tend to play competitive games in larger groups, which are hierarchical. High-status boys give orders, and low-status boys are pushed around. So boys learn to use language to preserve independence and negotiate their status, trying to hold center stage, challenge and resist challenges, display knowledge and verbal skill.

These divergent (有分歧的) assumptions about the purpose of language persist into adulthood, where they lie in wait behind cross-gender conversations, ready to leap out and cause puzzlement or grief. In the case of asking for directions, the same interchange is experienced differently by women and men. From a woman's perspective, you ask for help, you get it, and you get to where you're going. A fleeting connection is made with a stranger, which is fundamentally pleasant. But a man is aware that by admitting ignorance and asking for information, he positions himself one-down to someone else. Far from pleasant, this is humiliating. So it makes sense for him to preserve his independence and self-esteem at the cost of a little extra travel time.

Here is another scene from the drama of the differences in men's and women's ways of talking. A woman and a man return home from work. She tells everything that happened during the day: what she did, whom she met, what they said, what that made her think. Then she turns to him and asks, "How was your day?" He says, "Same old rat race." She feels locked out: "You don't tell me anything." He protests, "Nothing happened at work." They have different assumptions about what's "anything" to tell. To her, telling life's daily events and impressions means she's not alone in the world. Such talk is the essence of intimacy — evidence that she and her partner are best friends. Since he never spent time talking in this way with his friends, best or otherwise, he doesn't expect it, doesn't know how to do it, and doesn't miss it when it isn't there.

Another source of mutual frustration is the difference in women's and men's assumptions about "troubles talk." She begins to talk about a problem; he offers a solution; she dismisses it, with pique (赌气). He feels frustrated: "She complains, but she doesn't want to do anything to solve her problems."

Indeed, what she wants to do about it is talk. She is frustrated because his solution cuts short the discussion, and implies she shouldn't be wasting time talking about it.

The female search for connection and the male concern with hierarchy is evident here, too. When a woman tells another woman about a problem, her friend typically explores the problem ("And then what did he say?" "What do you think you might do?"); expresses understanding ("I know how you feel"); or offers a similar experience ("It's like the time I ..."). All these responses express support and bring them closer. But offering a solution positions the problem-solver as one-up. This asymmetry (非对称) is distancing, just the opposite of what she was after in bringing up the discussion.

A similar mismatch of expectations occurs when a woman complains about her boss, and a man tries to be helpful by explaining the boss' point of view. She perceives this as an attack, and a lack of loyalty to her. One man told me, incredulously, "My girlfriend just wants to talk about her point of view." He feels that offering opposing views is obviously a more constructive conversational contribution. But conversations among women are usually characterized by mutual support and exploration. Alternative views may be introduced, but they are phrased as suggestions and questions, not as direct challenges. This is one of the many ways that men value oppositional stances, whereas women value harmonious ones.

A woman was hurt when she heard her husband telling the guests at a dinner party about an incident involving his boss that he hadn't told her. She felt this *proved* that he hadn't been honest when he'd said nothing happened at work. But he didn't think of this experience as a story to tell until he needed to come up with material to put himself forward at the dinner party.

Thus, it isn't that women always talk more, while men are taciturn (沉默寡言的) and succinct (简约的). Women talk more at home, since talk, for them, is a way of creating intimacy. Since men regard talk as a means to negotiate status, they often see no need to talk at home. But they talk more in "public" situations with people they know less well. At a meeting, when questions are solicited (要求) from the floor, it is almost always a man who speaks first. When the phones are opened on a radio talk show, the vast majority of calls are from men, who are more likely to speak at length, giving introductions to their questions (if they have any) and addressing multiple topics.

Generalizing about groups of people makes many of us nervous. We like to think of ourselves as unique individuals, not representatives of stereotypes. But it is more dangerous to ignore patterns than to articulate them.

If women and men have different ways of talking (and my research, and that of others, shows that they do), then expecting us to be the same leads to disappointment and mutual accusation. Unaware of conversational style differences, we fall back on mutual blame: "You go on and on about nothing." "You don't listen to me."

Realizing that a partner's behavior is not his or her individual failing, but a normal expression of gender, lifts this burden of blame and disappointment. Surprisingly, years together can make the mutual frustration worse, rather than better. After 57 years of marriage, my parents are still grappling (争斗) with the different styles I have described. When my mother read my book (*You Just Don't Understand Women and Men*), she said, "You mean it isn't just Daddy? I always thought he was the only one."

Understanding gender differences in ways of talking is the first step toward changing. Not knowing that people of the other gender have different ways of talking, and different assumptions about the place of talk in a relationship, people assume they are doing things right and their partners are doing things wrong. Then no one is motivated to change; if your partner is accusing you of wrong behavior, changing would be tantamount (等于的) to admitting fault. But when they think of the differences as cross-cultural, people find that they and their partners are willing, even eager, to make small adjustments that will please their partners and improve the relationship.

Note: Please put down on *Answer Sheet 1* your answers to the questions in this part. (注意：此部分试题请在**答题卡** 1 上作答。)

1. Most men are reluctant to ask for directions because they would like to get more familiar with unknown territory at the cost of a little extra travel time.

2. Men and women have problems in conversing with each other because

they are raised to see the world in different ways.

3. Men generally see the world as a competitive place while on the other hand women often view themselves primarily in connecting with other people.

4. Barriers to effective communication between men and women contribute to the high divorce rate in the U. S.

5. The expression "cross-gender conversations" (Paragraph 5) means _____.

6. Americans often make jokes about women talking too much, but in fact, men _____.

7. When a woman starts to talk about a problem, she is expecting to find _____.

8. Men view talk as a means to _____.

9. The author points out that just like people from different cultures, men and women have problems with _____.

10. The author believes that a good knowledge of gender differences in ways of talking might eventually lead to _____.

Part III Listening Comprehension (35 minutes)
Section A

Directions: *In this section, you will hear 8 short conversations and 2 long conversations. At the end of each conversation, one or more questions will be asked about what was said. Both the conversation and the questions will be spoken only once. After each question there will be a pause. During the pause, you must read the four choices marked A), B), C) and D), and decide which is the best answer. Then mark the corresponding letter on* **Answer Sheet 2** *with a single line through the centre.*

Note: Please put down on **Answer Sheet 2** your answers to the following questions. (注意：此部分试题请在**答题卡 2** 上作答。)

11. A) $ 5.72.   B) $ 4.62.
    C) $ 4.92.   D) $ 5.64.

12. A) 24.   B) 12.
    C) 6.   D) 3.

13. A) At customs.   B) At the library.
    C) In a bank.   D) At the post office.

14. A) He wants to eat immediately.
    B) He wants to know when the game will be over.
    C) He's worried about what time it is.
    D) He's afraid he's dying.

15. A) The lectures were all boring.
    B) Not all the lectures were interesting.
    C) The lectures were rather interesting.
    D) The lectures were just so so.

16. A) Wait for the lecture to begin.
    B) Go immediately to their seats.
    C) Get something to drink first.
    D) Sit down and enjoy the lecture.

17. A) She didn't have any food for dinner.
    B) She ran out to get dinner menus.
    C) She ran out to buy food for dinner.
    D) She can't think of anything to make for dinner.

18. A) He was very slow in doing things.
    B) He was the right person to do such a thing.
    C) He is expected to do such a thing.
    D) He would never do such a thing.

Questions 19 to 21 are based on the conversation you have just heard.

19. A) Relaxing at the seashore.
    B) Visiting her parents.
    C) Sailing on a boat.
    D) Preparing for a race.

20. A) She was invited only for the weekend.
    B) The weather was too hot.
    C) She had an appointment.
    D) She had schoolwork to do.

21. A) She doesn't know how to swim.
    B) The water was too deep.
    C) The water was too cold.
    D) She didn't have enough time.

Questions 22 to 25 are based on the conversation you have just heard.

22. A) She comes to visit this famous town.
    B) She comes to visit her friend.
    C) She comes to Edinburgh on business.
    D) She is on her way to London on business.

23. A) Walk down the Royal Mile.
    B) Visit Holyrood Palace.
    C) Visit the Castle.
    D) Pay a visit to the Queen.

24. A) It's a narrow street of medieval houses.
    B) It's the palace where the Queen lives when she comes to Edinburgh.
    C) It's where the Scottish government used to be.
    D) It's where the Scottish kings and queens used to live.

25. A) Famous Scottish whiskey.
    B) Scottish sweaters.

C) Castle rocks.

D) A souvenir of Holyrood Palace.

Section B

Directions: *In this section, you will hear 3 short passages. At the end of each passage, you will hear some questions. Both the passage and the questions will be spoken only once. After you hear a question, you must choose the best answer from the four choices marked A), B), C) and D). Then mark the corresponding letter on **Answer Sheet 2** with a single line through the centre.*

Note: Please put down on **Answer Sheet 2** your answers to the following questions.（注意：此部分试题请在**答题卡**2上作答。）

Passage One

Questions 26 to 28 are based on the passage you have just heard.

26. A) Congressional secretary. B) Congressman.
    C) Senator. D) Vice president.

27. A) Childhood in his native home，Texas.

    B) Working as congressional secretary in Washington.

    C) Vacationing at his ranch in Texas.

    D) Presidency in the White House.

28. A) He laughed with the dog in his arms.

    B) He picked up the dog by the tips of its ears.

    C) He sat in a chair with the dog dangling beside him.

    D) He made people laugh by kissing the dog's ears.

Passage Two

Questions 29 to 31 are based on the passage you have just heard.

29. A) They help to cure anxiety.

    B) They help patients to gain insight into the cause of anxiety.

    C) They help to control anxiety.

D) They help patients to work efficiently.

30. A) They reduce a person's appetite.
    B) They make a person less persistent in face of trouble.
    C) They make a person's nervous system weak.
    D) They make a person more vulnerable to disease.

31. A) Prejudiced.   B) Enthusiastic.
    C) Indifferent.   D) Objective.

Passage Three

Questions 32 to 35 are based on the passage you have just heard.

32. A) Night clubs and theaters.   B) Fine universities.
    C) Historical places.   D) The world's largest stores.

33. A) There are more job opportunities.
    B) There are good universities.
    C) The city's cultural life is rich.
    D) All of the above.

34. A) Thousands every day.   B) Thousands every week.
    C) Thousands every month.   D) Thousands every year.

35. A) 7:30 to 9:00 a.m.   B) 4:00 to 6:30 p.m.
    C) 7:00 to 9:30 a.m.   D) 3:30 to 5:30 p.m.

Section C

Directions: *In this section, you will hear a passage three times. When the passage is read for the first time, you should listen carefully for its general idea. When the passage is read for the second time, you are required to fill in the blanks numbered from 36 to 43 with the exact words you have just heard. For blanks numbered from 44 to 46 you are required to fill in the missing information. For these blanks, you can either use the exact words you have just heard or write down the main points in your own words. Finally, when the* *passage is read for the third time, you should check what you have written.*

Note: The questions in this section are all shown on ***Answer Sheet 2***；please put down your answers on it as required.（注意：此部分试题在**答题卡**2 上；请在**答题卡**2 上作答。）

Part IV Reading Comprehension (Reading in Depth) (25 minutes)
Section A
Directions: *In this section, there is a short passage with 5 questions or incomplete statements. Read the passage carefully. Then answer the questions or complete the statements in the fewest possible words on **Answer Sheet 2**.*

The human brain is somewhat like an archaeological site, preserving within its layers the basic brain structures of its evolutionary predecessors — the lower mammals and reptiles（爬行动物）. Consequently，it has a relatively recent outer layer that is distinctly primate（灵长目动物的），with special developments and tissues that distinguish human beings from other primates. Nevertheless，we have not one brain，but at least three — that is，three connected parts carry out distinctive but interrelated functions.

The oldest part of the human brain is the "reptilian brain," which is found in the lower center of the brain. It resembles a basic part of the brain of reptiles and serves many of the same functions in humans that it serves in reptiles. It regulates a large number of innate behavior patterns that are related to preserving the species.

During the course of evolution，a new formation of brain cells developed in lower mammals giving them two brains. This ancient，mammal brain adds new things to the behavior repertoire（全部功能）of mammals. The business of this new brain is basically the desires and emotions that keep mammals moving，mating，and avoiding pain. For many mammals，evolution stopped here.

The brain continued to develop with the addition of a third layer called the "neocortex"（新皮层）. This new part of the brain reached its peak of development in human beings. This is the brain that gives humans the capacity of rational thought. Because of the new part of the brain we are able to engage in verbal communication, to read and write, to empathize (表同情) with others, and to contemplate our own existence.

Note: Please put down on *Answer Sheet 2* your answers to the questions in this section. (注意：此部分试题请在**答题卡** 2 上作答。)

47. What is the author mainly talking about in this passage?

48. What is the function of the neocortex?

49. What is the reason why lower mammals cannot speak?

50. The selection is most likely taken from _____.

51. The tone of the selection can best be described as _____.

Section B
Directions: *There are 2 passages in this section. Each passage is followed by some questions or unfinished statements. For each of them there are four choices marked A), B), C) and D). You should decide on the best choice and mark the corresponding letter on* **Answer Sheet 2** *with a single line through the centre.*

Passage One
Questions 52 to 56 are based on the following passage.

For me, scientific knowledge is divided into mathematical sciences, natural sciences or sciences dealing with the natural world (physical and biological sciences), and sciences dealing with mankind (psychology, sociology, all the sciences of cultural achievements, every kind of historical knowledge). Apart from these sciences is philosophy, about which we will talk shortly. In the first place, all this is pure or theoretical knowledge, sought only for the purpose of understanding, in order to fulfill the need to understand what is intrinsic and consubstantial (一体的) to man. What distinguishes man from animal is that he knows and needs to know. If man did not know that the world existed, and that the world was of a certain kind, that he was in the world and that he himself was of a certain kind, he wouldn't be man. The technical aspects of applications of knowledge are equally necessary for man and are of the greatest importance, because they also contribute to defining him as man and permit him to pursue a life increasingly more truly human.

But even while enjoying the results of technical progress, he must defend the primacy and autonomy of pure knowledge. Knowledge sought directly for its practical applications will have immediate and foreseeable success, but not the kind of important result whose revolutionary scope is in large part unforeseen, except by the imagination of the Utopians. Let me recall a well-known example. If the Greek mathematicians had not applied themselves to the investigation of conic (圆锥的) sections, zealously and without the least suspicion that it might someday be useful, it would not have been possible centuries later to navigate far from shore. The first men to study the nature of electricity could not imagine that their experiments, carried on because of mere intellectual curiosity, would eventually lead to modern electrical technology, without which we can scarcely conceive of contemporary life. Pure knowledge is valuable for its own sake, because the human spirit cannot resign itself to ignorance. But, in addition, it is the foundation for practical results that would not have been reached if this knowledge had not been sought disinterestedly.

Note: Please put down on *Answer Sheet 2* your answers to the following questions.（注意：此部分试题请在**答题卡**2上作答。）

52. The author includes among the sciences all the following EXCEPT _____.

    A) literature   B) economics

    C) anthropology   D) astronomy

53. The author indicates that most important advances made by mankind come from _____.

    A) technical applications

    B) apparently useless information

    C) the natural sciences

    D) the biological sciences

54. The author points out that the Greeks who studied conic sections

_____.

A) invented modern mathematical applications

B) were unaware of the value of their studies

C) worked with electricity

D) were forced to resign themselves to failure

55. The title below that best expresses the ideas of the passage is _____.

A) Technical Progress

B) Man's Distinguishing Characteristics

C) Learning for Its Own Sake

D) The Difference Between Science and Philosophy

56. It can be inferred from the passage that to the author man's need to know is chiefly important in that it _____.

A) allows the human race to progress technically

B) encompasses both the physical and social sciences

C) defines his essential humanity

D) has increased as our knowledge of the world has grown

Passage Two
Questions 57 to 61 are based on the following passage.

It is notorious that facts are compatible with opposite emotional comments, since the same fact will inspire entirely different feelings in different persons, and at different times in the same person; and there is no rationally deducible (可推论的) connection between any outer fact and the sentiments it may happen to provoke. These have their source in another sphere of existence altogether, in the animal and spiritual region of the subject's being. Conceive yourself, if possibly, suddenly stripped of all the emotion with which your world now inspires you, and try to imagine it as it exists, purely by itself, without your favorable or unfavorable, hopeful or apprehensive comment. It will be almost impossible for you to realize such a condition of negativity and deadness. No one portion of the universe would then have importance beyond another; and the whole collection of its things and series of its events would be without significance, character, expression, or perspective. Whatever of value, interest, or meaning our respective worlds may appear endowed with are thus pure gifts of the spectator's mind. The passion of love is the most familiar and extreme example of this fact. If it comes, it comes; if it does not come, no process of reasoning can force it. Yet it transforms the value of the creature loved as utterly as the sunrise transforms Mont Blanc from a corpse-like gray to a rosy enchantment; and it sets the whole world to a new tune for the lover and gives a new issue to his life. So with fear, with indignation, jealousy, ambition, worship. If they are there, life changes. And whether they shall be there or not depends almost always upon non-logical, often on organic conditions. And as the excited interest which these passions put into the world is our gift to the world, just so are the passions themselves gifts; — gifts to us, from sources sometimes low and sometimes high; but almost always non-logical and beyond our control. Gifts, either of the flesh or of the spirit; and the spirit blows where it lists, and the world's materials lend their surface passively to all the gifts alike, as the stage-setting receives indifferently whatever alternating colored lights may be shed upon it from the optical apparatus in the gallery.

Meanwhile the practically real world for each one of us, the effective world of the individual, is the compound world, the physical facts and emotional values in indistinguishable combination. Withdraw or pervert（使错乱）either factor of this complex resultant, and the kind of experience we call pathological ensues.

Note: Please put down on *Answer Sheet 2* your answers to the following questions.（注意：此部分试题请在**答题卡 2** 上作答。）

57. This passage mainly discusses _____.

    A) the dual nature of the world in which we humans live

    B) the effect of strong emotions

    C) emotion and reality

    D) emotions and passions — gifts of the spectator's mind

58. Our feelings about external reality have their origin in _____.

    A) our heart

B) events that affect us personally

C) our immediate environment

D) our subjective being

59. The passion of love is cited by the author to show how _____.

A) unable we are to control our emotions

B) unreal our practical world is

C) familiar passions are to us

D) our world can be transformed by our feelings

60. According to the author, all the following statements are true EXCEPT that _____.

A) whatever values our world has for us are imparted by our minds

B) our feelings about external reality flow from what is objective — outside facts in the environment

C) there seems no logical way to predict our reactions to a given set of conditions

D) our emotions and passions are gifts — no way of controlling or summoning them

61. We can conclude from the passage that a man who is about to be executed will feel _____.

A) emotions we cannot predict   B) desperate

C) apathetic   D) depressed

Part V   Error Correction (15 minutes)

Directions: *This part consists of a short passage. In this passage, there are altogether 10 mistakes, one in each numbered line. You may have to change a word, add a word or delete a word. Mark out the mistakes and put the corrections in the blanks provided. If you change a word, cross it out and write the correct word in the corresponding blank. If you add a word, put an insertion mark (∧) in the right place and write the missing word in the blank. If you delete a word, cross it out and put a slash (/) in the blank.*

Example:

Television is rapidly becoming the literature of our ~~periods~~. Many of the arguments
~~having~~ used for the study of literature as a
school subject are valid for∧ study of television.

1. time/times/period
2. _____
3. _____the_____

Note: The questions in this part are shown on ***Answer Sheet 2***; please put down your answers on the **Sheet**.（注意：此部分试题在**答题卡2**上；请在**答题卡2**上作答。）

Part VI Translation (5 minutes)

Directions: *Complete the following sentences by translating into English the Chinese given in brackets.*

Note: Please put down on ***Answer Sheet 2*** your answers to the questions in this part.（注意：此部分试题请在**答题卡2**上作答。）

72. It is decided that _____ （公共场所不容许吸烟）.

73. While the director is away on vacation，_____ （将由他的副手负责）.

74. _____ （那些不断让自己接触新思想的人）will certainly find that life is so interesting.

75. _____ （除非工人们的要求得到满足）there will be a strike soon.

76. We hung out a lantern _____ （免得他们在大雾中迷了路）.

Answer Sheet 1 (答题卡 1)

Part I   **Writing**   **(30 minutes)**

Directions: *For this part, you are allowed 30 minutes to write a short essay entitled **The Marvels of Medicine in the Twentieth Century**. You should write at least **150** words following the outline given below:*

Introduction：Advances in medical science — the most important achievements made in the twentieth century

1. Development of vaccines and antibiotics
2. Discoveries of new diagnosis methods
3. Advent of genetic engineering, a new branch of biology

Concluding remarks：Even greater wonders to be wrought in the 21st century

The Marvels of Medicine in the Twentieth Century

Answer Sheet 1 (答题卡 1)

Part II Reading Comprehension (Skimming and Scanning) (15 minutes)

1. [Y] [N] [NG]
2. [Y] [N] [NG]
3. [Y] [N] [NG]
4. [Y] [N] [NG]

5. _____

6. _____

7. _____

8. _____

9. _____

10. _____

Answer Sheet 2 (答题卡2)

Part III   Section A   Section B

11. [A] [B] [C] [D]   16. [A] [B] [C] [D]   21. [A] [B] [C] [D]   26. [A] [B] [C] [D]   31. [A] [B] [C] [D]
12. [A] [B] [C] [D]   17. [A] [B] [C] [D]   22. [A] [B] [C] [D]   27. [A] [B] [C] [D]   32. [A] [B] [C] [D]
13. [A] [B] [C] [D]   18. [A] [B] [C] [D]   23. [A] [B] [C] [D]   28. [A] [B] [C] [D]   33. [A] [B] [C] [D]
14. [A] [B] [C] [D]   19. [A] [B] [C] [D]   24. [A] [B] [C] [D]   29. [A] [B] [C] [D]   34. [A] [B] [C] [D]
15. [A] [B] [C] [D]   20. [A] [B] [C] [D]   25. [A] [B] [C] [D]   30. [A] [B] [C] [D]   35. [A] [B] [C] [D]

Part III   Section C

The truth is that radio has not been eclipsed by television and cable and the Internet. In fact, radio is as (36) _____ as it has ever been. According to the Consumer Electronics Manufacturers Association, 675 million radio receivers are (37) _____ in use in the United States; on average, Americans over the age of eleven spend three hours and eighteen minutes of (38) _____ listening to at least one of them.

I don't mention this to make the (39) _____ that radio is "better" than other electronic media, but I will say that it is different, very different. Radio is special to people. And in an (40) _____ when we in the West have so many other media (41) _____ to us, media that can "do" so much more than radio ever could, radio still (42) _____ a kind of loyalty that (43) _____ channels and Web sites cannot claim.

This loyalty is largely due to radio's very limitations. (44) _____

_____. That is, it has to speak to us, through either words or music. Couple this with the fact that radio is a curiously intimate medium: people tend to feel that they are connecting with their radios one-on-one. This is generally not the case with television, (45) _____

_____. But because radio is a "smaller" medium (many low-powered mom-and-pop operations, which were never part of television, still exist on radio), (46) _____

_____.

Answer Sheet 2 (答题卡 2)

Part IV Section A   **Part V   Error.Correction**   (15 minutes)

47. _____

_____

_____

48. _____

_____

_____

49. _____

_____

_____

50. _____

_____

_____

51. _____

_____

_____

Criticism is judgment. A critic is a judge. A judge

must study and think about the material presented to it,   62. _____

correct it or reject it after thinking what he has read,   63. _____

watched or heard.

  Another word for criticism is the appreciation.   64. _____

When I criticize or appreciate some object or another, I

look for its good points and its bad points. In reading

any printing or written matter, I always have a pencil in   65. _____

hand and put any comments in the book or on a separate

piece of paper. In other words, I never talk back to the   66. _____

writer.

  The sort of critical reading may well be called

creation reading because I am thinking along with the   67. _____

writer, asking him questions, seeing that he answers the   68. _____

questions and how well he answers them. I mark the

good passages to restore them in my memory and ask   69. _____

myself about every other part and about the complete

piece of writing: — where, how and why could or

should I improve upon them?   70. _____

  You might think that doing what I suggested is

work. Yes, it is, and the work is a pleasure because I   71. _____

can feel my brain expanding, my emotion reacting and

my way of living changing.

Part IV Section B

52. [A][B][C][D]
53. [A][B][C][D]
54. [A][B][C][D]
55. [A][B][C][D]
56. [A][B][C][D]
57. [A][B][C][D]
58. [A][B][C][D]
59. [A][B][C][D]
60. [A][B][C][D]
61. [A][B][C][D]

Part VI   **Translation**   (5 minutes)

72. _____

73. _____

74. _____

75. _____

76. _____

Practice Test 8

Part I Writing (30 minutes)

Note: The topic and directions for writing are shown on *Answer Sheet 1*. （注意：此部分试题在**答题卡** 1 上。）

Part II Reading Comprehension (Skimming and Scanning) (15 minutes)

Directions: *In this part, you will have 15 minutes to go over the passage quickly and answer the questions on Answer Sheet 1.*

For questions 1 – 4, mark

Y *(for YES)*　　　　*if the statement agrees with the information given in the passage;*

N *(for NO)*　　　　*if the statement contradicts the information given in the passage;*

NG *(for NOT GIVEN)*　*if the information is not given in the passage.*

For questions 5 – 10, complete the sentences with the information given in the passage.

Isn't It Time to Right the Wrong?

— By Tom Seligson

In the summer of 1944，Port Chicago — a Navy base 30 miles northeast of San Francisco — was the scene of a devastating explosion. Hundreds of lives were lost in what's considered the deadliest home-front disaster of the war. Most of the dead and injured were African-Americans，put in harm's way by a segregated military little concerned for their safety. Worse，racism lay at the heart of the disaster and later of an event that has been called one of the biggest miscarriages of justice in our history.

At the time，Port Chicago was the busiest ammunition depot on the West Coast. The sailors worked around the clock，loading bombs, depth charges and torpedoes onto ships headed for the Pacific theater. In the segregated U.S. Navy，the job of loading the deadly ammunition was performed only by black sailors.

147

"To find yourself loading ammunition was a disappointment," recalls Robert Routh, an African-American sailor from Memphis who was 19 at the time. "We all wanted to be actually fighting. But we knew that what we did was essential to the war."

Essential but risky. "Loading ammunition was extremely dangerous," explains Robert L. Allen, author of *The Port Chicago Mutiny* and the foremost authority on the events. "The sailors were given no training for it. On top of that, it was common practice for the officers to pit the men against each other, betting to see who could load their boat the fastest."

A Coast Guard detail working at the port warned the Navy that these unsafe conditions could lead to a disaster. The Navy refused to change its procedures, and the Coast Guard withdrew its men.

The Night Calm Was Shattered

On the evening of July 17, 1944, two cargo ships were tied up at the pier. The *E. A. Bryan* was almost fully loaded with 4600 tons of cluster bombs, depth charges and 40 millimeter shells. The *Quinalt Victory* had just docked. Robert Routh and fellow sailor Percy Robinson, 18, from Chicago, were in their barracks. At 10:19, the night calm was shattered.

"I was in my bunk when the explosion occurred," recalls Robinson. "I was looking out the window, and all of a sudden everything turned to sunlight. 1 jumped up to see what was happening, and then I felt the concussion. I instinctively covered my face with my arms. Then a second explosion lifted me up and knocked me to the floor."

Robert Routh also turned toward the window at the first explosion. "It was the greatest fireworks you ever wanted to see," he recalls. It also was the last thing he ever saw. "With the second explosion, glass went everywhere. It was a combination of the glass and the concussion that destroyed my eyes."

The second explosion was so powerful that seismographs （地震仪） at Berkeley recorded it as an earthquake. The *E. A. Bryan* was blown into tiny pieces. The *Quinalt Victory* was ripped apart, and Port Chicago's wooden pier was completely destroyed. The human cost was even worse. Everyone on the pier and aboard the two ships was killed. Of the 320 fatalities, 202 were black. And of the 390 injured, 233 were black.

As bad as it was, though, the disaster might not have made history if it weren't for what followed.

The Navy's Insult

A Navy court of inquiry ruled out sabotage. It heard testimony about the unsafe conditions at the port, but its final report absolved the white officers of any responsibility and blamed the tragedy on "rough handling" of the explosives by the black sailors. Then the white officers were granted 30-day leaves. "None of the black sailors were granted leaves," says Robinson, who suffered lacerations (裂伤) to his face, head and arms. "I requested 30 days of leave, which you're entitled to if you're wounded. I was turned down." Instead, they were given the grim task of collecting the remains of their fellow sailors. "You can imagine the psychological impact this had," says Routh. "My loss of sight was traumatic, but everyone had traumatic needs, physical or mental. And no help was given."

The Sailors Take a Stand

Instead, three weeks after the explosion, the black sailors were ordered back to work. But the men had had enough. Of the 328 ordered to resume loading ammunition, 258 refused. Routh's blindness had ended his military service, but Robinson — just released from the hospital — was among those who balked. "We all had our reasons for not going back to work," he explains. "Some were afraid of another explosion. I was angry that they wouldn't let me go home."

All 258 black sailors were locked up on a barge. "A few days later, we were led out and addressed by the admiral," recalls Robinson. "He told us that if we didn't go back to work, we would be charged with mutiny (哗变). And mutiny is punishable by death by a firing squad. I believed he meant it, so I was one of 208 men who stepped forward. I was put in prison anyway. I was charged with disobeying an order." The 50 sailors who still refused to go back to work were, in fact, charged with mutiny.

Mutiny Charged

It was the largest mass-mutiny trial in U.S. Navy history. "Their lawyer was a junior officer going up against senior officers," explains Robert L. Allen. "He took the position that the men were in shock and fear, and that led to a work stoppage. There was no conspiracy to commit mutiny. This was nothing but a peaceful sit-down strike." The trial received a lot of attention and was followed closely by Thurgood Marshall, the future Supreme Court justice who was then chief counsel for the NAACP (National Association for the Advancement of Colored People).

Fully aware of the conditions at Port Chicago and how segregation, unfair treatment and discriminatory orders had contributed to the incident, Marshall noted: "This is not 50 men on trial for mutiny. This is the Navy on trial for its whole vicious policy toward Negroes."

Injustice Continued

But after 32 days of hearings, the court deliberated only 80 minutes before finding all the sailors guilty. They were sentenced to 15 years in prison. The 208 sailors who had initially joined them were imprisoned for 90 days, then given summary courts-martial and bad-conduct discharges.

The verdicts caused a public uproar in black communities. Thurgood Marshall appealed the case to the Pentagon, and even Eleanor Roosevelt became involved. But the Navy refused to reconsider the convictions. It wasn't until 1946, in the general euphoria (兴奋) over the end of the war, that the Port Chicago sailors — along with many other imprisoned servicemen — were granted clemency and released.

Ironically, from behind bars, the accused had helped to achieve some of their objectives. "With all the protests, the Navy realized it had a public-relations problem," says Allen. "They brought in white sailors to help load ammunition. This began the process of desegregation in the Navy."

The survivors of Port Chicago returned home, but what had happened to them continued to weigh on their lives. "Many of the men were still living with a sense of humiliation and shame over their being imprisoned for mutiny," Allen says.

Can We Set This Right?

Over the past decades, many influential people have been trying to clear the names of the men. This whole event was a miscarriage of justice based on the racism of the time. What these men did by disobeying were acts of personal courage.

The Navy did review the cases in 1994, but it upheld the original convictions. "The Navy has a lot of trouble admitting mistakes," says Miller. "They keep saying the trials were fair. Well, the trials only took place because the sailors were African-American. They would not have been on trial if they hadn't been."

Finally, in 1999, President Clinton granted a pardon to one of the only surviving Port Chicago sailors convicted of mutiny — Freddie Meeks.

Percy Robinson's defiant spirit (he was once a boxer) is still evident. He told his lawyers he didn't want a pardon to erase the court-martial on his record. "A pardon means I'm forgiven for something I did wrong. I don't think I did anything wrong," he asserts. After 35 years as a research scientist in Los Angeles, Robinson is now on his second career as a commercial photographer.

Despite his blindness, Robert Routh went back to school, eventually earning a master's degree at Pepperdine University. Robust and good-humored, he still works fulltime as a benefits counselor with the Department of Veterans Affairs.

Port Chicago itself no longer exists. The site of the explosion is now part of the Concord Naval Weapons Station, which is used by the Army. The only sign of the tragedy that once occurred here are the pilings from the old pier.

In 1994, a monument was built and a chapel dedicated to commemorate the men who lost their lives. To further honor the memory of those men, there is an ongoing campaign to support the issuance of a Port Chicago stamp by the U.S. Postal Service. Forty members of Congress already are behind the initiative.

"A stamp will help make people aware of the great injustice that was done here," believes Robert L. Allen. "It would be an appropriate way to recognize this tragedy and honor these men."

Note: Please put down on *Answer Sheet 1* your answers to the questions in this part. (注意：此部分试题请在**答题卡** 1 上作答。)

1. There was something disastrous happening on an evening of mid-July in 1944: two ships, fully loaded with ammunition, were exploded in a Navy base near San Francisco.

2. Hundreds of people who were killed or injured in the explosion were all African Americans.

3. The root cause of this tragedy consisted in the prevalent racism in the U.S.

4. None were fully aware of the unsafe conditions for loading ammunition until the explosion occurred.

5. A Navy court of inquiry ruled that this accident was attributed to _____.

6. Three weeks after the explosion, when the black sailors were ordered back to work most of them _____.

7. There were 50 black sailors who firmly refused to go back to work even though they were threatened _____.

8. After 32 days of trial, the 50 black sailors were sentenced _____.

9. According to Thurgood Marshall, the then chief counsel for the National Association for the Advancement of Colored People, the mutiny trial was one of the biggest miscarriages of justice in American history: it was not 50 men on trial for mutiny, but _____.

10. In order to right the wrong by further honoring these people, a campaign is being launched to _____.

Part III　Listening Comprehension (35 minutes)
Section A
Directions: *In this section, you will hear 8 short conversations and 2 long conversations. At the end of each conversation, one or more questions will be asked about what was said. Both the conversation and the questions will be spoken only once. After each question there will be a pause. During the pause, you must read the four choices marked A), B), C) and D), and decide which is the best answer. Then mark the corresponding letter on* **Answer Sheet 2** *with a single line through the centre.*

Note: Please put down on *Answer Sheet 2* your answers to the following questions.（注意：此部分试题请在**答题卡**2上作答。）

11. A) Interviewer and interviewee.　　B) Teacher and student.
　　C) Saleswoman and customer.　　D) Policewoman and witness.

12. A) An exciting dream.　　B) A funny dream.
　　C) A frightening dream.　　D) A happy dream.

13. A) To the library.　　B) Picnicking in the woods.
　　C) Skiing in the mountain.　　D) To the beach.

14. A) By car.　　B) By bus.
　　C) On foot.　　D) By train.

15. A) John has traveled all over the world.
　　B) John is going to San Francisco.
　　C) John is glad to hear from his friend.
　　D) John likes postcards.

16. A) The two walkmans are very much alike.
　　B) She likes the smaller walkman.
　　C) The man's walkman can't record.
　　D) She likes a walkman with a recorder.

17. A) Secretary.　　B) Business administration.
　　C) Home economics.　　D) Biology.

18. A) He can drive slowly now.
　　B) He is sure that he is a good driver.
　　C) He thinks the class too slow for him.
　　D) He is making steady progress.

Questions 19 to 21 are based on the conversation you have just heard.

19. A) She would have stayed in her hometown for the rest of her life.

B) She would have made a great mistake in her life career.

C) She would have been happy to come to the city to look for a job.

D) She would have become a secretary to someone in her village.

20. A) She had left the place where she was born.

B) She has not been given much job opportunity in the city.

C) She has so far no promotion or transfer.

D) She can't avoid making mistakes in her routine work.

21. A) Her boyfriend.　　　　　　　B) Her colleague.

C) Her assistant.　　　　　　　D) Her former schoolmate.

Questions 22 to 25 are based on the conversation you have just heard.

22. A) On August 30th.　　　　　　B) On September 1st.

C) On September 6th.　　　　　D) On December 22nd.

23. A) Advanced grammar.　　　　　B) American literature.

C) Pronunciation.　　　　　　D) Conversation.

24. A) Monday, Wednesday and Friday.

B) Monday, Tuesday and Friday.

C) Tuesday, Thursday and Friday.

D) Tuesday, Wednesday and Thursday.

25. A) A language lab and videos.

B) Video and tape recorders.

C) Computers and recorders.

D) A language lab and computers.

Section B

Directions: *In this section, you will hear 3 short passages. At the end of each passage, you will hear some questions. Both the passage and the questions will be spoken only once. After you hear a question, you must choose the best answer from the four choices marked A), B), C) and D). Then mark the* *corresponding letter on Answer Sheet 2 with a single line through the centre.*

Note: Please put down on *Answer Sheet 2* your answers to the following questions.（注意：此部分试题请在**答题卡** 2 上作答。）

Passage One

Questions 26 to 28 are based on the passage you have just heard.

26. A) People don't understand the importance of learning to listen.
    B) Sometimes we should listen more than we speak.
    C) Listening is always more important than speaking.
    D) We can learn more from listening than from reading and speaking.

27. A) Because he was all ears to those who came for advice.
    B) Because he had a good mastery of communication skills.
    C) Because he had much business experience behind him.
    D) Because he could provide effective solutions to practical problems.

28. A) A salesperson.
    B) An experienced sales manager.
    C) A senior business executive.
    D) A government administrator.

Passage Two

Questions 29 to 31 are based on the passage you have just heard.

29. A) Anger is difficult to detect by looking at a person's face.
    B) Anger is frequently confused with other emotions.
    C) Anger is detected by women better than by men.
    D) Anger cannot be detected by a psychologically trained person.

30. A) They were less able to judge correctly than the average students.
    B) They did better than the average students in the group.
    C) They did as well as the women students.
    D) They did better than the women students in the group.

31. A) To prefer adults to students as judges.

    B) To ask students who have received psychological training to judge.

    C) To ask women rather than men to judge.

    D) To ask psychologists to judge.

Passage Three

Questions 32 to 35 are based on the passage you have just heard.

32. A) A senior executive.　　　　B) A professor.

    C) A playwright.　　　　　　D) A science teacher.

33. A) To study well accounting and finance.

    B) To be good at business management.

    C) To take a philosophy course.

    D) To be equipped with technical expertise.

34. A) Because it stretches our vision and challenges our problem-solving ability.

    B) Because it helps to develop insight into the essence of life.

    C) Because it helps us learn how to think in an analytical way.

    D) All of the above.

35. A) A great ancient thinker.

    B) A famous scientist.

    C) An outstanding Greek playwright.

    D) A well-known psychologist.

Section C

Directions: *In this section, you will hear a passage three times. When the passage is read for the first time, you should listen carefully for its general idea. When the passage is read for the second time, you are required to fill in the blanks numbered from 36 to 43 with the exact words you have just heard. For blanks numbered from 44 to 46 you are required to fill in the missing information. For these blanks, you can either use the exact words you have just heard or write down the main points in your own words. Finally, when the* *passage is read for the third time, you should check what you have written.*

Note: The questions in this section are all shown on **Answer Sheet 2**; please put down your answers on it as required. (注意：此部分试题在答题卡 2 上；请在答题卡 2 上作答。)

Part IV   Reading Comprehension (Reading in Depth) (25 minutes)
Section A

Directions: *In this section, there is a short passage with 5 questions or incomplete statements. Read the passage carefully. Then answer the questions or complete the statements in the fewest possible words on* **Answer Sheet 2.**

Joseph Weizenbaum, professor of computer science at MIT, thinks that the sense of power over the machine ultimately corrupts the computer hacker and makes him into a not very desirable sort of programmer. The hackers are so involved with designing their program, making it more and more complex and bending it to their will, that they don't bother trying to make it understandable to other users. They rarely keep records of their programs for the benefit of others, and they take rarely time to understand why a problem occurred.

Computer science teachers say they can usually pick out the prospective hackers in their courses because these students make their homework assignments more complex than they need to be. Rather than using the simplest and most direct method, they take joy in adding extra steps just to prove their ingenuity.

But perhaps those hackers know something that we don't about the shape of things to come. "That hacker who had to be literally dragged off his chair at MIT is now a multimillionaire of the computer industry," says MIT professor Michael Dertouzos. "And two former hackers became the founders of the highly successful Apple home computer company."

When seen in this light, the hacker phenomenon may not be so strange after all. If, as many psychiatrists say, play is really the basis for all human activity, then the hacker games are really the preparation for future developments.

Sherry Turkle, a professor of sociology at MIT, has for years been studying the way computers fit into people's lives. She points out that the computer, because it seems to us to be so "intelligent," so "capable," so "human," affects the way we think about ourselves and our ideas about what we are. She says that computers and computer toys already play an important role in children's efforts to develop an identity by allowing them to test ideas about what is alive and what is not.

"The youngsters can form as many subtle nuances and textured relationships with the computers as they can with people," Turkle points out.

Note: Please put down on **Answer Sheet 2** your answers to the questions in this section. （注意：此部分试题请在**答题卡 2**上作答。）

47. What is the passage mainly concerned with?

48. According to Prof. Weizenbaum, what led to the hackers' strange behavior is _____.

49. In Prof. Dertouzos' opinion, the hackers probably have _____.

50. What does the phrase "to develop an identity" (Paragraph 5) mean?

51. The passage tries to convey the idea that _____.

Section B

Directions: *There are 2 passages in this section. Each passage is followed by some questions or unfinished statements. For each of them there are four choices marked A), B), C) and D). You should decide on the best choice and mark the corresponding letter on* **Answer Sheet 2** *with a single line through the centre.*

Passage One

Questions 52 to 56 are based on the following passage.

In managing information resources, the medium may be the key to an effective system. The medium is a vehicle, a tool, or a container for holding information; the information itself is the thing of value.

Three popular categories of information media are paper, film, and electronic storage devices. The media choice must not be viewed as a choice among these three, however; it must be viewed as an opportunity to select from a multitude of media possibilities in combinations that build effective systems. In many instances the person responsible for information-resource management is not the person who determines the medium in which information will be created. In such a case, the manager of a firm's information resources faces a challenge in making a significant contribution to the organization's objectives.

For effective management of information resources, media conversion may be necessary. Examples include keying or scanning paper documents to convert them to electronic media. Other processes convert electronic media from one format to another. For example, disk files created on one system may not be compatible with another system. Various hardware and software combinations can be used to convert files to formats that equipment will accept. For information generated within organizations, this necessity of making systems compatible may be eliminated by cooperative planning. However, very little control can be exercised over the media used to generate information that comes to your organization from the outside.

The medium for information may be selected to satisfy a need that exists when information is created and communicated. For example, a paper record may be created because of its portability and because no special equipment is necessary for later references to that information; electronic transmission may be selected because it is the fastest means of communicating information. A firm may use electronic mail because a network already exists for on-line computer communication. The additional application may cost less than postage to mail paper memos.

Note: Please put down on *Answer Sheet 2* your answers to the following questions.（注意：此部分试题请在**答题卡** 2 上作答。）

52. Which of the following can best sum up the passage?
    A) Media Selection in Managing Information Resources.
    B) The Importance and Necessity of Media Conversion.
    C) Three Categories of Information Media.
    D). Various Means of Communicating Information.

53. The first paragraph aims to tell the reader _____ .
    A) the importance of information-resource management
    B) the relationship between the medium and information
    C) the great variety of media for holding information
    D) the numerous resources of information

54. According to the author, _____ .
    A) paper is the best storage device
    B) people have a choice of different information media
    C) it is better to let the person responsible for information-resource management determine the medium
    D) the manager should build an effective system by selecting a good combination of different media

55. For effective management of information resources, the manager should _____ .
    A) convert all paper documents to electronic media
    B) make media conversion when necessary
    C) control the media used to generate information both inside and outside his organization
    D) use one format in processing information

56. The main idea of the last paragraph is that _____ .
    A) paper record is the most convenient medium for later reference
    B) electronic mail costs less than postage to mail paper memos
    C) different media for information may be selected for different purposes
    D) by using different media, a firm can create various information for its objectives

Passage Two
Questions 57 to 61 are based on the following passage.

Many leading scientists down through the years from Galileo to Einstein have been deeply religious. They have been intrigued by the essential mystery of life and material existence, and have recognized that spiritual as well as scientific understanding is needed.

Two biologists might examine a living cell under a microscope. One will see there the handiwork of God; the other will see only what evolution has chanced to produce. And yet both will agree on the cell's biological history, its composition, its structure, and its function. One physicist will find God in the exquisitely organized and exact laws of the physical universe. Another physicist will not be able to see anything beyond the laws themselves. The religious views of a scientist do not come from his science; they come from his entire philosophy, his whole view of the world. But scientists are not unique in this matter; the same disparity of thinking is to be found among people from all walks of life.

In the modern world, science serves two important functions. One is to provide the basis for a scientific technology. It is in this way that science has the greatest influence on our daily living. Through technology, we advance the structure of civilization and gain increasing domination over the earth and adjoining portions of the universe. The other purpose served by science is one of understanding. Through science, we discover how phenomena occur and, to a limited extent, why they happen the way they do. Vital processes are analysed and studied, that we may know more of how organisms function, and how they have come to be what they are. Through science, we seek to know what a man is — how his body works and why he thinks and dreams. As we search to know ourselves and the workings of our minds, we expect to find solutions to problems of confusion and discontent. Science is a way to understanding, but in some ways it is a narrow path that does not touch on all the questions posed by the facts of human life. Science does not provide a way of life; it does not create a moral order. It is quite obvious that not all human knowledge can be reduced to scientific terms. Interpretations of the ultimate meaning and value of life will, in the final analysis, be made more on the basis of spiritual awareness than on scientific acuity.

Note: Please put down on *Answer Sheet 2* your answers to the following questions. (注意：此部分试题请在**答题卡** 2 上作答。)

57. According to the author, many leading scientists _____.

A) have acknowledged that only religion can explain the mystery of life

B) have been puzzled by the mystery of life and material things

C) have attempted to explain physical life from a religious point of view

D) have been so intrigued as to make great efforts to solve the mystery of life

58. The author suggests in the second paragraph that _____.

A) while some physicists conclude from the laws of nature that there is a God, others draw no such conclusion

B) it is only by studying philosophy that a man can develop religious beliefs

C) by examining a living cell under a microscope biologists can understand the process of evolution

D) there is a disparity of thinking between scientists and people from other walks of life regarding science and religion

59. In the last sentence of the second paragraph, "this matter" refers to _____.

A) the fact that a scientist's religious views derive from his whole outlook on life

B) the fact that some people believe in God while others do not

C) the disparity of thinking between scientists and people from other walks of life

D) the disparity in the religious conclusions drawn from the observation of natural phenomena

60. In he third paragraph "scientific technology" is _____.

A) the application of scientific knowledge to the skills of industry

B) the application of science and industry to daily life

C) science and industry as the basis of progress

D) the use of science and industrial techniques in gaining control of the universe

61. In the third paragraph it is mentioned that by means of science _____

are analysed and studied.

A) the ways in which cells formed
B) changes in organic life
C) the main ways in which organisms develop
D) processes on which organic life depends

Part V   Error Correction (15 minutes)

Directions: *This part consists of a short passage. In this passage, there are altogether 10 mistakes, one in each numbered line. You may have to change a word, add a word or delete a word. Mark out the mistakes and put the corrections in the blanks provided. If you change a word, cross it out and write the correct word in the corresponding blank. If you add a word, put an insertion mark (∧) in the right place and write the missing word in the blank. If you delete a word, cross it out and put a slash (／) in the blank.*

Example:

Television is rapidly becoming the literature of our ~~periods~~ . Many of the arguments
~~having~~ used for the study of literature as a
school subject are valid for∧ study of television.

1. time/times/period
2. _____
3. _____ the _____

Note: The questions in this part are shown on *Answer Sheet 2*; please put down your answers on the **Sheet**. (注意：此部分试题在**答题卡** 2 上；请在**答题卡** 2 上作答。)

Part VI   Translation (5 minutes)

Directions: *Complete the following sentences by translating into English the Chinese given in brackets.*

Note: Please put down on *Answer Sheet 2* your answers to the questions in this part. (注意：此部分试题请在**答题卡** 2 上作答。)

72. Things were getting along well _____ （却冒出个意想不到的问

题来）.

73. It takes me quite a long while to work it out. This question _____ （可不像看上去那么简单）.

74. _____ （如果我当时把事情搞糟了）, I would have been fired.

75. _____ （由于他们之间利益上的根本冲突） the two will never co-operate.

76. _____ （谈到音乐） I know nothing about it.

Answer Sheet 1 (答题卡1)

Part I   **Writing**   **(30 minutes)**

Directions: *For this part, you are allowed 30 minutes to write a composition based on the following graph. The title is* **Enthusiasm for Sports.** *You should write no less than 150 words and give your reasons why many TV viewers prefer to watch sports programs. Quote as few figures as possible in your writing and write neatly and clearly.*

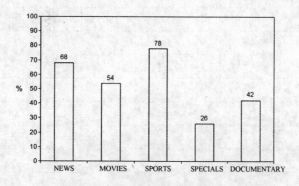

Percentage of TV Viewers of Various Programs

ENTHUSIASM FOR SPORTS

Answer Sheet 1 (答题卡 1)

Part II   Reading Comprehension (Skimming and Scanning) (15 minutes)

1. [Y] [N] [NG]   5. _____   8. _____

2. [Y] [N] [NG]   6. _____   9. _____

3. [Y] [N] [NG]

4. [Y] [N] [NG]   7. _____   10. _____

Answer Sheet 2 (答题卡 2)

Part III   Section A   Section B

11. [A] [B] [C] [D]   16. [A] [B] [C] [D]   21. [A] [B] [C] [D]   26. [A] [B] [C] [D]   31. [A] [B] [C] [D]

12. [A] [B] [C] [D]   17. [A] [B] [C] [D]   22. [A] [B] [C] [D]   27. [A] [B] [C] [D]   32. [A] [B] [C] [D]

13. [A] [B] [C] [D]   18. [A] [B] [C] [D]   23. [A] [B] [C] [D]   28. [A] [B] [C] [D]   33. [A] [B] [C] [D]

14. [A] [B] [C] [D]   19. [A] [B] [C] [D]   24. [A] [B] [C] [D]   29. [A] [B] [C] [D]   34. [A] [B] [C] [D]

15. [A] [B] [C] [D]   20. [A] [B] [C] [D]   25. [A] [B] [C] [D]   30. [A] [B] [C] [D]   35. [A] [B] [C] [D]

Part III   Section C

One of the basic ingredients of American popular culture is consumption, and it is the advertising industry that makes mass consumption possible. Advertising sells us (36) _____, beauty, youth, fashion, happiness, success, status and (37) _____. When Calvin Klein, for example, advertises blue jeans, he is selling us sex (38) _____, not jeans. Polo sells us fashion status and Miller beer offers us macho (男子的) good times.

Research has shown that the average adult can be (39) _____ to 500 advertisements each day from radio, television, newspapers and magazines.

In 1987 $109 billion was spent on advertising in the United States and these (40) _____ are growing at a faster rate than the (41) _____ national product. Although advertising costs are (42) _____ on to customers, advertising can also save consumers' money by (43) _____ more customers to manufacturers, thus making possible mass production and mass consumption, which leads to lower prices. Color television sets, for example, cost $800 to $1,000 when they first went on the market in the later 1950s, but (44) _____.

Advertising is an important element of our culture because it reflects and attempts to change our life styles. (45) _____.

It is estimated that, by the time a person raised in the United States reaches the age of 21, he or she has been exposed to 1 million to 2 million advertisements. (46) _____

_____. It influences our choice to wear Reebok running shoes, brush our teeth with Crest, and feed our cats Fancy Feast.

Answer Sheet 2 (答题卡2)

Part IV   Section A

47. _____
    _____

48. _____
    _____

49. _____
    _____
    _____

50. _____
    _____

51. _____
    _____
    _____

Part IV   Section B

52. [A][B][C][D]
53. [A][B][C][D]
54. [A][B][C][D]
55. [A][B][C][D]
56. [A][B][C][D]
57. [A][B][C][D]
58. [A][B][C][D]
59. [A][B][C][D]
60. [A][B][C][D]
61. [A][B][C][D]

Part V   Error Correction   (15 minutes)

A good way to get information for essays and
reports is to interview people who are experts in your   62. _____
topic or whose opinions may be interesting. Interviews
are also a good way to get a sampling of people's
opinions on various questions. Here are some
suggestions that will help you make most of a planned   63. _____
interview:

1. If the person to be interviewed (the interviewee) is
   busy, cancel an appointment in advance.   64. _____

2. Prepare your questions before the interview so that
   you make best use of your time. In preparing, think
   about the topic about what the interviewer is likely   65. _____
   to know.

3. Use your questions, but don't insist in sticking to   66. _____
   them or proceeding in the order you have listed.
   Often the interviewee will have important
   information that was never occurred to you, or one   67. _____
   question may suggest another very useful one.

4. If you don't understand something the interviewee
   has said, say politely and ask him or her to clarify it   68. _____
   or to give an example.

5. Take notes. If the interviewee goes too slowly for   69. _____
   you, ask him or her to stop for a moment, especially
   if the point is important. A tape recorder lets you
   avoid this problem. Therefore, be sure the   70. _____
   interviewee agrees to be taped.

6. As soon as possible after the interview, read over
   your notes. They may need clarified while the topic   71. _____
   is still fresh in your mind.

Part VI   Translation   (5 minutes)

72. _____

73. _____

74. _____

75. _____

76. _____

Practice Test 9

Part I Writing (30 minutes)

Note: The topic and directions for writing are shown on *Answer Sheet 1*. (注意: 此部分试题在**答题卡**1上。)

Part II Reading Comprehension (Skimming and Scanning) (15 minutes)

Directions: *In this part, you will have 15 minutes to go over the passage quickly and answer the questions on **Answer Sheet 1**.*

For questions 1 − 4, mark

Y *(for YES)*   *if the statement agrees with the information given in the passage;*

N *(for NO)*   *if the statement contradicts the information given in the passage;*

NG *(for NOT GIVEN)*   *if the information is not given in the passage.*

For questions 5 − 10, complete the sentences with the information given in the passage.

Big Blunders from Big Businesses

International marketing can be a tricky business. With the increase in global trade, international companies cannot afford to make costly advertising mistakes if they want to be competitive and profitable. Understanding the language and culture of target markets in foreign countries is one of the keys to successful international marketing. Too many companies, however, have jumped into foreign markets with embarrassing results. Out of their blunders, a whole new industry of translation services has emerged.

Faulty Translations

The value of understanding the language of a country cannot be overestimated. Translation mistakes are at the heart of many blunders in international advertising. Since a language is more than the sum of its words, a literal, word-by-word dictionary translation seldom works. The following examples prove this point. Otis Engineering Company once displayed a poster at a trade show in Moscow that turned heads. Due to a poor translation of its message, the sign boasted that the firm's equipment was great for improving a person's sex life. The Parker Pen Company suffered an embarrassing moment when it realized that a faulty translation of one of its ads into Spanish resulted in a promise to "help prevent unwanted pregnancies."

Automobile manufacturers in the United States have made several notorious advertising mistakes that have been well publicized. General Motors learned a costly lesson when it introduced its Chevrolet Nova to the Puerto Rican market. Although "nova" means "star" in Spanish, when it is spoken, it sounds like "no va" which means "it doesn't go." Few people wanted to buy a car with that meaning. When GM changed the name to Caribe, sales picked up dramatically. Ford also ran into trouble with the name of one of its products. When it introduced a low-cost truck called the "Fiera" into Spanish-speaking countries, Ford didn't realize until too late that the name meant "ugly old woman" in Spanish. Another American auto manufacturer made a mistake when it translated its Venezuelan ad for a car battery. It was no surprise when Venezuelan customers didn't want to buy a battery that was advertised as being "highly overrated."

Airline companies have also experienced problems of poor translation. A word-by-word translation ruined a whole advertising campaign for Braniff Airlines. Hoping to promote its plush leather seats, Braniff's ad urged passengers to "fly on leather." However, when the slogan was translated into Spanish, it told customers to "fly naked." Another airline company, Eastern Airlines, made a similar mistake when it translated its motto, "We earn our wings daily" into Spanish. The poor translation suggested that its passengers often ended up dead.

Marketing blunders have also been made by food and beverage companies. One American food company's friendly "Jolly Green Giant" became something quite different when it was translated into Arabic as "Intimidating Green Ogre." When translated into German, Pepsi's popular slogan, "Come Alive with Pepsi" came out implying "Come Alive from the Grave." No wonder customers in Germany didn't rush out to buy Pepsi. Even a company with an excellent international track record like Kentucky Fried Chicken is not immune to the perils of faulty translation. A lot of sales were lost when the catch phrase "finger lickin' good" became "eat your fingers off" in the Chinese translation.

A manufacturer of one laundry detergent made an expensive mistake in a promotional campaign in the Middle East. The advertisements showed a picture of a pile of dirty clothes on the left, a box of the company's detergent in the middle, and clean clothes on the right. Unfortunately, the message was incorrectly interpreted because most people in the Middle East read from right to left. It seemed to them that the detergent turned clean clothes into dirty ones.

Cultural Oversights Can Be Disastrous

Successful international marketing doesn't stop with good translations — other aspects of culture must be researched and understood if marketers are to avoid blunders. When marketers do not understand and appreciate the values, tastes, geography, climate, superstitions, level of literacy, religion, or economic development of a culture, they fail to capture their target market. For example, when a popular American designer tried to introduce a new perfume in the Latin American market, the product aroused little interest and the company lost a lot of money. Ads for the new fragrance highlighted its fresh camellia scent. What marketers had failed to realize was that camellias are traditionally used for funerals in many South American countries.

Procter and Gamble has been successful in marketing its products internationally for many years. Today, overseas markets account for over one third of its sales. However, the company's success in this area didn't happen overnight. Procter and Gamble initially experienced huge losses because marketing managers did not recognize important cultural differences. For instance, when P&G first entered the Japanese market with its popular Cheer laundry detergent, most Japanese housewives weren't interested. The promotional campaign that emphasized Cheer as an effective "all temperature" detergent was lost on the Japanese who usually wash clothes in cold water. Although the pitch had been quite successful in the United States where clothes are washed in all temperatures, it fell flat in Japan. All of this could have been avoided if P&G marketers had done more preliminary research before launching the campaign. Once P&G changed its strategy and promised superior cleaning in cold water, sales for Cheer picked up dramatically.

The use of numbers can also be a source of problems for international marketers. Since every culture has its own set of lucky and unlucky numbers, companies need to do their homework if they want to avoid marketing blunders. A U. S. manufacturer of golf balls learned this lesson the hard way when it packaged its product in groups of four for export to Japan. The company couldn't figure out why the golf balls weren't selling well until it realized that in Japanese the word for the number four also means death. In Japan four and nine are very unlucky numbers which should be avoided by marketers.

Even illustrations need to be carefully examined. A picture that is culturally offensive can ruin an advertisement even if the written message is properly translated. McDonnell Douglas Corporation made an unfortunate error in an aircraft brochure for potential customers in India. It included a picture of men wearing turbans, which was not appreciated by the Indians. A company spokesman reported, "It was politely pointed out to us that turbans were distinctly Pakistani Moslem." The artist for the ad had used an old National Geographic magazine to copy the picture.

Preventing Blunders

Having awakened to the special nature of foreign advertising, companies are becoming much more conscientious in securing accurate translations. They are also becoming much more sensitive to the cultural distinctions and variables that play such an important role in any international business venture. Above all, the best way to guard against errors is to hire trained professional translators who thoroughly understand the target language and its idiomatic usage. These translators should be very familiar with the culture and people of the country, and have a grasp of the technical aspects of the industry.

Many international companies are using a technique called "back-translation," which greatly reduces the possibility of advertising blunders. The process of back-translation requires one person to translate the message into the target language and another person to translate the new version back into the original language. The purpose is to determine whether the original material and the retranslated material are the same. In this way companies can ensure that their intended message is really being conveyed.

Effective translators aim to capture the overall message of an advertisement because a word-for-word duplication of the original rarely conveys the intended meaning and often causes misunderstandings. In designing advertisements to be used in other countries, marketers are recognizing the need to keep messages as short and simple as possible and to avoid idioms, jargon, and slang that are difficult to translate. Similarly, they avoid jokes, since humor does not translate well from one culture to another. What is considered funny in one part of the world may not be so humorous in another. The bottom line is that consumers interpret advertising in terms of their own cultures. As the global marketplace opens up, there is no room for linguistic or cultural blunders.

Note: Please put down on *Answer Sheet 1* your answers to the questions in this part. （注意：此部分试题请在**答题卡** 1 上作答。）

1. The first rule of advertising is to know your target market and this is especially true in today's global marketplace where cultural differences come into play.

2. Mistakes in global marketing can be embarrassingly humorous, but will inevitably weaken a company's position in the market.

3. The value of understanding the language of a foreign country should not be over-estimated, though many blunders in international advertising result directly from translation mistakes.

4. Many multinational companies are hiring more and more trained professional translators who thoroughly understand the target language and are very familiar with the culture of the country.

5. In Spanish（Puerto Rico is a Spanish-speaking island）, "nova" means "start", but when spoken, "no-va" means "it doesn't go." Very naturally, few people would _____.

6. Kentucky Fried Chicken's famous advertising phrase "finger lickin' good" became "eat your fingers off" in the Chinese translation, and this faulty translation caused the fast food chain _____.

7. A popular American designer put up ads for a new perfume in the Latin American market, emphasizing its fresh camellia scent. The marketers failed to know that _____.

8. A U.S. golf ball manufacturer wondered why its products did not sell well in Japan. Later it learned that this had much to do with its packaging of product in groups of four for export: in Japanese _____.

9. In order to prevent faulty translations in advertising, international companies are employing a technique known as _____.

10. By way of conclusion the author emphasizes that in designing advertisements, the most important factor that has to be considered is _____.

Part III   Listening Comprehension (35 minutes)
Section A
Directions: *In this section, you will hear 8 short conversations and 2 long conversations. At the end of each conversation, one or more questions will be asked about what was said. Both the conversation and the questions will be spoken only once. After each question there will be a pause. During the pause, you must read the four choices marked A), B), C) and D), and decide which is the best answer. Then mark the corresponding letter on Answer Sheet 2 with a single line through the centre.*

Note: Please put down on *Answer Sheet 2* your answers to the following questions.（注意：此部分试题请在**答题卡** 2 上作答。）

11. A) At 8:00.   B) At 10:00.
     C) At 12:00.   D) At 2:00.

12. A) At a hotel.   B) At a hospital.
     C) In a bank.   D) At a school.

13. A) He relaxes.   B) He goes fishing.
     C) He goes to work.   D) He works at home.

14. A) Her back hurt during the meeting.

B) She agreed that it was a good meeting.

C) The proposal should be sent back.

D) His support would have helped this morning.

15. A) On a bus.   B) On a train.

C) Over a phone.   D) In an elevator.

16. A) 10.   B) 11.

C) 12.   D) 13.

17. A) Once a few weeks.   B) Every month.

C) Seldom.   D) Every summer.

18. A) $ 4.25.   B) $ 4.75.

C) $ 17.00.   D) $ 8.50.

Questions 19 to 22 are based on the conversation you have just heard.

19. A) He's always got involved in traffic accidents.

B) He's nearly smashed into a wall several times.

C) He's sometimes run the risk of being killed.

D) He's run into another car in front of him.

20. A) During his last race.

B) During the British Grand Prix.

C) During the Mexican Grand Prix.

D) On his way to the studio.

21. A) The man was badly hurt.

B) He had a terrible accident and had his left leg broken.

C) Two racing cars collided.

D) Two racing drivers were killed.

22. A) He was chased by a number of racing cars.

B）He was stopped and fined by a policeman.

C）He had lost his way through London streets.

D）He had to drive through the busy streets in London.

Questions 23 to 25 are based on the conversation you have just heard.

23. A）To help people to organize their work in an effective way.

B）To help people to become efficient at their jobs.

C）To help people to arrange their time properly.

D）To help people to reduce stress.

24. A）Workers on assembly lines.

B）Government officials.

C）Business people.

D）College students.

25. A）Set time-limits with them.

B）Never make appointments with them.

C）Tell them to value other people's time.

D）Tell them you won't wait if they are not punctual.

Section B

Directions: *In this section, you will hear 3 short passages. At the end of each passage, you will hear some questions. Both the passage and the questions will be spoken only once. After you hear a question, you must choose the best answer from the four choices marked A), B), C) and D). Then mark the corresponding letter on* **Answer Sheet 2** *with a single line through the center.*

Note: Please put down on **Answer Sheet 2** your answers to the following questions.（注意：此部分试题请在**答题卡**2上作答。）

Passage One

Questions 26 to 29 are based on the passage you have just heard.

26. A）It has doubled.   B）It has increased by half.

C）It has an 85% growth.   D）It has grown out of proportion.

27. A) The pressure for high standards in American education.
    B) The kids' readiness for active participation in learning.
    C) The prevalent eagerness to improve academic performance.
    D) All of the above.

28. A) Heavy homework loads.   B) Long hours' work without play.
    C) Carrying heavy backpacks.   D) None of the above.

29. A) Limited improvements in some subjects.
    B) Remarkably better gains in reading scores.
    C) A subtle weakening of students' readiness for active participation in learning.
    D) Both A and C.

Passage Two
Questions 30 to 32 are based on the passage you have just heard.

30. A) Men of different social classes go to different kinds of pubs.
    B) Men of different social classes go to pubs for different reasons.
    C) Men often go to pubs with their wives or girlfriends.
    D) All of the above.

31. A) Women were forbidden to visit any pub.
    B) Men often took their wives to pubs.
    C) Only people of lower social classes went to pubs.
    D) Pubs were always crowded as they opened only at certain times.

32. A) They believe pubs are only suitable for men.
    B) They strongly oppose women's visit to pubs.
    C) They consider the pub an unrespectable place.
    D) They have changed their views on pubs.

Passage Three
Questions 33 to 35 are based on the passage you have just heard.

33. A) The smell of the food.   B) The quality of the food.

C) The distance of the food.   D) The amount of the food.

34. A) The direction to fly in.   B) The distance to fly.
     C) The height to fly.   D) The kind of food to find.

35. A) Diligent.   B) Interesting.
     C) Creative.   D) Cooperative.

Section C

Directions: *In this section, you will hear a passage three times. When the passage is read for the first time, you should listen carefully for its general idea. When the passage is read for the second time, you are required to fill in the blanks numbered from 36 to 43 with the exact words you have just heard. For blanks numbered from 44 to 46 you are required to fill in the missing information. For these blanks, you can either use the exact words you have just heard or write down the main points in your own words. Finally, when the passage is read for the third time, you should check what you have written.*

Note: The questions in this section are all shown on *Answer Sheet 2*; please put down your answers on it as required.（注意：此部分试题在**答题卡**2上；请在**答题卡**2上作答。）

Part IV   Reading Comprehension (Reading in Depth) (25 minutes)
Section A
Directions: *In this section, there is a short passage with 5 questions or incomplete statements. Read the passage carefully. Then answer the questions or complete the statements in the fewest possible words on Answer Sheet 2.*

Questions 47 to 51 are based on the following passage.

    Research that went into developing the highly specialized technology for space travel has resulted in many unexpected practical applications back on earth. Out of the engineering that produced rocket motors, liquid propellants, space suits, and other necessities of space flight came by-products that no one had anticipated. Equipment and procedures designed for astronauts and space flights have been successfully adapted for use in medicine, industry, and the home. These valuable products of space research, called spin-offs, have improved the quality of life on earth in many ways.

Some of the best-known examples of spin-offs from space research are found in hospitals and doctors' offices. One such example is the sight switch, which was originally developed to allow astronauts to control their spacecraft without using their hands. The sight switch is now used by handicapped people to operate devices using eye movements. Another spin-off is the voice command device, which was designed to enable astronauts to steer their spacecraft by voice command. This device is now being used to help deaf people learn to speak.

Doctors have also benefited from the technology required to make miniature electronic instruments small enough and durable enough for trips into space. From this technology have come hearing aids the size of an aspirin and television cameras small enough to be attached to a surgeon's head to give medical students a close-up view of an operation.

Biotelemetry, which was developed to monitor the physical signs of astronauts by checking their temperature, brain-wave activity, breathing rate, and heartbeat, offers doctors a new means of monitoring hospital patients. Biosensors attached to the body send data by wire or radio. This information is displayed on terminals for doctors to analyze.

Aerospace scientists in England developed a special bed for astronauts that is now used for burn patients. It enables them to float on a cushion of air. The burns can heal more quickly because they do not rub against the bed.

Note: Please put down on *Answer Sheet 2* your answers to the questions in this section. (注意：此部分试题请在**答题卡 2** 上作答。)

47. What does the technical term "spin-offs" refer to?

48. According to the author, the development of the highly specialized technology for space travel has not only made space travel possible but also _____.

49. Using word-part and contextual clues, we may infer that "biotelemetry" means the monitoring and measuring of a living organism's _____ by

179

the use of telemetry techniques.

50. What is the author primarily concerned with in this passage?

51. What would be the most likely topic for the author to address in succeeding paragraphs?

Section B
Directions: *There are 2 passages in this section. Each passage is followed by some questions or unfinished statements. For each of them there are four choices marked A), B), C) and D). You should decide on the best choice and mark the corresponding letter on* **Answer Sheet 2** *with a single line through the centre.*

Passage One
Questions 52 to 56 are based on the following passage.

A weather map is an important tool for geographers. A succession of three or four maps presents a continuous picture of weather changes. Weather forecasters are able to determine the speed of air masses and fronts; to determine whether an individual pressure area is deepening or becoming shallow and whether a front is increasing or decreasing in intensity. They are also able to determine whether an air mass is retaining its original characteristics or taking on those of the surface over which it is moving. Thus, a most significant function of the map is to reveal a synoptic picture of conditions in the atmosphere at a given time.

All students of geography should be able to interpret a weather map accurately. Weather maps contain an enormous amount of information about weather conditions existing at the time of observation over a large geographical area. They reveal in a few minutes what otherwise would take hours to describe. The United States Weather Bureau issues information about approaching storms, floods, frosts, droughts, and all climatic conditions in general. Twice a month it issues a 30-day "outlook" which is a rough guide to weather conditions likely to occur over broad areas of the United States. These 30-day outlooks are based upon an analysis of the upper air levels which often set the stage for the development of air masses, fronts, and storms.

Considerable effort is being exerted today to achieve more accurate weather predictions. With the use of electronic instruments and earth satellites, enormous gains have taken place recently in identifying and tracking storms over regions which have but few meteorological stations. Extensive experiments are also in progress for weather modification studies. But the limitations of modification have prevented meteorological results except in the seeding of super-cooled, upslope mountainous winds which have produced additional orographic（山岳形态的）precipitation（山岳雨）on the windward side of mountain ranges. Nevertheless, they have provided a clearer understanding of the fundamentals of weather elements.

Note: Please put down on *Answer Sheet 2* your answers to the following questions.（注意：此部分试题请在**答题卡 2** 上作答。）

52. All the following characteristics of weather maps are mentioned in this passage EXCEPT _____.
    A) barometric pressure   B) fronts
    C) thermal changes   D) wind speed

53. The thirty-day forecast is determined by examining _____.
    A) daily weather maps   B) upper air levels
    C) satellite reports   D) changing fronts

54. A "synoptic" weather map is a chart that _____.
    A) summarizes a great deal of general weather information
    B) appears daily and can be interpreted accurately
    C) presents data on atmospheric conditions over a wide area
    D) shows ever-changing fronts

55. The observation of weather conditions by satellites is advantageous because it _____.
    A) uses electronic instruments
    B) enables man to alter the weather
    C) makes weather prediction easier
    D) gives the scientist information not obtained readily otherwise

56. At the present time, experiments are being conducted in _____.

    A) manipulating weather

    B) determining density of pressure groups

    C) 30-day "outlooks"

    D) controlling storms

Passage Two

Questions 57 to 61 are based on the following passage.

Writing being largely a self-taught occupation, texts on how to get about it — though great in number — seldom are of much use.

You try, and fail. Then try again, and perhaps fail not quite so grievously. Until at last, if you have some aptitude for it, the failures become less frequent, or at any rate less noticeable.

It is this ability to conceal one's defects that passes, finally, for accomplishment.

Along the way there are the discouragements of unkind criticism, outright rejection, nagging insecurity and intermittent inability to meet debts.

It is uncommon, therefore, to come across a book containing advice of much practical value for anyone toying with the dangerous idea of embarking on a writing life.

An acquaintance recently loaned me such a book, however — one I wish I'd had the luck to read years ago, and which I would commend to any young person bent on making a career of words. It is the slender autobiography of the English novelist Anthony Trollope, first published in 1883, the year after his death.

Needing some means to support himself, Trollope at age 19 signed on as a junior clerk in the British postal service. He was at his desk at 5:30 each morning to write for three hours. And he remained in the mail service 33 years, long after reputation and prosperity had come to him.

Now, what of his advice?

1. For safety's sake, arm yourself with some other skills, some other line of work to fall back on. That way, failure at writing, though the disappointment may be keen, will not mean utter ruin.

2. Do not depend overly much on inspiration. Writing is a craft, which

Trollope compared to the craft of shoemaking. The shoemaker who has just turned out one pair of his work sets to work immediately on the next pair.

3. Have a story to tell, but, more important than that, people it with characters who will speak and move as living creatures in the reader's mind. Without memorable characters, story alone is nothing.

4. Meet your deadlines. Life is endlessly "painful and troublesome" for writers who can't finish their work on time.

5. Do not be inflated by praise. And, above all, do not be crushed by criticism.

6. Understand the risks of writing for a living. "The career, when successful, is pleasant enough certainly; but when unsuccessful, it is of all careers the most agonizing."

Note: Please put down on *Answer Sheet 2* your answers to the following questions. (注意：此部分试题请在**答题卡** 2 上作答。)

57. In this passage the author mainly discusses _____.
    A) the difficulties and risks of making a career of words
    B) the futility of instructions contained in writing manuals
    C) the autobiography of the 19th century English novelist Anthony Trollope
    D) some sound advice provided in Anthony. Trollope's autobiography

58. From the context we can figure out that the phrase "pass for" in Paragraph 3 means _____.
    A) pose as   B) be accepted as
    C) be equal to   D) act as

59. According to the author, writing _____.
    A) is basically a self-taught occupation and no instructions on how to deal with it are of any practical use
    B) is a "trial and error" process and it does not count whether you have the gift for writing or not
    C) for a living is the most difficult and risky of all careers, full of frustration and discouragement

D) sometimes provides good hopes of winning public praise and escaping humiliating poverty

60. The author admires Anthony. Trollope particularly for _____.

A) his brilliance   B) his diligence

C) his precaution   D) his pragmatism

61. From the passage we may infer that the author is most probably _____.

A) a professional writer   B) an instructor of writing

C) an educator   D) a publisher

Part V   Error Correction (15 minutes)

Directions: *This part consists of a short passage. In this passage, there are altogether 10 mistakes, one in each numbered line. You may have to change a word, add a word or delete a word. Mark out the mistakes and put the corrections in the blanks provided. If you change a word, cross it out and write the correct word in the corresponding blank. If you add a word, put an insertion mark (∧) in the right place and write the missing word in the blank. If you delete a word, cross it out and put a slash (/) in the blank.*

Example:

Television is rapidly becoming the literature of our ~~periods~~. Many of the arguments ~~having~~ used for the study of literature as a school subject are valid for ∧ study of television.

1. time/times/period
2. ~~~~
3.   the

Note: The questions in this part are shown on *Answer Sheet 2*; please put down your answers on the **Sheet**. （注意：此部分试题在**答题卡 2** 上；请在**答题卡 2** 上作答。）

Part VI   Translation (5 minutes)

Directions: *Complete the following sentences by translating into English the Chinese given in brackets.*

Note: Please put down on *Answer Sheet 2* your answers to the questions in this part.（注意：此部分试题请在**答题卡**2 上作答。）

72. You will find it is worthwhile ＿＿＿＿＿＿＿＿（和同事们保持良好的关系）.

73. I walked all the way to see her ＿＿＿＿＿＿＿＿（结果她却不在家）.

74. "It doesn't pay to be dishonest，does it?" "＿＿＿＿＿＿＿＿（那当然啦）！

75. The sales manager of this international company ＿＿＿＿＿＿＿＿.（由于玩忽职守而被降级）.

76. I tried hard to put across my idea to him but ＿＿＿＿＿＿＿＿（我所有的努力均归于无效）.

Answer Sheet 1 (答题卡 1)

<table>
<tr><td rowspan="2">学校：</td><td colspan="15" align="center">准　考　证　号</td></tr>
<tr><td>[0]</td><td>[0]</td><td>[0]</td><td>[0]</td><td>[0]</td><td>[0]</td><td>[0]</td><td>[0]</td><td>[0]</td><td>[0]</td><td>[0]</td><td>[0]</td><td>[0]</td><td>[0]</td><td>[0]</td></tr>
</table>

学校：	准 考 证 号
姓名：	
划线要求	

准 考 证 号

[0]	[0]	[0]	[0]	[0]	[0]	[0]	[0]	[0]	[0]	[0]	[0]	[0]	[0]	[0]
[1]	[1]	[1]	[1]	[1]	[1]	[1]	[1]	[1]	[1]	[1]	[1]	[1]	[1]	[1]
[2]	[2]	[2]	[2]	[2]	[2]	[2]	[2]	[2]	[2]	[2]	[2]	[2]	[2]	[2]
[3]	[3]	[3]	[3]	[3]	[3]	[3]	[3]	[3]	[3]	[3]	[3]	[3]	[3]	[3]
[4]	[4]	[4]	[4]	[4]	[4]	[4]	[4]	[4]	[4]	[4]	[4]	[4]	[4]	[4]
[5]	[5]	[5]	[5]	[5]	[5]	[5]	[5]	[5]	[5]	[5]	[5]	[5]	[5]	[5]
[6]	[6]	[6]	[6]	[6]	[6]	[6]	[6]	[6]	[6]	[6]	[6]	[6]	[6]	[6]
[7]	[7]	[7]	[7]	[7]	[7]	[7]	[7]	[7]	[7]	[7]	[7]	[7]	[7]	[7]
[8]	[8]	[8]	[8]	[8]	[8]	[8]	[8]	[8]	[8]	[8]	[8]	[8]	[8]	[8]
[9]	[9]	[9]	[9]	[9]	[9]	[9]	[9]	[9]	[9]	[9]	[9]	[9]	[9]	[9]

Part I　　　　　　　　　　Writing　　　　　　　　　　(30 minutes)

Directions: *For this part, you are allowed 30 minutes to write a composition based on the following graph which shows the changes in the number of college graduates who chose to be teachers or to go into business. The suggested title is* **To Be a Businessman or to Be a Teacher***. You should write no less than 150 words and your writing should contain the following ideas:*

1. 大学毕业生中选择教师职业的人越来越少。
2. 大学毕业生中在大公司里谋职从商的人越来越多。
3. 出现这种情况的原因：在大公司工作工资待遇较高，发展机会较多，可以较充分地实现个人的价值。

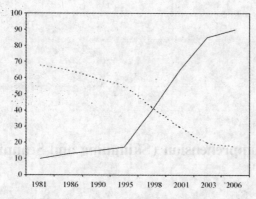

TO BE A BUSINESSMAN OR TO BE A TEACHER

Answer Sheet 1 (答题卡 1)

_____

Part II   Reading Comprehension (Skimming and Scanning) (15 minutes)

1. [Y] [N] [NG]   5. _____   8. _____

2. [Y] [N] [NG]
                     6. _____   9. _____
3. [Y] [N] [NG]

4. [Y] [N] [NG]   7. _____   10. _____

Answer Sheet 2 (答题卡 2)

Part III Section A   Section B

11. [A] [B] [C] [D] 16. [A] [B] [C] [D] 21. [A] [B] [C] [D] 26. [A] [B] [C] [D] 31. [A] [B] [C] [D]

12. [A] [B] [C] [D] 17. [A] [B] [C] [D] 22. [A] [B] [C] [D] 27. [A] [B] [C] [D] 32. [A] [B] [C] [D]

13. [A] [B] [C] [D] 18. [A] [B] [C] [D] 23. [A] [B] [C] [D] 28. [A] [B] [C] [D] 33. [A] [B] [C] [D]

14. [A] [B] [C] [D] 19. [A] [B] [C] [D] 24. [A] [B] [C] [D] 29. [A] [B] [C] [D] 34. [A] [B] [C] [D]

15. [A] [B] [C] [D] 20. [A] [B] [C] [D] 25. [A] [B] [C] [D] 30. [A] [B] [C] [D] 35. [A] [B] [C] [D]

Part III Section C

Despite recent court actions, time may prove America and tobacco to be inseparable. Tobacco was the "money crop" of the (36) _____ in the 1600s and 1700s. It was worth dying for in the Revolutionary War. Tobacco became a legal (37) _____ of exchange in Virginia, Maryland and North Carolina. Because of tobacco, the colonists (38) _____ two things in great supply — land and cheap labor. They killed and drove American Indians from their native soil and (39) _____ millions of Africans to toil in America.

Tobacco is rooted in two of the greatest (40) _____ of American history. Not to mention the damage that it does to smokers. You see them every day as they stand outside businesses because they can't live without one of the world's most (41) _____ drugs.

Don't expect lawmakers to legislate tobacco out of existence. And recent multibillion-dollar verdicts and settlements will not make cigarettes (42) _____. Our wonderful history and smoking are inseparable.

More folks now know cigarettes and other tobacco products are a cheap delivery system for powerful drugs that (43) _____ kill their faithful users. (44) _____
_____. We know smoking kills more than 400,000 Americans a year.

Yet, 48 million adults still smoke. Between 1993 and 1997, smoking was up 28 percent among college students, and (45) _____. 1.2 million Americans under age 18 started smoking daily in 1996 compared with 708,000 in 1988.

Movie stars and advertisements romanticize smoking, and what cannot be sold here is shipped overseas. (46) _____
_____.

Answer Sheet 2 (答题卡 2)

Part IV   Section A   Part V   Error Correction   (15 minutes)

47. _____

_____

_____

48. _____

_____

_____

49. _____

_____

_____

50. _____

_____

_____

51. _____

_____

_____

Part IV   Section B

52. [A][B][C][D]
53. [A][B][C][D]
54. [A][B][C][D]
55. [A][B][C][D]
56. [A][B][C][D]
57. [A][B][C][D]
58. [A][B][C][D]
59. [A][B][C][D]
60. [A][B][C][D]
61. [A][B][C][D]

Look at your watch for just one minute. During that short period of time, the population of the world had increased by eighty-five people. Perhaps you think that isn't much. In the next hour, more than 5,000 additional people will be living on this planet. So it goes, hour after hour. In one day, there are about 120,000 additional mouths to feed. Multiply this by 365. What will happen after 100 years?

This population explosive may be the greatest challenge of the present time. Within the next forty years, the world population may double. Can the new frontiers of science meet the needs of the crowded world of tomorrow?

If the present rate of population increase continues for the next 600 or 700 years, there will be standing rooms only. Each will have between 3 to 10 square feet of space in which to live. This contains the mountaintops, deserts, and the ice and snow fields of the polar areas. Of course, no one expects such a thing to happen. War, plague, famine or some other catastrophe can be expected to occur long when the population reaches this point. Actually, the danger is in an overcrowded world where people are huddled together so that they cannot move arms and legs, but in an upset balance between population and resources.

Since 600 years is so far away, take a look directly ahead. How can the hungry people be filled? About half of the babies born this year will not have enough to eat. Is the world going out of water? Will there be enough fuel? What will supply the energy need to run the machine of tomorrow's world? Certainly, man must look to the future and find new ways of providing for his needs.

62. _____
63. _____
64. _____
65. _____
66. _____
67. _____
68. _____
69. _____
70. _____
71. _____

Part VI   Translation   (5 minutes)

72. _____

73. _____

74. _____

75. _____

76. _____

Practice Test 10

Part I   Writing (30 minutes)

Note: The topic and directions for writing are shown on ***Answer Sheet 1***.（注意：此部分试题在**答题卡** 1 上。）

Part II   Reading Comprehension (Skimming and Scanning) (15 minutes)

Directions: *In this part, you will have 15 minutes to go over the passage quickly and answer the questions on **Answer Sheet 1**.*

For questions 1 – 4, mark

Y *(for YES)*   *if the statement agrees with the information given in the passage;*

N *(for NO)*   *if the statement contradicts the information given in the passage;*

NG *(for NOT GIVEN)*   *if the information is not given in the passage.*

For questions 5 – 10, complete the sentences with the information given in the passage.

Do's and Taboos: Cultural Aspects of International Business

— By M. Katherine Glover

Understanding and heeding cultural variables is one of the most significant aspects of being successful in any international business endeavor. A lack of familiarity with the business practices, social customs, and etiquette of a country can weaken a company's position in the market, prevent it from accomplishing its objectives, and ultimately lead to failure.

As business has become increasingly international and communications technology continues to develop, the need for clearly understood communication between members of different cultures is even more crucial.

Growing competition for international markets is another reason that companies must consider cultural distinctions. As Secretary of Commerce Robert Mosbacher indicated, "American companies have to rely on all available tactics for winning in the global marketplace today. Learning internation-

191

al business diplomacy should be the first step they take."

Customs vary widely from one country to another. Something with one meaning in one area may mean the opposite somewhere else. Some of the cultural distinctions that firms most often face include differences in business styles, attitudes towards development of business relationships, attitudes towards punctuality, negotiating styles, gift-giving customs, greetings, significance of gestures, meanings of colors and numbers, and customs regarding titles.

American firms must pay close attention to different styles of doing business and the degree of importance placed on developing business relationships. In some countries, business people have a very direct style, while in others they are much more subtle in style. Many nationalities value the personal relationship more than most Americans do in business. In these countries, long-term relationships based on trust are necessary for doing business. Many U. S. firms make the mistake of rushing into business discussions and "coming on too strong" instead of nurturing the relationship first. According to Roger Axtell in his book *Do's and Taboos of Hosting International Visitors*, "There is much more to business than just business in many parts of the world. Socializing, friendships, etiquette, grace, and patience are integral parts of business. Jumping right into business discussions before a get-acquainted interlude can be a bad mistake."

Charles Ford, Commercial Attaché in Guatemala, cites this cultural distinction as the greatest difference between the American and Guatemalan styles of doing business. The inexperienced American visitor, he claims, often tries to force a business relationship. The abrupt "always watching the clock" style rarely works in Guatemala. A better informed business executive would, he advises, engage in small talk about Guatemala, indicate an interest in the families of his or her business associates, join them for lunch or dinner, and generally allow time for a personal relationship to develop. Solid business opportunities usually follow a strong personal relationship in Guatemala. This holds true for Latin America in general.

Building a personal rapport is also important when doing business in Greece, according to Sondra Snowdon, President of Snowdon's International Protocol, Inc., a firm that trains and prepares executives in cross-cultural communications. Business entertaining is usually done in the evening at a local taverna (咖啡厅), and spouses are often included. The relaxed atmosphere is important to building a business relationship based on friendship.

Belgians, however, are the opposite, Snowdon says. They are likely to get down to business right away and are usually conservative and efficient in their approach to business meetings.

Attitudes towards punctuality vary greatly from one culture to another and unless understood can cause confusion and misunderstanding. Romanians, Japanese, and Germans are very punctual, while many of the Latin countries have a more relaxed attitude toward time. The Japanese consider it rude to be late for a business meeting, but it is acceptable, even fashionable, to be late for a social occasion.

In Guatemala on the other hand, according to Ford, a luncheon at a specified time means that some guests might be 10 minutes early, while others may be 45 minutes late.

When crossing cultural lines, something as simple as a greeting can be misunderstood. The form of greeting differs from culture to culture. Traditional greetings may be a handshake, hug, nose rub, kiss, placing the hands in praying position, or various other gestures. Lack of awareness concerning the country's accepted form of greeting can lead to awkward encounters.

The Japanese bow is one of the most well-known forms of greeting. The bow symbolizes respect and humility and is a very important custom to observe when doing business with Japanese. There are also different levels of bowing, each with a significant meaning. Japanese and Americans often combine a handshake with a bow so that each culture may show the other respect.

Handshakes are the accepted form of greeting in Italy. Italians use a handshake for greetings and goodbyes. Unlike the United States, men do not stand when a woman enters or leaves a room, and they do not kiss a woman's hand. The latter is reserved for royalty.

The traditional Thai greeting, the *wai*, is made by placing both hands together in a prayer position at the chin and bowing slightly. The higher the hands, the more respect is symbolized. The fingertips should never be raised above eye level. The gesture means "thank you" and "I'm sorry" as well as "hello." Failure to return a *wai* greeting is equivalent to refusing to shake hands in the West.

According to Snowdon, American intentions are often misunderstood and Americans are sometimes perceived as not meaning what they say. For example, in Denmark the standard American greeting "Hi, how are you?" leads the Danes to think the U. S. business person really wants to know how they are. She suggests that, "Hi, I'm pleased to meet you" is preferable and conveys a more sincere message.

People around the world use body movements or gestures to convey specific messages. Though countries sometimes use the same gestures, they often have very different meanings. Misunderstanding over gestures is a common occurrence in cross-cultural communication, and misinterpretation along these lines can lead to business complications and social embarrassment.

The "OK" sign commonly used in the United States is a good example of a gesture that has several different meanings according to the country. In France, it means zero; in Japan, it is a symbol for money; and in Brazil, it carries a vulgar connotation.

Assistant Commercial Attaché in the United Kingdom Thomas Kelsey advises that American businessmen should never sit with the ankle resting on the knees. They should instead cross their legs with one knee on top of the other. He also suggests avoiding their backslapping and putting an arm around a new acquaintance.

In Thailand, it is considered offensive to place one's arm over the back of the chair in which another person is sitting, and men and women should not show affection in public.

The use of a palm-up hand and moving index finger signals "come here" in the United States and in some other countries is considered vulgar. In Ethiopia, holding out the hand palm down and repeatedly closing the hand means "come here."

Proper use of names and titles is often a source of confusion in international business relations. In many countries (including the United Kingdom, France, and Denmark), it is appropriate to use titles until use of first names is suggested.

First names are seldom used when doing business in Germany. Visiting business people should use the surname preceded by the title. Titles such as

"Herr Direktor" are sometimes used to indicate prestige, status, and rank.

Thais, on the other hand, address each other by first names and reserve last names for very formal occasions, or in writing. When using the first name, they often use the honorific "Khun" or a title preceding it. In Belgium, it is important to address French-speaking business contacts as "Monsieur" or "Madame," while Dutch-speaking contacts should be addressed "Mr." or "Mrs." According to Sondra Snowdon, to confuse the two is a great insult.

Customs concerning gift-giving are extremely important to understand. In some cultures, gifts are expected, and failure to present them is considered an insult, whereas in other countries, offering a gift is considered offensive. Business executives also need to know when to present gifts — on the initial visit or afterwards; where to present gifts — in public or private; what type of gift to present; what color it should be; and how many to present.

Gift-giving is an important part of doing business in Japan. Exchanging gifts symbolizes the depth and strength of a business relationship to the Japanese. Gifts are usually exchanged at the first meeting. When presented with a gift, companies are expected to respond by giving a gift.

In sharp contrast, gifts are rarely exchanged in Germany and are usually not appropriate. Small gifts are fine, but expensive items are not a general practice.

Gift-giving is not a normal custom in Belgium or the United Kingdom either, although in both countries, flowers are a suitable gift if invited to someone's home. Even that is not as easy as it sounds. International executives must use caution to choose appropriate flowers. For example, avoid sending chrysanthemums (especially white) in Belgium and elsewhere in Europe since they are mainly used for funerals. In Europe, it is also considered bad luck to present an even number of flowers. Beware of white flowers in Japan where they are associated with death, and purple flowers in Mexico and Brazil.

Negotiating can be a complex process between parties from the same nation. Negotiating across cultures is even more complicated because of the added chance of misunderstanding stemming from cultural differences. Negotiating styles differ from nation to nation. In addition, a host of cultural variables must be dealt with all at once.

For example，it is essential to understand the importance of rank in the other country and to know who the decision makers are. It is equally important to be familiar with the business style of the foreign company. Is it important to be direct or subtle? Is it necessary to have an established relationship with the company before beginning negotiations? Executives negotiating with foreign companies must also understand the nature of agreements in the country，the importance of gestures，and negotiating etiquette.

These cultural variables are examples of the things that U. S. executives involved in international busi-ness must be aware of. At times in the past，Americans have not had a good track record of being sensitive to cultural distinctions. However，as business has become more global，Americans have become more sensitive to cultural difference，and the importance of dealing with them effectively. Still，some companies fail to do their homework and make fatal or near-fatal mistakes that could have easily been prevented. A number of firms have learned the hard way that successful domestic strategies do not necessarily work overseas and that business must be adapted to the culture. A company ultimately must not only have a sensitivity to other cultures but also have a good understanding of its own culture and how other countries see American culture.

Note: Please put down on *Answer Sheet 1* your answers to the questions in this part. （注意：此部分试题请在**答题卡 1**上作答。）

1. Adapting to cultural variables is a significant part of an international business endeavor.

2. Learning about a country's culture is a show of respect and is always deeply appreciated.

3. Business executives who are not alert to cultural differences simply cannot function efficiently overseas and failure to research and understand a culture has led to many international business blunders.

4. Americans have had a good track record of being sensitive to cultural distinctions.

5. In Latin America, solid business opportunities usually result from
   _____.

6. When it comes to something as simple as a greeting, lack of awareness
   concerning _____ can lead to awkward encounters.

7. Misunderstanding is very common in communication between different
   cultures, and misinterpretation in this respect may cause _____.

8. In many European countries, such as Great Britain, France and Denmark, it is proper to use titles till the use of first name is suggested,
   while in Germany _____.

9. While gift-giving is an important part of doing business in Japan, it is not
   a normal custom in such countries as _____, _____, and _____.

10. Generally, negotiating is a complicated process by itself, and negotiating
    across cultures is even more intricate because of _____.

Part III   Listening Comprehension (35 minutes)
Section A

Directions: *In this section, you will hear 8 short conversations and 2 long conversations. At the end of each conversation, one or more questions will be
asked about what was said. Both the conversation and the questions will be
spoken only once. After each question there will be a pause. During the
pause, you must read the four choices marked A), B), C) and D), and decide which is the best answer. Then mark the corresponding letter on **Answer
Sheet 2** with a single line through the centre.*

Note: Please put down on **Answer Sheet 2** your answers to the following questions.（注意：此部分试题请在答题卡 2 上作答。）

11. A) The woman types too slowly.
    B) The woman types too fast.
    C) The woman types faster than he does.
    D) The woman couldn't type fast.

12. A) At a dentist's.　　　　　　B) In a hospital.
　　 C) In a drugstore.　　　　　　D) At a doctor's.

13. A) She will pay Mr Stewart a visit.
　　 B) She will give Mr Stewart a call.
　　 C) She will buy Mr Stewart a phone book.
　　 D) She will buy herself a phone book.

14. A) There will be more people in the restaurant at dinner time.
　　 B) There are fewer people than usual.
　　 C) They don't have any lunch special today.
　　 D) It's very busy.

15. A) Before 12:45.　　　　　　　B) At 12:55.
　　 C) At one o'clock.　　　　　　D) After one o'clock.

16. A) He has other hobbies now.
　　 B) He went fishing once.
　　 C) He had to quit fishing.
　　 D) He goes fishing sometimes.

17. A) He doesn't like New York.
　　 B) He likes Orlando better than New York.
　　 C) He was a businessman.
　　 D) He is very busy with his work.

18. A) He wants to be independent.
　　 B) It's about time for him to make the decision.
　　 C) He is not sure whether he'll live with his children permanently or not.
　　 D) He wants to live with his children but not permanently.

Questions 19 to 22 are based on the conversation you have just heard.

19. A) She is a job interviewer.　　　B) She is a university professor.

C) She is a career adviser.　　D) She is a psychologist.

20. A) Just keep calm and do your best.
    B) Face the interviewer, while answering questions.
    C) Never take your eyes off the interviewer.
    D) Sit straight on the edge of your chair.

21. A) Pretend to be what the company wants.
    B) Tell the truth, exclude for what you don't want them to know.
    C) Tell the whole truth.
    D) Answer it in a roundabout way.

22. A) Apply for the kind of work you want to do.
    B) Apply to the firm that you would enjoy working for.
    C) Be confident that you will get the job you want.
    D) Answer and ask questions sensibly.

Questions 23 to 25 are based on the conversation you have just heard.

23. A) He has got a part-time job.
    B) He is still on the waiting list.
    C) He has not yet started to look for a job.
    D) He is planning to look for a job.

24. A) Because they expect too much from part-time jobs.
    B) Because they are too optimistic about job markets.
    C) Because they are lacking in experience.
    D) Because the unemployment figures are up again.

25. A) Look at the jobs in the classifieds in the local paper.
    B) Search on the Internet and send out his resume by e-mail.
    C) Print out his resume and send it to the relevant companies.
    D) Both A and C

Section B

Directions: *In this section, you will hear 3 short passages. At the end of each passage, you will hear some questions. Both the passage and the questions will be spoken only once. After you hear a question, you must choose the best answer from the four choices marked A), B), C) and D). Then mark the corresponding letter on* **Answer Sheet 2** *with a single line through the center.*

Note： Please put down on **Answer Sheet 2** your answers to the following questions.（注意：此部分试题请在**答题卡 2** 上作答。）

Passage One

Questions 26 to 28 are based on the passage you have just heard.

26. A）50 years old.   B）45 years old.
    C）40 years old.   D）55 years old.

27. A）He was a warrior.
    B）He was the Shawnee war chief.
    C）He was an adopted son of Chief Blackfish.
    D）Both A and C.

28. A）Becoming a war chief.
    B）Travelling across the country and speaking to the public.
    C）Getting back some of the land taken by the settlers.
    D）Getting all the Indian tribes united.

Passage Two

Questions 29 to 31 are based on the passage you have just heard.

29. A）The group in a messy storeroom.
    B）The group in a nice office.
    C）The group in a poorly designed living room.
    D）All of the above.

30. A）Visitors to an art museum in Kansas City.
    B）Visitors to a university museum.

C) Visitors to an exhibit of paintings.

D) Visitors to an exhibit of photos.

31. A) People in the dark brown room walked more quickly.

B) People spent more time in the white room than in the dark room.

C) Dark brown stimulated more but shorter activity.

D) Dark brown stimulated more and longer activity.

Passage Three

Questions 32 to 35 are based on the passage you have just heard.

32. A) Human relations. B) Personality.
    C) Interpersonal skills training. D) Interpersonal competence.

33. A) To train effective leaders.

B) To improve managers' interpersonal skills.

C) To teach communication skills to introverted supervisors.

D) To build up closer relations between management and employees.

34. A) Positive. B) Negative.
    C) Indifferent. D) Strongly supportive.

35. A) Interpersonal skills can be improved through training.

B) Interpersonal skills can never be learned.

C) Interpersonal skills can be effectively taught in training programs.

D) Interpersonal skills can neither be taught nor learned.

Section C

Directions: *In this section, you will hear a passage three times. When the passage is read for the first time, you should listen carefully for its general idea. When the passage is read for the second time, you are required to fill in the blanks numbered from 36 to 43 with the exact words you have just heard. For blanks numbered from 44 to 46 you are required to fill in the missing information. For these blanks, you can either use the exact words you have just heard or write down the main points in your own words. Finally, when* *the passage is read for the third time, you should check what you have written.*

Note：The questions in this section are all shown on *Answer Sheet 2*；please put down your answers on it as required.（注意：此部分试题在**答题卡**2上；请在**答题卡**2上作答。）

Part IV　Reading Comprehension（Reading in Depth）（25 minutes）
Section A
Directions: *In this section, there is a short passage with 5 questions or incomplete statements. Read the passage carefully. Then answer the questions or complete the statements in the fewest possible words on Answer Sheet 2.*

During the 1990s we will witness many technological changes in the way we communicate. Even books, like the one you are reading, will probably change from their 500-year-old format to exciting "user-friendly" forms enhanced by the computer page. According to futurist Alvin Toffler, books in the future will be read on book-sized video screens. These electronic devices will be able to immediately translate foreign language editions, enlarge or reduce the size of the type, change the type styles, adjust the degree of reading difficulty, and allow the readers of novels to increase or decrease the levels of violence and sexual explicitness to fit individual tastes.

All of these new "user-friendly" options along with the content itself will be delivered on tiny microchips or CD-ROMs（now used in libraries to deliver large amount of information to computer screens）.

Toffler has been forecasting technological changes since his first successful book, *Future Shock*, was published in 1970. His vision of changing trends has been remarkably accurate. In 1980, his book *The Third Wave* explained how civilization was in transition between the second and third great cycles of human history. The first cycle was the agrarian society, which existed until the second cycle, the industrial age, was ushered in during the late eighteenth and early nineteenth centuries. The third cycle, which is now replacing the industrial society, is the information age.

In his latest book, *Powershift*, published in 1990, Toffler tells how the information explosion is causing turmoil among established institutions — such as governments, banks, trade unions and the media — as the industrial age gives way to the information age. According to Toffler, power is directly linked with knowledge and knowledge has become central to economic development. He sees a shifting of power in our culture, transforming such institutions as finance, politics and media. These powershifts, he contends, will create a radically different society.

In addition to economic turmoil, the information age is bringing us a wide range of new communication technologies. This technological explosion began escalating during the 1980s and seems to be gaining snowball-like momentum. Sociologist Daniel Bell pointed out that by the 1980s the United States had more people working in the production of information than in manufacturing and agriculture combined.

Note: Please put down on *Answer Sheet 2* your answers to the questions in this section. (注意：此部分试题请在**答题卡** 2 上作答。)

47. In its context the expression "user-friendly" means _____.

48. Why does the author give us an account of the "exciting" features of "electronic books"?

49. What does the author think of Toffler's foresight of changing trends?

50. Why is knowledge playing a decisive role in the shifting of power in almost all established institutions?

51. The "information age" is characterized by _____.

Section B

Directions: *There are 2 passages in this section. Each passage is followed by some questions or unfinished statements. For each of them there are four choices marked A), B), C) and D). You should decide on the best choice and mark the corresponding letter on **Answer Sheet 2** with a single line through the centre.*

Passage One

Questions 52 to 56 are based on the following passage.

No other country spends what we do per capita for medical care. The care available is among the best technically, even if used too lavishly and thus dangerously, but none of the countries that stand above us in health status have such a high proportion of medically disenfranchised （被剥夺了公民权利的） persons. Given the evidence that medical care is not that valuable and access to care not that bad, it seems most unlikely that our bad showing is caused by the significant proportion who are poorly served. Other hypotheses have greater explanatory power: excessive poverty, both actual and relative, and excessive affluence.

Excessive poverty is probably more prevalent in the U. S. than in any of the countries that have a better infant mortality rate and female life expectancy at birth. This is probably true also for all but four or five of the countries with a longer male life expectancy. In the notably poor countries that exceed us in male survival, difficult living conditions are a more accepted way of life and in several of them, a good basic diet, basic medical care and basic education, and lifelong employment opportunities are an everyday fact of life. In the U. S. a national unemployment level of 10 percent may be 40 percent in the ghetto while less than 4 percent elsewhere. The countries that have surpassed us in health do not have such severe or entrenched problems. Nor are such a high proportion of their people involved in them.

Excessive affluence is not so obvious a cause of ill health, but, at least until recently, few other nations could afford such unhealthful ways of living. Excessive intake of animal protein and fats, dangerous intake of alcohol and use of tobacco and drugs （prescribed and proscribed）, and dangerous recreational sports and driving habits are all possible only because of affluence. Our heritage, desires, opportunities, and our machismo （大男子气概）, combined with the relatively low cost of bad foods and speedy vehicles, make us particularly vulnerable to our affluence. And those who are not affluent try harder. Our unacceptable health status, then, will not be improved appreciably by expanded medical resources nor by their redistribution so much as by a general attempt to improve the quality of life for all.

Note: Please put down on *Answer Sheet 2* your answers to the following questions. （注意：此部分试题请在**答题卡 2** 上作答。）

52. All of the following are mentioned in the passage as factors affecting the health of the population EXCEPT _____.
    A) the availability of medical care services
    B) the genetic endowment of individuals
    C) the nation's relative position in health status
    D) an individual's life style

53. The author is primarily concerned with _____.
    A) condemning the U.S. for its failure to provide better medical care to the poor
    B) evaluating the relative significance of factors contributing to the poor health status in the U.S.
    C) comparing the general health of the U.S. population with world averages
    D) advocating specific measures designed to improve the health of the U.S. population

54. Which of the following conclusions does the passage best support about the relationship between per capita expenditure for medical care and the health of a population?
    A) The per capita expenditure for medical care has relatively little effect on the total amount of medical care available to a population.
    B) The genetic makeup of a population is a more powerful determinant of the health of a population than the per capita expenditure for medical care.
    C) A population may have very high per capita expenditure for medical care and yet have a lower health status than other populations with lower per capita expenditure.
    D) The higher the per capita expenditure on medical care, the more advanced is the medical technology of a country; and the more advanced the technology, the better is the health of the population.

55. The author refers to the excessive intake by Americans of alcohol and tobacco and drug use in order to _____ .
    A) show that some health problems cannot be attacked by better medical care
    B) demonstrate that use of tobacco and intoxicants is detrimental to health
    C) cite examples of individual behavior that have adverse consequences for health status
    D) illustrate ways in which excessive affluence may contribute to a poor health status

56. Which of the following questions does the passage provide information to answer?
    A) What is the most powerful influence on the health status of a country's population?
    B) Which nation in the world leads in health status?
    C) Is the life expectancy of males in the U. S. longer than that of females?
    D) What are the most important genetic factors influencing the health of an individual?

Passage Two

Questions 57 to 61 are based on the following passage.

Intelligence used to be seen as a fixed entity, some faculty of the mind that we all possess and which determines in some ways the extent of our achievements. Since the Intelligence Quotient was relatively unaffected by bad teaching or a dull home environment, it remained constant. Its value, therefore, was a predictor of children's future learning. If they differed markedly in their ability to learn complex tasks, then it was clearly necessary to educate them differently — and the need for different types of school and different ability groups within schools was obvious.

Today, we are beginning to think differently. In the last few years, research has thrown doubt on the view that innate intelligence can ever be measured and on the very nature of intelligence itself. Perhaps most important, there is considerable evidence now which shows the great influence of the environment both on achievement and intelligence. Children with poor home backgrounds not only do less well in their school work and in intelligence tests — a fact which could be explained on genetic grounds — but their performance tends to deteriorate gradually compared with that of their more fortunate classmates. Evidence like this lends support to the view that we have to distinguish between genetic intelligence and observed intelligence. Any deficiency in the appropriate genes will obviously restrict development, no matter how stimulating the environment. But we cannot observe or measure innate intelligence; whereas we can observe and measure the effects of the interaction of whatever is inherited with whatever stimulation has been received from the environment. Changes may occur in our observations or measurements, if the environment is changed. In other words, the Intelligence Quotient is not constant.

Researches over the past decade have been investigating what happens in this interaction. Work in this country has shown that parental interest and encouragement are more important than the material circumstances of the home.

Two major findings have emerged from these studies. Firstly, that the greater part of the development of observed intelligence occurs in the earliest years of life. 50 percent of measurable intelligence at age 17 is already predictable by the age of four. In other words, deprivation in the first four or five years of life can have greater consequences than any of the following twelve or so years.

Secondly, the most important factors in the environment are language and psychological aspects of the parent-child relationship. Much of the difference in measured intelligence between "privileged" and "disadvantaged" children may be due to the latter's lack of appropriate verbal stimulation and the poverty of their perceptional experiences.

These research findings have led to a revision in our understanding of the nature of intelligence. Instead of it being some largely inherited fixed power of the mind, we now see it as a set of developed skills with which a person copes with any environment. These skills have to be learned and, indeed, the fundamental one is learning how to learn.

Note: Please put down on *Answer Sheet 2* your answers to the following questions.（注意：此部分试题请在**答题卡2**上作答。）

57. Which of the following might serve as a suitable title for the passage?
    A) Intelligence: A Changed View
    B) Intelligence and Intelligence Quotient
    C) Genetic Intelligence vs Observed Intelligence
    D) Innate Intelligence and Developed Skills

58. The term "fixed entity" in the first paragraph can best be interpreted as _____.
    A) an invariable constant
    B) a stable faculty of the mind
    C) an inherited fixed capacity
    D) a specific innate potential

59. The old view of intelligence would seem to justify _____.
    A) comprehensive education and un-streamed classes
    B) grouping of children into different classes
    C) sending the duller children out to work at an early age
    D) taking "disadvantaged" children away from their home environment

60. A "disadvantaged" child is one _____.
    A) who is unintelligent
    B) who is incapable of learning well
    C) who comes from a deprived home environment
    D) whose parents are poor and segregated

61. Intelligence is now believed to be _____.
    A) a set of developed skills
    B) incapable of any kind of measurement
    C) closely related to a child's actual learning experiences
    D) Both A and C

Part V Error Correction (15 minutes)

Directions: *This part consists of a short passage. In this passage, there are alto-gether 10 mistakes, one in each numbered line. You may have to change a word, add a word or delete a word. Mark out the mistakes and put the cor-rections in the blanks provided. If you change a word, cross it out and write the correct word in the corresponding blank. If you add a word, put an inser-tion mark (∧) in the right place and write the missing word in the blank. If you delete a word, cross it out and put a slash (/) in the blank.*

Example:

Television is rapidly becoming the literature of our ~~periods~~. Many of the arguments
~~having~~ used for the study of literature as a
school subject are valid for∧ study of television.

1. time/times/period
2. _____
3.   the

Note： The questions in this part are shown on **Answer Sheet 2**；please put down your answers on the **Sheet**.（注意：此部分试题在**答题卡 2** 上；请在**答题卡 2** 上作答。）

Part VI Translation (5 minutes)

Directions: *Complete the following sentences by translating into English the Chinese given in brackets.*

Note: Please put down on **Answer Sheet 2** your answers to the questions in this part.（注意：此部分试题请在**答题卡 2** 上作答。）

72. While she was at college, she _____.（让自己尽可能多地参与各项课外活动）.

73. _____（这富婆总算领悟到）that money can not buy her much happiness.

74. Reading between the lines, you'll be able to _____（觉察到作者对受害者深切的同情）.

75. _____ （在我看来，他算不上是个了不起的科学家） although he won the Nobel prize in physics decades ago.

76. This commentator points out，"What should be debated is _____ （为什么科技与经济的进步并没有给大多数美国家庭带来多大的好处）.

Answer Sheet 1 (答题卡1)

Part I   **Writing**   **(30 minutes)**

Directions: *For this part, you are allowed 30 minutes to write a composition on the topic* **Job Problems for College Graduates.** *Study the following charts carefully and your composition must be based on the information given in the charts.*

Write to：

（1） state the changes in college graduates' choices of careers；

（2） give possible reasons for the changes；

（3） suggest some solutions to the problem.

1981   2006

⊠ Graduates who continue to study

◩ Graduates who take jobs irrelevant to their majors

☐ Graduates who hold jobs in their majors

Your composition should be no less than **150** words. Please write neatly.

JOB PROBLEMS FOR COLLEGE GRADUATES

....

....

....

Answer Sheet 1 (答题卡 1)

_____

_____

_____

_____

_____

_____

_____

_____

_____

_____

_____

_____

_____

_____

_____

_____

_____

_____

_____

_____

_____

_____

_____

Part II Reading Comprehension (Skimming and Scanning) (15 minutes)

1. [Y] [N] [NG]   5. _____   8. _____

2. [Y] [N] [NG]

3. [Y] [N] [NG]   6. _____   9. _____

4. [Y] [N] [NG]   7. _____   10. _____

Answer Sheet 2 (答题卡2)

Part III   Section A   Section B

11. [A] [B] [C] [D]   16. [A] [B] [C] [D]   21. [A] [B] [C] [D]   26. [A] [B] [C] [D]   31. [A] [B] [C] [D]

12. [A] [B] [C] [D]   17. [A] [B] [C] [D]   22. [A] [B] [C] [D]   27. [A] [B] [C] [D]   32. [A] [B] [C] [D]

13. [A] [B] [C] [D]   18. [A] [B] [C] [D]   23. [A] [B] [C] [D]   28. [A] [B] [C] [D]   33. [A] [B] [C] [D]

14. [A] [B] [C] [D]   19. [A] [B] [C] [D]   24. [A] [B] [C] [D]   29. [A] [B] [C] [D]   34. [A] [B] [C] [D]

15. [A] [B] [C] [D]   20. [A] [B] [C] [D]   25. [A] [B] [C] [D]   30. [A] [B] [C] [D]   35. [A] [B] [C] [D]

Part III   Section C

Our sleep time over the past century has been (36) _____ by almost 20 percent.

Generally, adults need to sleep one hour for every two hours (37) _____, which means that most need about eight hours of sleep a night. Of course, some people need more and some less. Children and teenagers need an average of about ten hours.

The brain keeps an exact (38) _____ of how much sleep it is owed. My colleagues and I (39) _____ the term *sleep debt* because (40) _____ lost sleep is like a (41) _____ debt: it must be paid back. If you get an hour less than a full night's sleep, you carry an hour of sleep debt into the next day — and your (42) _____ to fall asleep during the daytime becomes stronger.

During a five-day (43) _____, if you get six hours of sleep each night instead of the eight you needed, (44) _____. Because sleep debt accumulates in an additive fashion, (45) _____. From this perspective, sleeping until noon on Saturday is not getting enough to pay back the ten lost hours as well as meet your nightly requirement of eight; you would have to sleep until about 5 p.m. to balance the sleep ledger.

(47) _____

_____.

Answer Sheet 2 (答题卡2)

Part IV Section A

47. _____

_____

48. _____

_____

49. _____

_____

50. _____

_____

51. _____

_____

_____

Part IV Section B

52. [A][B][C][D]
53. [A][B][C][D]
54. [A][B][C][D]
55. [A][B][C][D]
56. [A][B][C][D]
57. [A][B][C][D]
58. [A][B][C][D]
59. [A][B][C][D]
60. [A][B][C][D]
61. [A][B][C][D]

Part V Error Correction (15 minutes)

Old age in the United States presents many problems and opportunities. With the result of improved medical services, people live longer than they used to. This increase in longevity creates a wide range of social needs that didn't exist when the average life expectancy was higher. The medical specialty of gerontology (老年医学) has opened research areas and careers related to the elderly.

Because of changes in the family structure from extended to nuclear, the elderly has to create existences apart from basically small family units. This situation is complicated by the fact many of their friends may have died and their children may have moved away.

The elderly person must set up a new life. Often, the elderly must rely on a fixed income — Social Security and pensions — and gradually diminished savings. While some live with their children, many more live by themself, with a friend, or in a nursing home.

Moreover, the increasing proportion of elderly people has given them a new political power. They have formed organizations such as the Grey Panthers to voice their own need and concerns over local , state, and federal agencies. Lobbying (国会院外游说活动) for such issues as increased Social Security benefits, better healthy care, income tax benefits, and rent controls have brought to the public an increased awareness of the determination of the elderly to assert their ability to deal effectively with their own lives.

62. _____

63. _____

64. _____

65. _____

66. _____

67. _____

68. _____

69. _____

70. _____

71. _____

Part VI Translation (5 minutes)

72. _____

73. _____

74. _____

75. _____

76. _____

Appendix I

Key to Practice Tests (1-10)

Practice Test 1

Part I   Writing

(For reference)

SCHOOLBAGS: TOO HEAVY FOR SCHOOLKIDS

These days we often hear schoolkids grumbling about their heavy homework load. This is not surprising when we see their schoolbags bulging with all sorts of textbooks and workbooks. They are required to take so many courses that they have to sit up late struggling with their assignments.

In spite of the clamor of the public for an end to this situation, the excessive pressure imposed on the pupils has not been relieved. The reasons for this are not difficult to figure out. First, a great part of the pressure comes from the parents, who have gone all lengths to help their children improve academic performance and urge them for early intellectual achievements: calling in private tutors or sending them out to various tutoring centers. Pupils at large seem to be driven by one message: Excel in academic performance. It has, in fact, been echoing in their heads ever since they started school. They have been pushed to score high, test well, and finish first.

On the other hand, teachers should be held responsible, too. To them, scores are not only the mark of success or failure for a particular student but also a measure of professional performance of their own. Many of them do not try with great efforts to enhance efficiency by improving their teaching methods. Instead, they just assign more drills and exercises, thrust more books into the pupils' backpacks, and stuff their heads with as many rules or facts as possible.

More and more people are crying out for "lightening kids' schoolbags." To my mind, it appears comparatively easy to relieve pupils of some pressure — to assign less homework and to cut off a few courses — although it calls for much care and efforts on the part of both teachers and parents. But what is more important is to "humanize" the current educational system — to make education ready for the future. Just as many educators have pointed out, when it comes to a child's well-being, we should be as concerned with character as with success. If we have reared a well-mannered, good, decent person, we should take pleasure and pride in that fact. More likely than not, if we have achieved these goals, the child's success will take care of itself.

Part II   Reading Comprehension (Skimming and Scanning)

1. N   2. Y   3. N   4. NG

5. working from home using equipment such as telephone, fax machines and modems to contact colleagues and customers

6. more productive

7. a sense of belonging/feel part of a team

8. promote connection and creativity

9. to strengthen personal connections already forged

10. develop a harmonious relationship

Part III   Listening Comprehension

Section A

11. D   12. A   13. D   14. C   15. C
16. B   17. A   18. B   19. D   20. C
21. B   22. C   23. A   24. D   25. B

Section B

26. D   27. C   28. A   29. B   30. C
31. D   32. D   33. B   34. B   35. A

Section C

36. unbelievable   37. claims   38. incomes   39. per
40. older   41. worth   42. disagree   43. observers

44. to play rock music doesn't require much training

45. Rock music has become a kind of religion

46. by writing his own music, McLean earns some extra money

Part IV Reading Comprehension (Reading in Depth)

Section A

47. relate the humanities to real social problems (or: help students apply the humanities to real problems)
48. with little or no practical value
49. It means "this generation".
50. Interfering with individuals' genes to produce superior and subordinate classes.
51. educational

Section B

52. B   53. A   54. B   55. C   56. D
57. C   58. B   59. D   60. B   61. A

Part V Error Correction

It was once thought that air pollution affected only the area immediately around large cities with factories and/or heavy automobile traffic. Today we know that ~~because~~ these are the areas with the worst air pollution, the problem is literally world-wide. ~~At~~ several occasions over the last decade, a heavy cloud of air pollution has covered the entire half of the United States and ~~lead~~ to health warnings even in rural areas away from any ~~minor~~ concentration of manufacturing and automobile traffic. ~~What~~ has been found that air pollution is killing trees in the mountains of California and melons on the farms of Indiana. In fact, the very ~~weather~~ of the entire earth may be affected by air pollution. Some scientists feel that the increasing concentration of carbon dioxide in the air ~~resulted~~ from the burning of fossil fuels (coal and oil) is creating a "greenhouse effect" — holding in heat reflected ~~to~~ the earth and raising the world's average temperature. If this view is correct and ~~that~~ the world's temperature is raised only a few degrees, much

62. ___although___
63. ___On___
64. ___led___
65. ___major___
66. ___It___
67. ___climate___
68. ___resulting___
69. ___from___
70. _____

of ice cap will melt and cities such as New York,
Boston, Miami, or New Orleans will be under water.　　71. _____ and _____

Part VI　　Translation

72.　is now under way
73.　Caught in a sudden downpour （or: a thunderstorm）
74.　what you fail to get by force （or: in war）
75.　the project of the exhibition center be completed on schedule
76.　Rather than they do it

Practice Test 2

Part I　Writing

(For reference)

WHAT A COLLEGE EDUCATION MEANS TO ME

　　What does a college education mean to me? This is a good question but I have never given much thought to it. Finishing the primary and secondary school as a top student, I just took it for granted that I should go on to college for higher education. Now that I am asked to write on this topic, I have to cudgel my brains, trying to provide a presentable answer to it.

　　To begin with, I believe a college or university is the best place where I can satisfy my desire for learning. I remember as I proceeded through high school into junior and senior years, I became genuinely interested in chemistry and physics. I felt that I wanted to further my studies in these subjects, and that I would never be content to end up as a high school graduate. It was then that I began to feel a deep yearning for knowledge. And as my high school years drew to a close, the decision to attend college seemed only too natural.

　　Up to now, I have been at college for more than two years. I have learned from my own experience that the college is not merely a good place to seek scientific truth but also an ideal place to broaden one's horizon. With courses and lectures available in different fields, college life keeps me in close contact with a variety of new social and political ideas. And living on campus also gives me the opportunity to meet different people, accumulate new experiences and know well about the world we live in.

Here, I don't want to conceal my motivation on the practical side. In today's society, college education has become an essential part of career preparation for students. The job market is so competitive and this trend will surely continue in the coming years. A bachelor's degree or a master's degree is all but indispensable if one wishes to find a satisfying professional job. And in this sense, I do hope our current educational system can teach us young people the skills, both scholastic and financial, that we will need not only to survive but to flourish in today's world as well.

Part II Reading Comprehension (Skimming and Scanning)
1. Y   2. NG   3. N   4. Y
5. looking at nature and our relationship with nature
6. is not always possible/a good idea
7. she finished high school
8. English/biology
9. She already published three books: *Under the Sea Wind, The Sea Around Us,* and *The Edge of the Sea*
10. enjoyable/informative

Part III Listening Comprehension
Section A
11. C   12. A   13. B   14. D   15. B
16. C   17. A   18. B   19. C   20. C
21. C   22. D   23. D   24. A   25. A

Section B
26. B   27. A   28. D   29. A   30. C
31. B   32. D   33. C   34. B   35. A

Section C
36. flashier   37. evolve   38. appreciation   39. emphasis
40. developing   41. declining   42. dropping   43. marginal
44. In the developed countries supply is surpassing demand with regards to this kind of technology

45. answers to environmental problems could not come from further advances in the same technologies

46. in finding ways to produce goods to meet the world's needs, using less of the raw materials

Part IV Reading Comprehension (Reading in Depth)

Section A

47. they can help employees in their career development in many ways

48. "To put somebody in charge of."

49. to improve the employees' chances for career success

50. limited power, lack of proper appreciation, and unnecessary office gossip

51. revealing weaknesses might affect their chances of job promotions and salary increases

Section B

52. C   53. D   54. A   55. D   56. D
57. C   58. D   59. A   60. C   61. C

Part V Error Correction

Time spent in a bookstore can be enjoyable, if you
are a book-lover or merely there to buy a book as a
present. You may even have entered the shop just to
find shelters ~~away~~ a sudden shower.

Whatever the reasons, you can soon become totally
unaware of your surroundings. The desire to pick up a
book with an attractive dust-jacket is irresistible, ~~even~~
this method of selection ought not to be followed, as
you might end up with a rather ~~bored~~ book. You soon
become engrossed in some book or other, and usually it is
only much later that you realise you have spent far ~~far~~
much time there and must dash off to keep some
forgotten appointment — without buying a book, of
course.

This opportunity to escape the realities of everyday

62.	whether
63.	from
64.	although
65.	boring
66.	too

life is, I think, the main attraction of a bookshop. There are not many places where it is ~~impossible~~ to do this. A music shop is very much like a bookshop. You can wander round such places to your heart's content. If it is a good shop, no assistant will approach ~~to~~ you with the inevitable greeting: "Can I help you, sir?" You needn't buy anything if you don't want. In a bookshop an assistant should remain ^ the background until you have finished browsing. Then, only then, are his services necessary. Of course, you may want to find out where a particular section is, ~~since~~ when he has led you there, the assistant should retire discreetly and look as ^ he is not interested in selling a single book.

67. possible

68. —

69. in

70. but

71. if

Part VI   Translation

72. I have to call in sick
73. putting it into effect is quite another
74. but it is worth seeing
75. keep pace with the economic and technological development in the world today
76. reality always remains far apart from the ideal

Practice Test 3

Part I   Writing

(For reference)

ENERGY SHORTAGE: HOW TO SOLVE IT

China was sweating a lot over the last summer, not only because of the continual heat waves. Lack of coal and oil also resulted in a power shortage. According to news reports, many cities had to restrict the power usage for air-conditioning and illumination, and thousands of manufacturers in Shanghai had to reschedule their production to evenings or weekends.

As it is, energy has become one of the biggest problems the world is faced with today. Many scientists and economists point out that our natural resources are very much limited. If we keep consuming our resources at the present rate, they warn, the world will soon be running out of oil, coal and metals, and this will certainly lead to a serious energy crisis threatening mankind's survival.

The majority of the world's people have responded with a clamor for more strict conservation of our natural resources. This is urgently necessary, indeed. It must be realized that much of our energy, in the form of oil, coal, gas, or electricity, has been wantonly consumed. If things go on like that, we will eventually leave for our descendants a devastated world, a vast stretch of wasteland. So, from now on, we will have to make serious efforts to enhance energy efficiency, reduce the number of high energy-consuming projects, and cut down energy waste of any form so as to slow down the present drain on our limited resources.

But conservation alone is not all the answer. It is obvious that, even if we save much energy by using it carefully, our natural resources, however abundant, will run out ultimately. And when they are gone they are gone forever, for resources can not reproduce themselves. In the long run, developing new sources of energy and increasing the use of new and renewable energy are more important ways to solve the energy problem. As we know, governments of some European countries, such as Germany and Italy, have worked out all sorts of incentive programs to encourage people to use solar energy. And recently some scientists have asserted that China has abundant wind energy reserve, which could be vital to properly solve the country's energy issue. So, searching unexplored areas for new supplies seems to be the only way out of our energy-shortage predicament.

Part II Reading Comprehension (Skimming and Scanning)

1. N   2. Y   3. Y   4. NG
5. long-term memory
6. constant intellectual stimulation
7. they belong to us exclusively — they not only determine our personalities but also help shape our outlook on life
8. its amazing capacity, its accuracy, and its fascination as a tantalizing mystery

9. research findings over the past decade
10. analogy

Part III Listening Comprehension

Section A
11. B	12. C	13. D	14. A	15. A
16. D	17. D	18. C	19. B	20. C
21. C	22. C	23. B	24. A	25. D

Section B
26. A	27. B	28. C	29. B	30. C
31. A	32. D	33. B	34. A	35. C

Section C
36. headquarters   37. valuable   38. attended   39. Consequently
40. reputation   41. accused   42. allegations   43. credibility
44. London's art dealers and auction houses are facing a bigger threat
45. when a newspaper reporter claimed that Sotheby's was involved in smuggling
46. the program shows Sotheby's got illegally imported art treasures regularly

Part IV Reading Comprehension (Reading in Depth)

Section A
47. The rapid growth in academic contact and international co-operation.
48. A great variety of subjects is studied.
49. keep up with current developments
50. friendships formed by scholars at meetings
51. They make scholars aware of problems outside their own field.

Section B
52. B	53. A	54. C	55. D	56. D
57. B	58. B	59. A	60. D	61. C

Part V   Error Correction

As we mentioned earlier, there is a wide variety of sports activities available ~~to~~ the United States both to watch and play. Most large cities have teams that play the most popular American sports — baseball, in the spring and summer, football, in the autumn and winter, and basketball, in the winter and spring. Tickets to games may be easy or difficult to obtain, ~~depend~~ on the team and the city. You can find the ticket ~~news~~ by reading the newspapers or by calling the ticket office of the teams. (These are listed in the Alphabetical Telephone Book.) ~~Moreover~~, most major sporting events are on radio and television. Most hotels and motels in the United States have television sets in each room, many of them ~~with~~ color.

If you would rather play a sport ~~not~~ watch it being played, there are certainly many opportunities to do. If you are interested in swimming or any indoor sports, go to the Young Men's Christian Association (YMCA) or the Young Women's Christian Association (YWCA). These are organizations for men and women ~~who~~ offer sports programs to the public at inexpensive rates. During the summer months, there are public and private beaches and swimming pools available. In every city you visit, ~~they~~ are public parks and play areas for picnics, sports, or walks. ~~Informations~~ about other sports can be found in the newspapers or frequently in the Yellow Pages of the telephone book.

62. ___in___

63. ___depending___

64. ___information___

65. ___However___

66. ___in___

67. ___than___

68. ___so___

69. ___that/which___

70. ___there___

71. ___Information___

Part VI   Translation

72. check up all the facts before he writes a report

73. seem to be about all that young people are really interested in

74. It's just as well I've brought plenty of money

75. he did not catch on to the joke made by the Chinese teacher

76. But for your strong support

Practice Test 4

Part I   Writing

(For reference)

THE VALUE OF SCIENCE

At the mention of the value of science, people will immediately associate it with beneficial results of scientific discoveries — the joys and conveniences which science has brought into human life. It is true that science has revolutionized our way of life and transformed the lives of billions of people. It has become the new "magic" which is capable of doing everything. The latest devices and gadgets around you for better living have all come about as a result of the application of scientific knowledge. And people now can hardly live without telephones, TV sets, jet planes and computers.

But the true value of science does not merely lie in those things. It is fully appreciated by the way in which science contributes to man's intellectual growth and spiritual well-being. It lies rather with its process than with its results. Why are people so eager to become scientists? Why do scientists spend their whole life on observation, experiments, and researches? Scientists are compelled by certain basic human urges. One is the urge to explore. The spirit of Columbus, of Galileo, and of Einstein — the spirit of conquering uncharted places, discovering unknown facts and climbing untrodden mountain peaks — is an inborn gift we are all endowed with. Another is the urge to create. It is not only embodied in the countless inventions made by Edison, the world famous inventor, but also expressed in what an ordinary carpenter does — he tends to stand aside admiring at that exquisite piece he has just finished. Obviously, science does more than provide man with material things — it helps man to satisfy his strong desire for exploration and to fully develop his intellectual potentials.

Science is man's most powerful weapon, with which man has freed himself from the yoke of ignorance and consequent fear. Science is man's treasure house, which has constantly provided him with vitality, hopes, ambitions, understanding and insights. Science is man's best friend, who is always ready to help — help elevate him spiritually and intellectually. And science, in its true sense, is a celebration of the human spirit itself.

Part II Reading Comprehension (Skimming and Scanning)

1. N   2. NG   3. Y   4. N
5. fight very hard to keep such information a secret
6. the population is so big/smoking is so popular
7. keep their markets open to foreign cigarettes
8. surpass that from (better known causes like) tuberculosis and AIDS
9. the increasing prosperity of large Asian countries
10. statistics

Part III Listening Comprehension

Section A

11. A   12. C   13. A   14. B   15. A
16. D   17. B   18. C   19. C   20. A
21. B   22. B   23. D   24. B   25. D

Section B

26. A   27. B   28. D   29. A   30. B
31. C   32. C   33. C   34. D   35. D

Section C

36. involve   37. technically   38. alternative   39. ethical
40. conception   41. conceiving   42. delivery   43. orphaned
44. A human egg might be kept for a long while before it is implanted in the mother's body
45. who is paid to carry the baby for another woman
46. Should it belong to the woman who gave birth, or to the biological parents?

Part IV Reading Comprehension (Reading in Depth)

Section A

47. Serious attempts made in the 18th century to regulate English.
48. They felt that English (as the language of scholarship) was growing too

wildly.

49. decide officially what people can and can not say
50. They were inappropriately (or: indiscriminately) developed on the Latin model.
51. a rapid growth in English as a living language

Section B

52. C   53. A   54. D   55. B   56. D
57. C   58. B   59. A   60. B   61. A

Part V Error Correction

In every city and town there are people ~~named~~ as real estate agents who will help you find a house to rent. But they may charge a fixed ~~number~~ of money, such as a month's rent or a percentage of the year's rent, to help you find a place. Some companies pay the amounts for their workers; others do not. If you have a ~~work~~ in the United States, be certain that you ask ~~if~~ your company will pay for this service or not ~~after~~ you sign any papers with a real estate agent. You can also find a house by yourself by noticing "For Rent" signs and following newspaper advertisement. The sign will list a telephone number for you to call.

When you rent a house, in addition to the rent, you will generally be expected to pay for what ~~we~~ called utilities — gas and electricity, heat and hot water — ~~besides~~ for simple electrical and other repairs. However, ~~this~~ is a good idea to be sure what the rent does and does not include. As ~~there~~ is often the case with most house rentals, you will probably be expected to have certain ~~demands~~ for the care of the house, such as grass-cutting and snow removal. For example, in most cities, you, not the city, are responsible for clearing the walk of snow in front of the house within a

62. known
63. sum/amount
64. job
65. whether
66. before
67. are
68. and
69. it
70. ___
71. responsibilities

few hours after each snowfall.

Part VI   Translation

72. When one feels an impulse to soar
73. had to be at the mercy of the imperialist powers
74. a small town to the west of New York City
75. anger flared from her eyes
76. but an indication that a person is prepared for life

Practice Test 5

Part I   Writing

(For reference)

THE NEWSPAPER: A BETTER SOURCE OF NEWS

Over the past hundred years, newspapers have played an important role in our social, political, and economic life. But for most of us today, television has become our main source of news. According to a questionnaire on "ways of obtaining information," nearly 72 per cent of the people watch TV, and only 12 per cent read newspapers for their daily news. Perhaps the great disparity of ratio results from the easy access to television nowadays. This, however, puts us in a very disadvantageous position, for the newspaper is a better source of news in many ways.

Although television news excels in bringing into our living room dramatic events of singular importance: spacecraft launchings, natural disasters, record-breaking sports events, wars and so on, yet it cannot cover important stories in the depth they may deserve because of its time limit. Newspapers, however, can devote to a news item as much space as necessary and flesh it out with more details.

Furthermore, television by nature is a passive medium. It deprives viewers of the freedom of selection. Whether you like or dislike a particular piece of news, you have to sit before the tube and watch it, following its pace passively. But by reading newspapers, you can select the most interesting news, and skip over what you think is boring or irrelevant. You can read some news in great detail or just run through it briefly. Also, watching TV involves very little, if any, mental activity, and a constant diet of television journalism leads to the decline in general intellectual skills such as reading and writing. In contrast to this, the print media encourages active involvement in what is being reported. Readers have to make greater efforts than TV viewers to follow and absorb a news report.

When we consider television news versus newspaper news in terms of format, coverage and nature, is there any question as to which is a better source of news?

Part II Reading Comprehension (Skimming and Scanning)
1. Y   2. N   3. Y   4. NG
5. Smaller chances of having a child to feel proud of/higher cost of child rearing/eagerness to take charge of child rearing
6. pushy
7. stress disorders/personality problems/behavior problems
8. demonstrating cause or effect through examples
9. character/success
10. a unique pattern of qualities and abilities

Part III Listening Comprehension
Section A
11. A	12. B	13. C	14. A	15. B
16. A	17. B	18. C	19. C	20. D
21. C	22. D	23. A	24. C	25. D

Section B
| 26. B | 27. C | 28. D | 29. C | 30. B |
| 31. A | 32. D | 33. C | 34. B | 35. C |

Section C
36. identifying 37. trigger   38. incidence   39. significantly
40. temporal   41. susceptible 42. phenomenon 43. stimulating
44. may lead to the occurrence of heart attacks in the morning
45. heart attack rates increase in the few days before and after their birthdays

46. Though stress is thought to be linked to above-mentioned risk factors, sci-entists are still researching in this field in order to know more about how and why heart failure occurs

Part IV Reading Comprehension (Reading in Depth)

Section A

47. The role of mental stimulation in preventing mental aging.
48. brain power
49. Education, chronic illness, and standard of living.
50. social interconnections
51. the process of mental aging has started/an important part of brain power

Section B

52. D	53. C	54. C	55. B	56. A
57. C	58. D	59. C	60. D	61. D

Part V Error Correction

The key to being a winner is to have desire and a goal from which you refuse to be deterred （被吓住）. That desire fuels your dreams and the special goal keeps you ~~focusing~~.   62. ___focused___

~~Deeply~~ down we all have a hope that our destiny is   63. ___Deep___
not to be average and prosaic. Everyone talks about a good game, but the winner goes out and ~~do~~ something.   64. ___does___
To win, there has to be movement and physical action. Attitudes and persistence can help us become ~~who~~ we   65. ___what___
want to be.

Competition is the best motivator. ~~Because~~ many   66. _While/Although_
people use competition as an excuse for not doing something, those who really want to ~~success~~ see   67. ___succeed___
competition as an opportunity, and they are willing to do the tough work ~~necessarily~~ to win.   68. ___necessary___

Learn to deal with fear. Fear is the greatest deterrent to taking ~~risk~~. People worry so much about   69. ___risks___

failing that their fear paralyzes them, ~~drained~~ the   70. _draining_
energy they might otherwise be using to grow.

　　You can cultivate self-respect by developing a
commitment to your own talents. It may be necessary
to do the thing you fear the most in order to put that
fear ~~in~~ rest, so that it can no longer control you.   71. _to_

Part VI　　Translation

72. will we be able to make great efforts to overcome our complacency
73. smoke and steam rising continually from the crater
74. range in price between $300,000 and half a million
75. Owing to a shortage of electric power as many as two thousand factories
76. has cashed in on the actress' predicament

Practice Test 6

Part I　Writing

(For reference)

SCHOOLKIDS GOING TO EVENING SCHOOL

　　Yesterday evening I dropped in on a friend of mine and found his ten-year-old daughter having an early supper by herself. Why didn't she have supper with the family? "She's going to English classes in an evening school," explained her father.

　　This is not a rare case. My friend's daughter is just one of thousands of schoolkids around the city who are learning foreign languages in evening schools. A survey conducted by Shanghai's Municipal Education Bureau indicates that in 2005, the enrollment of school pupils in different evening schools jumped to 80 per cent, compared with 4 per cent fourteen years ago. Evening schools and various tutoring centers have mushroomed all over the city to cater not only for on-the-job adults but for school pupils as well.

　　Why are so many schoolkids attending language evening classes? The most obvious reason is that parents are attaching much importance to having their children mastering a foreign language. In this age of economic reforms, more people have come to realize that the command of a second language often means a good opportunity for a successful career — a passport to a prosperous future.

It is true that most primary schools in China make English a compulsory part of the curriculum, but a pupil begins to learn English only when he is in his third or fourth grade, and there are only three lesson periods per week. Many parents, who cannot wait till then or do not settle for the little amount of English taught at school, send their children to language schools in the evening in the hope that they will learn it at an ever earlier age and learn much more to be ahead of the pack.

And good teachers and advanced equipment also play a part in the ever-increasing enrollment of evening school students. Most of the teachers there are from colleges and universities. Senior lecturers or professors, they have much experience in teaching foreign languages. "With so many good teachers and such modern audio-visual aids," said my friend, "it is worthwhile to send my daughter there." Yeah, for most of the parents, a successful child is the ultimate proof of their success.

Part II　Reading Comprehension (Skimming and Scanning)

1. N　　2. NG　　3. Y　　4. Y
5. through relaxation
6. tensing each muscle group separately
7. self-talk, distraction, and imaging
8. directing our thoughts and feelings
9. less painful or unpleasant
10. reduce stress through successful management

Part III　Listening Comprehension

Section A

11. B　　12. B　　13. A　　14. C　　15. D
16. D　　17. A　　18. D　　19. D　　20. B
21. C　　22. C　　23. D　　24. C　　25. A

Section B

26. D　　27. C　　28. C　　29. C　　30. B

31. A　　32. C　　33. C　　34. D　　35. D

Section C

36. mental　　37. Among　　38. established　　39. adults
40. outside　　41. surrounded　　42. insists　　43. normal
44. will live in apartments or in a house, learning to perform various tasks of daily life
45. They will learn: you've got to pay for the phone calls you make
46. Much of the job training is done outside the school

Part IV　Reading Comprehension (Reading in Depth)
Section A

47. we are creating environmental problems that will eventually destroy our planet
48. It is a typical example of overblown environmental rhetoric.
49. speeches or writings that are very fine-sounding but widely exaggerated.
50. bring about much lighter distress to human beings
51. environmental problems are a sort of necessary evil (or: some unavoidable harmful effects that come alongside with economic growth)

Section B

52. C　　53. D　　54. B　　55. A　　56. D
57. D　　58. C　　59. C　　60. A　　61. B

Part V　Error Correction

　　Some people, in all seriousness, say that humans
will be living in space within the next hundred or so
years. Planet Earth will be crowded, dirty and ~~lack~~ of　　62.　　short
resources. A sort of exodus (移居) of mankind will
begin.

　　Spaceships will be assembled so that they revolve
around the earth. Some may orbit around Mars. These
space stations will be serviced by space buses. We saw
the first space bus ~~launch~~ in April 1981. This was　　63.　　launched
"Columbia", ~~it~~ made several orbits around the earth and　　64.　　which

233

then returned, landing on a huge dry lake bed in California. "Columbia" will be used again. Previous spaceships have been abandoned, only the nose cone being used to bring the ~~crews~~ back to earth.

65. _____ crew _____

Upon established, each space station will generate its own atmosphere and have its own agriculture. It will need to ~~rotation~~ to provide an artificial gravity; people will be forced ~~inwards~~ from the centre by centrifugal （离心力）force.

66. _____ Once _____

67. _____ rotate _____

68. _____ outwards _____

The moon and Mars could become new sources of new materials. Driving through space ~~will~~ no longer need Earth fuel — the energy would come from the sun. This energy would be converted ~~from~~ electricity to work magnetic rockets.

69. _____ would _____

70. _____ into _____

That all sounds quite ~~fantastically~~ but, with the rapid development of modern technology, who knows about what the future holds?

71. _____ fantastic _____

Part VI Translation

72. ended up in a draw
73. distinguished himself as a space rocket expert
74. There is no denying
75. our very existence may be threatened
76. does she let me know (or: does she tell me) what happened that summer

Practice Test 7

Part I Writing

(For reference)

THE MARVELS OF MEDICINE IN THE TWENTIETH CENTURY

Looking back, the twentieth century has seen numerous scientific and technologic achievements, and what stand out high above others are advances in medical science. Their results have clearly been shown in three areas: development of vaccines and antibiotics, discoveries of new diagnosis methods, and the advent of genetic engineering as a new branch of learning.

Ever since medical researchers started to devise ways of preventing germs invading the body, and of fighting them once they did, the quality of life for people in the world has remarkably improved. Today smallpox is a forgotten disease, and vaccinations are no longer required. Polio is under control and the vaccine is widely available. The development of such antibiotics as penicillin has helped many people recover from serious illness.

Over the past decades more and more doctors have come to realize the importance of detecting changes in the body at an early stage. Modern diagnosis began in the early 1900s with the discovery of X-rays. With the passage of time, new methods for viewing the interior of the body were brought out one after another. In recent years, ultrasonic waves, magnetic resonance and other techniques have made it possible to detect anything in the body that is beginning to be abnormal.

Medical advances have been moving in even more fundamental directions. Scientists have found that the body machinery is directed by the genes. Researches in this field have evolved into a new branch of learning — genetic engineering. It was only in the 1950s that scientists discovered the kind of structures the genes have. And at the end of the twentieth century the first "rough map" of the human genetic code was completed. This was referred to as a "major scientific milestone," which might lead to a more fully understanding of the genes that make people susceptible to cancer, AIDS, Parkinson's or Alzheimer's.

With each important discovery, the practice of medicine has undergone a revolution. The medical advances made in the twentieth century have not only improved the lives of many people but also laid a solid foundation for further development in medicine. And I do believe that in the 21st century scientists will work even greater wonders in the area of medical science and eventually find cures to what are now called "incurable" diseases.

Part II Reading Comprehension (Skimming and Scanning)

1. N   2. Y   3. Y   4. NG
5. conversations between males and females
6. talk much more in public situations

7. support, understanding, and exploration

8. negotiate status (or: build up prestige)

9. cross-cultural communication

10. improved relationships between husband and wife

Part III　Listening Comprehension

Section A

11. C　　12. B　　13. C　　14. A　　15. C

16. B　　17. D　　18. D　　19. A　　20. D

21. C　　22. D　　23. D　　24. A　　25. B

Section B

26. D　　27. C　　28. B　　29. C　　30. B

31. D　　32. B　　33. D　　34. C　　35. A

Section C

36. popular　　37. currently　　38. weekday　　39. case

40. era　　　　41. available　　42. inspires　　43. premium

44. Radio has to hold our attention using words and music instead of dazzling pictures

45. for a TV viewer usually feels that he or she is a nobody among a large audience

46. a radio listener tends to believe that the program is just prepared for, and broadcast to, him or her alone

Part IV　Reading Comprehension (Reading in Depth)

Section A

47. The evolutionary basis of the structure of the human brain.

48. It is the part of the brain that reasons.

49. Because they lack a neocortex.

50. the script of a television program produced for science students

51. scholarly

Section B

52. A　　53. B　　54. B　　55. C　　56. C

57. C   58. D   59. D   60. D   61. A

Part V   Error Correction

Criticism is judgment. A critic is a judge. A judge
must study and think about the material presented to ~~it~~,   62.   him
correct it or reject it after thinking ^ what he has read,   63.   about
watched or heard.

Another word for criticism is ~~the~~ appreciation.   64.   —
When I criticize or appreciate some object or another, I
look for its good points and its bad points. In reading
any ~~printing~~ or written matter, I always have a pencil in   65.   printed
hand and put any comments in the book or on a separate
piece of paper. In other words, I ~~never~~ talk back to the   66.   always
writer.

The sort of critical reading may well be called
~~creation~~ reading because I am thinking along with the   67.   creative
writer, asking him questions, seeing ~~that~~ he answers the   68.   whether
questions and how well he answers them. I mark the
good passages to ~~restore~~ them in my memory and ask   69.   store
myself about every other part and about the complete
piece of writing: — where, how and why could or should
I improve upon ~~them~~?   70.   it

You might think that doing what I suggested is
work. Yes, it is, ~~and~~ the work is a pleasure because I   71.   but
can feel my brain expanding, my emotion reacting and
my way of living changing.

Part VI   Translation

72. no smoking be allowed in public places
73. his assistant will be in charge
74. Those who constantly expose themselves to new ideas
75. Unless the workers' demands are met
76. lest (or: for fear that) they (should) get lost in the heavy mist

Practice Test 8

Part I   Writing

(For reference)

ENTHUSIASM FOR SPORTS

Modern sports are becoming more spectator-oriented than participant-oriented. Just think of millions and millions of people who spend countless hours before TV sets watching sports of all sorts: Olympic Games, World Series Games and the World Cup Soccer Games. According to a survey, sports have the greatest number of viewers (78%) among various televised events. When an important football match is televised live, the streets of a big city are often left deserted. Even if it makes spectators dog-tired the next day, they can not tear themselves away from the screen. They are eager to know for sure the final scores. "True, the scores will be available in the morning paper," says a football fan, "but that's not the same thing: what's going on here!"

A passion for sports takes possession of thousands of people who go to stadiums, watch games on TV or listen to broadcasts. One of the primary causes perhaps is that sports can provide alternative outlets for emotions and alternative sources of satisfaction. Modern science and technology has reduced most of work and life to a routine. There is no variety, nor challenge, nor risk. Everything is predictable and controllable. Among the activities through which people seek release from their colorless existence or pent-up emotions, sports offer the purest form of escape and healthiest outlet. Sports can obliterate awareness of everyday reality, discharge the tensions of a day at work, satisfy the starved need for free fantasy and aggressive urge, and lift one to a moment of intense excitement and exhilaration.

Enthusiasm for sports also reflects the public "feeling." For most people it represents a common background, a shared interest. It has a binding power that transcends social classes and political views. Strangers may share nothing in the way of religion, education and politics, but the shared interest in sports is strong enough for them to get along and even become friends. Sports give people the opportunity to become a part of a community. Just because of the nature of sport itself and of human beings, sports can always incite in them a passionate enthusiasm.

Part II   Reading Comprehension (Skimming and Scanning)

1. NG   2. N   3. Y   4. N
5. the "rough handling" of the explosives by the black sailors
6. refused to resume loading ammunition
7. with a charge of mutiny (or: to be charged with mutiny)
8. 15 years in prison
9. Navy on trial for its whole vicious policy toward African-Americans
10. support the issuance of a Port Chicago stamp by the U.S. Postal Service

Part III   Listening Comprehension

Section A

11. A   12. C   13. D   14. A   15. D
16. D   17. B   18. D   19. A   20. C
21. B   22. C   23. C   24. A   25. B

Section B

26. B   27. A   28. C   29. A   30. A
31. C   32. B   33. C   34. D   35. A

Section C

36. sexuality   37. luxury   38. appeal   39. exposed
40. expenditures   41. gross   42. passed   43. delivering
44. mass production and consumption make low TV price possible
45. Advertisements help to turn new trends and fashions into mass culture
46. Advertisements, in fact, exert great influence on our behavior, social beliefs and values

Part IV   Reading Comprehension (Reading in Depth)

Section A

47. The different opinions concerning the hacker phenomenon.
48. their strong desire to control the computer
49. better insight into the future than other people

50. To seek a unique answer of their own（Or：To get a specific response in their own way）.

51. perhaps the hacker phenomenon is not bad at all

Section B

52. A   53. B   54. D   55. B   56. C

57. B   58. A   59. A   60. A   61. D

Part V   Error Correction

A good way to get information for essays and reports is to interview people who are experts ~~in~~ your topic or whose opinions may be interesting. Interviews are also a good way to get a sampling of people's opinions on various questions. Here are some suggestions that will help you make ^ most of a planned interview：

62. ____on____

63. ____the____

1. If the person to be interviewed（the interviewee）is busy, ~~cancel~~ an appointment in advance.

64. ____make____

2. Prepare your questions before the interview so that you make best use of your time. In preparing, think about the topic about what the ~~interviewer~~ is likely to know.

65. ____interviewee____

3. Use your questions, but don't insist ~~in~~ sticking to them or proceeding in the order you have listed. Often the interviewee will have important information that ~~was~~ never occurred to you, or one question may suggest another very useful one.

66. ____on____

67. ____/____

4. If you don't understand something the interviewee has said, say ^ politely and ask him or her to clarify it or to give an example.

68. ____so____

5. Take notes. If the interviewee goes too ~~slowly~~ for you, ask him or her to stop for a moment, especially if the point is important. A tape recorder lets you avoid this problem. ~~Therefore~~, be sure the

69. ____fast____

70. ____However____

interviewee agrees to be taped.

6. As soon as possible after the interview, read over your notes. They may need ~~clarified~~ while the topic   71.   _clarifying_ is still fresh in your mind.

Part VI   Translation

72. when a problem popped up
73. is not as simple as it appears
74. If I had messed (it) up
75. Owing to the basic conflict of interest between them
76. When it comes to music

Practice Test 9

Part I   Writing

(For reference)

TO BE A BUSINESSMAN OR TO BE A TEACHER

In recent years college graduates have been flooding the job market, expecting to find a position in joint ventures, foreign-funded firms or big banks even at the expense of their specialties. Although many high schools and colleges are wringing their hands over the lack of teaching staff, very few graduates are willing to take a teaching job. Even those who graduate from teachers' colleges would refuse to give thought to it. According to a recent study, there are 100 candidates competing for every vacancy in joint ventures, while there is only one applicant for a job at a high school where ten teachers may be needed.

Why do so many graduates gravitate into business instead of teaching? The ever-widening pay gap between these two professions is the obvious reason. A secretary or an office clerk in a joint venture earns 3 – 5 times as much as does a teacher, and if one is promoted to the position of a business executive or manager (which is most likely to be the case in a couple of years in a firm or company, if he or she is really smart and intelligent), the salary may jump even higher. It is no wonder that college graduates are attracted into more lucrative fields.

As a matter of fact, college students in general have a strong desire as much for success as for comforts a decent income could provide. Working in a foreign-funded enterprise, college graduates, young and capable, tend to have easy access to actualizing their own uniqueness. Freed from bureaucracy and nepotism, they are able and eager to participate in charting the course of their own future. While experiencing the reality of their own by knowing themselves and being themselves, they can enjoy extra happiness and satisfaction by expressing their full range of abilities and talents.

It is quite obvious that the pursuit of a spiritual as well as material well-being is the main reason for college graduates' preference for business over teaching.

Part II　Reading Comprehension (Skimming and Scanning)

1. Y　　2. NG　　3. N　　4. NG
5. have liked to buy a car that "doesn't go"
6. much loss of its sales
7. camellias are traditionally used for funerals in many South America countries
8. four is a very unlucky number and the word for the number four also means death
9. "back-translation"
10. consumers interpret advertising in terms of their own cultures

Part III　Listening Comprehension

Section A

11. C　　12. B　　13. D　　14. D　　15. D
16. C　　17. C　　18. A　　19. C　　20. B
21. C　　22. D　　23. A　　24. C　　25. A

Section B

26. B　　27. A　　28. C　　29. D　　30. D
31. D　　32. C　　33. C　　34. B　　35. D

Section C

36. colonies　　37. medium　　　38. craved　　　39. enslaved
40. horrors　　41. addictive　　42. vanish　　　　43. eventually

44. Many of us know smoking cigarettes might lead to cancer, heart disease, strokes, and some other diseases

45. in spite of the efforts to prohibit young kids from smoking, the number of teenage smokers increased by 73 percent from 1988 to 1996

46. We are sharing with people in other countries the worst part of American history

Part IV　Reading Comprehension (Reading in Depth)
Section A

47. (It refers to) Unexpected, valuable by-products from scientific research projects.

48. improved the quality of people's life on earth

49. physiological function

50. Describing examples of space technology adapted for use in medicine.

51. Examples of equipment and procedures adapted for industrial use.

Section B

52. C	53. B	54. C	55. D	56. A
57. D	58. B	59. C	60. D	61. A

Part V　Error Correction

Look at your watch for just one minute. During that short period of time, the population of the world ~~had~~ increased by eighty-five people. Perhaps you think that isn't much. In the next hour, more than 5,000 additional people will be living on this planet. So it goes, hour after hour. In one day, there are about 120,000 additional mouths to feed. Multiply this by 365. What will happen ~~after~~ 100 years?

This population ~~explosive~~ may be the greatest challenge of the present time. Within the next forty years, the world population may double. Can the new frontiers of science meet the needs of the crowded world of tomorrow?

62. ＿＿＿＿＿

63. ＿＿＿in＿＿＿

64. ＿explosion＿

If the present rate of population increase continues for the next 600 or 700 years, there will be standing ~~rooms~~ only. Each will have between 3 to 10 square feet of space in which to live. This ~~contains~~ the mountaintops, deserts, and the ice and snow fields of the polar areas. Of course, no one expects such a thing to happen. War, plague, famine or some other catastrophe can be expected to occur long ~~when~~ the population reaches this point. Actually, the danger is ^ in an overcrowded world where people are huddled together so that they cannot move arms and legs, but in an upset balance between population and resources.

65.   room
66.   includes

67.   before
68.   not

Since 600 years is so far away, take a look directly ahead. How can the hungry people be ~~filled~~? About half of the babies born this year will not have enough to eat. Is the world ~~going~~ out of water? Will there be enough fuel? What will supply the energy ~~need~~ to run the machine of tomorrow's world? Certainly, man must look to the future and find new ways of providing for his needs.

69.   fed

70.   running
71.   needed

Part VI   Translation

72. to keep on good terms with colleagues
73. only to find her out
74. Certainly not
75. has been degraded to a lower position for negligence of duty
76. all my efforts were to no avail

Practice Test 10

Part I   Writing

(For reference)

JOB PROBLEMS FOR COLLEGE GRADUATES

Each year thousands upon thousands of graduates flood into the job market, waving their college diplomas and certificates, expecting better jobs in their specialized fields, only to be frustrated and disappointed. According to the charts, only 35 per cent of graduates in 2006 could find jobs related to their majors, compared with 89 per cent in 1981 when China had its first college graduates after the Cultural Revolution. Why do college graduates find it increasingly difficult to get a satisfactory and rewarding job?

One reason perhaps is that many colleges and universities fail to gear their curricula to the development of industries. Degree courses offered in many colleges and universities are so outdated and irrelevant and impractical that employers as well as students themselves find it hard to translate their book knowledge into real job skills. No employers want to know about their mind-broadening and horizon-widening qualities, and few are willing to spend time and budget training raw recruits.

Secondly, there is an oversupply of graduates with a certain specialty, and this oversupply is increasing. Already there is an overabundance of lawyers, executive secretaries, sales engineers and other specialists. Yet colleges and graduate schools continue every year to turn out more graduates of these specialties to compete for jobs that aren't there. The result is that many of them cannot enter the professions for which they are trained and have to take other jobs which even do not require a college degree.

On the other hand, there is tremendous need for teachers, research workers and public officials. But the disparity in pay between intellectual work and business management has frustrated the hope and ambition of graduates who major in education, administration and liberal arts.

College graduates are, so to speak, valuable resources in our country and no one has the right to waste the wealth of talent. The problems they encounter in job hunting deserve more attention from the colleges and the government. The colleges should get students out of the ivory tower and gear their courses to the real needs of industry and business; while the government should provide college graduates with more vocational opportunities, better working conditions and decent salaries so that more and more graduates would like to devote their life to academic studies and scientific research.

Part II Reading Comprehension (Skimming and Scanning)

1. Y   2. NG   3. NG   4. N

5. a strong personal relationship

6. its generally accepted form

7. business complications and social embarrassment

8. first names are seldom used

9. Germany/Belgium/the United Kingdom

10. the added chance of misunderstanding resulting from cultural differences

Part III Listening Comprehension

Section A

11. A   12. C   13. A   14. B   15. B

16. D   17. D   18. C   19. C   20. B

21. B   22. D   23. B   24. D   25. D

Section B

26. B   27. D   28. D   29. B   30. C

31. D   32. C   33. B   34. A   35. A

Section C

36. reduced   37. awake   38. accounting   39. coined

40. accumulated   41. monetary   42. tendency   43. workweek

44. you would owe yourself a sleep debt of ten hours

45. by the fifth day your brain would be as sleepy as if you had stayed up all night

46. But for most people it is difficult to sleep that long because of the function of our biological clock

Part IV Reading Comprehension (Reading in Depth)

Section A

47. "readily adaptable to meet the particular needs of individual readers"

48. To illustrate that many technological changes will occur in communications.

49. Remarkably accurate.

50. It is central to economical development，directly linked with power.

51. an ever-quickening technological explosion (or: a technological explosion gaining snowball-like momentum)

Section B

52. B   53. B   54. C   55. D   56. A
57. A   58. C   59. B   60. C   61. D

Part V   Error Correction

Old age in the United States presents many problems and opportunities. ~~With~~ the result of improved medical services, people live longer than they used to. This increase in longevity creates a wide range of social needs that didn't exist when the average life expectancy was ~~higher~~. The medical specialty of gerontology (老年医学) has opened research areas and careers related to the elderly.

Because of changes in the family structure from extended to nuclear, the elderly ~~has~~ to create existences apart from basically small family units. This situation is complicated by the fact ^ many of their friends may have died and their children may have moved away.

The elderly person must set up a new life. Often, the elderly must rely on a fixed income — Social Security and pensions — and gradually ~~diminished~~ savings. While some live with their children, many more live by ~~themself~~, with a friend, or in a nursing home.

~~Moreover~~, the increasing proportion of elderly people has given them a new political power. They have formed organizations such as the Grey Panthers to voice their own need and concerns ~~over~~ local , state, and federal agencies. Lobbying (国会院外游说活动) for such issues as increased Social Security benefits, better ~~healthy~~ care, income tax benefits, and rent controls

62. ____As____

63. ____lower____

64. ____have____

65. ____that____

66. __diminishing__

67. __themselves__

68. __However__

69. ____to____

70. ____health____

247

have brought to the public an increased awareness of the 71. _____has_____ determination of the elderly to assert their ability to deal effectively with their own lives.

Part VI Translation

72. got herself involved in as many extra-curricular activities as possible
73. It has dawned on the rich lady
74. sense the author's deep sympathy with the victims
75. To my mind，he is not much of a scientist
76. why technological and economic progress has done so little good to most American families

Appendix II

Tape Scripts For Listening Comprehension

Practice Test 1

Section A

Directions: *In this section, you will hear 8 short conversations and 2 long conversations. At the end of each conversation, one or more questions will be asked about what was said. Both the conversation and the questions will be spoken only once. After each question there will be a pause. During the pause, you must read the four choices marked A), B), C) and D), and decide which is the best answer. Then mark the corresponding letter on **Answer Sheet 2** with a single line through the centre.*

Now, let's begin with the eight short conversations.

11. W: I'm sorry you failed the physics course, Todd.
    M: Let's face it. I'm just not cut out to be a scientist.
    Q: What do we learn about Todd?

12. W: I certainly would like to buy the brown suit I saw in the department store, but don't have enough money.
    M: Well, if you would budget your money more carefully, you would be able to buy it.
    Q: How does the man feel about the woman?

13. W: If we hurry we can take the express train and save an hour, couldn't we?
    M: Yes. The express takes only three hours to get to New York.
    Q: How long does it take the local train to get to New York?

14. W: Tom, there is something wrong with my bike. Will you please fix it for me now?
    M: Sorry. I've got my hands full.
    Q: What's Tom's problem?

15. M: Would you go to the tennis court with me if it doesn't rain?

W：No. It's very hot outside and I burn easily.

Q：Why won't the woman go to the tennis court?

16. W：I don't know what the problem is. You'd better give me the works.

M：Okay. I'll change the oil and check the brake.

Q：Whom is she talking to?

17. M：Isn't that the umbrella I lent you last week?

W：I'm afraid I'm very bad at returning things.

Q：What describes the woman's emotion?

18. M：You've been here three years. Have you had much of a chance to travel?

W：Not much. Last year I planned to go to Yellow Stone Park in December, but I had to postpone the trip. Then a few months later, I finally made it there.

Q：When did the woman go to Yellow Stone Park?

Now you'll hear two long conversations.
Conversation One

M：Well, now, Mrs. Davis, do you have any questions about your job?

W：Yes, I do, really. I'm a bit worried about this word processing.

M：There is no need to worry about it. Your application form says that you can type pretty fast. We'll give you training on the word processor. In fact it is just an advanced typewriter. And it has a memory so that you don't have to type a regular letter again and again. You'll get used to it, I can assure you. The training just takes a few weeks. And you'll find that it's easier to check and correct mistakes than on a normal typewriter.

W：Oh, that sounds good. Em, how about this computer? I'm not sure about that either. Actually, I'm a computer illiterate.

M：Well, we'll give you training on that as well. But that comes later — after you've worked with the word processor. Again, it's very much like a typewriter. You'll be using it to get information from its memory. Really it's just like a large filing cabinet that there is no paper involved. You type out the reference number or the subject and the information appears on a television screen.

W: Oh, that doesn't sound too difficult. How long would the training for that take?

M: Probably a couple of months. We hope you can do that part-time during your working hours.

W: Hm. That sounds fine. So that first bit of training would be with the word processor.

M: Yes, that's about aright. Exact details can be worked out later, of course.

Questions 19 to 21 are based on the conversation you have just heard.

19. What is the woman worried about?

20. What is not mentioned about the word processor?

21. How would the woman be trained?

Conversation Two

M: Doctor Brook, I just don't know what's wrong with me. I always feel tired and rundown. My wife finally persuaded me to visit you to find out what the trouble is.

W: Looking at your case history I see that you had pneumonia four years ago and that you also had a minor operation last year. Did you have any long aftereffects?

M: Well, I don't remember so ...

W: For instance, how long did you stay at home each time?

M: Just a couple of days. But about six months ago I was home for about two weeks with a cold or something.

W: Did you see a doctor at that time or did you just stay home?

M: No, I didn't see a doctor. The symptoms were about the same as this time. When I began to feel better, I returned to work.

W: And when did you start feeling so tired again?

M: It must have been about ten days ago. When I came home from work one night there just didn't seem to be any reason to go back the next day.

W: Well, it sounds as if your problem may be the kind of work you do. The tests I just made don't show anything really wrong. But I would like to make some further tests in the hospital.

M：That's fine with me.

W：All right，you can check in tonight and I'll make the tests tomorrow morning.

Questions 22 to 25 are based on the conversation you have just heard.

22. Why is the patient seeing the doctor?

23. How long did the man stay home after he had pneumonia?

24. When did the man return to work the last time he was sick?

25. What does the doctor suggest this time?

Section B

Directions: *In this section, you will hear 3 short passages. At the end of each passage, you will hear some questions. Both the passage and the questions will be spoken only once. After you hear a question, you must choose the best answer from the four choices marked A), B), C) and D). Then mark the corresponding letter on **Answer Sheet 2** with a single line through the centre.*

Passage One

After two decades of growing student enrollments and economic prosperity, business schools in the United States have started to face harder times. Only Harvard's MBA Schools has shown a substantial increase in enrollment in recent years. Both Princeton and Stanford have seen decrease in their enrollments. Since 1990, the number of people receiving Masters in Business Administration（MBA）degrees has dropped about 3 percent to 75,000, and the trend of lower enrollment rates is expected to continue.

There are two factors causing this decrease in students seeking an MBA degree. The first one is that many graduates of four-year colleges are finding that an MBA does not guarantee a satisfactory job on Wall Street or in other major financial districts of major American cities. Many of the entry-level management jobs are going to students graduating with Master of Arts degrees in English and the humanities as well as those holding MBA degrees. Students have asked the question, "Is an MBA degree really what I need to be best prepared for getting a good job?" The second major factor has been the cutting of American payrolls and the lower numbers of entry-level jobs being offered. Business needs a changing, and schools are struggling to meet the new demands.

Questions 26 to 28 are based on the passage you have just heard.

26. What is the passage mainly talking about?
27. Which of the following business schools has NOT shown a decrease in enrollment?
28. What are two causes of declining business school enrollments?

Passage Two

Ever since Philo T. Farnsworth assembled the first television set in his Indiana garage in 1927, the basic technological principles for bringing electronic pictures into the home have remained the same. There have been only two major changes in the way TV sets work: the introduction of color in 1954, and the shift from tubes to transistors in the 1970s.

Now a radical change is about to take place. Digital television — which uses a different method of signal transmission — will significantly alter the way future television sets will look and perform.

The digital set, already on sale in Europe and scheduled to be introduced in the United States this fall, is a cross between a computer terminal and a TV set. Although the differences it will bring may not be dramatic, its improved quality will be increasingly appreciated, as zoom effects, stereo sound, and freeze-frame views of live shows become commonplace. Digital TV promises to give viewers a clearer, more consistent picture than has been available so far.

Questions 29 to 31 are based on the passage you have just heard.

29. When was the first color TV introduced?
30. What effect will digital TV sets have?
31. Which of the following is NOT true?

Passage Three

A person's social prestige seems to be determined mainly by his or her job. Occupations are valued in terms of the incomes associated with them, although other factors can also be relevant — particular the amount of education a given occupation requires and the degree of control over others it provides. The holders of political power also tend to have high prestige.

Unlike power and wealth, which do not seem to be becoming more equally shared, the symbols of prestige have become available to an increasing number of Americans. The main reason is the radical change in the nature of jobs over the course of this century. In 1900 nearly 40 percent of the labor force were farm workers and less than 20 percent held white-collar jobs. At the beginning of the 1980s, however, less than 5 percent of the labor force worked on farms and white-collar workers were the largest single occupational category. Blue-collar workers, the largest category in the mid-fifties, now constitute less than a third of all workers. The increase in the proportion of high-prestige jobs has allowed a much greater number of Americans to enjoy these statuses and the life-styles that go with them.

Questions 32 to 35 are based on the passage you have just heard.

32. Which is the least important factor relevant to a person's social status?

33. Which is the main factor for the rise in the proportion of high-prestige jobs?

34. What are a growing number of Americans becoming?

35. Who made up the largest occupational category in 1900?

Section C

Directions: *In this section, you will hear a passage three times. When the passage is read for the first time, you should listen carefully for its general idea. When the passage is read for the second time, you are required to fill in the blanks numbered from 36 to 43 with the exact words you have just heard. For blanks numbered from 44 to 46 you are required to fill in the missing information. For these blanks, you can either use the exact words you have just heard or write down the main points in your own words. Finally, when the passage is read for the third time, you should check what you have written.*

Around the world young people are spending (36) **unbelievable** sums of money to listen to rock music. *Forbes Magazine* (37) **claims** that at least fifty rock stars have (38) **incomes** of between two million and six million dollars (39) **per** year.

"It doesn't make sense," says Johnny Mathis, one of the (40) **older** music millionaires, who made a million dollars a year when he was most popular, in the 1950s. "Performers aren't (41) **worth** this kind of money. In fact, nobody is."

But the rock stars' admirers seem to (42) **disagree**. Those who love rock music spend about two billion dollars a year for records. They pay 150 million to see rock stars in person.

Some (43) **observers** think the customers are buying more than music. According to one theory, (44) **rock music has a special appeal because no real training is needed to produce it**. There is no gulf between the audience and the performer. Every boy and girl in the audience thinks, "I could sing like that." (45) **So rock has become a new kind of religion, a new form of worship**. Young people are glad to pay to worship a rock star because it is a way of worshipping themselves.

Luck is a key word for explaining the success of many. In 1972 one of the luckiest was Don McLean, who wrote and sang "American Pie." McLean earned more than a million dollars from recordings of "American Pie." Then, too, (46) **like most performers, McLean writes his own music, so he earns an additional two cents on every single record of the song**.

Practice Test 2

Section A

Directions: *In this section, you will hear 8 short conversations and 2 long conversations. At the end of each conversation, one or more questions will be asked about what was said. Both the conversation and the questions will be spoken only once. After each question there will be a pause. During the pause, you must read the four choices marked A), B), C) and D), and decide which is the best answer. Then mark the corresponding letter on Answer Sheet 2 with a single line through the centre.*

Now, let's begin with the eight short conversations.

11. M: Hello. This is Tom Davis. I have an appointment with Mrs. Jones for nine o'clock this morning, but I'm afraid I'll have to be about fifteen minutes late.

    W: That's alright, Mr. Davis. She doesn't have another appointment scheduled until ten o'clock.

    Q: When will Mr. Davis most probably meet with Mrs. Jones?

12. M: Don't worry about the meter ma'am. It's broken. I'll charge you a flat five dollars for the ride.

    W: If the traffic is this bad everyday, it's worth twice as much.

    Q: What's the man's occupation?

13. W: It's so hot today I can't work. I wish there were a fan in the library.

    M: So do I. I'll fall asleep if I don't get out of this stuffy room soon.

    Q: What are these people complaining about?

14. W: I just made up a quart of orange juice this morning, and now I can't find it anywhere. Did you know what happened to it?

    M: Did you hear a crash earlier? That was it. I'm just as clumsy as ever.

    Q: What is the problem?

15. M: Janet's quite enthusiastic about camping, isn't she?

    W: Yes, she often goes for weeks at a time.

    Q: What does the woman say about Janet?

16. W: May I please have a roll of twenty exposure Kodacolor II?

    M: Certainly. Here you are. I think you'll find that your shots will be just as good outdoors as in with a flash, of course.

    Q: Where are they?

17. W: There are so many children at the school. I wonder how the teacher keeps track of them.

    M: I used to get cold feet at the thought of teaching a class of 50.

    Q: What was the man's attitude toward teaching?

18. M: The Student Club is planning a Chinese Speech Competition during

the Chinese New Year. How about getting some help from the school authority?

W: Good. That will get the ball rolling.

Q: What does the woman mean?

Now you'll hear two long conversations.

Conversation One

W: Hello.

M: Hi, Sarah, this is Mike.

W: Great to hear from you Mike! How have you been doing these days?

M: To tell you the truth, I'm very worried about our final examinations next month. For one thing, I'm suffering from insomnia. I can't fall asleep, even after I've swallowed some sleeping pills.

W: I sympathize! I went through the same thing last year.

M: That's exactly why I'm calling you. Do you have any suggestions for coping with anxiety? You know how I hate exams!

W: Well, take a walk or have a shower before you go to sleep.

M: I have tried. All seems to be of no use.

W: OK. I know, last year the university offered a stress-management course at about this time. Have you been in contact with the student health services?

M: No, I have always been pressed for time!

W: Funny, isn't it? Just when students need help most, we can't afford the time to get it!

M: Well, perhaps I should find out more about this stress-management course. Things have got to get better!

W: I suggest you call the health services tomorrow. They open at nine a.m.

M: Thanks, Sarah. I'll let you know how it goes.

W: Best of luck! And have a good night's sleep!

M: That's easier said than done! Thank you just the same.

Questions 19 to 21 are based on the conversation you have just heard.

19. Why is Mike worried?

20. Why does Mike turn to Sarah for advice?

21. Why has Mike not contacted the student health services?

Conversation Two

W: This is Frida and this is her husband — Diego Rivera. She can't have fallen in love with him for his look. I reckon he must have been either very rich or very intelligent.

M: Actually, he was both highly intelligent and very rich. At first, Frida's father was against her marrying Diego because he was from an infamous family. But later on he agreed to it because he couldn't pay his daughter's medical expenses any more. Frida must have spent a fortune on doctors and operations over the years.

W: Oh, yes, what a terrible life — first polio and then that awful accident. It's amazing she produced so many paintings, isn't it?

M: Yes, she must have been an incredibly brave woman.

W: But the marriage didn't work out too well, did it?

M: Well, it had its ups and downs.

W: She painted this one with the cropped hair while they were separated, didn't she?

M: Yes, that's right.

W: She really looked like a man here. In fact, she looked as if she's got a moustache! And why was she dressed in a man's suit? I thought it might have had something to do with women's liberation. You know — she cut off her hair to symbolize equality or something.

M: Er, no — the reason she cut off her hair and put on a man's suit is because Diego Rivera loved her long hair, and also loved the traditional women's Mexican dresses she used to wear. She did it to hurt him.

Questions 22 to 25 are based on the conversation you have just heard.

22. What was Frida?
23. Why did Frida's father approve of her marriage to Diego?
24. Why did Frida put on a man's suit?
25. Which of the following inferences can be made about Frida?

Section B

Directions: *In this section, you will hear 3 short passages. At the end of each passage, you will hear some questions. Both the passage and the questions* will be spoken only once. After you hear a question, you must choose the best answer from the four choices marked A), B), C) and D). Then mark the corresponding letter on **Answer Sheet 2** with a single line through the centre.

Passage One

The World Social Forum met for the first time at the end of last month in Porto Alegre, Brazil. The World Social Forum is a new international conference that will meet every year. Its goal is to create and exchange social and economic projects. The projects will support human rights, social justice and development that does not waste natural resources.

Most of the representatives at the recent World Social Forum oppose globalization. They do not agree with the economic theory of a worldwide economy. Some people attending the forum wanted to end the movement toward a global economy. Others wanted to reform it.

Activists at the World Social Forum say globalization policies have caused a greater inequality between the poorest and the richest people in the world. The Forum met to find ways to support economic policies based on the needs of poor people and the environment.

United Nations studies show that the poorest 20% of the world's people have lost half of their share of the world's income since 1960. Their share dropped from 2.4% to 1.1%. During the same years, income increased for the richest twenty percent of the population. The rich people increased their share of world income from 69% to 86%.

Questions 26 to 28 are based on the passage you have just heard.

26. What is the purpose of the World Social Forum?
27. Why do most representatives at the conference oppose globalization?
28. According to United Nations studies, how much have the richest people increased their share of world income since 1960?

Passage Two

What happens when a merchant displays an item in his store window with a price tag on it? Must the merchant sell the item if the money is offered? It is a fact of law that a display of goods in a store window is not an offer to sell those goods, which can be accepted by a customer saying he will buy them. Instead, the display is known as an invitation by the merchant to receive offers from potential customers. The customer makes the offer to buy and the merchant may accept that offer. Then the goods are sold. But the merchant need not accept the offer, and without such acceptance, the customer cannot obtain the goods or sue the merchant for not letting him have them.

Unless the seller accepts the offer by taking cash from the customer, the seller is allowed to change his mind. The merchant may want to take back the goods because they have been displayed by mistake or had the wrong price written on them, and he or she would have the legal right to do this.

Questions 29 to 31 are based on the passage you have just heard.

29. Where is the price tag put?

30. When can goods be sold?

31. Can the seller have his goods back if they have the wrong price written on them?

Passage Three

Ladies and gentlemen, welcome aboard your Scenic Cruiser Bus to Saint Louis, Memphis, and New Orleans with changes in Saint Louis for Kansas City and points west.

This coach is scheduled to arrive in Saint Louis at eight o'clock. You will have a fifteen minute rest stop at Bloomington at three o'clock and a half-hour dinner stop at Springfield at five-thirty.

Passengers on this Coach are scheduled to arrive in Memphis at seven o'clock tomorrow morning and in New Orleans at five o'clock tomorrow afternoon. Please don't forget the number of your coach when re-boarding. That number is four-one-eight.

Let me remind you that federal regulations prohibit smoking cigarettes or cigars anywhere in the coach.

This coach is restroom-equipped for your comfort and convenience. Please watch your step when moving about in the coach. Relax and enjoy your trip, and thank you for traveling Scenic Cruiser Bus Lines.

Questions 32 to 35 are based on the passage you have just heard.

32. When will the bus arrive in Saint Louis?
33. Where will the passengers change buses to Kansas City?
34. When will the dinner be over?
35. What is the federal regulation with regard to smoking?

Section C
Directions: *In this section, you will hear a passage three times. When the passage is read for the first time, you should listen carefully for its general idea. When the passage is read for the second time, you are required to fill in the blanks numbered from 36 to 43 with the exact words you have just heard. For blanks numbered from 44 to 46 you are required to fill in the missing information. For these blanks, you can either use the exact words you have just heard or write down the main points in your own words. Finally, when the passage is read for the third time, you should check what you have written.*

A growing number of scientists insist that answers to the world's problems will not come from a (36) **flashier** array of electronics and machines. Instead, as they see it, solutions must (37) **evolve** from a better understanding of the humans that drive the system and from a fuller (38) **appreciation** of the limits and potential of the earth's resources.

What this means is an increased (39) **emphasis** on the life and earth sciences, on sociology, psychology, economics and even philosophy.

More and more of the best minds in science, particularly young researchers, are being drawn into these (40) **developing** fields.

Industry officials are concerned by a (41) **declining** rate of innovation in technology. Patent applications by Americans have been (42) **dropping** in the U. S. since 1971. Yet many scientists seem to be saying: The need for better televisions, bigger power plants and faster airplanes — markers of rapid-fire technological creativity — is becoming (43) **marginal** at best. (44) **The market in the industrialized nations for this kind of technology is reaching a saturation point**.

All this is not to say that technological creativity will not play a critical role in solving energy and food shortages, or that (45) **answers to environmental** difficulties will not come from further advances in the same technologies that may have helped cause the problems.

Where the real challenge lies is (46) **in finding ways to produce goods to meet the world's needs, using less of the raw materials that are becoming scarce**.

Practice Test 3

Section A

Directions: *In this section, you will hear 8 short conversations and 2 long conversations. At the end of each conversation, one or more questions will be asked about what was said. Both the conversation and the questions will be spoken only once. After each question, there will be a pause. During the pause, you must read the four choices marked A), B), C) and D), and decide which is the best answer. Then mark the corresponding letter on* **Answer Sheet 2** *with a single line through the center.*

Now, let's begin with the eight short conversations.

11. M: Now, what seems to be the trouble, Mrs. Stephens?
    W: I've been very dizzy lately, and last night I had some chest pain.
    Q: What's the probable relationship between the two speakers?

12. W: Was Robert elected to the committee?
    M: Yes, in fact he was made chairman but he only agreed to take the job if they'll let him make all the decisions himself.
    Q: What does Robert intend to do?

13. W: Have Chris and Sally left for school yet? It's a quarter to nine now.
    M: Sally left at 8:15 a.m., and Chris hurried off twenty minutes later.
    Q: What time did Chris leave home?

14. M: Frank is always complaining about his job.
    W: Maybe if you tried waiting on tables, you'd see what it's like.
    Q: What does the woman mean?

15. M: I'd love to dance, but I don't know the steps.
    W: It doesn't matter; no one will be looking at us in this crowd.
    Q: What does the woman mean?

16. M: Does the boss check up on you often?

    W: Indeed she does. It seems as though she's in here three or four times an hour, although I'm sure it's not that often.

    Q: What does the boss do?

17. M: Was the movie as good as you expected?

    W: It's hard to say. I only saw the tail end of the film.

    Q: What does the woman mean?

18. W: I'd like to leave this prescription to be filled please.

    M: Certainly Mrs. Brown. By the way Mr. Brown telephoned a few minutes ago. He wanted me to remind you to buy toothpaste, soap and some cough medicine.

    Q: Where did this conversation most probably take place?

Now you'll hear two long conversations.

Conversation One

W: I think there should be greater restrictions placed on the press and the stories they print. I can't open a newspaper or magazine without reading stories full of false information about myself or people I know. It's getting ...

M: Sorry, but I can't believe that you're actually complaining about free publicity. I mean I remember, Shelley, before you were famous, you were begging us to write features about you ... anything ...

W: If you would just let me finish — of course the press have been important. I'm an actress and I understand the power of the press. But the thing is, I rarely seem to read anything true about myself these days ... The point I'm trying to make here is that famous people have families with feelings.

M: Oh, sorry. You're really hurt by that particular article last week.

W: To increase circulation and make more money, certain newspapers continue to print those stories when it's obvious that they're not true.

M: But I think we have to consider the relationship between fame, the public and the press. The public are fascinated by fame and scandal, and they love to read about their favorite stars.

W: I'm sick of gutter-press making up stories. It's irresponsible and it messes up people's life.

M: The problem is, it's not always clear what's true and what isn't. I mean, if a newspaper prints something scandalous or embarrassing about a famous person, they're bound to deny it, but that doesn't mean it's not true.

W: Are you trying to say ...

M: No smoke without fire, if you ask me.

Questions 19 to 21 are based on the conversation you have just heard.

19. What is the probable relationship between the two speakers?
20. What does the woman think of the press?
21. What does the man suggest at the end of conversation?

Conversation Two

W: Mark really needs to see this article in *Psychology Weekly*.

M: Why? What's it on?

W: Reasons for negative behavior patterns — like habitual lateness ...

M: You're right. That's Mark. He's never on time. So what does it say?

W: That people who are always late often do it for a reason — either conscious or unconscious. It could be an expression of anger and resentment — or a way of resisting authority. It could even be anxiety.

M: Well, I don't know. In Mark's case, I think it's because he wants to be noticed.

W: That's the next reason in the article — the need for attention. They give the example of movie stars who used to make these grand entrances.

M: That's not really Mark's style though — he's so quiet.

W: What gets me is that he's late for his friends all the time — but not for other things, like work.

M: Well ... but they might deduct pay for that.

W: Exactly. You know, sometimes I'm tempted to tell him to come at, say, seven, and everybody else at 7:15. Then maybe we wouldn't have to wait so long.

M: We have to try something. You know, he confessed to me one day that he was even late for his sister's wedding. She was really angry.

W: I remember that. He was in the wedding — so they couldn't start until he got there.

M: Maybe you should slip that magazine under his door. And hope he gets the message.

Questions 22 to 25 are based on the conversation you have just heard.

22. What is the main subject of the magazine article?
23. What do Mark's friends think is the reason for his problem?
24. What do the speakers say about Mark's recent behavior?
25. What solution does the woman consider?

Section B

Directions: *In this section, you will hear 3 short passages. At the end of each passage, you will hear some questions. Both the passage and the questions will be spoken only once. After you hear a question, you must choose the best answer from the four choices marked A), B), C) and D). Then mark the corresponding letter on **Answer Sheet 2** with a single line through the centre.*

Passage One

I knew it wouldn't be long before they discovered my escape from the boat house where they had locked me up, but now I had no choice except to go on. I stumbled up the path which rose steeply to the top of the cliff. Once there, I stopped for a moment to get my breath back, looking out as I did so across the sea. I could see the steamer which came across once a week from the mainland making its way towards the harbour. From where I stood, it looked like a toy or model someone had built. I began waving my arms in the air, then I removed my jacket and used that too to attract attention. But it all seemed hopeless as the steamer sailed steadily on towards the mouth of the harbour. I began to shout, in a last desperate attempt to stop her, and when my throat was quite dry, and my arms aching from the effort I had made, then at the last moment the miracle happened. The steamer began to slow up, and then to move in, away from the harbour and what awaited her there.

Questions 26 to 28 are based on the passage you have just heard.

26. Where did the story take place?
27. Why did the speaker feel hopeless?
28. What happened in the end of the story?

Passage Two

A good way to see the USA is by car. Americans love their automobiles and in the past fifty years they have developed a vast network of roads and freeways to help them reach their destinations. As few visitors have their own cars, renting one is the next best thing. You will need a valid driver's license and either international credit cards, or a deposit.

You should start out with a working knowledge of the road. Regulations vary from state to state and this can be very confusing to a newcomer. For example, in some states it is legal to turn right at a red light if there is no approaching traffic, while in other states you will be fined for this action. Throughout the country it is forbidden to pass a school bus when it has stopped to let off children.

The size of the country may startle you at first and you may be surprised at the spectacular physical beauty. When the first pioneers began to expand west into the wildness, the natural resources of the land seemed inexhaustible. Nearly 1,000 million acres of land was covered by virgin forest. Much of this was burnt off for farmland and it soon became apparent that the government would have to take action or the natural beauty of the land would be lost forever.

Questions 29 to 32 are based on the passage you have just heard.

29. What is not needed for a visitor to rent a car?
30. What is forbidden when one is driving in America?
31. What may startle you at first when you're traveling in America by car?
32. Why would the government have to take some actions?

Passage Three

Hong Kong is a city inclined toward red; in Thailand the color is yellow; India leans toward reds and oranges. To an Asian colors are infused with beliefs, religious and otherwise. To the Chinese, red is very lucky, but to Thais yellow brings good fortune. The combination of blue, black, and white is, to the Chinese, suggestive of a funeral.

Many Western businessmen believe that most Asians have become Westernized in their outlook, but Westernization and education do not usually completely replace the culture and beliefs of an Asian's forefathers. They tend instead to make a more intricate alliance between his culture and religious bonds. The approach required to sell an Asian any commodity must follow the basic formula of catering to national pride, acknowledging equality, and understanding the Asian's beliefs.

Color is a touchy thing. Advertisers are advised to take into consideration the religious and superstitious beliefs connected with colors before using them. The color combinations of green and purple are acceptable throughout Asia, but using one or both of these colors is no guarantee of sales, as a prominent manufacturer of water-recreation products learned in Malaysia. Its home office received heated requests from its Malaysian distributors to stop shipments on all products colored green. The distributors reported that numerous customers associated the color green with the jungle and illness.

Questions 33 to 35 are based on the passage you have just heard.

33. What does the speaker emphasize in his talk?
34. What color do the Thais think may bring good luck?
35. What did Malaysians associate the green color with?

Section C

Directions: *In this section, you will hear a passage three times. When the passage is read for the first time, you should listen carefully for its general idea. When the passage is read for the second time, you are required to fill in the blanks numbered from 36 to 43 with the exact words you have just heard. For blanks numbered from 44 to 46 you are required to fill in the missing information. For these blanks, you can either use the exact words you have just heard or write down the main points in your own words. Finally, when the passage is read for the third time, you should check what you have written.*

London is the center of the international art market and Sotheby's, which has its (36) **headquarters** there, is the world's biggest and oldest seller of art and antiques. If you were lucky enough to own a priceless "Old Master", an Impressionist, or a (37) **valuable** antique, and you wanted to sell it, you would probably put it up for auction at Sotheby's.

Sotheby's auctions are (38) **attended** by some of the world's richest people, who spend millions of pounds on art and antiques each year. (39) **Consequently**, the company is very proud of its status and its 250-year-old (40) **reputation**. But, earlier this year, that reputation came under threat, when a journalist (41) **accused** Sotheby's staff of bringing art treasures to London illegally. If these (42) **allegations** are true, they will severely damage London's (43) **credibility** as a center of the world's art trade.

As if that were not bad enough, (44) **London's art dealers and auction houses are facing an even bigger threat** from European Union regulations. If passed in Britain, the EU laws would make London a much less attractive place to purchase art treasures. Buyers and sellers would then look elsewhere for the best prices and could stop coming to London altogether.

The problems began last year, (45) **when a journalist from Britain's Times newspaper, Peter Watson, claimed that senior staff at Sotheby's were at the center of a widespread smuggling operation**. He made his allegations in a book and television program, which used hidden camera to film Sotheby's staff. Watson says (46) **the program, which was shown last February, proves that art treasures were being illegally exported to London on a regular basis**, and that the international art trade needs to be cleaned up.

Practice Test 4

Section A

Directions: *In this section, you will hear 8 short conversations and 2 long conversations. At the end of each conversation, one or more questions will be asked about what was said. Both the conversation and the questions will be spoken only once. After each question there will be a pause. During the pause, you must read the four choices marked A), B), C) and D), and decide which is the best answer. Then mark the corresponding letter on Answer Sheet 2 with a single line through the centre.*

Now, let's begin with the eight short conversations.

11. M: The front tire is flat, and the seat needs to be raised.

W: Why not take it to Mr. Smith?

Q: What kind of work does Mr. Smith probably do?

12. W: How do you like your new tenant who moved to your apartment last Monday?

M: Well, she is a nice lady, though I'm having a hard time getting used to her.

Q: What's the man's problem?

13. M: What would you do if you heard a strange noise in the middle of the night?

W: I'd lie awake a little while, waiting to see if it happened again. And if it did, I'd get up.

Q: How would you describe the woman?

14. W: My husband isn't very athletic. But he is an excellent cook, and he can sew, iron ... He is a good husband.

M: Really? That's interesting. Is he English?

Q: What does the man mean?

15. W: Peter must have been joking when he said that he was going to quit his job.

M: Don't be too sure. He told me that he was trying to sell his house.

Q: What does the man think of Peter?

16. M: Is it raining out?

W: Is it raining? Look at my clothes: they're soaked.

Q: What does the woman mean?

17. W: After I've finished reading this book, I can lend it to you if you are interested.

M: If I'm interested! I've been trying to borrow it everywhere.

Q: What does the man mean?

18. M: Have you called John to come and fix the faucet in our bathroom?

W: I called several times but his phone was out of order.

Q: What can we learn from the conversation?

Now you'll hear two long conversations.

Conversation One

M: What's Neil going to do when he leaves school?

W: Until a few months ago he was going to go to university, but he's changed his mind. Now he reckons he's going to make it in the pop world.

M: And how do you parents feel about that?

W: We think he's making an enormous mistake.

M: But surely he can go back to his studies if his music career fails.

W: That's true, but once he gets a taste of freedom, he'll find it more difficult to go back to college. I just think it's such a waste — in three years' time, he'll have got his degree and he'll still be young enough to try out the music business. At least if it doesn't work out he'll have a qualification behind him.

M: Have you discussed this with him?

W: Of course, but he's made up his mind. We're just hoping that he'll get out of his system and then come to his sense and go back to his studies. When I left school I didn't go on to university, and I've regretted it ever since. I just don't want him to make the same mistake as I did.

M: Will you support him while he's trying to be a pop singer?

W: You mean financially? No. He won't be living at home, and we can't afford to pay for him to live in London, so it's up to him to make it work.

Questions 19 to 21 are based on the conversation you have just heard.

19. What is Neil going to do after his graduation from high school?
20. What do the parents hope Neil to do?
21. Why do the parents strongly oppose Neil's decision?

Conversation Two

W: So what are the two main times of the day that you watch TV?

M: Well, a little around breakfast time and then it tends to be really late — eleven or even midnight — when I've finished work.

W: And what sort of programs do you go for?

M: Some news bulletins but I also really like to put my feet up with some of the old comedy shows.

W: Fine. And turning to the new channel ... which type of programs would you like to see more of?

M: Well, I certainly don't think we need any more factual programs like news and documentaries. I think we need more about things like local information ... you know, providing a service for the community. And in the same vein, perhaps more for younger viewers ... you know, good quality stuff.

W: Ah ha. And if you had to give the new directors some specific advice when they set up the channel, what advice would you give them?

M: I think I'd advice them to pay more attention to the quality of the actual broadcast, you know, the sound system. They ought to do lots more of these kinds of interview, you know, talking with their potential customers.

W: Oh, I'm glad you think it's valuable!

M: Certainly ... yeah.

W: Good. Ok, this will be a commercial channel of course, but how often do you think it is tolerable to have adverts?

M: Well out of that list I'd say every quarter of an hour. I don't think we can complain about that, as long as they don't last for ten minutes each time!

W: Quite. And ... would you be willing to attend any of our special promotions for the new channel?

M: Yes, I'd be very happy to, as long as they're held here in my area.

W: Thank you very much for your time.

Questions 22 to 25 are based in the conversation you have just heard.

22. What kind of programs would the man like to see on the new channel?
23. What advice would the man give about the new channel?
24. How often does the man think advertisements should occur on the new channel?
25. Under what circumstances would the man like to attend the special promotions for the new channel?

Section B

Directions: *In this section, you will hear 3 short passages. At the end of each* *passage, you will hear some questions. Both the passage and the questions will be spoken only once. After you hear a question, you must choose the best answer from the four choices marked A), B), C) and D). Then mark the corresponding letter on **Answer Sheet 2** with a single line through the centre.*

Passage One

The Internet computer system is helping many people start and operate businesses. But to use the Internet, a person has to learn how to use a computer. A person also needs a telephone line or satellite connection. However, about half the world's population has never even made a telephone call. And most poor people do not own a computer. For these people a "digital divide" exists.

Two meetings were held in the United States to discuss what can be done. One was called the "Digital Dividends Conference." It was held in Seattle, Washington. Officials from large American information technology companies attended. Representatives from non-governmental organizations also attended.

These people are working to make it easier for poor people to use the Internet. The head of Microsoft, Bill Gates, spoke at the meeting. Mr. Gates has given hundreds of millions of dollars to help people in developing countries fight diseases like malaria and AIDS. He said that people have to be healthy before they can use computers and the Internet.

Another conference was held at the World Bank headquarters in Washington, D. C. It was called "Voices of the Poor." It was supported by the British Department for International Development. About 100 people from different organizations attended. They learned that many organizations around the world are using computers and the Internet to help reduce the digital divide.

Questions 26 to 28 are based on the passage you have just heard.

26. What does the term "digital divide" mean?
27. What does Bill Gates think in that regard?
28. What do we learn from the conference "Voices of the Poor"?

Passage Two

During World War II, Great Britain and the United States tried to deal with the problem of an international agreement on money. The two countries tried to set up a formal system which everyone would use to exchange money between countries. The system they set up is usually called the Bretton Woods System. The system got this name from the town in New Hampshire in the United States where the international agreement was signed. The Bretton Woods agreement was signed in 1944. When it was signed, it seemed to be a good system.

The Bretton Woods agreement had two main parts. The first part concerned exchange rates. All of the countries that signed the agreement promised to regulate their exchange rates. The countries promised not to change their exchange rates too often. This was a very important part of the agreement. It helped to stabilize the international finance system. The second part of the Bretton Woods agreement concerned a currency fund. The fund was supposed to help countries that needed currency. All the countries contributed some of their currency to the fund. They could borrow the necessary currency from the fund. This helped all of the member countries to do business with each other. This second part of the agreement was called the International Monetary Fund (IMF).

Questions 29 to 31 are based on the passage you have just heard.

29. How did the Bretton Woods System get its name?
30. What did countries that signed the agreement promise to do?
31. Who contributed money to the International Monetary Fund?

Passage Three

Captain Joseph Mackey's airplane was flying over the ocean on its way to Great Britain when engine trouble started. He turned back and made a crash-landing at night in the deep snow of Newfoundland. All the men in the plane were killed except Captain Mackey, who was badly hurt.

Captain Mackey waited all the next morning for an airplane to come in search of him. In the afternoon he set out to find help. He went about a mile but found that he was too weak to go on through the snow. Half walking and half crawling, he made his way back to the plane.

The second day many planes passed above him, but none of the pilots saw him. The third day Captain Mackey heard a plane coming nearer and nearer, flying very slowly. It flew right over him and passed on. Then he gave up hope of being found. In a few minutes the plane returned, and the pilot dipped one wing to get a clearer view.

The pilot came down closer for a better look, and then he saw Captain Mackey waving his arms. The pilot quickly climbed higher and sent a radio message. In a short time a plane came and dropped a sleeping bag, food, medicine, and tools for Captain Mackey.

Questions 32 to 35 are based on the passage you have just heard.

32. What made Captain Mackey turn back?
33. Where did the plane crash?
34. How many men were either hurt or killed?
35. How long did Captain Mackey wait before an airplane found him?

Section C

Directions: *In this section, you will hear a passage three times. When the passage is read for the first time, you should listen carefully for its general idea. When the passage is read for the second time, you are required to fill in the blanks numbered from 36 to 43 with the exact words you have just heard. For blanks numbered from 44 to 46 you are required to fill in the missing information. For these blanks, you can either use the exact words you have just heard or write down the main points in your own words. Finally, when the passage is read for the third time, you should check what you have written.*

In the medical profession, technology is advancing so fast that questions of law and ethics cannot be discussed and answered fast enough. Most of these questions (36) **involve** ending or beginning a human life. For example, we have the medical ability to keep a person (37) **technically** "alive" for years, on machines, after he or she is "brain dead". But is it ethical to do this? And what about the (38) **alternative**? In other words, is it (39) **ethical** *not* to keep a person alive if we have the technology to do so?

And there are also many ethical questions involving the (40) **conception** of a human baby. External fertilization, for example, is becoming more and more common. By this method, couples who have difficulty (41) **conceiving** a child may still become parents. At a cost between $70,000 and $75,000 for the (42) **delivery** of one such baby, should society have to pay for this especially when there are many (43) **orphaned** children who need parents? (44) **A fertilized human egg might be frozen for a long time before it is implanted in the mother's body**; is this fertilized egg a human being? If the parents get a divorce, to whom do these frozen eggs belong? And there is the question of surrogate mothers. There have been several cases of a woman (45) **who is paid to carry the baby of another woman who is medically unable to do so**. After delivering the baby, the surrogate mother sometimes changes her mind and wants to keep the baby. Whose baby is it? (46) **Is it the surrogate's because she gave birth? Or is it the biological parents'?**

Practice Test 5

Section A

Directions: *In this section, you will hear 8 short conversations and 2 long conversations. At the end of each conversation, one or more questions will be asked about what was said. Both the conversation and the questions will be spoken only once. After each question there will be a pause. During the pause, you must read the four choices marked A), B), C) and D), and decide which is the best answer. Then mark the corresponding letter on **Answer Sheet 2** with a single line through the centre.*

Now, let's begin with the eight short conversations.

11. W: Help me with this stack of books, will you, Jack?
    M: Help you! Do you think I work here?
    Q: What does Jack mean?

12. W: Do you think we should invite Peter over for dinner?
    M: His mother's here for a visit.
    Q: What does the man mean?

13. M: Let's have a festival at the beginning of the school year to raise some

money for the club.

W: Good. That will get the ball rolling.

Q: What does the woman mean?

14. W: May I make a recommendation, Sir? The clams with our special sauce are good. They are fresh from the Ocean.

M: Thank you, but I don't care for shellfish.

Q: Where did this conversation probably take place?

15. W: You didn't say anything at yesterday's meeting. Don't you think it was a success?

M: I was really fascinated by what every speaker said.

Q: Why didn't the man say anything at the meeting?

16. W: Cathy seemed to be quite satisfied with the results of her exams.

M: Satisfied? She could hardly contain herself.

Q: How did Cathy feel about her exams?

17. M: We've worked long enough for a Saturday afternoon.

W: OK. Let's call it a day.

Q: What did the woman mean?

18. M: I'd like to take a trip to Florida for my spring vacation. Can you give me any ideas on where to go?

W: I could tell you about the places I've visited, but I think you'd better get a professional to make your arrangements.

Q: What advice did the woman give the man?

Now you'll hear two long conversations.

Conversation One

M: Hey, Christine, remember how we were complaining that we wanted to see the drama series but couldn't afford the tickets? I've found a solution.

W: Yeah? Won the lottery, huh?

M: Huh-uh. But, seriously, I did find a way for us to see all the plays — and we don't have to pay a cent.

W: Come on, Jim. That's impossible.

M: No, really, we can. I called Stanhope Theater to ask if they had student discounts. They didn't, but they did have another suggestion.

W: What's that?

M: The man there told me they just lost four of their ushers so they have openings.

W: Really?

M: Yeah. You don't get paid, but you do get to stand in the back and watch the play after you've helped everyone find their seats. No seat, but a good view. Then during intermission you help sell refreshments.

W: But Jim, each play is performed on six nights. Can we make that big a commitment?

M: We don't have to. That's the best part. They have enough ushers so that each person works only two nights at the same play.

W: I never imagined we'd be able to see the whole series. Let's take a look at the schedule right now.

Questions 19 to 21 are based on the conversation you have just heard.

19. Why did Christine and Jim think they would not be able to see the drama series?

20. What did Jim learn when he called the theater?

21. At the end of their conversation, how does Christine feel about Jim's solution?

Conversation Two

W: Professor Wilson, can you spare me a few minutes?

M: That's OK. Actually, I'm on my way to an appointment with students, so please make this quick.

W: My name is Maria Taylor, and I'm in your Psychology class at 2:00.

M: Oh, yes. I recall now. You always ask good questions about the lectures. What can I do for you now?

W: You say in your lecture last week that IQ changes little from childhood, but the skills of emotional intelligence can be learned at any age.

M: Right, it's not easy, however. You know, growing your emotional intelligence takes practice and commitment and improving your emotional intelligence takes time, say, several months.

W: Why do you say improving an emotional intelligence takes months rather than days?

M: Well, you know, the emotional centers of the brain are involved.

W: The emotional centers of the brain?

M: Yes. The thinking brain learns technical skills and purely cognitive abilities. It gains knowledge very quickly, but the emotional brain does not.

W: Why?

M: Because to master a new behavior, the emotional centers need repetition and practice.

W: So it takes time.

M: Yes. Improving your emotional intelligence, then, is similar to changing your habits. You have to change your old habits and replace them with the new ones.

W: Oh, I see. And another question I want to ask you is: can we say emotional intelligence is the opposite of IQ?

M: No. You know some people are blessed with a lot of both while some with little of either. What we are doing now is trying to find out how they complement each other.

Questions 22 to 25 are based on the conversation you have just heard.

22. Who are the speakers?

23. What did the man say in his last lecture?

24. How long does it take to improve one's emotional intelligence?

25. What are the man and his colleagues trying to find out?

Section B

Directions: *In this section, you will hear 3 short passages. At the end of each passage, you will hear some questions. Both the passage and the questions will be spoken only once. After you hear a question, you must choose the best answer from the four choices marked A), B), C) and D). Then mark the corresponding letter on **Answer Sheet 2** with a single line through the centre.*

Passage One

Many Americans are moving to big cities. At the same time, many

Americans are leaving the cities and looking for the "good life" in the country. Although they think they know what they want, they don't always find it.

Unless you know something about small-town life, you may be in for some big surprise. There are not so many job opportunities there. People are not always happy about having newcomers move in. They like to keep things the way they are. And although there is usually a movie theater and a couple of restaurants, there isn't a lot to do at night.

But if you're looking for a more relaxed way of life, if you want to save money, and if you can make your own good times, small-town life may be for you. Before you decide whether or not to leave the city, spend a couple of weeks in a village. Look around and talk to people. Think what it would be like to live there fifty two weeks a year. And then, if you're sure, you can make the big move.

Questions 26 to 28 are based on the passage you have just heard.

26. Why are many Americans leaving cities for the country?
27. Which is NOT true about small-town life?
28. What should one do before making the big move?

Passage Two

The estimated one-fifth of children in London's schools who cannot read simple sentences by the age of eight should be given special help. This is the main conclusion of an independent report on London's 700 primary schools. The report, which is the result of a year's work, tells London's primary schools that they must demand more of their children.

Most parents were happy with the schools, but some said that their children's pace of learning might be too slow. The report confirmed this by stating that much of the new work must have been taught at the same level of difficulty as the old.

The report emphasized that children should not be tortured but more should have been expected of them in schools. This would mean that some children might have achieved much more than the limited demands made on them by comprehension exercises or copying out from textbooks.

Mrs. Morrel, who commissioned the report, said that all London's schools must put into effect a framework of reform. Every child ought to be able to read by the age of eight.

Other reforms mentioned in the report were that parents should be better represented on school governing committees and that each school ought to draw up a development plan, listing what improvements it can make. Parents should also be represented on the education committee.

Questions 29 to 31 are based on the passage you have just heard.

29. What should primary schools do according to the report?
30. What should eight-year-old children be able to do?
31. What did Mrs. Morrel do?

Passage Three

During the past decade, there has been a multifold increase in violent crimes throughout the world. Not only has there been a frightening increase of murders and rapes, but chances of being attacked and robbed have grown so that the elderly avoid leaving their apartments.

The exact cause of this horrifying development has not been found. Some sociologists feel that the growth of crime on TV is related with the growth of violence on our streets. Others blame the constant threat of complete destruction from nuclear explosives. If the world is going to be blown up, why not enjoy yourself fully!

Regardless of the cause or causes, a fundamental change in attitude among people is easy to see. Years back, the old saying "Practice what you preach" was a prevalent one. People had moral standards that they could follow: people were concerned about their fellow human beings.

Today, people have become "I-centered." They are more interested in achieving immediate, selfish pleasures. The best advice they can give in the rare instances when they do is "Do what I say, not what I do." They are saying, "There are moral principles to follow if you want to, but don't use me as a guide since I no longer follow them."

The major difference that I see in the quotations points out the tragic change in our morality and social ways. Until people once more learn to replace "I" with "we," we shall continue to move toward destructive self-centeredness.

Questions 32 to 35 are based on the passage you have just heard.

32. What has increased greatly in the past decade?
33. What does the speaker think is the cause or causes for this frightening development?
34. What changes have taken place in people's morality?
35. Which of the following is most suitable to describe the author's attitude?

Section C

Directions: *In this section, you will hear a passage three times. When the passage is read for the first time, you should listen carefully for its general idea. When the passage is read for the second time, you are required to fill in the blanks numbered from 36 to 43 with the exact words you have just heard. For blanks numbered from 44 to 46 you are required to fill in the missing information. For these blanks, you can either use the exact words you have just heard or write down the main points in your own words. Finally, when the passage is read for the third time, you should check what you have written.*

As heart disease continues to be number-one killer in the United States, researchers have become increasingly interested in (36) **identifying** the potential risk factors that (37) **trigger** heart attacks. High-fat diets and "life in the fast lane" have long been known to contribute to the high (38) **incidence** of heart failure. But according to new studies, the list of risk factors may be (39) **significantly** longer and quite surprising.

Heart failure, for example, appears to have seasonal and (40) **temporal** patterns. A higher percentage of heart attacks occur in cold weather, and more people experience heart failure on Monday than on any other day of the week. In addition, people are more (41) **susceptible** to heart attacks in the first few hours after waking. Cardiologists first observed this morning (42) **phenomenon** in the mid-1980s and have since discovered a number of possible causes. An early-morning rise in blood pressure, heart rate, and concentration of heart (43) **stimulating** hormones, plus a reduction of blood flow to the heart, (44) **may all contribute to the higher incidence of heart attacks between the hours of 8:00 a.m. and 10:00 a.m.**

In other studies, both birthdays and bachelorhood have been implicated as risk factors.

Statistics reveal that (45) **heart attack rates increase significantly for both females and males in the few days immediately preceding and following their birthdays**. And unmarried men are more at risk for heart attacks than their married counterparts. (46) **Though stress is thought to be linked in some way to all of the aforementioned risk factors, intense research continues in the hope of further comprehending why and how heart failure is triggered.**

Practice Test 6

Section A

Directions: *In this section, you will hear 8 short conversations and 2 long conversations. At the end of each conversation, one or more questions will be asked about what was said. Both the conversation and the questions will be spoken only once. After each question there will be a pause. During the pause, you must read the four choices marked A), B), C) and D), and decide which is the best answer. Then mark the corresponding letter on Answer Sheet 2 with a single line through the centre.*

Now, let's begin with the eight short conversations.

11. M: It's always so hot and humid in here.
    W: That's because there are so many plants and windows.
    Q: Where did this conversation most likely take place?

12. W: I had such a bad start in the last race; it was hard to catch up. All I could see was the backs of the others' heads.
    M: We'll work on your start. The most important thing is concentration.
    Q: What is the probable relationship between these two people?

13. W: I love the beach when the sand is fine and the water is just barely making waves.

M: I prefer an angry sea. That makes me feel better whenever I'm sad.

Q: What does the man like?

14. M: If you'd like to take the package with you, Miss, it won't take long to wrap.

W: There's no rush. Could you please have it delivered this week?

Q: What does the woman mean?

15. M: I heard that the newspaper gave that book a terrible review.

W: It depends on which newspaper.

Q: What does the woman mean?

16. M: Aren't there any direct flights?

W: I'm sorry. Your best bet would be at nine a. m. departure on United flight twelve arriving in Chicago at eleven a. m., with five-hour wait for your connecting flight to Los Angeles.

Q: What time will the man leave Chicago?

17. W: John, can you help me? I couldn't work out this math problem.

M: I'm sorry. You can hardly expect me to do that.

Q: What does the man mean?

18. W: How long can I keep these out?

M: Two weeks. After that you will be fined for every day they are overdue.

Q: Where does the conversation take place?

Now you'll hear two long conversations.
Conversation One

W: Hi Tim! How are you?

M: Fine, thank you.

W: I'd been wondering when I'd run into you. Have you been here long?

M: I arrived yesterday, on Sunday. How about you?

W: I got here a few days ago, on Saturday. No — wait a minute, what's today? — Sorry Friday, not Saturday.

M: But we didn't have to be here till today.

W: Yes, I know, but I wanted to get my things moved into my room, and just take a look around. So, did you decide to do English in the end?

M: No, I changed my mind and opted for history instead. And you're doing biology, if I remember correctly.

W: Yes, although to start with I couldn't decide between that and geography.

M: How much reading have you got? I was given an amazingly long list of books to read. See!

W: Wow, it does look pretty long.

M: Well, I counted 57. I could hardly believe it! What's your list like?

W: Well, it's not as long as yours, but there are 43 altogether. I don't know how I'm going to get through them all.

M: Well you don't have to read them all this week! You just have to stay ahead of the lectures and seminars. Have you got your class schedule yet?

W: Yep. It came with the reading list. When's your first lecture?

M: Tuesday. How about you?

W: The day after. It's my busiest day; I've got two lectures in the morning and one in the afternoon.

Questions 19 to 22 are based on the conversation you have just heard.

19. When did Tim arrive at school?
20. What major has Tim decided on?
21. When will Jane have her first lecture?
22. What suggestion does Tim make for the reading assignments?

Conversation Two

M: Ow! That hurts!

W: What happened? Did you cut yourself?

M: Yes — on the edge of this paper. How can such a little cut hurt so much? I'm not even bleeding, but my finger really hurts.

W: You know, I read something about that. It turns out that a little cut on a finger can hurt a lot more than a big cut somewhere else.

M: Why? That doesn't make any sense.

W: Actually, it does. There are more nerve endings in your hands than almost anywhere else in the body, and it's the nerve endings that allow you to feel pain.

M: I guess that's true.

W: Also, a little cut like yours won't damage the nerve endings, just irritate them. If they were damaged, you would feel less pain, but the wound could be more serious.

M: So I suppose I should be happy my finger hurts so much?

W: Right. Now go get yourself a bandage.

M: Why? You just told me it's not serious.

W: It's not, but it does seem to be bothering you. Putting a bandage over the cut will keep the skin from drying and will help keep the skin together. If the skin stays together, the nerve endings won't be exposed, and the cut will hurt less.

Questions 23 to 25 are based on the conversation you have just heard.

23. How did the man cut himself?

24. According to the woman, what caused the pain when the man cut himself?

25. What advice does the woman give the man?

Section B

Directions: *In this section, you will hear 3 short passages. At the end of each passage, you will hear some questions. Both the passage and the questions will be spoken only once. After you hear a question, you must choose the best answer from the four choices marked A), B), C) and D). Then mark the corresponding letter on* **Answer Sheet 2** *with a single line through the centre.*

Passage One

Dangerous occupations tend to be exciting and well paid. They often involve foreign travel or meeting famous and interesting people. Here is a look at someone who likes his dangerous occupation in spite of the danger, and at why he does it.

Gilbert Michael Pitts is a freelance cameraman. He does a lot of his work underwater. Michael has been diving since he was about nine years old. He says that he was on holiday with his parents and a friend had a snorkel. He tried it and "that was it — ever since I first put my head under water I've been fascinated by diving." Later on he went on a four month commercial diving course. His commercial diving career included underwater photography — stills and video (to inspect oil rigs), underwater burning, planting explosives and connecting pipelines.

"I'm not frightened or apprehensive," he says, "because it's a medium I've been working in for such a long time. It's something that I love. I am frightened of certain things, but they certainly don't include diving in water. I think it's a matter of experience and just being at ease in that environment."

Questions 26 to 29 are based on the passage you have just heard.

26. What is Gilbert Michael Pitts?
27. Which of the following statements is TRUE?
28. Which of the following is NOT included in a commercial diving career?
29. Why did Michael say he was not frightened?

Passage Two

Phone books have white, blue and yellow pages. The white pages list people with phones by last name. The blue pages contain numbers of city services, government services, and public schools. Businesses and professional services are listed in a special classified directory — the Yellow Pages.

The area covered by one area code may be small or large. For example, New York City has one area code, but so does the whole state of Oregon. There is an area code map of the U. S. and Canada in the front of the white pages.

Pay phones have numbers in the U. S. This means you can arrange to call a friend at a phone booth. Or if you are making a long distance call and run out of money, give the number on your phone to the person you're talking to. Then hang up the receiver and they can call you back.

If you make a long-distance call and get a wrong number, call the operator and explain what happened. This means that you can make the call again to the right number without having to pay more money; or you can have the phone company mail you a credit coupon that has the same value as the phone call.

Questions 30 to 32 are based on the passage you have just heard.

30. What kind of phone numbers are listed in the blue pages?
31. What is the advantage for pay phones to have numbers?
32. Why should you let the operator know if you get a wrong number?

Passage Three

An advertisement says "Learn English in six weeks, or your money back". Of course, it never happens quite like that. As we know, no language is easy to learn except one's mother tongue. And think how much practice that gets. Before the Second World War people usually learned English in order to read English literature. Now most people want to speak English. Every year many millions of people start to learn English. How do they do it?

Some people try at home, with books and tapes, some use radio or television programmes, others go to school or attend evening classes. If they use English only two or three times a week, it will take a long time to learn it, like English learning at school. A few people try to learn English fast and study six or more hours a day. It is clearly easier to learn English in England, Canada, Australia or the United States. However, most people cannot afford this, and for many it is not necessary. They need English in order to do their work better. For example, most scientists and engineers chiefly need to be able to read books and reports in English. Whether English is learnt quickly or slowly; it is hard work. Good teachers, books and machines will help, but they cannot do the student's work for him.

Questions 33 to 35 are based on the passage you have just heard.

33. What does an advertisement say about English learning?
34. Why did most people learn English before World War II?
35. Which of the following is NOT true?

Section C

Directions: *In this section, you will hear a passage three times. When the passage is read for the first time, you should listen carefully for its general idea. When the passage is read for the second time, you are required to fill in the blanks numbered from 36 to 43 with the exact words you have just heard.*

For blanks numbered from 44 to 46 you are required to fill in the missing information. For these blanks, you can either use the exact words you have just heard or write down the main points in your own words. Finally, when the passage is read for the third time, you should check what you have written.

Some people cannot learn in ordinary schools. Often some physical or (36) **mental** handicap prevents a child from learning. In education today new methods are being used in special schools to help the handicapped learn.

(37) **Among** the many interesting schools for handicapped persons, there is one which is being (38) **established** in the southern part of New Jersey, U.S.A. It is called the Bancroft Community. Here handicapped young (39) **adults** will be trained to support themselves and to get along in the (40) **outside** world.

The Bancroft Community is not (41) **surrounded** by walls of any kind. Its director (42) **insists** that it be open so that students may gradually develop (43) **normal** relations with the rest of the world. Bancroft Community students (44) **will live in apartments or in a house, cooking their own meals, washing their own clothes, and learning to perform other tasks**. Gradually, as they become able, they will buy their own furniture, paying for it out of their own earnings. They will pay rent and pay for their food, too. (45) **They will learn to expect telephone bills for the calls they make every month**.

As a step toward the goal of becoming independent, each handicapped person will decide what kind of work he wants to be trained to do. (46) **While some of the training will be carried on within the Bancroft Community itself, most of the students will receive job training in nearby towns**. They will be trained by townspeople for whom they will work without pay.

Practice Test 7

Section A

Directions: *In this section, you will hear 8 short conversations and 2 long conversations. At the end of each conversation, one or more questions will be asked about what was said. Both the conversation and the questions will be spoken only once. After each question there will be a pause. During the* pause, you must read the four choices marked A), B), C) and D), and decide *which is the best answer. Then mark the corresponding letter on Answer Sheet 2 with a single line through the centre.*

Now, let's begin with the eight short conversations.

Section A

11. W: How many stamps do I need to send this package airmail?

    M: Well, that's going to be expensive. Airmail postage is 52 cents for the first ounce and 44 cents for each additional ounce. You have eleven ounce here.

    Q: How much will it cost the woman to mail her package?

12. M: This candy was cut into 6 squares.

    W: Let's cut them in half, so that each person can have one.

    Q: How many persons would have candy?

13. M: I've forgotten my passbook, but I'd like to make a deposit to my savings account if I may.

    W: No problem, just bring this receipt with you the next time you come in, along with your passbook, and we will adjust the balance.

    Q: Where does the conversation take place?

14. W: Let's get a snack when the baseball game is over.

    M: When it's over? I am dying of hunger now.

    Q: What does the man mean?

15. M: How about yesterday's lectures on American Folklore?

    W: They weren't at all boring.

    Q: What does the woman think of the lectures?

16. M: The bell will ring in two minutes, but I'd like to get something to drink before the lecture begins.

    W: Shall we take our seats now? You can get some later.

    Q: What does the woman suggest that they should do?

17. M: Dear, what shall we have for dinner today?

    W: Oh, I've run out of ideas for dinner menus.

Q：What does the woman mean?

18. M：Why not ask Tim to go skating with us in the mountain?

    W：He'd be the last person to do such a thing.

    Q：What can we know about Tim?

Now you'll hear two long conversations.

Conversation One

M：Hey, Karen. Looks like you got some sun this weekend.

W：Yeah, I guess so. I spent the weekend at the beach.

M：Oh, yeah? That's great! Where did you stay?

W：Some friends of my parents live out there and they invited me for as long as I wanted to stay.

M：So what are you doing back here already?

W：Oh, I have a paper I need to work on, and I just couldn't do any serious studying at the beach.

M：I don't blame you. So what did you do out there ... I mean besides lie out in the sun, obviously?

W：I jogged up and down the beach and I played some volleyball. You know, I never realized how hard it is to run on sand. I couldn't even get through a whole game before I had to sit down. It's much easier to run in the wet sand near the water.

M：Not to mention cooler. Did you go swimming?

W：I wanted to, but they said the water isn't warm enough for that until a couple of months from now, so I just waded in up to my knees.

M：It all sounds so relaxing. I wish I could get away to the beach like that.

W：It looks like you could use it. Don't tell me you spent the weekend in the library again.

Questions 19 to 21 are based on the conversation you have just heard.

19. How did the woman spend last weekend?

20. Why did the woman come home so soon?

21. Why didn't the woman go swimming?

Conversation Two

W: Excuse me. Do you live here?

M: Yes, I've lived here in Edinburgh all my life. My name's Rory McDonald. How do you do?

W: Hi, I'm Chris Hudson from Phoenix, Arizona. I'm an oil engineer. I'm on my way to London on business.

M: How long are you staying in Edinburgh?

W: Just a day. What can I see here in twenty-four hours?

M: Well, most tourists want to visit the Castle. It's on Castle Rock. It's where the Scottish government used to be. From there you can walk down the Royal Mile.

W: What's the Royal Mile?

M: It's a narrow street of medieval houses. It's worth seeing. Then you really should visit Holyrood Palace.

W: Who lives in the Palace?

M: No one, except the Queen when she comes to Edinburgh, which is usually once a year. But the kings and queens of Scotland used to live there before Scotland was united with England.

W: When was that?

M: That was … er, let me see … in 1603.

W: You seem to know a lot about Scottish history.

M: Aye, well, I'm a McDonald of the McDonald clan. You know there are clans in Scotland, and we're all proud of our history.

W: I'd like to buy something as a souvenir of the trip. What should I buy?

M: Why don't you buy some sweaters? Scottish sweaters are famous for their quality. And you must buy some whiskey. Of course you know that's our national drink.

W: Yes, I've already bought the whiskey.

M: Good. But remember you mustn't put ice in it. That spoils the flavor!

W: Oh, we Americans put ice in everything!

Questions 22 to 25 are based on the conversation you have just heard.

22. Why is the woman in Edinburgh?
23. Which of the following is not suggested to her?

24. What is the Royal Mile?
25. What does the man suggest she buy?

Section B

Directions: *In this section, you will hear 3 short passages. At the end of each passage, you will hear some questions. Both the passage and the questions will be spoken only once. After you hear a question, you must choose the best answer from the four choices marked A), B), C) and D). Then mark the corresponding letter on **Answer Sheet 2** with a single line through the centre.*

Passage One

Lyndon B. Johnson was the 8th Vice president of the United States to take the place of a President who died in office, and he was surely one of the most colorful.

Johnson came to Washington in 1930 as a congressional secretary, and he spent the next 38 years in the Nation's Capital. Despite all this time away from his native Texas, he never lost the speech or manners of his western, rural home. He told his close friends that his happiest times were when he was vacationing at his ranch in Johnson City, Texas, or walking along a dirty road. Much of his behavior seemed more suited for the ranch than for the more formal atmosphere of a cosmopolitan city.

Johnson kept two dogs at the White House, and he loved to play with them. Once when reporters and photographers asked to be allowed to take pictures of the President playing with his pets, Johnson surprised everyone by picking up one of the animals by its ears. People were shocked. The President of the United States was laughing while a 20-pound dog dangled by the tips of its ears.

Questions 26 to 28 are based on the passage you have just heard.

26. What was Johnson's job immediately before he became president?
27. When was Johnson's happiest time?
28. What did Johnson do when reporters asked to see him playing with his dog?

Passage Two

Many people suffer from some form of extreme anxiety. Some experience occasional attacks of panic for no apparent reason. Others go around in a state of continual uneasiness. The usual way of controlling anxiety is with drugs, which cure none of the conditions described but do help patients manage their anxiety. Patients who take these drugs say that they are able to work, to sleep, and to go to places they had feared to visit. But the effects of the drugs on the human body, especially on the nervous system, have been unknown.

We have started a series of studies to identify the effects of the drugs on the brain and have gained some insight into the costs and benefits of the anti-anxiety drugs. They are valuable because they can reduce the effects of anticipated failure, frustration, and disappointment. But their value demands a price. Two effects of the drugs are obviously harmful. They reduce a person's ability to react to changes in the environment; and more important, they keep a person from developing persistence in the face of unexpected troubles. Since it is fairly sure that people will meet problems they had not expected, this effect may make the price of anti-anxiety drugs too high.

Questions 29 to 31 are based on the passage you have just heard.

29. What is the function of anti-anxiety drugs?
30. Which of the following is the harmful effect that the drugs have on a person?
31. What is the author's attitude towards anti-anxiety drugs?

Passage Three

Every month thousands of tourists visit New York City. Their reasons for choosing New York are many. Some come to see historical places like the Statue of Liberty. Others are attracted by the night clubs and theaters. Many enjoy shopping in the world's largest stores, and some come to New York just because it's big.

People from other parts of the United States move to New York by the thousands each year. Some come to get better jobs. Others want to attend one of New York's fine universities. Dancers, actors, and painters are attracted by the city's rich cultural life. Still others are bored with small-town life and want the excitement of the big city.

Careful planning is needed to make your stay in New York City a success. Be sure that you don't arrive during the rush hour. Weekdays from 7:30 to 9:00 a. m. and 4:30 to 6:00 p. m. travel on the streets is slow and difficult. Choose a hotel that is near the center of the city. And be sure to bring plenty of money. It's no fun to see hundreds of exciting things and not have the money to do them.

Questions 32 to 35 are based on the passage you have just heard.

32. Which of the following might NOT be an attraction to tourists in New York City?

33. Why do so many Americans move to New York?

34. How many tourists come to New York?

35. When is the rush hour in New York City?

Section C

Directions: *In this section, you will hear a passage three times. When the passage is read for the first time, you should listen carefully for its general idea. When the passage is read for the second time, you are required to fill in the blanks numbered from 36 to 43 with the exact words you have just heard. For blanks numbered from 44 to 46 you are required to fill in the missing information. For these blanks, you can either use the exact words you have just heard or write down the main points in your own words. Finally, when the passage is read for the third time, you should check what you have written.*

The truth is that radio has not been eclipsed by television and cable and the Internet. In fact, radio is as (36) **popular** as it has ever been. According to the Consumer Electronics Manufacturers Association, 675 million radio receivers are (37) **currently** in use in the United States; on average, Americans over the age of eleven spend three hours and eighteen minutes of (38) **weekday** listening to at least one of them.

I don't mention this to make the (39) **case** that radio is "better" than other electronic media, but I will say that it is different, very different. Radio is special to people. And in an (40) **era** when we in the West have so many other media (41) **available** to us, media that can "do" so much more than radio ever could, radio still (42) **inspires** a kind of loyalty that (43) **premium** channels and Web sites cannot claim.

This loyalty is largely due to radio's very limitations. (44) **Radio can't dazzle us with visual spectacles; it has to capture and hold our attention aurally**. That is, it has to speak to us, through either words or music. Couple this with the fact that radio is a curiously intimate medium: people tend to feel that they are connecting with their radios one-on-one. This is generally not the case with television, (45) **where the individual viewer invariably senses that he or she is nothing more than an anonymous, statistically insignificant part of a huge and diverse audience**. But because radio is a "smaller" medium (many low-powered mom-and-pop operations, which were never part of television, still exist on radio), (46) **the individual listener can somehow believe that the signal is traveling direct and uninterrupted from the studio microphone to his set alone, that the announcer is speaking and playing records just for him**.

Practice Test 8

Section A

Directions: *In this section, you will hear 8 short conversations and 2 long conversations. At the end of each conversation, one or more questions will be asked about what was said. Both the conversation and the questions will be spoken only once. After each question there will be a pause. During the pause, you must read the four choices marked A), B), C) and D), and decide which is the best answer. Then mark the corresponding letter on **Answer Sheet 2** with a single line through the centre.*

Now, let's begin with the eight short conversations.

11. W: I wonder if you'd like to answer a few questions. We are doing a market survey.

    M: That depends. What sort of questions are they?

    Q: What is the probable relationship between the woman and the man?

12. M: I had a dream about parrots the other night. A whole flock of par-

rots was flying around as I was climbing up the streambed. It's rather worrying.

W: Would you describe that as a nightmare?

Q: What kind of dream did the man have?

13. W: Did you pack the car?

M: Yes, I put in our bathing suits, some towels, the suntan lotion, and our two library books.

Q: Where are they going?

14. W: If I were you I'd take the bus to work. Driving in that rush hour traffic is terrible.

M: But by the time the bus gets to my stop, there aren't any seats left.

Q: How does the man prefer to go to work?

15. M: I'll send John a postcard from San Francisco when I go there on holiday.

W: I'm sure that he'd be glad to get one. He has a collection of cards from all over the world.

Q: What do we learn about John?

16. M: The walkman I bought yesterday is just like yours, isn't it?

W: Almost. Mine is a little bit smaller, but it can't record. I'd rather have had one like yours.

Q: What does the woman mean?

17. M: I heard Helen's going to college. What's she studying?

W: She's taking courses in statistics, economics and accounting.

Q: What career does Helen probably plan to follow?

18. W: Rob, how is your driving class? You are learning to drive well, aren't you?

M: Slowly but surely.

Q: What does Rob mean?

Now you'll hear two long conversations.
Conversation One

M: You're back. And right on schedule too. How was your holiday?

W: It was all right, I suppose.

M: You don't sound as though you enjoyed it very much. Where did you go?

W: I went home. I stayed with my family.

M: Where is your home?

W: It's in West Virginia. It's a quite small village in West Virginia. You know, going home really made me think how different my life would have been if I'd stayed there.

M: Why? What would you have done?

W: Well, first of all, I probably would have married the boy I went steady with while I was in high school.

M: Would it have been a mistake if you had married him?

W: It would have been different, that's all. If I had married him, I probably would have stayed there in West Virginia for the rest of my life.

M: Would that have been so bad?

W: I would never have come to the city. I never would have tried to get a job.

M: But you've come to the city and had several jobs.

W: That's true. The thing is that after all these years of working, I am still a secretary or assistant to someone. No transfer. No promotion. It's so annoying and frustrating. I didn't come all the way up to the city for that, did I?

M: Do you think you'll ever go back to West Virginia to live?

W: Someday, maybe, but not until I've had more experience. I'd like to know that I could have real career if I wanted to.

M: Well, the first step in a successful career is to get some work done. Here are some letters that have to be answered right away.

W: All right, I'll take care of them. But you just wait. Someday I might be your boss!

Questions 19 to 21 are based on the conversation you have just heard.

19. According to the woman, what would have become of her had she married her boyfriend?

20. Why is the woman complaining now?

21. Who is the man?

Conversation Two

M: Excuse me.

W: Yes, can I help you?

M: Yes, uh ... I want to take an English course in September and I need some information.

W: Sure. Courses start on September 6th and finish right before Christmas on December 22nd. Um ... the advanced classes meet every Monday, Wednesday and Friday, from 6 to 8 in the evening, registration is one week before classes begin, so that's August 30th.

M: So there are no classes on Tuesday and Thursday?

W: No, not for advanced students. Only Monday, Wednesday and Friday.

M: And how much is the tuition for one course from September 6th to December 22nd?

W: It's 350 dollars. And if you want to continue in January, that will be another 350.

M: 350 dollars. Hmm. Could you tell me what's in the advanced courses?

W: Let me see. There's advanced grammar, American literature and conversation.

M: Is there any work on pronunciation?

W: No, not at this level.

M: How about writing? Is there anything on composition?

W: Yes, they do some writing, but most of the work is on grammar, literature and conversation.

M: I see. And just a few more questions. Do you have a language lab where I can work on my pronunciation? And what about videos and computers?

W: Well, we don't have a language lab. The building is too small. But we do have video and we also have tape recorders in every room.

M: And computers?

W: No, none at present.

M: I see. Well, thank you very much. You're very helpful.

W: You're welcome. Good-bye.

M：Good-bye.

Questions 22 to 25 are based on the conversation you have just heard.

22． When will the courses start?
23． Which of the following is not in the advanced courses?
24． When does the class meet?
25． What facility do they have?

Section B

Directions: *In this section, you will hear 3 short passages. At the end of each passage, you will hear some questions. Both the passage and the questions will be spoken only once. After you hear a question, you must choose the best answer from the four choices marked A)，B)，C) and D). Then mark the corresponding letter on **Answer Sheet 2** with a single line through the centre.*

Passage One

All through school we're taught to read, write, and speak — we're never taught to listen. But while listening may be the most undervalued of all the communication skills, good managers are likely to listen more than they speak. Perhaps that's why God gave us two ears and only one mouth.

Some of the most successful managers are also the best listeners. I remember one manager in particular. He had been hired by a large corporation to assume the role of sales manager. But he knew absolutely nothing about the specifics of the business. When salespeople would go to him for answers, there wasn't anything he could tell them — because he didn't know anything! Nonetheless, this man really knew how to listen. So no matter what they would ask him, he'd answer, "What do you think you ought to do?" They'd come up with the solution; he'd agree; and they'd leave satisfied. They thought he was fantastic.

He taught me this valuable listening technique, and I've been applying it ever since. Many of the problems I hear don't require me to offer solution. I solve most of them by just listening and letting the complaining party do the talking. If I listen long enough, the person will generally come up with an adequate solution.

Questions 26 to 28 are based on the passage you have just heard.

26. What does the speaker mean by saying "God gave us two ears and only one mouth"?

27. Why could the manager successfully play the role of sales manager at a large company?

28. What kind of person is the speaker?

Passage Two

Tests conducted at the University of Pennsylvania's Psychological Laboratory showed that anger is one of the most difficult emotions to detect from facial expression. Professor Dallas E. Buzby confronted 716 students with pictures of extremely angry persons, and asked them to identify the emotion from the facial expression. Only two percent made correct judgments. Anger was most frequently judged as "pleased." And a typical reaction of a student confronted with the picture of a man who was mad was to classify his expression as either "bewildered," "quizzical," or simply, "amazed." Other studies showed that it is extremely difficult to tell whether a man is angry or not just by looking at his face. The investigators found further that women are better at detecting anger from facial expression than men are. Paradoxically, they found that psychological training does not sharpen one's ability to judge a man's emotions by his expressions but appears actually to hinder it. For in the university tests, the more courses the subject had taken in psychology, the poorer judgment scores he turned in.

Questions 29 to 31 are based on the passage you have just heard.

29. What is the main idea of the passage?

30. How were students with psychological training doing in the test?

31. What would be the best thing to do to achieve the greatest success in detecting anger from the facial expression?

Passage Three

In preparing a book, I asked several successful executives to tell me what they thought students should study if they wanted to succeed in business. They listed only a few technical subjects — accounting and finance, for example.

But time and again, these executives identified philosophy as one of the most important areas you can study for learning how to think in a disciplined, analytical, and imaginative way.

The way that philosophy helps you see the world is no less real than its practical benefits to your career. Studying philosophy exposes you to a wide range of problems that you wouldn't meet otherwise. It simply lets you see more of the world. It stretches your imagination. It challenges you to come up with your own answers to tough issues that do not have ready-made solutions.

Studying philosophy helps you to develop insight into some of life's great puzzles and to fashion your own vision of what life is all about. As you go through life, you will be challenged all along the way to make decisions about who you are and what's important to you. Philosophy helps you develop a sense of what life is all about and where you're going.

In fact, Socrates, one of the first great philosophers, thought that philosophy is the single most important element in making our lives worthwhile. "The unexamined life," he said, "is not worth living." In Socrates' mind, at least, philosophy makes it possible for us to control our own destiny.

Questions 32 to 35 are based on the passage you have just heard.

32. What is most probably the speaker's profession?

33. According to some successful executives, what is a must for a college student if he or she wants to succeed in business?

34. Why does the speaker emphasize the importance of studying philosophy?

35. Who was Socrates?

Section C

Directions: *In this section, you will hear a passage three times. When the passage is read for the first time, you should listen carefully for its general idea. When the passage is read for the second time, you are required to fill in the blanks numbered from 36 to 43 with the exact words you have just heard. For blanks numbered from 44 to 46 you are required to fill in the missing information. For these blanks, you can either use the exact words you have just heard or write down the main points in your own words. Finally, when* *the passage is read for the third time, you should check what you have written.*

One of the basic ingredients of American popular culture is consumption, and it is the advertising industry that makes mass consumption possible. Advertising sells us (36) **sexuality**, beauty, youth, fashion, happiness, success, status and (37) **luxury**. When Calvin Klein, for example, advertises blue jeans, he is selling us sex (38) **appeal**, not jeans. Polo sells us fashion status and Miller beer offers us macho good times.

Research has shown that the average adult can be (39) **exposed** to 500 advertisements each day from radio, television, newspapers and magazines.

In 1987 $109 billion was spent on advertising in the United States and these (40) **expenditures** are growing at a faster rate than the (41) **gross** national product. Although advertising costs are (42) **passed** on to customers, advertising can also save consumers' money by (43) **delivering** more customers to manufacturers, thus making possible mass production and mass consumption, which leads to lower prices. Color television sets, for example, cost $800 to $1,000 when they first went on the market in the later 1950s, but (44) **thanks to mass production and consumption, some sets now sell for less than $200**.

Advertising is an important element of our culture because it reflects and attempts to change our life styles. (45) **New cultural trends and fashions are first transmitted to the mass culture through advertisements**.

It is estimated that, by the time a person raised in the United States reaches the age of 21, he or she has been exposed to 1 million to 2 million advertisements. (46) **The cumulative effects of this lifelong exposure play a significant role in shaping our behavior, social beliefs and values**. It influences our choice to wear Reebok running shoes, brush our teeth with Crest, and feed our cats Fancy Feast.

Practice Test 9

Section A

Directions: *In this section, you will hear 8 short conversations and 2 long conversations. At the end of each conversation, one or more questions will be* asked about what was said. Both the conversation and the questions will be spoken *only once*. *After each question there will be a pause. During the pause, you must read the four choices marked A), B), C) and D), and decide which is the best answer. Then mark the corresponding letter on **Answer Sheet 2** with a single line through the centre.*

Now, let's begin with the eight short conversations.

11. M: Miss Smith, I told Dr. Brown that I would call him in the Houston office at ten o'clock their time. Please find out the time difference for me so that I'll know when to place the call.

    W: It's two hours earlier in Houston, Sir. I know without looking it up because my sister lives there.

    Q: When should the man place his call to Houston?

12. M: Could you please tell me what room Robert Davis is in?

    W: Yes, he's in the Intensive Care Unit on the fourth floor.

    Q: Where does the conversation take place?

13. W: You're always working around the house on Saturday, painting and doing repairs. You must enjoy it.

    M: Not really. I'd rather relax or go fishing, but Saturday is the only day I have to get anything done. By the time I get home from work during the week, I'm too tired.

    Q: What does the man usually do on Saturday?

14. M: I agreed with your proposal at the meeting this morning, it was a good one.

    W: You should back me up then, when I need it.

    Q: What does the woman mean?

15. W: Nine, please.

    M: This is the express, Madam. The first stop is the first floor.

    Q: Where did this conversation take place?

16. W: I set up the conference table for a dozen people, but Mr. Wilson called and said he can't make it.

    M: Don't change anything yet. We didn't expect Mr. Miller, but I just

303

heard he intends to come after all.

    Q: How many people are now expected at the meeting?

17. W: It is certainly good to hear your voice. When are you coming for a visit?

    M: Not for a few months, I'm afraid, Mom. But I hope we can come for a few weeks this summer, probably in June.

    Q: How often does the man visit his Mom?

18. W: We went to the new restaurant at the corner last Saturday and had two fish dinners for the price of one.

    M: Tom told me you had a delicious and filling meal all for ￥8.50.

    Q: What is the special price for one fish dinner?

Now you'll hear two long conversations.

Conversation One

W: Mr. Deluca, you've been a racing-driver for more than ten years. You've had a very dangerous life, haven't you? I mean, you've almost been killed a couple of times during these years, haven't you?

M: Yes, I suppose that's right.

W: When was your worst accident?

M: I'd say last years. It was during the British Grand Prix last September. In the middle of the race I smashed into a wall. The car was completely ruined and my left leg was broken. Luckily, nobody was killed.

W: Is that the only time you've been .. er .. close to death?

M: No. Once, during the Mexican Grand Prix, two cars in front of me had a bad accident. One of them ran into the other. I swerved to avoid them and hit a fence. My car was badly damaged but luckily I wasn't even hurt.

W: You must enjoy danger. I mean, you wouldn't be a racing-driver if you didn't, would you?

M: I don't know about that. I had a very frightening experience quite recently. I was frightened to death! I thought I was going to be killed at any moment.

W: Really? When was that? During your last race?

M: No. It was on my way to this studio. I had to drive through London streets during the lunch hour. There were so many cars all around me and they were so close to each other.

Questions 19 to 22 are based on the conversation you have just heard.

19. Why does the woman think the man has led a dangerous life?
20. When does the man think his worst accident occurred?
21. What happened during the Mexican Grand Prix?
22. What frightening experience did the man recently have?

Conversation Two

W: In the studio today we've got Roberta Wilson, who's a time management consultant. Good morning, Roberta.

M: Good morning, Cindy.

W: Roberta, what exactly do time management consultants do?

M: Well, Cindy, it's all about helping people to organize their work in an effective way: maximum efficiency; minimum stress.

W: Hah, sounds like something I need. Who are your clients?

M: Um, mainly business people, but I've also worked with politicians, civil servants and university lecturers.

W: Um, quite a range, then. And what sort of things help people to organize their time? I suppose punctuality is important.

M: Um, yes and no. It's easier to finish a meeting on time if it starts on time. But in international contexts, you do have to be aware of cultural differences.

W: For example?

M: Well, in Britain big, formal meetings usually start on time, but less formal meetings often begin a few minutes late. In Germany, on the other hand, people expect all meetings to begin on time. In some countries, er, for example, in Latin America, there's a more relaxed attitude. So, you do have to adapt to circumstances.

W: Um, it sounds like even if you manage your own time very well, you still can't control what other people do.

M: Well, you can set limits. If you're meeting a friend who always arrives late，you can say，"Well，I'm going to wait for 15 minutes. If they aren't there by then，I'll leave,"

W：Hmm. I've got one friend who's always late. I don't think I'd ever see her if I did that.

M：Hah，but people who are always late are the ones you need to set limits with. If they know that you won't wait，then，perhaps they'll make an effort.

W：Isn't that rather harsh?

M：No，not really. Someone who constantly turns up late is putting a low value on your time. Let them know you've got other things to do. And I'm not suggesting you do that with everyone — just the persistent latecomers.

Questions 23 to 25 are based on the conversation you have just heard.

23. What does a time management consultant exactly do?
24. Who are the main clients of the time management consultant?
25. What does the man suggest people do with the persistent latecomers?

Section B

Directions: *In this section, you will hear 3 short passages. At the end of each passage, you will hear some questions. Both the passage and the questions will be spoken only once. After you hear a question, you must choose the best answer from the four choices marked A), B), C) and D). Then mark the corresponding letter on **Answer Sheet 2** with a single line through the centre.*

Passage One

Ask any kid about homework，and you'll get the same response：There is too much of it，and too much of it is worthless.

Ah，kids. What do they know?

Maybe more than you think.

The push for high standards in American education has driven schools to pile on the homework. Twenty years ago elementary school children averaged 85 minutes of homework a night，according to a University of Michigan study. Today that's grown to more than two hours a night，a 50 percent increase.

That's not the only thing that's grown. So have the number of children who report having back, shoulder and neck pain as a result of hauling back-packs heavy with homework, according to the American Academy of Ortho-pedic Surgeon.

Results are mixed. The U.S. Department of Education tests progress in math, reading and science under a program called the National Assessment of Educational Progress. And in the twenty years, while fourth-graders have made moderate improvements in math and science, reading scores actually have declined slightly.

Junior and senior high students have made better gains in test scores. But despite that, a vocal anti-homework movement has emerged the last few years that argues that too much homework takes away from important family time and actually creates a counterproductive backlash in some students who simply get tired of the grind. What's more, they argue, few studies have established any concrete benefits to heavy homework loads.

Questions 26 to 29 are based on the passage you have just heard.

26. How is today's primary school children's homework load, compared with 20 years ago?
27. What is the reason for this increase of homework load?
28. What makes many kids have back or neck pain?
29. What are the results from the increase of homework load?

Passage Two

According to government statistics, men of all social classes in Britain visit pubs quite regularly, though the kind of pub they go to may be different and their reasons for going there vary, too. Nowadays they often take their wives or girlfriends, which used not to be the case.

The fact is that the typical English pub is changing, partly because of the licensing laws not being so strict as they were, but also because publicans (酒店老板) are trying to do away with the old Victorian image of the pub. Pubs now provide couples with an atmosphere where they can both enjoy them-selves. Pubs used not to open except at certain times. The result was that they were usually crowded with men who seemed to be drinking as much as possible in the time available. But that kind of pub is rapidly becoming a thing of the past.

Opening hours are still limited to eight hours a day, but the publican can now choose which hours suit him best. And these days you can even get a cup of coffee if you prefer it to beer. But in spite of this the Puritans would never dream of admitting that a pub could become a respectable place.

Questions 30 to 32 are based on the passage you have just heard.

30. What do government statistics show?

31. How were things going with pubs in the past?

32. How would the Puritans feel about the pubs today?

Passage Three

Bees are very small animals which fly through the air to look for flowers for food. Bees have been studied by Karl von Frisch who won a Nobel Prize for his work. He studied bees' activities when they returned to their home called a hive. When a bee found some food, it returned to the hive and danced. The dance was the way the bee communicated to other bees the fact that it had found food.

Bees do two kinds of dances to tell other bees of their discovery of food. First, there is a round dance. In this dance, the bee moves in a circle inside the hive. The round dance is used when food is close by. The food must not be more than ten meters away. If a bee comes back and does a round dance, other bees know they must go out and look nearby for food. The bees also smell the bee that has found the food. The smell tells them what kind of flower to look for. After watching the round dance and smelling the bee that has found the food, the other bees can find the food source.

A second kind of dance done by the bees is a tail-wagging dance. In this dance, the bee wiggles the end of its body as it moves in a straight line. The tail-wagging dance is used when the food is far away. The food must be more than ten meters away. The bees know from the speed of the tail-wagging dance just how far away the food source is. The line the bee dances on shows the direction that the bees must fly in to find the food. In the tail-wagging dance, the bees also smell the bee that has found the food. The smell tells them what kind of flower to look for. After watching the tail-wagging dance and smelling the bee that has found the food, the other bees know three things. They know how far to fly, what direction to fly in, and what kinds of flowers to look for.

Questions 33 to 35 are based on the passage you have just heard.

33. What do the bee's round dance and tail-wagging dance indicate?
34. What does the speed of the tail-wagging dance tell other bees?
35. How can the bees in the passage be described?

Section C

Directions: *In this section, you will hear a passage three times. When the passage is read for the first time, you should listen carefully for its general idea. When the passage is read for the second time, you are required to fill in the blanks numbered from 36 to 43 with the exact words you have just heard. For blanks numbered from 44 to 46 you are required to fill in the missing information. For these blanks, you can either use the exact words you have just heard or write down the main points in your own words. Finally, when the passage is read for the third time, you should check what you have written.*

Despite recent court actions, time may prove America and tobacco to be inseparable. Tobacco was the "money crop" of the (36) **colonies** in the 1600s and 1700s. It was worth dying for in the Revolutionary War. Tobacco became a legal (37) **medium** of exchange in Virginia, Maryland and North Carolina. Because of tobacco, the colonists (38) **craved** two things in great supply — land and cheap labor. They killed and drove American Indians from their native soil and (39) **enslaved** millions of Africans to toil in America.

Tobacco is rooted in two of the greatest (40) **horrors** of American history. Not to mention the damage that it does to smokers. You see them every day as they stand outside businesses because they can't live without one of the world's most (41) **addictive** drugs.

Don't expect lawmakers to legislate tobacco out of existence. And recent multibillion-dollar verdicts and settlements will not make cigarettes (42) **van-**

ish. Our wonderful history and smoking are inseparable.

More folks now know cigarettes and other tobacco products are a cheap delivery system for powerful drugs that (43) **eventually** kill their faithful users. (44) **Many of us know cigarettes have been linked to cancer, heart disease, strokes, and emphysema**. We know smoking kills more than 400,000 Americans a year.

Yet, 48 million adults still smoke. Between 1993 and 1997, smoking was up 28 percent among college students, and (45) **despite the ban on underage smoking, the daily habit of puffing cigarettes jumped 73 percent from 1988 to 1996 among teens**. 1.2 million Americans under age 18 started smoking daily in 1996 compared with 708,000 in 1988.

Movie stars and advertisements romanticize smoking, and what cannot be sold here is shipped overseas. (46)**We are sharing the worst about America and its history with everyone else**.

Practice Test 10

Section A

Directions: *In this section, you will hear 8 short conversations and 2 long conversations. At the end of each conversation, one or more questions will be asked about what was said. Both the conversation and the questions will be spoken only once. After each question there will be a pause. During the pause, you must read the four choices marked A), B), C) and D), and decide which is the best answer. Then mark the corresponding letter on **Answer Sheet 2** with a single line through the centre.*

Now, let's begin with the eight short conversations.

11. M: Couldn't you type any faster?
    W: This is the fastest I've ever typed.
    Q: What does the man think of the woman's typing?

12. W: Could you give me something for the pain? I didn't go to sleep until 3 o'clock this morning, and I don't have an appointment with my dentist until next week.
    M: I'm sorry to hear that. Aspirin is the strongest medicine I can give you without a prescription.

Q: Where does this conversation most probably take place?

13. M: Goodbye Mrs. Tobin. Please do look us up. We are in the phone book.

   W: I'm sure I will, Mr. Stewart. So nice meeting you.

   Q: What will Mrs. Tobin do?

14. W: Can you believe we got a seat so quickly?

   M: It's usually crowded here at lunch time.

   W: I know. I wonder why it's not today.

   Q: What does the woman imply about the restaurant?

15. M: How did I miss you at the bus stop? I was there at 1:00.

   W: I got there at a quarter to one and I left ten minutes after I got there.

   Q: When did the woman probably leave the bus stop?

16. M: I've gotten so busy that I can hardly find time for any outside activities.

   W: Do you still have time for fishing?

   M: Only once in a while now, but I still consider it my hobby.

   Q: What does the man mean?

17. M: Didn't your husband come to New York with you?

   W: He would like to. But he couldn't take off time to come. He went to Orlando on business.

   Q: What can we learn about her husband?

18. W: Are you going to live with your children permanently?

   M: Well ... they want me to, but it's too early to know for sure. I'm pretty independent.

   Q: What does the man mean?

Now you'll hear two long conversations.

Conversation One

M: In the studio today we have Eve Startling, a career adviser at a well-known comprehensive school. Glad to have you with us, Eve.

W: Thank you.

M: A lot of young people are very nervous when they go to a job interview for the first time. What's the best way of dealing with this?

W: The obvious answer isn't much help, really, I'm afraid: "Just keep calm and do your best." If you're nervous to start with, this advice probably has the opposite effect. And in fact, a certain amount of tension is probably a good thing. It's the same with the way you sit when the interviewer asks you to sit down.

M: How do you mean?

W: Well, if you balance on the edge of you chair, it shows you're nervous, but if you relax and make yourself too comfortable, that won't do, either. You should sit naturally, but straight, to show you're paying attention.

M: And I suppose you should face the interviewer when you answer questions.

W: Yes, eye contact is important then, but that doesn't mean you never take your eyes off the interviewer. And it's all right to be naturally pleasant, but don't try too hard.

M: One of the things that upset people most at interviews, I think, is that interviewers often ask trick questions. Even quite innocent questions like "How do you spend your spare time?" can contain traps in certain cases. Suppose the company would prefer an outdoor person but you spend every weekend looking at your stamp collection. What should you do? Should you always tell the truth or pretend to be what the company wants?

W: Tell the truth, yes, but not necessarily the whole truth. It's no good pretending to be what you're not — an experienced interviewer would soon find out — but you needn't go out of your way to tell them anything you don't want them to know.

M: One last piece of advice before we sign off?

W: Yes, and it may surprise you. That is that very often young people get carried away just with the idea of winning. It's hard to remember when there's a lot of unemployment, as there is nowadays, but you should be sure that this is the kind of work you want to do and the firm is one that you would enjoy working for. Otherwise you may get the job and then find out that you hate it. So remember to ask sensibly questions as well as to answer sensibly.

Questions 19 to 22 are based on the conversation you have just heard.

19. Who is Eve Startling ?
20. What does Eve suggest a job interviewee do?
21. What should a job interviewee respond when asked a trick question?
22. What advice does Eve offer by way of conclusion?

Conversation Two

W: Hi, John!

M: Hi, Beth!

W: Congratulations! I heard you've got a part-time job.

M: No. I wish I had. I'm still on the waiting list.

W: Seems like it's hard to get a good part-time job these days.

M: You bet. I've been searching online for days, but there's little chance ...

W: Funny, isn't it? You're a Management major concentrating on Marketing. Now you've got to learn how to market yourself! Why not look in the local paper? There're often lots of jobs in it.

M: Are you kidding? The unemployment figures are up again this month!

W: Don't be so negative. Look at the jobs in the classifieds in today's paper ... so many openings. Just print out your resume and send it to them.

M: I usually apply online. I send a short cover letter in the text of the email, and then attach my resume. It's convenient. What about you? Any luck?

W: Well, I haven't even started planning to look for a job yet. If only I had more time, I could do it.

M: Why so busy?

W: Well, I didn't get good grades last semester and failed two tests ...

M: Sorry to hear that. I think no one deserves good grades more than you!

W: Thank you. The main reason, I guess, was that I didn't get accustomed to the way of learning here. Well, where there's a will, there's a way. I wish you good luck on your job search.

Questions 23 to 25 are based on the conversation you have just heard.

23. What do you know about John?

24. Why is it hard for students to get a good part-time job?

25. What does Beth suggest John do?

Section B

Directions: *In this section, you will hear 3 short passages. At the end of each passage, you will hear some questions. Both the passage and the questions will be spoken only once. After you hear a question, you must choose the best answer from the four choices marked A), B), C) and D). Then mark the corresponding letter on **Answer Sheet 2** with a single line through the centre.*

Passage One

Tecumseh was a Shawnee Indian warrior who was born in Ohio in 1768. He saw little peace during his life, but he never gave up his dream of getting all the Indian nations together to protect their land.

When Tecumseh was only six years old, white settlers started flocking onto land belonging to the Shawnee. His father, who was the Shawnee war chief, was killed by the settlers.

After being adopted by Chief Blackfish and learning all he could about warfare, Tecumseh was determined to do what he could to stop frontiersmen from taking more and more land belonging to Indians.

Tecumseh knew that the Indians didn't have a chance unless they united. So he spent the next twenty years traveling and speaking for Indian unity. He covered thousands of miles across the country, sharing his dream with thousands of other Indians. He did all he could to persuade them to unite. The dream seemed impossible, but Tecumseh didn't give up hope. By the early 1800s, the name of Tecumseh was known throughout the land.

Then, in 1812, war broke out between Americans and Great Britain. Hoping to get back some of the land taken by the settlers, many Indians sided with the British. Tecumseh fought with great courage, and in 1813, he died during one of the battles.

Tecumseh's dream was never realized, but his memory has not been lost. He stood firm, fighting for his beliefs.

Questions 26 to 28 are based on the passage you have just heard.

26. How old was Tecumseh when he died?

27. Who was Tecumseh?

28. What was Tecumseh's dream?

Passage Two

At the University of Kansas art museum, investigators tested the effects of different colored walls on two groups of visitors to an exhibit of paintings. For the first group the room was painted white; for the second, dark brown. Movement of each group was followed by an electrical system under the carpet. The experiment revealed that those who entered the dark brown room walked more quickly, covered more area, and spent less time in the room than the people in the white environment. Dark brown stimulated more activity, but the activity ended sooner. Not only the choice of colors but also the general appearance of a room communicates and influences those inside. Another experiment presented subjects with photographs of faces that were to be rated in terms of energy and well-being. Three groups of subjects were used; each was shown the same photos, but each group was in a different kind of room. One group was in an "ugly" room that resembled a messy storeroom. Another group was in an average room — a nice office. The third group was in a tastefully designed living room. Results showed that the subjects in the beautiful room tended to give higher ratings to the faces than did those in the ugly room.

Questions 29 to 31 are based on the passage you have just heard.

29. Which group gave higher ratings to the faces?

30. Whom did investigators test on?

31. Which of the following is NOT true?

Passage Three

Business and public organizations spend tens of millions of dollars each year on development programs to improve their managers' interpersonal skills. You'd think, therefore, that there would be little debate over whether such skills can be effectively taught. But there are diverse opinions on this question.

On one side are those who view interpersonal skills as essentially personality traits that are deep-rooted and not inclined to change. Just as some people are naturally quiet, while others are outgoing, the anti-training side argues that some people can work well with others while many cannot. That is, it's a talent you either have or you don't. They believe that no amount of training is likely to convert individuals with highly offensive interpersonal styles into "people-oriented" types.

The skills advocates have an increasing body of experimental research to support their case. For instance, there is evidence that training programs focusing on the human relations problems of leadership, supervision, attitudes toward employees, communication, and self-awareness produce some improvement in managerial performance.

Nothing in the research suggests that skills training can magically transform the interpersonally incompetent into highly effective leaders. But that should not be the test of whether interpersonal skills can be taught. The evidence strongly demonstrates that these skills can be learned. Although people differ in their baseline abilities, the research shows that training can result in improved skills for most people.

Questions 32 to 35 are based on the passage you have just heard.

32. What does the passage mainly discuss?
33. What is the purpose of the training programs?
34. What is the speaker's attitude towards the training programs?
35. What does the speaker try to convince us?

Section C

Directions: *In this section, you will hear a passage three times. When the passage is read for the first time, you should listen carefully for its general idea. When the passage is read for the second time, you are required to fill in the blanks numbered from 36 to 43 with the exact words you have just heard. For blanks numbered from 44 to 46 you are required to fill in the missing information. For these blanks, you can either use the exact words you have just heard or write down the main points in your own words. Finally, when the passage is read for the third time, you should check what you have writ-*

ten.

Our sleep time over the past century has been (36) **reduced** by almost 20 percent.

Generally, adults need to sleep one hour for every two hours (37) **awake**, which means that most need about eight hours of sleep a night. Of course, some people need more and some less. Children and teenagers need an average of about ten hours.

The brain keeps an exact (38) **accounting** of how much sleep it is owed. My colleagues and I (39) **coined** the term *sleep debt* because (40) **accumulated** lost sleep is like a (41) **monetary** debt: it must be paid back. If you get an hour less than a full night's sleep, you carry an hour of sleep debt into the next day — and your (42) **tendency** to fall asleep during the daytime becomes stronger.

During a five-day (43) **workweek**, if you get six hours of sleep each night instead of the eight you needed, (44) **you would build up a sleep debt of ten hours (five days times two hours)**. Because sleep debt accumulates in an additive fashion, (45) **by day five your brain would tend toward sleep as strongly as if you'd stayed up all night**. From this perspective, sleeping until noon on Saturday is not getting enough to pay back the ten lost hours as well as meet your nightly requirement of eight; you would have to sleep until about 5 p.m. to balance the sleep ledger.

(46) **But for most people it is difficult to sleep that long because of the alerting mechanism of our biological clock**.